DISCARDED

SUMMER

IN THE

CITY

PS
3569
.T4517
S9
1984

SUMMER

IN THE

CITY

A NOVEL BY

MARK

STEVENS

RANDOM HOUSE NEW YORK

HILBERT COLLEGE
McGRATH LIBRARY
5200 SOUTH PARK AVE.
HAMBURG, N. Y. 14075

50,701

Copyright © 1984 by Mark Stevens
All rights reserved under International
and Pan-American Copyright Conventions.
Published in the United States by Random House, Inc., New York,
and simultaneously in Canada by Random House
of Canada Limited, Toronto.

Library of Congress Cataloging in Publication Data

Stevens, Mark, 1951–
Summer in the city.

I. Title.
PS3569.T4517S9   1984   813'.54   83–17841
ISBN 0–394–53187–6

Manufactured in the United States of America

9   8   7   6   5   4   3   2

First Edition

For Annalyn

PART
ONE

CHAPTER

ONE

I

Below the towers touched with pink, commuters veered around several points of resistance: a hawker shouting "Only a dollar! Dollar each!," a man returning home after a night shift, a boy selling the *Daily News*. They muttered at the young woman, who was slowing to a stop, until she looked at them with her surprising eyes. At times they were blue, at others gray; they shone in her dark face like a splash of light. She put down her shoulder bag, then murmured with a small smile, "Well, I'm back." She stared straight ahead for a full minute, as a person might stare at a former lover. Then she glanced at the early sun winking against the buildings. She looked down the canyon of Thirty-second Street, breathed in the sweet and sour air, listened to the tramp of feet. The great gray city—her great gray city.

She stepped toward a pay phone. Her first business was to call Penelope, who had found a sublet for her on the Upper West Side. What would that funny creature be up to? Some quick mischief played across her face; it was too cheerful a morning, she thought, to talk to someone who was always so tired. She turned instead toward the taxis outside Penn Station. But no, she preferred to walk awhile after her year in the country. A walk was the right way to say hello to a city. And Grand Central was a better place than Penn Station to begin and end a journey. So she headed uptown, welcoming what she loved about New York. Especially the compression of energy that forced the buildings skyward. What to do! Where to go! She enjoyed the way the city kept forming new pictures before her, and she began once again to use the corners of her eyes. She noticed the model prancing down the street like a racehorse and the addict nodding. She studied the vendors, the lovers, the arguers. A band of Puerto Rican boys swung toward her with a radio blaring. She stepped aside, knowing they would not. A girl wore a T-shirt printed with the logo of a department store. Why turn yourself into an ad? She relished the rub of extremes, the flash of styles, the declarations of I, I, I—everything that rendered the world vivid, risky, varied, important.

But she did not give herself over to the city, not entirely. She held something back out of the feeling that her crowded city did not include enough. A bearded man, flagging a taxi, reminded her of her former lover; and then of her former celebrity. His beard was sprouty enough to imply he was imaginative, she thought, and trim enough to indicate he was reliable. He seemed surrounded by something intangible, a perfume that suffused the world she had once moved in. Most people in the arts, including her old boyfriends, lived for that perfume, which emanated from the mix of gossip, art, money, and fame in New York. She herself enjoyed the perfume on occasion, but no longer found it sustaining. She trailed her hand across the face of a building, then glanced at a street sign.

Forty-second was too sleazy for a May morning, so she cut toward Grand Central along a narrow street that was still deep in shade. The city, which had been airy and light on Seventh, pressed down around her. She passed some dank-smelling newspapers on a garbage pail and noticed the old-fashioned lettering, CUSTOM TAILORING, on a darkened storefront. Suddenly she stopped short. Who—what? It was only a New York derelict, but he was doing something odd, scampering spider-fast here and there, fumbling in his rags for drumsticks. Soon he padded to the curb, whistling against his teeth, and began to drum the sticks on the street, swaying to a private song; somewhere, far off, an orchestra was warming up. She edged along. And then, after he met her eyes, she hurried past.

A year ago, before she left New York, her mind had sometimes played that old trick on her. An ordinary event, such as a bicyclist skidding around a corner, became a vague but important omen: the city seemed to point its finger, opening a seam in her heart. She felt especially rational during these mad moments; the everyday world simply separated into something else, the way the focusing device on a camera divides an image in two. It was the man's ragged drumming, she thought, or some queer exaltation in his look, that had penetrated her usual reserve. And she remembered her way of escaping the terror of his eye—with a knowing smile. She stopped and with two fingers pressed her eyes closed. The skin tightened on her face; her cheekbones, delicate but strong, like the bones of a bird, gave her look conviction. This time, she reminded herself, she meant to see the world as it was, without portents and knowing smiles.

She dropped her fingers and smiled. Wasn't there a better way to make an entrance? "Ready"—she joked—"set"—the quick light in her face turned outward—"go!" She strode down the street toward Fifth Avenue, glancing around and around and up while her bag swung from her like an anchor. Even New York, she decided, looked innocent when the air was fresh and morning-cool and the northern light, slowly strengthening, turned the windows to silver. Down the street the Chrysler Building appeared almost medieval—a prince among buildings, she thought, with windows like mail and a lance at its tip. She passed two men and shivered gently, having met the eyes of one. She liked him because he seemed to look at her, to talk to his friend, and to think of some third thing, all at the same time. He might have been a little firmer, she thought, not so steeped in the easy ennui of those who read French novels on rainy afternoons in college. But he had what she most wanted in men: he provoked the right curiosity, the kind not easily exhausted.

The touch of his eye deepened the blue in her own, and her legs went a little soft. She kept her musings fairly distant, however, the way a teasing lover restrains his hand. Kept vague, lovemaking could assume any of its forms, from the fierce to the gentle; it retained its promise and some of the character of its fine sad end, the relaxing into a forgetfulness without shape.

Hardly the right mood, she thought, teasing herself, for looking at Grand Central Station. She decided the building looked pretty foolish, dwarfed by high rises but full of earnest importance; she liked it anyway, partly for its humbug, partly because it was old and aimed at greatness. She wandered to Fifth to study the clothes and enjoyed the stony elegance of the avenue, now giving way to the glassy hauteur of boutiques.

A row of buses, roaring and spitting, pulled away from the curb. Buses reminded her of herd animals, dumb plodding creatures like cattle which, when her uncle got behind a string of them, lumbered away shitting steamily. She remembered her uncle smelling of cheap cologne and chewing tobacco; his eyes were wet when she left. Right now, she thought, it would be very still on his place: only the hoot of a tired owl or the bang of a solitary hammer. But she had wanted to come back, she told herself, she had wanted to come back very much. She considered the next year so important that she had even taken the train—though taking the train seemed a little precious—to give her trip some ceremony. She returned to New York, after fleeing to a small Western town, convinced that her life to date was a failure. She regarded the coming months as a test, though of what she could not quite say. She wanted to be both loving and acid-smart. She wanted to attain a private balance in New York.

Before calling Penelope—before plugging into the city—she took one more moment. She glanced at her reflection in a store window. Her dress had been carefully chosen: blue, with a simple cut and some playful slink. Then she searched in the shoulder bag for her brush. She drew it slowly through her hair, enjoying the rhythm of pull and tug. Her hair was shorter now, cut to shoulder length, but she could still gather it up in bunches for the pass of the brush. As she brushed, her expression grew remote; and then suddenly she was done. Where else could she live? Some cussedness in her temperament demanded a life in one of the great places. New York was old, corroding, increasingly ridiculous. But it was a city with a past, a city of density and height, where the small human drives played themselves out against a significant backdrop. Perhaps, she thought, she could become a heretic in the cathedral city! She smiled at the melodrama in her imagination—her friends did not know about that—then listened for the strident voice of the city. That voice could usurp your pulse, she thought, but she would master it. She would orchestrate its music. Its shapelessness offered her the freedom to remake herself: she was twenty-eight and there was time. She dropped the dime into the pay phone. The line was busy. Then there was no answer. And then a machine came on, asking her to leave her name. New York!

2

When her phone rang, Penelope took a sip of coffee. Would her new answering machine work? She was not optimistic. She took another sip, and when the ringing stopped, said "Hallelujah, you dumb . . ." Dumb what? It was hard to know how to insult a machine. She made a mental note to reflect upon this in her diary. Then she depressed a button, planning to listen to her own message and the response of her first caller. A guitar struck a dramatic chord—something camp she had discovered on a Spanish record—and a voice murmured, "Greetings . . . Hello . . . This is Penelope . . . This is also a recording . . . Sorry I'm not here . . . Or, to be frank, I might be working . . . Or, I might want to be alone . . . If you would like to leave a message, wait until you hear the chord . . . Goodbye."

Excellent. It had taken her some time to achieve the right tone, rather clever but offhand. She leaned back on her sofa with satisfaction, then coiled herself around the Rolodex and answering machine. She balanced a coffee cup on one knee. She still wore her nightgown, and the loft was almost dark. An ominous sculpture stood in a corner; a ficus was fading near the blinds; a slight scent, like that of a wine cork, perfumed the air. She pressed the button marked "message." The chord struck again, and she sat up a little.

"Penelope, this is Kelly Martin. I'm back, but I don't want to talk to a machine. I'll call later." There was a loud click.

She stretched. Why was Kelly always so brisk? She took a deep breath—and had an idea. But first she raised the blinds on her view. From one end of her loft she could see the Empire State Building, from the other the World Trade Center. In the daylight she despaired of clearing away the vague disorder—papers, magazines, cups, a choked bookcase. She supposed all imaginative people, with more important things on their mind than superficial order, faced this problem. As she watched the modern dancer in the loft across the street perform her morning exercises, Penelope, a long, thin woman with an air of Pre-Raphaelite fatigue, gave her own stomach an admiring pat—no excess there.

Armed with a second cup of coffee, she began to approach her idea. She curled up on the couch and carefully rearranged the Rolodex, the phone, a purple felt pen, and a yellow pad. On the pad she drew two columns, one of which was headed "Today," the other "This Evening." Her idea belonged to "This Evening," but she began with "Today." Under that heading she wrote, in capital letters, 1) PRIVACY, 10:00—11:45 A.M. This period of solitude was designed for the dreaming and free association she considered necessary to her work. During this time she must not be disturbed, must feel under no pressure. She often said it was the most demanding part of her day, adding that she expected only artists to understand what she meant. Penelope first knew she was an artist, she liked to tell friends, at the age of three. She did not limit herself to one art form; the arts, she said, were converging. She was a poet, diarist, potter, conceptual sculptor, film-maker, critic, short-story writer, and photographer.

Next she wrote, 2) PROJECT, 11:45—1:00 P.M. This referred to her ongoing work of art, which a magazine had already praised for "its exact, self-referential, yet strangely mysterious quality." On two identical tripods Penelope had set up two identical cameras, one aimed at the Empire State Building, the other at the World Trade Center. Every day at noon an automatic timer simultaneously fired the shutter of each camera. This was to be done each day for a year; the results were to be made into a book. It was to be a sculpture in and of time. To date the subtle variation and progression of light in the photographs had surpassed her highest expectations. As she considered the project, however, she was momentarily afflicted by doubt; she felt lonely and singular. And yet, she reminded herself, to be uncertain, to suffer—that was the fate of all great artists.

Then she wrote, 3) SALT MINES, 1:00—4:00 P.M. To help pay the maintenance, she photographed celebrities for book jackets, record covers, and magazines. If only artists did not have to pay the rent, she thought—imagine what art had been lost to landlords! Despite her scorn for this work, she made a great deal of money. Part of her loft was a studio; her specialty was the writer. Usually she chose to light the writer from the side, leaving one part of the face mysteriously dark and the other brightly revealed, and she was very particular about clothes. The writer should look as if he or she had been walking beside the ocean or, if male, chopping wood. An old shirt from L. L. Bean's was best, but a turtleneck was all right and sometimes, for a certain kind of writer, an old sports jacket worked well. She refused to photograph a male writer with a pipe, even if he actually smoked one: that was a cliché. Her greatest secret, however, was wrinkles. She played them up. The young writer always displayed the first delicate cuts of age—wrinkles, she said, were the geography of experience—while old writers looked like Father Time.

Her anticipation increased. In a few minutes she would consider "This Evening." She flipped through her Rolodex. One day she herself expected to be famous; until then she took considerable pleasure in knowing the celebrated. Picking numbers at random from the Rolodex, she began to rain calls upon people she knew, talking to publicists, agents, friends, editors. She spoke with no one for more than two minutes, and she was always first to say she had to run. In this way she seeded her name throughout the city; the result would be assignments, invitations, lunches. Then, shortly before the start of her period of privacy, she replaced the receiver. After dawdling a moment she took up her felt pen. Under "This Evening" she wrote the name "Billy Bell." She underlined it twice.

It was too bad, she thought, that he gave himself to television. Of course, he had grown up in California; she must remember that, given his medium and background, he did admirable work. On his program he interviewed not only common celebrities, but also the more interesting achievers—people unacquainted with television, she thought, not unlike herself. He seemed successful with all levels of brow. An honest popularizer: what was wrong with that? Someone had to do it. No doubt he owed part of his success to good looks, but that was not his fault, and he did not blow-dry his hair. For a couple of minutes she daydreamed about how unimportant his looks were to her.

They had met one afternoon, while shooting publicity photos for his television show. That night, both being free, they had slept together. Since then she had seen him several times, and she had arranged a vague date for tonight, under the guise of inviting him to a party at her loft. Unfortunately, there was no party. She could think of a number of men—she smiled at the thought—who would be delighted to arrive at a party and find only Penelope Lamb. But she was not certain about him. Suppose he was offended? She stared at some photographs of him on a contact sheet, as if to ask whether he would mind. But she could not tell. As always, he looked open and cheerful. Certainly nothing would appear to be wrong. But privately . . . That was it—he was deep, even though he was good-looking. This was delightful, but did not solve her problem.

She stretched like a cat on the sofa: her idea. A very small party. No more than four. Kelly Martin would be invited when she called back. If Kelly could not make it, or if she did not call, so much the better. Then they would be three: not Penelope's fault. If she did come, Billy would not pay much attention to her. Kelly was pretty enough, but she had once written savagely about television. She was also said to have had some kind of breakdown; and her work was going nowhere, as she herself admitted. It would be nice of Penelope to invite her. No doubt Kelly, tired from her trip, would leave early.

The fourth would be Jennings . . . she could not remember his last name. He was Billy's assistant, someone of no particular importance, without serious intentions—and a sloppy, arrogant person who liked to bait her. But he was Billy's best friend, a college friend. She took a moment to be touched: Billy was loyal. Below his name she added "Kelly Martin" and "Jennings?" Then, after looking up the station number in the Rolodex, she smiled and shut her eyes. It was almost time for her period of privacy.

3

Jennings took the phone call from Penelope in front of his editing monitor, where he was putting together a video clip of Billy Bell's recent visit to an institution for handicapped children in Queens. Beside him the new summer intern, a girl whose name he did not know, stopped talking. He tucked the phone between his shoulder and ear to keep his hands free. "Yes, I'm all right," he told Penelope. He junked a piece of tape that showed Billy getting out of a car: too awkward. He began instead with some footage of the cold brick façade of the institution—also an awkward opening, but a certain amateur quality came across as personal on television. "Can't reach Billy? I think he's taping a show . . . Okay, I'll ask him." The director of the institution in Queens was an officious man with a small mustache. Jennings added some footage of him; the ugly façade and the officious director would set off Billy's charm. "Tonight, right—what time? You want me too? Don't think I can . . . an emergency?" Then a sharp cut to Billy in his white suit, moving lightly up the stairs. He looked nice, he seemed concerned.

"Just a minute." Jennings put Penelope on hold, then dialed Billy on the intercom. "That photographer is calling again. What's up?" The footage of Billy walking down a long corridor with the director was only fair: Billy said nothing interesting. But the corridor was gloomy. That was good. Jennings cut the sound of their conversation, sending them down the murky green corridor in silence. "You promised? How can you like her? . . . All right. She wants me to come too . . . Come down in a few minutes, okay?" He kept five seconds of a shot of a roomful of handicapped children, then reconnected himself to Penelope. "We're both coming. What time?" Unfortunately, the shot seemed too general; at a distance not enough looked wrong. He studied some closeups of the children. One girl had a sweet face. She'd be useful later. "You want me to bring wine? How many people?" But first—he selected a clip of a badly handicapped child whose lower lip twitched—"Penelope, I'm on deadline now, we can talk tonight."

For a moment Jennings leaned back. He seemed neither concerned nor unconcerned with his work. This impressed the intern, who smoked cigarettes with great intensity. She tucked some hair behind one ear, then began to chatter again. Jennings cut sharply to Billy shaking hands, in the exaggerated way adults greet children: patting a cheek, the top of a head, bending low to talk to a certain child. The intern said, "He'd be a really good politician, I think. I mean, let's face it, he couldn't be any worse than what we have, though I have some doubts about whether it's a good idea to mix journalism and politics. I almost wrote a paper on that. The thing about him, I know this sounds corny, but he actually seems to care." There was a superb shot of Billy seated on a chair, balancing a child on his knee. The child was trying to talk, unsuccessfully. Billy was patient—five seconds would seem patient on television—and then he gently sealed the child's lips with one finger. He smiled kindly. The child smiled too. Excellent. "Yale has a radio station, but it also might get a television station, one of those short-range things. I know they're looking for a rich alumnus. There are a couple that want to give the money." She paused. "Tax reasons."

"It's lung cancer if you keep that up," Jennings told her, his eyes bothered by the smoke.

"Nothing to worry about yet." She seemed delighted to have earned a response. "I've got time."

This was the first of her remarks to make an impression on Jennings. He looked at her strangely. She made him feel significantly, uncomfortably, older than a college student. The puppy. "You've got time," he slowly repeated—and punched a button. He inserted a full minute of Billy's conversation with a little boy who was missing an arm. What did the boy want to be when he grew up? It was too much—but then nothing was too much for a clip about handicapped children—he wanted to be a fireman. Billy was perfect, as straight as anyone could wish. "Of course I know I should give up smoking and I will. Besides, people are getting to be very unpleasant about it. Maybe Bill Bell should do a show about smoking. There's great viewer interest. In a politics course once I read some studies about—"

For a moment Jennings wondered how to wrap it up, then inserted a few seconds of the sweet-faced child. This left the impression that Billy had improved matters, somehow made the children cuter. In a final shot, Billy asked the children to visit him at the studio in New York City. They clapped and Billy smiled. Jennings checked the running time: exactly four minutes. It would be a strong introduction to Billy's interview of officials responsible for the care of handicapped children in New York.

"How is it?" the intern asked.

Jennings looked at her. "I don't know what you mean," he said slowly.

He kept his eyes on her. And for the first time she was at a loss for words. Did she have a crush on him? Why did anyone like

12

him, he wondered, when he could be so disagreeable? He softened and said, "It's okay." She relaxed into a smile, to suggest she was not one to miss a joke. He asked her to write a paragraph—not more than thirty seconds—which they could use to introduce the film clip. He would rewrite it, keeping a few of her words. That would make her happy. "All right," he said, "once more." On the monitor a man in a white suit stepped out—but the door behind them opened, and Jennings knew, without looking, that Billy himself had entered the room. Behind one shoulder Jennings felt the pressing warmth, smelled the minty breath, bent to the pull of the charm that glowed behind them like a soft white light.

"Who is *that* guy?" teased Billy, watching himself walk down the gloomy green corridor.

Jennings did not turn around. Beside him the girl shifted in her seat. Her attention, he noticed, began to falter. The eyes trembled and slipped—then locked into a new orbit.

"How we doing, Carol?"

"Great!"

"Just fair," said Jennings.

"Looks good, looks good," said Billy's voice—a voice as clean and smooth as freshly ironed sheets.

"This goes too far," Jennings objected, when the man in the white suit walked into the room full of children. "It makes me want to laugh."

"Not at all. It's a good editing job."

"It's a terrible clip." The edge in his own voice surprised him.

"You're a perfectionist."

"That's not—" He stopped himself. Compared to Billy's good will, his irritability seemed cheap. "I guess it's all right," he said.

"Always my toughest critic."

4

Billy leaned closer to the monitor. "I like this bit with the kid on my knee," he said. "Really was a nice little kid." The intern, watching the monitor, sat very still. She hardly dares to look up, Billy thought, she's that shy. He liked to watch her watch him, and he liked her shyness. It made him feel generous. He smiled. She shouldn't worry so much.

"Jennings, I hope you've taught her everything you know."

The intern almost looked up: very, very shy.

"She doesn't need any help from me."

"I'll bet. That poor kid—can you believe he wants to be a fireman?"

Billy studied the man in the white suit. Not his best work, he thought. The children did not respond warmly enough; the give and take was not as lively, as elastic, as it should be. The strain made the sudden dip of the man's head to hear a child's whisper look artificial. At awkward moments, he told himself, he should remember to appear relaxed, natural, intrigued.

Still, the clip wasn't bad.

"Let's go through it again," he said.

Jennings, on the next run-through, stopped the tape suddenly. He trimmed a few seconds. He threw it into reverse. Billy was indulgent. He knew that Jennings, for whatever reason, was testy —that was just Jennings. Nonetheless, the constant interruption of the moving image disturbed him. He did not like the rough chop-chopping. He did not like the machine itself: damp hands had worn down the paint, soiling the knobs. He did not like to watch the man in the white suit, at the flick of someone's fingers, dance like a puppet.

"Leave it alone," he said.

"Okay."

Jennings wore one shirt sleeve rolled up, Billy noticed, the other rolled down.

"Once more through," Billy said. "Without messing around."

Jennings began to rewind the tape.

Billy, staring into the blank picture, began to daydream. He stood on the steps of the institution for handicapped children. Officials were gathered on all sides; clusters of microphones, spiky with authority, stood before him. He'd be damned, he told the crowd, if he wasn't going to do something about the disgraceful treatment of handicapped children in the state of New York.

Jennings started up the tape.

Yes, Billy thought, it was all right. He studied the tape. It was all right, it was—

"Mr. Bell?"

He was startled. So the girl could talk!

"Call me Billy," he reminded her. "Billy."

"Billy—"

"That's better," he said. He dropped one hand on her shoulder, the other on Jennings'.

"Now, where were we?"

CHAPTER

TWO

I

Jennings often found himself with scraps of time—the odd hour, a ragged afternoon—that he did not know how to use. With almost two hours before Penelope's party, he walked across Columbus Circle to the pleasingly ridiculous Maine Memorial. On fine afternoons he liked to buy hot dogs and sauerkraut from a Greek vendor, then sit on a stone ledge under the monument. The corner was always busy with strollers leaving or entering the park, pushers muttering "uppers, smoke," workers hurrying to the subway. He liked his detached position amid the rush; the city was his foil and he was at home. After that day's editing, however, he could not settle down. He was angry, and his anger did not make sense to him. Why should he be irked by Billy? Or exasperated with the intern? Or nettled by Penelope? Their crimes were nothing more than charm, youth, and usury. Paying for the wine! A percentage on a party he did not want to attend! He walked further into the park. The softness of spring calmed him, without easing his spirit.

He lay down on a bench and shut his eyes. He was too young, he thought, to worry about age. Yet he was conscious that time—

his own time—was beginning to speed up. He could not remember without effort what he had done two weeks, four months, or six years ago. Did the years between thirty and seventy pass more rapidly than those between ten and thirty? And why, suddenly, did he care? He knew why. His oldest friend had changed. Something extraordinary had happened: certain people were touting Billy as a politician. Jennings did not know what lay behind this abrupt interest; it seemed to happen by itself, like the weather. No important elections would be held for some time, but the gossip columns, the articles about city politics, and the questions addressed to Billy on television all implied that Billy Bell was a potential candidate for Congress, the city council, or even the mayoralty. For the first time Jennings was surprised at something that had happened to Billy—and uneasy because, for the first time, he had had nothing to do with it.

Their friendship, he thought, had not changed in ten years. Now, teased by worry, he began to wonder about its origins, for Billy was not the sort of person he usually liked. Jennings remembered Billy in college as handsome in the corn-fed American way—clear features, gray eyes, sandy hair. He appeared at first to be one of those young men whose life was charmed. He seemed straight of mind and heart, yet he also possessed force, a curiously innocent energy that appealed to Jennings. He did not seem to pursue, or even to want, success; and yet success claimed him. He was always in the spotlight, not through his own effort but because he was drafted, or the obvious choice, or the compromise candidate. Since he did not push for position he was not envied, and he did all jobs well. At times his innocence seemed cold or his warmth abstract. This only enhanced his appeal. People were grateful, Jennings thought, to receive the full force of his attention, thankful for anything personal.

Jennings was less certain why Billy liked him. Perhaps Billy enjoyed his sophisticated edges—his New Yorkness. When young, Jennings had taken full possession of the fashionably serious attitudes of the time, which mostly came from advanced novels and movies. He was clever, ironic, knowing, casual, and suffused with ennui. His character did not end there, however. He had never believed in his own strong appeal, but he tried for a moment— as he lay on the bench—to identify what others might like . . . He

17

did not whine, hate, or aim to hurt. His humor was oblique and deflationary, his intelligence beguiling. He expended his talent with democratic carelessness, doing well enough by not trying; he thought little of himself, his smile suggested, but still less of the common run of ambition. To some his reluctance before the world seemed spoiled, to others the product of a deep and serious disappointment, a refusal to yield his best self to the tawdry and sentimental. For such people he possessed a centered if dormant power—and they sought his approval.

He kicked off his shoes, then opened his eyes with a thought. He brought to Billy, who required a motivating spark from outside, ideas, opinions, and quickness of mind. In return, Billy achieved a success that, because of his innocence, seemed acceptable. Jennings himself refused to seek power, but he had a fugitive liking for the public eye—for the beautifully made object presented to a crowd. Wasn't it he, Jennings, who first suggested that Billy go into TV? Only two years later Billy became host of a late-afternoon talk show, after substituting for another host. As Billy's assistant, Jennings offered advice. He took credit for developing the blend of the serious and the lighthearted that characterized the show: the next topic, after handicapped children, was the circus trapeze. His eye for style, its efflorescence and decay, was brilliant. Having noticed that Billy habitually wore light-colored clothing, Jennings encouraged him to wear an off-white that was not quite ostentatious; the accent was provided by a warmly colored tie. Billy soon developed a reputation as a man of lively taste who was not corrupt. Not least, Jennings acquired a technical flair for television. Who, he thought with disgust, sitting up on the bench, would have thought he'd end up splicing videotape?

He wondered why he gave himself to such work. Out of heedlessness perhaps: his talent and his success were the measure of his scorn. Out of pleasure too, for he enjoyed shaping Billy's image. He liked cutting, splicing, selecting; he liked getting the right rhythm or a good composition into running film. All his life he had tended to hang back and watch. It seemed natural to develop, out of his detachment and discontent, a taste for the amended image, for the drama that improved upon life. And now he no longer enjoyed doing that for Billy. Nor could he take pride in his concealed power. He had provided only the frame, he thought, for Billy's extraordinary talent. He remembered that Billy was the only student trusted by both the students and the administration during the antiwar strikes in college. This had astonished Jennings, who could not join the free flow of feeling on either side, since Billy did not also appear wishy-washy. There was no dumb-jock look in his face, no annoying reasonableness, no glint of the self-righteous. He seemed serious, though not without wit, and he seemed open. He was always what the moment called for and he was always himself. His ability to strike the right balance, together with his confidence, gave his actions moral force.

On television Billy was a great listener. He looked at his guests, Jennings thought, with a faintly wrinkled brow. He let silences linger. Often his guests said more than they intended, having dropped their guard. Billy himself, though he said little, was never upstaged. He had a way of asking a sudden sharp question, gently phrased. His guest usually faltered or answered incompletely. On the follow-up Billy did not press too hard, which suggested that he was polite and his guest calculating. He also had a talent for soliloquy. At the beginning or end of a show he often spoke directly to the audience about important issues. He never criticized without finding reason to hope or praised without finding ground for improvement. Yet he spoke with true feeling, without the blandness of a man presenting the balanced view. On the air he often seemed more intimate than in person: public issues became a private matter.

But now—politics! Billy could no longer be called innocent, Jennings thought, for he was the pursuer as well as the pursued. And Jennings did not want to follow him into politics. Television was a well-paid living without real responsibility. Politics was more important. Jennings stood up and sat down. Politics! It was probably his own fault: he had encouraged Billy to spend one full week every other month investigating an issue important to New Yorkers. His intention had been to win awards for the show, but the result was political attention. Politics! And yet it was not just politics that had strained their friendship, for Billy was not the only one to have changed.

Jennings walked away from the monument. Until recently he had taken pride in his malaise and his freedom, permitting himself anything forbidden by instinct or tradition. He had used dangerous drugs and stayed out all night. He had experimented with many kinds of sex, done any kind of work. It was the most respectable kind of life. In the last couple of years, however, he had become aware that his jaded approach was itself a cliché. He considered himself free, but his freedom was a box. He remembered what the intern had said: "I've got time."

At the liquor store, his mood improved. He predicted to himself, with pleasure, what Penelope's loft would look like. Most were the same: enormous bed, too many plants, expensive pots and pans, divisions that doubled as bookcases, something ugly in an interesting way—perhaps a bathroom imprisoned in pipes. The ugly dollop was important. It lent respectability; it was a memorial to the avant-garde. He wondered what Billy saw in Penelope, whom he considered pretty but limp. She smiled like a young woman dying of leukemia on a made-for-TV movie, and she had a comical way of whispering. Her voice would trail off, so that people were always leaning toward her, uncertain whether her remark was sarcastic, ironic, or brilliant.

He spent half an hour selecting the wine. Although he was not a connoisseur, he enjoyed the descriptions that the store's owner, a man with nervous fingers, wrote beside each wine: "witty, with some charm of fruit"; "full-bodied, a sincere accompanist to your roast." Jennings wondered how much to spend. He looked at some inexpensive wines with extravagant labels, but in the end purchased something very expensive with a proletarian label. He often took solace in private jokes. It was an old habit.

2

Jennings, first to arrive at Penelope's, brought word that Billy would be delayed. He enjoyed seeing how closely Penelope's loft conformed to his model and admired the outsized paint-spattered elevator and the barbed-wire sculpture. Penelope, wearing a flowing purple dress (he remembered that she usually dressed in purple), presented her cheek for a kiss. And then, sounding overworked, asked him to wash the lettuce.

"Why's Billy late?"

"Something about a series we're doing on handicapped children."

Penelope, reviewing the wine, sighed. "What that man must go through! I could never do something with handicapped children. It's really admirable, you know. It's so *easy* not to pay attention. And Billy, Billy Bell with all that influence—the culture is terrified by the power of television, even if we're not—will actually *improve* matters. You know, I think he would make a good politician, and I don't think he should be embarrassed about it. People forget that politicians are a *necessary* evil, they forget that word *necessary*. I don't. Someone's got to do it. Those handicapped children . . ." She shook her head respectfully. "Billy would make a good politician and I'm going to tell him so, although it could be argued—and I've heard it argued—that his present position is more powerful than any political role he might want."

She asked Jennings to open his wine. "Let it breathe, I guess." Then she continued, "You know when I first realized that Billy could do politics? When I really saw that he was in touch? It was when we were together at a Village restaurant, Mario's, you probably know it, terrible food but sort of special anyway. Well, we were deep in conversation, *deep*, and all of a sudden there was this man who came over and started haranguing him about something like budgets. And Billy just smiled brightly at him, as if he'd finished a good set of tennis, and told the guy, 'I'm sorry but I'm busy.' And the remarkable thing was the man walked away beaming, as if Billy had just solved Brooklyn."

Jennings smiled and made an exaggerated motion with his hands, to indicate he could not hear her over the sound of the faucet. This gave him the chance, when the lettuce was done, to escape from the kitchen. He did not know what to make of the extraordinary view from Penelope's window. He remembered that when he had lived in the Village, a few years before, the Empire State Building was always in the corner of his eye.

"Cheese," Penelope called out from the kitchen.

"What?"

"Cheese."

Penelope unwrapped an aged Corsican goat cheese, and he surrounded it with crackers. "Do you know Kelly Martin?" she asked. "She was supposed to come tonight, and she still will if she calls."

21

Jennings said he didn't know her.

"Oh yes, you remember," she said, dipping a spoon into her lamb stew. She sipped. "You remember, she wrote that series of—what would you call them? Spoofs." She spun her tray of spices, and added a pinch of something.

He did remember. "I loved them. I—"

"Poor woman. You probably don't know what happened to her. No one really does. *Very* romantic. Almost gothic. I heard she had a breakdown over some songwriter. Anyway, one day she was just gone, poof, like that, somewhere out west. Bloomsbury types, when they had their breakdowns, went to Italy." She added another pinch. "Don't bring it up if she comes, but I think she's going to teach . . . grade school." Another pinch. "Did you like her work?"

Jennings said he did.

"I was talking to someone who said the stories didn't wear very well, though, and I think there's some truth to that. Of course she was just getting started, but it's basically all there in the beginnings. Sad. Even her editor, I've heard, thinks those little spoofs are rather thin and dated. Of course, what doesn't date? Michelangelo dates. They just seemed a little pale, not really carried through. Did you put enough crackers with the cheese?"

Jennings left to check the crackers. He remembered thinking that, had he been a writer, he would have liked to write stories like hers. They were cutting, and close to his chilly view, yet they occasionally possessed a soft, unanticipated warmth. He brightened with anticipation. Then suddenly he asked himself, wasn't one of her sketches modeled on Penelope? He looked at the view, remembering one of Kelly's rare vulgar asides: if you hung a hammock from the World Trade Center to the Empire State Building, the giant's ass would fall on—

The telephone rang. Wasn't there also a sketch about a woman who spoke in italics? Penelope called out, "Get it, would you, that's probably Kelly."

Jennings, conscious of the eeriness that attended coincidence—when the world at large stole into his private thoughts—picked up the telephone. "Hello?" There was a moment's silence. Then a questioning voice: "Penelope?" Jennings smiled. "No, this is—but never mind, you have the right number. Is this Kelly?"

"Yes, how did you—"

"We're all expecting you," Penelope said, taking the phone from Jennings. "You have to come immediately, no ifs or buts . . . We've set a place already. To celebrate your return . . . No, nothing elaborate, just a few friends . . . Oh, that's all right, we'll start without you."

"Now you probably want a drink," Penelope told Jennings. "White wine? For me too—there's a bottle in the refrigerator." She sagged into some pillows. "Yes, it's too bad about Kelly," she said. "It will be interesting to see how she's changed." She sighed. "It's very hard to do *anything* well today. It may be a cliché to say so, but it's true: a culture in decline. Have you *read* or *seen* anything good lately? I know you don't look at art much."

He could not forget Kelly's voice—the music and shade.

"Come on now," Penelope prompted, "tell me something to go see."

And so he told her, as he poured the wine, about a new movie he liked. Penelope smiled, shook her head sadly, disagreed. "I was just . . . disappointed. Of course, I'm the only person I know who *didn't* like that movie. On the other hand, I'm the only person I know who *did* like that ridiculous movie about the country singer. Not great art, but then no one meant it to be."

Penelope often found a success disappointing, Jennings noticed, and a failure promising. He wanted to prick her.

"You seem to like failure more than success."

"Failure? Success? It's all relative, isn't it?" She paused. "But, Jennings, you haven't told me, what have *you* been up to recently?"

The doorbell interrupted him. Penelope stood up with alarming speed. "Would you get it?" she asked, settling back.

3

"No Penelope?" asked Billy at the door. His smile, fond and private, teased away the strain between them. "Where is she?" He gave Jennings a brotherly punch on the arm. "Not in the kitchen I hope." He said this in a joking voice meant to be overheard, making his earlier intimacy with Jennings seem more pronounced.

He kissed Penelope's cheek, extricated the spoon from her fingers, and took a sip of the stew. "Fabulous! Where did you, of all people, learn your way around a kitchen!"

Penelope beamed. "Women are still allowed in the kitchen, you know that. They just want men there too."

"Well, here we are!" Billy declared. "Do you mind?" he asked, holding up a bottle of Scotch. Penelope shook her head, testing the stew again. "Almost right." She studied the spice rack gravely. Billy's presence made the question of how much salt to use seem of more than ordinary importance. He stood on the outskirts, drink in hand, smiling occasionally, and said little. His silence encouraged Jennings and Penelope to talk more than usual, while orienting themselves toward him. It felt right to entertain Billy.

Jennings would have preferred to think of other things. And he was aware that his volubility only enhanced Billy's silence: compared with Penelope and himself, who were arguing about goat cheese, Billy seemed very intelligent. At the dinner table he and Penelope discussed the secret of her stew and her real estate investments. Then they reviewed the merits of various forms of exercise. When at last she asked Billy what had delayed him at the office, Billy seemed reluctant to answer. When she insisted upon knowing—"It won't go beyond this table"—Billy only smiled. Penelope looked delighted. "You're being coy."

"Not me."

"Yes you are."

"Not *me*."

Then, with easy authority, Billy refilled each wineglass. "I was just on the phone—for too long—with the director of a home for handicapped children. He didn't like what I said in the summing-up portion of my interview about the way these children are treated in New York. He wants to sue, believe it or not. I convinced him, I hope, that it was not a personal attack on him—just on the legislation." Billy smiled, then put down the wine bottle. "Those children got under my skin. You know, usually they're invisible, just not around. Or you see one at a distance. But never so many at once, so close up."

His words had power, being the first he had volunteered. "You hardly know what to do. You try to be cheerful, but they know if you don't mean it. Even if you do mean it, and I mean it,

50,701

they don't take much comfort. They've seen it before, the embarrassed cheerfulness of the healthy. You're not sure, but it's possible they smile sweetly to make *you* feel better. They seem . . . so old."

It was impressive that someone in a position of power, who did not have to pay attention to such things after hours, should be so affected by the sight of handicapped children; impressive too that he should speak of serious feelings when others discussed goat cheese. Jennings was surprised. It was hardly a great insight that the handicapped often reassured the healthy, but Billy did not usually put that sort of thing into words. He must have failed with them in some unexpected way, Jennings thought. "I'm amazed," said Jennings, "that that man, loathsome as he was, would think of suing. You weren't critical of him at all. Besides, any attention caused by a suit would only—"

"He won't sue. There's too much talk in the government right now about welfare and Medicare fraud."

"Corruption?" said Penelope.

"He doesn't want attention."

"How much corruption?"

"No one knows."

"Maybe we should continue the series," Jennings said.

"The director was stealing from *cripples*?"

"We've already done five programs, though, and the ratings are tapering off. No, I don't think he's stealing. And it would be hard to break the issues format. I'm hoping some journalists will pick it up."

"I'll bet he's corrupt," Penelope said. "Even if it's difficult to prove. Anyway, you know what I've always said—"

"Next fall, we could repeat the series, take a different angle on it."

"What I've always *said*," continued Penelope, "is that politicians are guilty until proven innocent."

"Why do you think everyone is corrupt?"

"Am I wrong?"

Billy laughed—an easy laugh, not an eruption. "You may be right." Then he was silent again, busying himself with salad. His discussion of handicapped children, lawsuits, and corruption made gossip difficult, and it was awkward to proceed to any other serious topics without him.

HILBERT COLLEGE
McGRATH LIBRARY
5200 SOUTH PARK AVE.
HAMBURG, N. Y. 14075

"You've been busy," Penelope said after a moment. "All this talk."

"About what?"

"About what!"

"You mean politics."

"Well, is it true?"

"Let's hope not," said Jennings.

"Billy's not saying. Coy again."

"Not at all. It's just talk."

"Come on."

Billy, leaning back, did not seem to mind questions, but he would neither confirm nor deny the reports. He smiled and shook his head; he touched up their glasses with wine. At last he said, "Who would wish politics on me? With all these bad reviews!" The tease excited Penelope, who pleaded for something off the record. She helped him to more food. She held his hand. Billy laughed—and they began a long conversation about the corruption, shallowness, and calculation of politics. Politicians, local and national, fell before their attack. A cozy feeling of accord, of putting the world to rights, settled over the table. In the shared candlelight even Jennings, as he mocked the mayor, believed that Billy would be different, and that his friends would share in the difference.

The doorbell startled them. It was as disorienting as daylight after a movie. "I almost forgot Kelly," said Penelope, rising slowly to open the door. Somewhat shyly, but without hesitation, Kelly embraced Penelope. "The apartment is fine," she whispered, and then, separating from her, turned to meet the others. Billy stood up, followed by Jennings. "You probably know Billy Bell and this is Jennings—"

"White," said Jennings.

"Now what are we going to feed you?"

Penelope raised one hand to her eyes. It would be necessary to reheat the stew, everyone was happy to wait, it wasn't any trouble.

Kelly said, "No."

She broke away from the group, moving with a light step in a wide circle around the loft. "I forgot about your view! I didn't remember what it was like."

She looked at the men, who looked at her.

"Who wants Sacher torte?" asked Penelope. "Cappuccino, espresso, et cetera?"

As they cleared the table, Jennings studied her closely, but without obtrusiveness; whenever she turned toward him his expression lost its focus. His first impression was of delightful quickness, and then, curiously, of something old-fashioned. It was not her clothing, appearance, or manners that created this impression, for there was nothing precious or ladylike about her. It was a fineness of grain—a way of speaking with her eyes, for example, when words were unnecessary—that seemed to come from another period. And behind her banter with Penelope there was a seriousness Jennings could not quite understand, since she was not earnest or self-important.

After helping pass around dessert and coffee, Kelly sat down opposite Jennings. Then she looked at him. He glanced away—having encountered, when their eyes touched, a startling warmth. Blue eyes were rarely warm, but when they were were as beautiful as sunlight on water. Jennings, uneasy, began to talk with foolish animation to Penelope. Then his words seemed to die away. Kelly's beauty was not of the blinding kind, which absorbs the surrounding light. It did not demand attention and flustered compliments, but it did require some significant response—some meeting of her expression. Jennings looked up and away. He felt dull. Not elegantly dull, as in his earlier ennui, but simply flat.

Penelope, having dutifully quizzed Kelly on her trip and apartment, returned the conversation to politics. But Jennings noticed something odd: Billy was no longer the center of attention. Penelope refilled Kelly's glass. "Come on," she chided, "you're behind us. Drink up."

4

Kelly had not wanted to come. To turn down Penelope's invitation, however, seemed ungracious. Hadn't Penelope found her an apartment? And so she flagged a cab—the subway was too jarring for the first day back—and sped down Eleventh Avenue. She relished the surge against the potholes and yellow lights. The shot down the dark, deserted West Side, she thought, was one of the great rides in New York. She put the meter out of mind, then felt a moment's fear at the prospect of the party.

A year ago her old boyfriend, who loved parties, would have made everything easy. He was a pianist-composer, with a charming Broadway bravado, who wanted to elevate musicals into something like opera. Whatever his success, she thought, he would not amount to much in her eyes. He was forceful on the surface, but timid of heart. He was too desperate to impress. She could have forgiven him all that, but not his failure to be serious and kind when it mattered. Two images from their last meeting entered her mind: his black turtleneck and the lifeless green of a hospital wall. She leaned back in the seat. Yet he was wonderful with a crowd. And he could be sweet when he was not being successful.

She recalled her pointed little phrase "priapic pride" and wondered if her sudden notoriety had made the black turtleneck jealous. Would anyone remember those satirical pieces, written in a mood of developing disgust? Their subjects varied from her friends and the places she went to fashionable ideas and the yearning for fame. She hoped no one remembered them. They were self-centered and cold. They took the richness from the world. The spark of her humor had crystallized into fine hard irony; and the clarity of her insight had hardened into ice. She did not want it that way! Her friends would be surprised, she thought, to hear that she was teaching ninth graders, as she had out west. Although her job as an editor at a good magazine remained open, she preferred to spend the year in more modest work. Teaching was a way for her to ease into the city, while considering what she wanted to do. Besides, she found something touching in the gawky arrogance of a good adolescent mind.

She rolled down the window to feel the wind. It was best, she thought, to develop a detachment that was neither cold nor bloodless—to be a skeptic, but with a gentle, wry humor and a gift for spontaneous pleasure. Why was that so hard? Perhaps it wasn't. On the way up to Penelope's loft, she enjoyed the peculiar artiness of the elevator, which was once used for freight. It smelled of garbage and French bread: the SoHo flavors, she thought, of dirt and chic. Inside the loft, where the more intimate smells of bodies, food, and wine made her feel like an intruder, she simply spun herself away from Penelope to praise the view. She demanded agreement from the men while she helped Penelope serve the Sacher torte.

Then she sat down and looked at each person in turn. Penelope was unchanged. Jennings was quiet, tightly furled. Billy Bell she knew by reputation. She could appreciate his great success as a talk-show host, since he began to shower the table with attention, becoming by turns serious and amusing. It was pleasant to be coaxed by his charm. It did not seem slick, since he was sometimes shy; often his words would end on a slightly tentative note, a faint question or appeal. So taken was she that when the questions to her ended she looked him full in the face, expecting to smile. Something queer happened: it was as if she had fallen through his eyes and that somewhere in the surprise of the fall he had stolen a look at things not meant to be seen.

She turned away, and the conversation lagged. She felt put on the spot. They were staring at her. And so, straightening in her chair, she surveyed the table and asked with some strictness, "Who here's been to Montana?" This time the silence pleased her. She liked, sometimes, to take center stage.

"I drove across the state to college," Penelope said. "Northern route to California, and what I remember is long—long, long, *long*, though of course very beautiful. Mountains and cows."

"Billy?"

Again she looked him full in the face, determined not to fall. This time there was no problem. "Not Montana," he said, "but I've spent some time in northern Wyoming. Beautiful. We were hiking."

"Must be good for hiking," Penelope said. "And canoeing and fishing and horseback riding and cowboys and sentimental photography. You know what I'd photograph? Campers and mobile homes. Not so pretty, but true—am I wrong?"

"It's more than that," said Billy, with an air of friendly correction. He glanced at Kelly. "She's an awful snob."

Penelope took happy offense.

"It must be very interesting to live there for a while," he continued. "To involve yourself in the way people live, not just as a tourist. I hope you're going to write about it."

29

"No," said Kelly, staring at him. "I don't want to write about it."

"Did you meet any organic farmers?" asked Penelope. "Or writers acting manly?"

"No."

"You ought to write something," Billy said, as if she could do them a favor. "The issues developing out there, the rise of land values, the squeeze on small landholders, oil of course, alcoholism—"

"I just lived there."

Whenever she looked at Billy, it was with cheerful indifference. And when she spoke, her eyes moved naturally from one person to the next. She continued, "The main issue around where I lived was when so-and-so would die of cancer, since he couldn't keep down the pills, or maybe if the football team would win more than one game; when so-and-so's baby would walk was very important. And Jack Creeley drove his pickup through his neighbor's new fence. He was a terrible drunk. Taxes. A girl got divorced, that was news. You know what? On Saturdays I liked listening to "Blue Suede Shoes" on a jukebox and on Sundays I sometimes went to church."

There was another moment of silence.

She felt wonderful.

Penelope, looking like a wit, said, "I know! You've become a Republican! No need to be embarrassed. All kinds of people do it."

"Then why'd you come back?"

The question surprised her. She was found out, her game uncovered. She was not unhappy, however, to be ambushed in this way. She peered at Jennings. "Well—"

"Pretty obvious why she came back," Penelope said. "Weren't you listening to what life was like on the range?" Her own wit amused her: she took time to shake her head. "Sometimes I've thought of making a photographic tour of the West. I would try to capture what the *people* were like—shoot unusual things, like the truck stops, the five and ten, not the cowboy stuff except for those rhinestone types. Maybe a picture portrait of the new West, the Sunbelt, is in order. Don't you think, Billy? But I'm so tied up here. It's true, I have a timer for my project, and I could have an assistant, of course, but to get it done right you've got to do it yourself. You must have some projects underway?" She glanced at Billy and Kelly simultaneously.

Kelly leapt in once again. "Teaching school." She looked at Jennings, but could not read his expression.

"It's very hard to support yourself with art or writing," Penelope said. "I know, I've suffered, still suffer; it's tough, really tough, really outrageous having to spend your time driving a taxi, teaching, not eating. Imagine the work that's been lost."

Did he ask why I came back, Kelly wondered, because he noticed the self-congratulation in my description of Montana? The clichés? Was his remark barbed? "I really don't plan to do any writing," she said. "Maybe a little journalism, a couple of free-lance articles."

There was another pause. Billy was watching intently, which was not displeasing; some part of her enjoyed attracting his interest, if only to ignore him. But she kept an eye on Jennings. She found his smile very disarming. It sometimes seemed un-pleasantly tight, yet also suggested an attractive kind of restraint. It was the smile of someone with taste enough not to spill his personality into the world. And it was imbued with a ghostly gentleness, of which he could not be aware.

Billy asked, "What will you be teaching?"

"History. Plain old boring American history."

Penelope leaned on the table. "Billy, would you like a cigar? I have some Cubans, and I'm going to have one of my usuals." Billy nodded. "There's also brandy for anyone who wants it." Then, with great deliberation, she lit a very thin cigar.

"You must have a Ph.D.," Billy said.

"No, I'm teaching ninth grade."

"Disadvantaged children?"

"I read a wonderful piece by a teacher who taught drug addicts to write poetry," said Penelope. "That would be intriguing, to say the least."

"No, mostly white, mostly rich."

Still looking at Billy, she asked him to pass the cigars. He struck a match for her: everyone watched the flame touch the tip. Then she glanced at Jennings. She already knew him, she thought, hav-ing known others of his kind. He was intelligent, unkempt, sleepy around the eyes. Cynical, of course, and jaded. No doubt his parents had money. She wanted to shake him, push his head under the tap, hand him a brush. What provoked her interest, though, was the odd integrity of his cynicism, for he did not seem to grant exceptions, even to himself. He was not finished thinking: an internal dysfunction left room for change. She liked that as much as the disarming smile.

"My poetry's not going too well," Penelope said, "a fallow period for the moment. Billy, did you get that collection of prose poems I sent you?"

"I liked them very much."

"Which in particular?"

"The one—oh, the one . . . with surreal overtones." He smiled. "Overlapping imagery."

"My favorite too."

Billy turned toward Kelly. "You're right, the most effective and innovating teaching goes on in the exclusive schools. They're cutting back the money for public schools in New York. Between us, I'd never work in a public school. Among other things, it's dangerous." He spoke as if he were alone with her.

"I guess you're right," she said.

Billy's expression became vague. The hand that held his cigar tapped on the table. Then his eyes focused. "I'd like to try teaching," he said slowly. "I don't know, maybe it would be rewarding. What do you think?" His expression became vague again. "Give up the show."

"Billy!" exclaimed Penelope.

He looked at Kelly.

"You might like teaching," Kelly said, matter-of-factly. "Go ahead, try it." Then she added, "If you want I could set up a job interview with our headmistress."

"That I'd like to see!" cried Penelope. "That would be something else, let's write the headline, 'Billy Bell Retires To Teach Adolescents.' I didn't know this brandy was so strong. Just before you came," Penelope told Kelly, "we were all talking about politics. They don't just want him for teaching, they want him for politics, though I've advised him to stay out. Politics to me is . . . *politics!*"

Billy smiled. "It's getting out of hand. Teitelman of all people wants to have lunch. He didn't say what he wants to talk about."

"You didn't tell me that," Jennings said.

"You'd left."

"Who's Teitelman?" asked Kelly.

"Who's Teitelman!"

"Wouldn't we like to know," Billy said, speaking as one not to be taken seriously. "He's—I don't know quite how to put it—one of the most important investment bankers. He puts together deals, but he also has close ties to both parties, knows labor leaders, advises presidents, wrote a book about welfare reform—"

Jennings, pretending to whisper to her, said, "He's always in those stories on the front page of the *Times* that nobody reads."

She smiled.

"He probably wants to find out what my intentions are. There's been all this talk in the air, all of it unsubstantiated, about my running—for what is not clear." Billy shook his head. "Today the office seems to find the man, not the other way around."

Kelly was certain she was right: Jennings did not, in the fashion of so many people she knew, exclude himself from criticism. Light with wine, she looked in his direction. So rumpled! Not unappealing—and his brown eyes moved here and there, or hid behind his smile, or gleamed behind a glass. She became aware that the party was silent. Billy had directed a question at her. She reeled back the conversation: he had asked her her opinion of his entering city politics.

She looked at him, surprised at the stiffness of his manner. He had seemed so supple before. "I don't know what to say . . . Yes, no"—she laughed—"I hope you do. I bet you'd help."

5

Billy tap-tapped the ash off his cigar. He considered going home. That would be too abrupt, though, with so much of the cigar left. He rested, raising the glass of brandy to his lips once, twice, three times. He breathed in deeply. The after-dinner table was a warm and fine place, a place of comforting disarray. He plucked a grape from a basket of fruit. A place to relax and enjoy. "Well, we'll see about politics," he said. "We'll see." He took another deep breath and looked up. This friend of Penelope's seemed to talk a lot. "My particular problem," he said, "is to decide what office to run for."

Penelope asked him his first choice.

"I don't really know. That's what I'm going to have to look

into, to try to balance my own choice—if I decide to run at all—with what's politically feasible."

There was a pause.

"The apartment couldn't be better," Kelly told Penelope. "If you stick your head out the window you can see the Hudson. And it's not too noisy, either."

Penelope smiled. "I can't imagine anyone calling you Mayor Bell!"

"Friends would never have to call me Mayor Bell."

"Where's the apartment?" Jennings asked.

"Upper West Side, in the Eighties."

"That's an issue you'd have to figure out," said Penelope. "Rent control. People turn savage about rent control. I know a marriage that practically broke up over whether ending rent control was immoral. The husband became a neo-conservative. Let's ask Mayor Bell—"

"I haven't made up my mind yet. That part of the West Side where your apartment is—I've never seen such rapid change. Is your building one of those beautiful old barns?"

"Well, only partially renovated. And I just have a small one-bedroom, but high ceilings."

"Imagine Mayor Bell rewriting the housing laws. Of course he'd never give us inside information. Would you, Billy?"

"No, but—are you going to redecorate it or is it already furnished?" He smiled at her. He wanted her to tell him, right away, what she was going to do to her apartment.

"Who cares?" Jennings said. "She probably has a bunch of old stuff from Montana coming by pickup."

"Actually," she told Jennings with a teasing sparkle, "I have hardly anything. And what do you mean, old stuff! You ought to see what we've got in Montana. Some of the best rec-room paneling east of Los Angeles!"

"No doubt!"

Penelope also seems to talk a lot, Billy thought.

"I'm not sure," Penelope was saying, "that I want you to be Mayor Bell."

Billy tap-tapped the ash. Then, unexpectedly, he tapped his spoon against a glass. "Attention, attention," he declared in a mock-comic voice, "your attention please. Enough of boring politics. I have a question to put to the table. Hold on, quiet—

silence. How can Jennings and I, Jennings being a great but still fallible genius, improve the show? What subjects, serious subjects I mean, should we look at on the issue side of the program?" He asked Kelly, "What do you think?"

Penelope leaned back. Her eyes narrowed. "Everything is a problem, but the poverty of artists, that's important. Why not do that next?"

"Pornography is next," Jennings said.

"Why not be positive for once? The poverty of artists is a great theme. It's got a great history. The people you interview will be articulate. On the other hand . . . the degradation of women is a great, eternal theme, too." She shook her head. "*That's* something I know about." She took a moment to reflect. "I may have to publish my diary. I don't want to, but . . ." She appeared to awake. "Billy, I would seriously suggest the plight of the artist. We should discuss it."

"I'll give you a call next week." He looked at Kelly.

"I don't know how to answer," Kelly said, after a moment. "I've been away, I haven't seen the show. There must be no end of issues." He held her eyes, but her expression was merely polite.

There was a pause.

She asked Billy, "Why is Jennings such a fallible genius?"

"I was just teasing."

There was another pause.

"Will you watch?" Billy asked her. "I'll blame it all on Jennings if it's terrible."

"Sure, when I get a television."

Billy drew the ashtray close; and slowly, carefully, rubbed out the cigar. "Penelope, thank you. I have to be going."

"You can't go yet."

"I must."

All their chairs scraped. "I wanted to show you some photographs in the other room," she said. "Of you . . ."

"A rain check? I have to be up at seven tomorrow."

Penelope refused Kelly's offer to help with the dishes. She planned to stay up all night, she told the assembled company, printing in her darkroom. A flurry of goodbyes and thank-yous, and the three found themselves in the elevator. Without Penelope they seemed very close, but not much was said. Outside it was soon determined that each lived in a different part of town, and that three taxis would most quickly be found on Houston Street, several blocks north. They set off, with Kelly flanked by the two men.

"Jennings," Billy said, "let's see if we can get more people from the arts on, not the usual top celebrities but some of the really important people, even if they're not so well known outside their fields. I think that's something we ought to do that's not being done—" He hesitated. "I want you to look into that tomorrow. It would be interesting for me too, because some of these people we interview are boring. They don't matter.

"In that," he explained to Kelly, as if to apologize for not amusing her with lighthearted matters, "I'm like Penelope. Can't escape work. This doesn't mean," he said to Jennings, "turning away from actors and writers, of course, only that we should always talk to the really serious people in the other areas too—the most respected judges, civil servants, even the best auto mechanic." As they walked past the iron buildings, he continued to give Jennings orders. Now and then, over the crunch of their footsteps, he directed a polite word at Kelly. He closed the door of one taxi, and another, and at last was alone.

6

In the darkness Billy blushed. He leaned against a wall until the spreading warmth prickled the tips of his fingers. After the glare of the party the evening seemed very kind. He looked at the black-browed buildings and some phrases from an old special on SoHo came into his mind: iron-proud warehouses . . . Albanians, Lithuanians . . . the Brooklyn Bridge. Then he decided to walk to his apartment on West Tenth Street, which was only twenty minutes away. He did not review the party. Instead, with practiced violence, he cleansed himself of thought and let the city begin to work on him. At a red light the thrust of the towers lifted his eyes; the drama of black and white quickened his breath. The light changed. A pair of lovers passed him, and he wondered if they knew who they had passed.

After a few blocks he considered the evening, but on his own terms. Penelope's friend, for example, must wait until he attended to more serious matters—politics. A field of greater significance than television. An important politician was the first principle, Billy thought, the generator of conversation and consequence. An important politician seemed to stand, hidden and enhanced, behind an aura of light, attention, power, hope. Politics. He remembered the stab of JFK's finger. How warm it was in Los Angeles after the assassination! And how cool it looked in Washington! He remembered admiring on television the gleaming uniforms of the soldiers, the muffled drums, the hushed announcers, the perfection of the family—sad daughter, little son, pretty wife rich and young. There had been joy in his mourning, the exhilaration of distant grief. But, he wondered, what did politicians actually do? In print and on television they announced and attacked. He knew he would excel at that. But the rest?

Billy murmured, "Jennings'll come around." He walked awhile without thinking, then shook his head fondly. Someday Jennings would be good at politics. Once he decided to concentrate, Jennings had the insider's knack for getting things done—a knack that seemed inseparable from his general disdain for the operations of the world. Billy loved both this knack and this disdain, when modified by one other trait. Jennings might be immune to celebrity, he might keep his own counsel, he might not court anyone's good opinion—but he was loyal. Except . . . Jennings and his knobs! Teitelman, extraordinary man! A person, Billy thought, for whom doubts did not exist. Teitelman *knew*. Rich through his own efforts, a first-name friend to everyone, the holder of numerous keys, Teitelman possessed an assurance that impressed Billy. With pleasure he remembered the man in the white suit, walking, walking, walking down the corridor.

Several couples spilled out of a bar. His thoughts moved, without seeming to, from politics to women. He remembered breaking up recently with his lover of six weeks: she was crying, he was tender. What a lovely person, he thought, both in bed and out. He planned to keep up with her, as he had with most of his lovers; he prided himself on staying friends. He walked a little more. Then with a calm feeling of having shaped the world to his sense, he let himself remember Penelope's friend. She was an attractive woman, he thought, quite friendly, certainly very opinionated. She appeared aloof, of course, and he rarely liked such women. But, he had to admit, she was very nice. He continued to parade the poor gray compliments through his mind, then became aware it wasn't working. He could not properly adjust her in his thoughts. And pressure was building elsewhere. It took terrific energy to continue the gray compliments, to march the man in the white suit down the corridor. His hold began to slip: and he blushed for the second time.

It was sometimes like this. His first meeting with a pretty woman, when she did not know his reputation, was very important. Relations between them would never again seem so simple, pure —naked. He would never again know her so well or be so well known himself. Those first undressed moments, before the usual business began, were all Billy knew of charm and rest and innocence: what he loved about Kelly was her brown and blue coloring, the brown of her complexion promising shade, the blue of her eye yielding a soothing light, without vulgar flash. First meetings, however, also made him shy. Until she knew about him, he felt exposed and vulnerable. And so he quickly began a performance, which hung between them like a transparent scrim.

He loved best the moment when he was not seen, the sudden catch in her perception as she thought, "I'm not talking to an ordinary person, I'm talking to Billy Bell." He remembered lighting Kelly's cigar—and tightened. Not once had he found, after their introduction, the right reflection in her eyes. He had the impression instead that her view of him never changed, that she looked at him and couldn't care less, that she was even making fun of him. He knew that sometimes he fell obsessively, idiotically, for one of the women who did not like him. And as he walked down the street he berated himself for this stupid behavior. That sort of thing shouldn't happen any more. Earlier in his life there had been some embarrassments, confessions and mopings, but he had subsequently learned to blunt the pain of his various obsessions with women. He would ignore her, or sleep with her once, or decide she was gay.

At a second red light he remembered his failure to warm up the handicapped children. Well, he thought, that will change. As a politician he would make his unexpected visit, having authorized money for an expensive machine. He would write the new legislation. He would see the surprised looks in damaged faces and give the impromptu speech from the steps. He would be generous to a fault. And the same night he would take someone out—someone he really liked that he'd met somewhere. And he would toast her, rolling the stem of the wineglass between his fingers to raise a sparkle.

CHAPTER

THREE

I

Despite a week of shopping, Kelly could not find the furniture she wanted—inexpensive, with straightforward lines. This didn't bother her, since she planned to take as much time as necessary. Where she lived mattered. She disliked haphazard arrangements, or the kind of room, still popular with some friends, that was decorated in dormitory style. Her plan was to buy the bones first— table, couch, bed, chair—then to add the smaller things that gave character to a place. The look of an apartment, she thought, should develop almost unnoticed, like the character of a child.

Except for boxes of linen, books, and kitchen utensils, nothing remained from before. She had given most things away. Her new apartment, which was on the seventh floor, had a cramped bedroom without much light, a living room, a narrow kitchen, and a bathtub with a crack like a spider. Often the hot soupy smell of the Hudson River sloshed through her rooms. She liked the old beleaguered Hudson. And she liked the silence, for she was in a protected corner at the end of a corridor. After shopping she believed, without thinking about it, that she was returning home.

Her first days were quiet. In the mornings she read in preparation for her class; after lunch she walked through the neighborhood. She wanted everything ordinary, and it was. The vivid day of her return was not forgotten, but she was pleased that, having settled in, she had no more colorful moments. She did not try to contact old friends. Some stopped by, but she knew they found her apartment at the end of the corridor depressing. They were polite about her job. If they were friends, she thought, they would stick by her. If not— She was saddened but not surprised by the small betrayals of friends. Once her telephone was installed, she heard from several more people, who spoke vaguely of lunch. When Jennings called, however, her spirits suddenly picked up.

She could hardly understand him: his sentences kept tacking back and forth. She hoped she knew the reason. When she told him her apartment was unfurnished, he offered to take her to Prendergast's, where he could arrange a discount. Prendergast's, which had become even more popular than Bloomingdale's, did not appeal to her much. But she wanted to see him, so they agreed to meet for lunch and shopping.

The restaurant was small and French-flavored, with red-checked tablecloths, old travel posters, and paper flowers in wine bottles. Young midtown professionals waited in line with friends from the office. The specialty was hearty soup. She arrived first and Jennings came soon after, but could not find her in the crowd. Seeing him lost among the pinstriped lawyers, she could not help but like him. She smiled as he sat down complaining about midtown congestion. He began, with the air of taking matters in hand, to question her. How was the shopping? Where had she gone? What did she need? After each short answer there was a long pause, since he was less good at follow-up questions. She could not resist teasing him. "I forgot," she said. "You're a journalist."

He looked startled. But only for a moment: the shadow in his expression melted away, and he said with mock horror, "Not me! That's Billy!"

She enjoyed his slight awkwardness, regarding it as a compliment to herself. After a while, however, she began to pity him and busied herself with a monologue about how hard it was to find furniture. Men uneasy with small talk were well-known to her, and she knew how to fill the gaps in their conversation. She asked him, once the wine softened the edge between them, how he could arrange a discount.

"The best way of all."

"Which is?"

"I know Tom Prendergast—you can guess how he came to be the boss." There was a pause. "Don't think I don't know anybody but the people I went to college with, but that's also where I met him. I've managed to stay in touch. Have you read about him?"

"I've heard something."

"He's incredible. He lives on top of his store, acting crazy—dashes around a sort of vast warehouse up there, talking too fast, wearing anything from rags to silk undershirts. Everyone talks about his isolation, how he never sees anybody but two or three friends; the rich recluse, whispers of orgies and so on. But I don't believe half the rumors—I think he starts them."

His words were touched with wonder, the first she had discerned in him.

"Do you know," he continued, "that in the five years since he took over, the store has changed from being just another of those old ladies in midtown to being by far the most popular place to shop in New York? He's a genius at marketing. People go there to be entertained, the way they go to the movies."

There was a pause. And, then, as she watched, his expression contracted with intelligence and doubt. "Of course, the madness makes him money. I know that."

"You're one of those people he sees?"

"I've never asked him for anything." He met her eyes. "Nothing except discounts." He looked down, picked up a spoon. "I guess I was one of the few people who was nice to him in college. He wasn't like he is now. Then he was quiet, sort of pudgy, not the sort of person anyone noticed . . ." She stopped paying attention to his words and listened to his voice, which had some gravel in it. "So you see, I don't think anyone knew who he was. How much do you think you'll spend?"

She shrugged, and glanced at him. He studied his menu. Their silence, though a little embarrassed, was not uncomfortable. His quiet seemed natural to her, not because he lacked things to say, but because he was by nature a little remote. He was one who waited, doubted, appraised, one to whom not much in the world

42

was worth the words. He looked up. She met his eyes—and spun off, the blood rising to her face. She studied her menu. It must take great energy, she thought, to keep eyes so warm inside such a cool manner.

"What are you going to have?" he asked, when their waiter began to hover.

She wasn't sure.

He said, "Maybe I'll have the celery soup."

That sounded wrong to her. He should order something more nourishing, a strong peasant soup like goulash. "That won't fill you," she said. "You should have —" She mentioned the heavier soups.

"And you?" he asked.

She planned to order a salad. That sounded wrong to him. "You shouldn't just order a salad in a soup restaurant," he said.

"Well?"

"Well?"

There was a pause.

"I'll have the bouillabaisse," he said.

"Me too."

They smiled together.

After a moment, their conversation turned to other people, since it was too early to talk about themselves. They found themselves in delighted agreement about the failings of mutual friends. "He uses every portentous reference, every lousy shred of alliteration," Jennings said, dismissing a critic his own age. "It makes you sick after a while, all that fancy tonguing of the page."

"Well, what's really sickening," she said, "is that you can never forget he's writing, never just read, because he's always so close, always saying look at me do this, look at me do that, isn't this pretty, aren't I clever?"

Jennings nodded.

There was a pause.

She thought, He's wearing camouflage.

He dressed so that it could not be said how he dressed: each article of clothing canceled the effect of another. That day he wore a faintly checkered jacket, rather preppy; the shirt was not worn or woodsy or Oxford, however, but business blue and shiny, as if yanked fresh from a cellophane wrapper. And he left it open at the neck, though it should have been worn with a tie. She leaned over—trousers pressed, shoes scuffed.

"Or," she said, when their soup came, "do you know that friend of his?" She mentioned a name.

"Do I ever!"

"He's worse. I never met someone whose ambition is so—*rank*."

With Jennings what she disliked about New York could be shaken out like laundry.

"Just pride—"

"But unmodified by any sort of doubt or self-ridicule."

"That's him."

There was a pause.

He raised his spoon to his lips. She raised hers. Up and down, up and down. She relaxed as the hot thick soup sent shivers along her arms. It was so easy to see through his manner! Perhaps that explained his elusive charm. What seemed cold and passive in his character, she thought, was little more than an ill-fitting cloak, cleverly worn.

Jennings, having finished his soup, smiled at her—a conspiratorial smile that asked, "Well, who do we savage next?" When she did not answer, his eyes darkened, and her mood turned sweet and murky. She liked his difficulty. She wanted to tease, awaken, provoke—to clarify the vague promise in his expression. And to fail at such ticklish work? She imagined a kind of stillness.

He sat up. "Penelope!" he exclaimed. "Penelope was one of the subjects in your sketches!"

"Very close," she said slowly, "but not an exact fit." It was hard for her to discuss the sketches. It would mean, in the end, describing her earlier life in New York. She was prepared to do so, but Jennings did not pursue the point. His discretion touched her. "But you know," she said, "she never suspected a thing. People rarely do. They're blind to themselves. Two people thought they were models, and they were wrong. So long as you're not literal, so long as you don't make the character live exactly where someone real lives. None of the actual models had the faintest idea."

She finished the soup. "Anyway, I would never use models again."

"No?"

"No."

Once more he skirted the "why?"

There was a long pause.

Then she asked him about Billy. She did not understand the friendship, since the two men seemed neither similar nor complementary in outlook.

"Has he called you?"

"What?"

"I think he likes you. He hasn't called?"

She shook her head, flattered and dismayed.

"We're very old friends, but I don't really know what else to say about him. You saw how he was at the party. He's under a lot of pressure now, since he has to decide whether to go into politics. He'd probably be good at politics—he's superb at television."

She wanted to ask Jennings more, but thought it would seem girlish. And she did not want him to think she preferred Billy. "He doesn't sound like your best friend."

"He is."

Something in his praise was ungenerous. The touch of meanness in his character, however, enhanced her sense of his potential. It gave his existence drama; it meant he would have to earn a good life. Not an easy person—but then a peaches-and-cream personality could never please her. She repeated, "Superb at television." Then, looking up, she teased him. "Does that mean you're superb at television too?"

"Hardly. I don't even watch television much."

There was a pause.

"But I don't know what else to do."

His smile was friendly but sealed. She knew she would learn little more—at least, not then. In any case, his success or failure at work was not very important to her. What mattered was that his life had an inner shape that could hold her interest. "No, let me help!" she insisted, when he reached for the check. Their hands touched. He refused. She insisted. Then, when their hands did not part of their own accord, she leaned back in her chair. Jennings was indifferent to traditional manners, she told herself, so this was not a routine gesture. She accepted it as another compliment.

2

At the restaurant door Jennings stopped abruptly. He had to call Tom, he said, to arrange for the discount. What he really wanted, however, was a moment alone. Not since the age of fourteen or fifteen, when every exchange with a girl seemed significant, had he felt so bewildered—so charmed by the sweet, awkward savor of coming to know someone. Long ago he had learned to convert his shyness into wry superiority; the soft smile became impregnable. But now . . . "Tom's not available," he reported. "Doesn't matter, we'll just go over." As they walked toward Prendergast's his arm sometimes brushed against hers, but he rarely spoke or looked at her. The light in her face was too surprising: it always forced him to turn away, leaving his perception of her partial, his sense of her beauty blurred.

They walked and walked—and then something was said. He glanced at her, then repeated the only word he remembered as a question.

"Shoes?"

"Shoes," she said. "I've always been amazed at how many shoe stores there are in New York. I don't see how they all survive— must be everyone is going somewhere."

Shoes? Instinct told him to say something droll. About shoes? But her observation did not demand a reply. She was not even looking at him. A different question came to him: how had she written those chilly pieces? He could not reconcile the sketches with what he knew of her character. He stretched his imagination as far as he could. But no, he could not connect the two. The woman beside him was not chilly. He was so perplexed that he did not know how to behave. To appear superior in the usual way might seem artificial to the woman beside him, while to appear naïve or unknowing—or in love—might provoke the scorn of the sketch-writer. So he became quiet. He blanketed his mind in a fine peaceful haze.

At Prendergast's, however, she required guidance. Was the store the kind of place she wrote about with ironic distaste? He announced, "Well, here we are."

"Really!"

His stupidity astonished him.

He adopted the role of guide. This allowed him to talk a great deal, while behaving in a colorless way—not far in spirit from his hazy silence. He spoke with authority. To illustrate Tom's genius he pointed to the façade, where the name "Prendie's" ran in a long neon diagonal from the upper to the lower corner of the store. "It used to be a stone colossus," he said. "Florentine banker's style, very forbidding. So Tom ran the zippy name across the front, which provoked enormous controversy. He tried to keep the argument going as long as possible, since it was good free advertising. Some people think Tom violated the architectural integrity of the building, while others say he added contrast, excitement, surprise."

"I see."

"He wants to get every kind of person with any money to come. Foreigners visit Prendergast's before anything else in New York—a prime minister gave a luncheon here. Tom tells me girls from Teaneck list "Walking through Prendie's" in their yearbooks under "hobbies." But the amazing thing is that even the highbrow condescending intellectuals sort of like the place. They hate Bloomingdale's, but they think Prendergast's is camp, I guess. Tom takes all the department store stuff and makes it—I don't know—self-conscious, a sort of put-on; makes all the clichés obvious. He announces in a huge ad that he wants to make an outrageous amount of money."

They passed through the whirling doors. A great space opened before them—so charged with color and movement that it could not be held whole in the eye. "Tom wants to stun the entering customers," Jennings explained. "Make them forget themselves for a moment. Good for sales." They watched as shoppers hurried past or stopped short. Tall ladies drifted toward them, squirting wrists with perfume; scarves, bangles, bracelets, and knickknacks shimmered on mirrored counters; here and there someone sniffed his watch. "The store pulls in so many directions," Jennings said, "that buying something is the best way to keep your balance."

Kelly edged away, browsing. Now and then she glanced at him, but paid little attention to what he said. He stood where he was: she looked so free. Then she tossed a scarf into the air, smiling.

She rejoined him. "This place is dangerous."

He resumed his tour. He rather admired Tom, he told her. In the way Tom squeezed each style until it popped there was a kind of mad conviction; conviction, too, in the endless theater and celebration of camp.

She slipped away to rap a frying pan with her knuckles.

He waited alone, but continued the speech to himself. The store mixed the sauce of style in New York. Every ingredient, from European svelte to American cowboy, was represented; each new trend in fashion was soon absorbed; only the polyester style of the suburban shopping malls was excluded. In the newspapers, beneath the ads that described this tasty brassiere or that sexy cookie, the motto of the store always appeared: "Everything that's anything."

Their eyes met.

"That's one of Tom's typical techniques," he said, pointing to a man dressed as a town crier, who was beating a drum and shouting in an English accent, "Come ye, come ye, to the floor fifth, Taste the splendor of the court medieval."

"Tom's been playing up the Middle Ages because of a new television program and the festival at Lincoln Center."

"Where are the beds?"

She tugged him toward the escalators, asking, "Do you think they have bedsprings?"

He liked being tugged.

"It's amazing," he said. "Everything you don't need. Sometimes I come here to visit Tom and I think it's the most—" He searched for the right word. Then he realized that, once again, she had not been sarcastic. Her remark was playful. "I don't know, bad taste in a way, a reflection"—here, foundering, he became intellectual—"of the basest side of a well-off group, a rich group—"

"Shshshshsh," she interrupted, putting one finger on her lips and another on his arm. "Listen."

He did.

She stood stone still, as if listening in the woods.

"Do you hear?"

He heard tiny bells; and somewhere, everywhere, a chirrup.

"Crickets," she said, dropping the finger from his arm. It left a warm spot. "I can't explain the bells"—a comic gleam entered her eye—"strange spirits of some kind, but what else could make the chirruping sound?" He did not know what to do or say. "Lots of crickets here," she said, looking around as if they were a lonely couple in a forest deep. "Don't you think?" Was she teasing him? "And spiders," she said. "Here comes a spider now; careful."

A languorous lady, adrift on a perfumed breeze, squirted his wrist with cologne; a second asked if he would like to open a charge account. When he resumed the role of guide, he found it grotesquely pompous. He deepened his voice to make fun of himself rather than the store. When she smiled, however, he pointed to The Crescent, a cavalcade of shops that formed a semicircle at one end of Prendergast's. Along the crescent, he said, were boutiques that carried stereo equipment, plants, health food, camping equipment, jogging shoes. The central shop, to which he drew her attention, was called Le French Fry. It sold junk food. "He's always rearranging the order of the other shops," Jennings said, "always retuning them, as he says. He thinks he can never get the order or pitch quite right, never stay exactly abreast of what people want—"

He looked around. A young woman nearby picked through towels. It was Kelly, but he might have been looking at a stranger. He felt a prick of pain—and then of pleasure, for he was able to admire her figure. He liked the flare of her hip as she reached for a towel and the tightening around her breasts when she held up the towel to the light. Her body did not bulge in her clothes, but came alive in movement: revealed now, hidden again. The spot where she had touched his arm glowed.

"Nothing," she said, turning away.

On the escalator Jennings leaned against the banister. "Tom's theory," he said, "is called 'bounce.' He studies how people visit the shops on The Crescent, and if the order is right they bounce—that's why it's a curve, to help the caroming. If they begin at Le French Fry they might feel guilty, so they'll bounce to jogging to take off weight, to health to ward off cancer, to stereo to forget it all. If you begin with something moral like sports you bounce to junk food or stereo as a reward. Even if you resist junk food the delicious smell gets you so worked up that you have to buy something—a flowering plant, maybe. Le French Fry is the keystone of the arch . . ."

They walked to the next escalator bank. As he spoke, her expression became increasingly dutiful. "Around here somewhere is one of his greatest successes," he said. "You've heard of it, a place called 'Private Parts' that sells underwear and lingerie—open only to women, so the ACLU has sued. Tom's made a fortune there. Furniture is up here too, fourth floor. Let's see, bedsprings."

Was she slightly irritated? Or just pretending?

He said, "Amazing, don't you think?"

"Yes—" Her tone was vague.

In a designer's enclave he pointed to clothes that would flatter her. "This scarf . . . that belt . . . a shift." He was conscious of sounding obnoxious, of acting bossy rather than flirtatious. He hesitated—silence was always possible.

At last she asked, her words flat, "Do you dislike the way I'm dressed?"

"No."

"Well, I don't like the way you dress." Was she serious? "In fact," she said, "I would guess you remove the designer labels from your clothing."

"What?"

She sees through me, he thought.

"You heard me."

Inside him a knot parted.

"Oh, that's just good taste," he said, "Not to—"

"No better, no worse. Another kind of design."

Found out.

"You're right."

"I do it too."

Jennings, swept into happiness, abandoned the guide. Touching her arm, he whispered, "A spider behind you." Then, playing, he regarded her with vast import.

During their walk to the right department they often nodded gravely, like a pair of silent conspirators. This delighted Jennings: he had not been ridiculous since childhood. Best of all was when, at the approach of a spider, she stiffened—and the spider passed by. At last he muttered, "We're here." The sound of his voice let some air out of his spirits, but he remained playful as they surveyed the hundreds of beds positioned with careful asymmetry. Then Kelly shut her eyes, stretched out her arms, and fell backwards onto one. Her eyes opened wide. "Too soft."

"May I help you?"

They looked at each other.

50

A salesman had come upon them. His charcoal suit was elegant, which led Jennings to think: salesman-spider-snob. Kelly explained what she wanted. The salesman did not look surprised when almost everything proved to be too expensive, even with the discount. When she stopped in front of a small double bed the salesman glanced at his watch; the glance was surreptitious, but not so they could fail to notice. "Why don't you each try it?" he suggested, smiling a little. "After all, you'll be spending one-third of your life there."

Kelly lay flat on her back.

"You too," said the salesman.

He did not look at her, though the salesman was an excellent subject for ridicule.

"Go on."

"I'll take her word for it."

Something went very wrong.

Kelly sat up.

Without thinking, Jennings lay down beside her. It was odd to lie on a bed in this great open arena, with his shoes on and the sound of business everywhere. He stared at the ceiling. Then he recalled their conspiratorial glances. He remembered what it was to be ridiculous. He crossed his legs, stretched his arms, and said with mock satisfaction, "I think I'll take a nap."

"Write it up," she told the salesman.

It seemed too quiet once they arranged delivery. On an impulse he stepped behind a display of soap dishes. "Are you a *demure* lady?" he asked, exhibiting an azure dish on which was printed "Call me DEMURE."

She smiled. "Of course not."

"Are you *loud*?" He showed her how a red soap dish worked. She shook her head.

"Are you melancholy?" A blue dish.

"There it is!" Kelly said.

"What?"

"The crickets!"

"What?"

She pointed to a machine that, when digesting a credit card, made cricket sounds. "The sound of money."

3

They walked lazily uptown, then broke quickly to prevent embarrassment. For awhile Jennings hardly noticed anything; the sting of parting was too sweet. Then he realized that a great difficulty had entered his life. Love did not fit him, or not quite. His reawakened feelings hurt. They asserted themselves, having been dormant so long, with the force of an adolescent crush. They made his present life, no less adolescent in its way, seem dead. He shuddered: so much would have to change. An awful reluctance, like a dank cloud, closed in around him.

He looked for distraction. When an old, fairly well-preserved Mustang pulled up at a traffic light, he examined it with devotion. When did they first come out? Was it 1964? A couple of years before he got his license? He drew abreast of the car and heard its radio—and then the driver turned up the sound. It was one of the old AM radios. Before Jennings recognized the song, he knew that loud, bad radio sound: the cracked treble, the wallowing bass, the vibration inside the box. The song was "Duke of Earl," which had come out before his time, when he was about eleven. But he could repeat the words by rote.

Their sense did not interest him. All that mattered was the sharp convulsion of his memory, as he remembered those times with girls when he was much younger. This convulsion was less a case of nostalgia than an affront, the harsh jab of a crowded and offended past. He felt as if, having been elbowed from behind, he'd whirled around in anger—to find someone he loved. He yielded a little, and relaxed into a single image: he was in the driver's seat of his parent's Volvo, having recently received his license. Beside him was his girlfriend. It was summer, they wore bathing suits, he had stopped for gasoline. That was all. But he could grasp, as he stood on Park Avenue, the warm slick plastic of the wheel. He could smell the hot leather of the seat, and he could see the fall of sunlight across her arm.

Next to this, his recent past looked dim. He could recall certain events—going to work for Billy in 1972, moving into his apartment, dining across from Kelly at Penelope's—but only in the indifferent fashion of an almanac. This frightened him. It was as if time were beginning to slide; as if, instead of a step-by-step progression, his twenties were passing in a skid. The song came to an end. He continued to repeat the words: "Nothing can stop me now, 'cause I'm the Duke of Earl."

When the Mustang, trailing inky exhaust, rumbled across Park Avenue, he repressed an embarrassing desire to run after it. He heard the opening bars of another song . . . a Phil Spector number . . . and then was left with the sound of New York. He resumed his walk, beginning to think more analytically. A few years before he had taken up jazz, which he preferred to rock. And yet—he realized that for him rock would always be the really significant music. This was true for almost everyone his age, whether or not they listened to much of it. How good or lasting the music was, how helpful or damaging its effect, seemed insignificant next to the overwhelming fact of it. Rock music was in his bones; it was in the air he breathed. It was the chorus that accompanied almost every act of sex, politics, drugs, or study taken during his youth. Steppenwolf was the moment on the highway to California, the Stones were the touch of tongues inside a girl's mouth, Hendrix was Woodstock or the march on Washington. A rock song, he thought, was often more than itself. It assumed the coloring of the moment when it was first heard. It tagged time. For a moment he had the unpleasant feeling that his hope for the future was consigned to the past.

4

Jennings said hello to the summer intern, then shut his door. His office, slightly more than a cubicle, was famously messy. Newspapers and magazines built up around the desk until, three or four times a year, the secretaries threw everything out; it was often said, with fond condescension, that Jennings did not notice this periodic cleaning. No sooner had he shut the door than Billy opened it.

"Unbelievable day," he said. "I've been looking all over for you."

He sat down—a cleaning had recently been carried out—but soon suggested they move to his office. "Unbelievable day," he repeated, motioning Jennings to a leather chair beside the desk. "The newspapers have been calling, all of them, all at once, I don't have any idea what set them off. They want to know what my political plans are. I told them I was seriously considering my options, I hadn't made up my mind, I was happy where I was—et cetera, et cetera. The usual."

The shine in Billy's eyes annoyed Jennings.

"That's fabulous. Great."

"I also had lunch with Teitelman, who said the political situation in the city was soft. That was his word. He thinks there's a good opening for me, if I make a move soon. I'd have to let everyone get used to the idea, pay my respects to the old pros, do some legwork, all that kind of thing." He waved his hand in dismissal.

"It sounds like you have everything figured out."

"He's smart, Teitelman."

"What's your first—move—going to be?"

"That's what I want to talk about."

"Didn't Teitelman have any ideas?"

"Oh-oh." Billy's face darkened with mock dismay. "I think you're feeling left out."

There was some truth to that. But Billy's polish offended Jennings more.

"Teitelman's just someone out there," Billy continued. "A power to be addressed. He can be helpful, that's all."

"Don't be so sure."

There was a small, understanding smile on Billy's face. If Jennings gave in to its allure, if he admitted his jealousy, the smile would flower. "Oh, I know I have to be careful," Billy said. "He's very tentative. Probably always will be." He paused. "Now, come on," he coaxed. "What's the matter?"

Jennings had not thought his uneasiness was so obvious. But Billy's perspicuity was only a matter of detail, he thought, of noticing whatever had some direct bearing on Billy himself. He wanted to startle those half-open eyes.

"Forget it, then. But you should know that Teitelman, as I said, is simply a power out there. He's not working for us. Besides,

I don't think his instincts are as good as yours, not in the matters that concern us. You know infinitely more about television—about me, to be frank—than he does. The way you edited the handicapped tape, for example. Teitelman could never do something like that."

Jennings despised this flattery.

"I just don't think you should go into politics."

"I can see that."

The small smile folded up.

Jennings, having won, regretted his victory. "I could be wrong," he said. "I'm probably wrong."

"Is it because you hate politics?" Billy asked, friendly again. "I know you do, and I do too in a way. It goes back to Vietnam and Watergate. I agree. Politics is vile, but someone should do it. I don't usually talk to you like this, I know, but I actually think I could *do* something. I told you this at Penelope's. Get some good accomplished. Not a lot, maybe, but something. Perhaps in a small way I could help restore a sense of health to politics."

"You sound like you're on TV."

Billy looked at his watch. "Well, think about it. Show in forty-five minutes."

"It's just that . . . well, we've become established here and now you want to move."

Billy smiled—the flowering smile.

"I have been thinking about politics. But you know I don't have much to say about—"

"Your instincts are always right. The technique you can pick up later."

"What I think is this." One part of Jennings was sickened, another relieved, by this surrender. Wasn't Billy his oldest friend? "You're going to have to demonstrate that you're very serious, almost earnest, especially since you're so young. That doesn't mean you shouldn't be splashy sometimes. Just that it's not common for TV people, or journalists, to go into politics, and there'll be some resistance. You're going to have to appear to be something more than an entertainer—"

"I hope I do already."

"You do, but more so. The issues programs are good for that, but you'll have to get a few issues, I think, that seem to be yours.

Not issues that you've discovered as a journalist, in a dispassionate way, but issues that you yourself will do something about. People are going to complain that you're using the program to advance your own interests, but that won't matter in the end, so long as you keep suggesting that this idea of entering politics is somebody else's idea, that you are being tapped, sort of against your wishes."

"Everyone has the same issues."

"You can claim some. Whatever you ran for you'd probably get most of the young professional vote—Upper West Side, the Village, and so on. That's probably your natural group, so you want to aim a little at the other groups, especially the boroughs if you're running citywide, without offending your own bunch."

"And you think pornography's—"

"No. Not the main issue. It's a special interest issue. If you pushed it too hard you'd become a single-issue candidate, and a conservative to boot, and it's not a single issue broad enough to win with. But it's good, I think, as a color issue. It gives some spark, a little spice. Feminists, maybe women in general, might jump aboard, especially if you didn't oppose abortion. Some blue-collar workers, some conservatives would like it too. It touches on the Mafia. There have been some horrible sex-related murders recently. People are frightened of rape, frightened for their children. So long as you didn't seem prudish I don't think you'd offend your regular group."

"Maybe."

"Anyway, just a thought."

"Yes, just a thought. What about the other main issues?"

"The usual—you don't have any choice. Something economic, of course. Taxes, crime." Had he said too much? His mood swung back against Billy. "I don't know, you'd need some important-looking advisers."

"Teitelman."

"Certainly not me."

"How about some baseball?"

"What?"

"We haven't gone in a long time. Yankees are playing Boston tonight."

"Sure."

56

"I have to go warm up that union leader."

Billy stood up, but seemed reluctant to go.

Jennings returned to his office. Suddenly going to a baseball game was one of their traditions. It began during the spring of their freshman year when, for the hell of it, they gave up studying for an exam to go to the stadium. Since then, they had often gone to a game when it seemed important to play hooky. They bought a ticket in the bleachers, drank warm pissy beer, and cheered for players whose names they did not know. In the last couple of years, however, it had become more difficult to get away, since Billy was always busy.

Jennings glanced at the sports page, then thought back to the time when he loved sports. As a child he woke before seven and lay by the door of their apartment, waiting for the slap of the morning papers. He would separate the sports page from the rest and, alone in the foyer, with no sound but the clock, would read each article, saving the most important for last. Only rarely was he taken to Yankee Stadium, where the great swath of space always impressed him. The unearthly shimmer of light on the too-green grass—you could not see that on television, or follow the arc of a sailing fly, or listen to the bawling of the vendors, or mark the dance of the nine players in their geometric garden.

He looked uneasily at the clock in the hall. The taping would soon begin.

In college, his approach to baseball changed. He took a campy interest. He watched the crowd. He and Billy made a practice of rooting for opposing teams, with Jennings pretending to admire the big-city Yankees. He hailed competence, luck, and the victory of capitalism over sentiment, while Billy the outlander opposed the damn Yankees in the name of virtue. Both of his approaches to the game—campy and awestruck—were lost to him now. Not to perform the ritual with Billy in the proper spirit, however, seemed disrespectful. So he decided to drink too much.

The studio was in the basement. Against one wall was a glass-enclosed booth, where technicians sat. Opposite was a carefully scaled, romantic photograph of the Manhattan skyline. Thick wires coiled between the cameras, which looked strangely lost until pointed, and cigar stubs lay on the linoleum. Jennings entered the glass booth, then watched workmen roll a platform into position under the photograph. There was a pair of swivel chairs on the platform, colored a reddish orange that looked elegant on television. There was also a coffee table and a crystal pitcher with two glasses. A workman filled the pitcher with a hose. As Billy took his seat Jennings thought, for the first time, that the translation from the scuffed, artificial set to the polished image onscreen was not very interesting. He did not savor the contrast. He did not find the irony rich.

Billy's guest, Pete Gargola, led the sanitationmen's union. When he called a strike the city stank and the rats gorged. As a man of some importance in Democratic politics, he was unlikely to prefer Billy Bell to one of the political pros; but he might, Jennings thought, start to like him. Billy introduced Gargola to the camera with great warmth, then asked a number of tough questions. Should Gargola ask for large wage increases, for example, when the city was so poor? Was that acting in the public interest? Gargola, ticking off points on his fingers, proved that sanitation men earned less for their suffering than other workers. When Billy asked why some blue-collar workers voted Republican, Gargola spread comfortably in his chair.

"First things first, Mr. Bell. This is a free country. Am I wrong? Sometimes people get crazy ideas about the guy that works for a living. I'm serious now, Mr. Bell. Our men vote Democrat, Republican, Independent, Kangaroo—you name it. Most vote Democrat because they know Democrats take care of the guy that works for a living." He shook his head. "But Democrats better not get comfortable, that's my constant refrain to the leadership of my party: Democrats . . . don't . . . get . . . too . . . comfortable. The guy that works for a living doesn't want the politicians looking too comfortable." To cap his point, he twisted in the chair.

Gargola belonged to the old backslapping school of city politics. His face resembled a fire hydrant, and he drove a beefy Cadillac without embarrassment. He could also sound and look more sophisticated, when necessary, than the guy that works for a living. He wore a pale blue shirt, Jennings noticed, and a red silk tie—possibly Gucci. That would look fine on the air. His shoes were old; they would not be visible This contrast in the man, unlike that between the scuffed studio and the polished screen, did not bore Jennings. What was the difference? He was not certain. Just flesh and blood, perhaps.

"I don't think any New York City politician will get comfortable while you're around, Mr. Gargola."

"What's this?" Gargola sat up straight. "What's going on here?" Then he winked like a grandfather telling a joke to children. "I got people that *love* me. My wife of forty years. Even my daughter loves me. You ought to see my daughter."

Billy laughed. He rarely laughs off the air, Jennings thought.

"Mr. Gargola," Billy asked, "what can we look forward to this summer, good news or bad?"

"We have another year on our contract," said Gargola, flattered. "But we were awfully easy on the mayor last time. You're a young man, you might not remember it, but it's God's truth. *Easy.* The city was in bad shape, so we went easy as a public service. But you can't expect us to carry the city on our backs all our life. Like I said, don't . . . get . . . too . . . comfortable. But listen—no need to fear. We're reasonable men. Sure . . ." He leaned back, about to become philosophical.

"Hey, you know—" Before Gargola became dull, Billy, looking puzzled, cut in. He sat back. His eyes squinted. "I didn't know you were such an elegant dresser. That tie!"

The old man gaped. He fingered his tie. He said, "Yeah, thanks, that's my daughter got it for me. Yes—" He fingered it some more, at a loss for words. "Very nice."

Billy told the camera, "We'll be right back."

Jennings stared. A feisty union leader turned into an old man fingering his tie. By contrast, Billy looked like a well-tailored young man, kind enough to compliment a doddering fool. Jennings continued to stare. Billy was sipping a glass of water. Gargola was smoothing his hair. What Billy had done, Jennings thought, possessed a kind of beauty. With one stroke he had taken the image from the man. Gargola seemed diminished, suddenly almost naked, mere flesh and blood. The image of Billy Bell, however, was enhanced. Jennings tapped on the glass. He liked Gargola's foolishness, but he wondered if Billy knew what he had done. He wanted him to know. With one minute until broadcast, knowing that Billy hated to be interrupted on the set, Jennings walked up to the platform.

"What time should we meet?"

"For what?"

"The game."

59

"Good Christ, we'll talk about it after the show." He turned away. "A Yankee fan," he told Gargola.

5

Billy did not allow interruptions on the set. He worked without a live audience to avoid distraction.

"Thirty seconds," said a technician.

With a twist of the will he postponed his anger.

"You were great," he told Gargola.

"Ten seconds."

A softness passed over and through his body. Each sense came alive and into focus.

"Five—"

He looked into the red eye.

"We're back with Mr. Pete Gargola, leader of the sanitation men's union. We've been talking about politics, economics, strikes, policy—lots of high-flown things. I'd like to do something a little different now." He smiled at Mr. Gargola. "And I don't mean to discuss your shirt size. What I want to talk about is your actual job—to put it bluntly, the job of handling garbage. It's not funny, I know that, and it can be dangerous. It's not something any of us likes to think about too much. Perhaps we ought to."

Billy spoke to the camera. An interview could sustain only so much strut and threat, and it was time to move away from the prospect of strikes. Besides, people loved to hear about the unpleasant work of others.

"Thank you, Mr. Bell. Thank you. I would be happy to inform your viewers of the many trials, the many tribulations of our life. What would you be interested in knowing?"

"What are some of the dangers?"

"There are the obvious. Razor blades and rats, to name two, broken glass, hangers and utensils, all kinds of terrible things. When I was young I sliced the tip off my thumb on a rusty can." He held up his thumb. "But, Mr. Bell, I cannot on this family program inform you of some of the things my men discover." He shook his head.

"Tell us some of the horrors rated PG."

"Limbs."

"I said PG!"

"Dead cats."

Billy looked surprised. Then a smile slipped into his eyes. "You should all win medals. A dead animal would win you the purple heart. Wasn't I reading about a tractor trailer filled with eggs that overturned on the Long Island Expressway? Didn't your men have to . . . "

"What an unholy mess that was."

The red light passed to the camera trained on Gargola.

"Slick as ice. My men wore galoshes. A lot of cars, of course, slid right off the expressway. We were hoping a truck filled with Ajax would turn over—no, seriously, that wasn't any joke. Took us all night, all that glop. My men said they were off scrambled eggs for weeks. The way we finally got the stuff off—"

Billy let Gargola continue to the point of silliness. Then he shook his head in amazement. His engineer, who recognized the cue, switched to the camera that picked up both men. "Unbelievable," Billy said, interrupting Gargola. The red light passed to Billy's camera. "Unbelievable," he repeated, feeling a sort of tenderness as the silence lengthened. On television screens he looked comfortable, at ease in millions of homes. Then he began to change the tempo, letting the sound of his voice replace Gargola's. In the last five minutes the conversation must be serious, though Gargola had seemed happy enough with silly subjects. "If I were a garbage man I'd scream murder too, sometimes. But I wanted—except I'm not supposed to use—wait a minute, I'm getting all tangled up here . . ." Billy smiled at the red eye. His expression was beguiling, trusting. In this unexpected freefall he seemed without fear.

"Let's start again," he said. His voice was strong. "Some people think the word 'sanitation engineer' is a terrible example of inflation, that the word 'garbage'—"

This was a point of passion for Gargola.

"Mr. Bell, it is perfectly true that, in fact we pick up refuse. How would you feel, however, if your daughter had to say, 'My

61

daddy is a garbage man'? Her daddy's not a garbage man, he *picks up refuse*. There is a real difference."

Some fire came into the conversation. Then when the heat was right, when the moment came for the serious discussion, Billy asked Gargola if he could change the subject. Gargola nodded. Turning toward the camera, Billy addressed himself to the common belief that New York City was in decline. As he spoke he was not conscious of a particular audience, but only of himself before some vague significance—an invisible crowd. And something inside him, as he looked into the red eye, was securely fixed. He could trust his instincts; he could move smoothly to what must be said, feeling as light as air. None of this seemed false. It was merely different—better.

"What I'm trying to say, Mr. Gargola, is: what do you, speaking as an individual, not the leader of a great union, have to say about the decline of New York? You have spent a lifetime in Queens."

"Mr. Bell, I have one word to say. Nuts. That is, if I may say so, the real garbage. In addition, let me say something about an even bigger question." He hesitated. "I know a lot of the young folks out there are going to laugh, and I would have laughed once too. But it starts in the home, and if I may say so, you can laugh all you want: there's no respect for the family."

He looked at the camera as if daring it to throw a tomato. "And I'm going to say that again. There's no respect for the family. Hell, I'll go you one further. There's no respect for motherhood."

There was a pause.

Billy's serious question hung suspended. Gargola's answer was not yet an answer.

"Mr. Gargola, believe me. No one's going to laugh at you."

To one part of his audience, Billy's remark sounded tongue in cheek. To another it sounded respectful.

"It was different in my day. Why, your hide was tanned if you didn't do your homework. Now—oh, my God—there are girls, twelve, thirteen, from good families, shooting up, selling themselves, every damn thing. I don't have much against the young kids, you know—" Then Gargola reined himself back. "You should see my daughter," he said, in a voice without accent. "She's an en-do-cri-nol-o-gist."

Billy, smiling, was silent. The red light on his camera continued to glow.

"I couldn't really tell you what it is. Hell, I can't even spell it. But I think it has to do with—" He winked and pointed to his rounded stomach.

Billy shook his head. "Our time is almost up. Mr. Gargola, you're a revelation." Billy's smile was without condescension, yet somewhat mysterious. It continued for some time. "Thanks for coming by." The old man nodded uncertainly, like someone who did not know in which direction to point. Then Billy faced his camera: "We have been talking to Mr. Pete Gargola, leader of our sanitation men. We've had a few sharp words." He smiled again. "After all, these men wake us at five in the morning, reveive higher wages than tenured teachers, and sometimes—to put it diplomatically—go on strike at awkward moments. Mr. Gargola is also, as I hope you've seen, a warm man who helps some awfully hard-working guys. Somehow I think New York's future can't be too bad with people like him around." Billy turned to his guest. "Mr. Gargola, you're a pretty good social philosopher, too." He looked back at his camera. "I hope we've learned something. I know I have. Until tomorrow, this is Billy Bell."

6

Billy never lingered on the set. He shook hands with his guest and closed himself in his office. His mood after every show was gentle, euphoric, and vulnerable, and he always followed the same ritual. He dropped three ice cubes, one after another, into a glass. He measured three fingers of Scotch into the glass. Then he slowly seated himself behind his desk. He sipped; he thought of nothing. It was one of the few moments when his mind was utterly clear. The sensation resembled the sweet exhaustion of a runner who, having pushed his body to its limit, lets himself rest.

This private happiness was rarely deeper than two of the three fingers of Scotch. The emptiness that began as something to which nothing need be added soon ripened into a sense of loss; from there melancholy gave way to depression. At that point Billy often added a couple more fingers of Scotch. And sometimes dozed. After a while questions, phrases, and scraps of thought began to tease his mind. He would settle on the couch. He would think of what he should have said, or whom to interview next . . . Jennings . . . Teitelman. . . . Often he became angry. The office pressed upon him until he finally burst out to give orders to his secretary. That day he telephoned Kelly Martin. He knew her number by heart.

He was reassured when she answered.

"Billy Bell here. Listen, I wanted to talk a few things over with you . . . Oh, just some matters where your expertise might be helpful . . . About teaching and writing. . . . No, lunch is not good for me in the next couple of weeks. All this politics . . . Let's have dinner. Saturday okay? I'll call with details. Yep. Bye." He thought: she's eager. He would have to watch out. He felt proud of his businesslike approach, but he did not dwell on the conversation. Instead, he wondered what Jennings could have meant by walking onto the set like that. Earlier he had been so unpleasant, so discouraging about political attention.

He buzzed Jennings on the intercom.

"Let's meet at seven," he said. "Take the subway up."

Although a driver was available, Billy preferred to do what they had always done. He looked at his watch: still plenty of time. He returned some calls, then began to brood. Jennings disapproved of politics, Jennings was an East Coast snob. Were his ideas about politics any good? Probably not, but Billy could not be sure. He remembered how he once admired Jennings' condescension; and how impressed he was that Jennings, nonetheless, seemed anxious to befriend him. Billy recalled how funny Jennings could be—that was gone now—when, on their early visits to the stadium, he would drink too much, and smiling at Billy, join the rowdies in the right-field bleachers. He would become one of the chief crows. Did anyone else, Billy wondered, know Jennings could behave that way?

He was about to call when Jennings himself appeared. "The New York *Times* has called to check on some of Gargola's quotes. Apparently they've been wanting to talk to him for some time about strikes but he's been mum—except for today, when he was a little encouraging. The show will get full credit." Jennings, about to go, turned back. "You had the *Times* watching, but I also think you did well with the boroughs. The old ladies in Queens must think you married the endocrinologist and go home each week for Sunday dinner with the folks."

"Let's have a drink before we go."

But Jennings had some errands, so Billy sat alone for an hour. He dabbled at his work, thinking of the many games they had seen together; he remembered the huge roaring crowd—brought into focus with the single swing of a bat. Then, a few minutes before seven, he changed into dark clothes and an outrageous cap. He did not want to be recognized. In the old days, among the rowdies, he was never recognized.

7

On the subway the regular riders eyed the stadium-bound crowd with sullen curiosity. They saw young lawyers, nattily bow-tied, who rarely rode the West Side lines; gum-chewers in T-shirts, who carried six-packs in brown-paper bags; eccentrics, who wore fixed stares under their Yankee caps; children, who brought mitts and parents. In the midst of the male bonhomie—crude jokes and warm beer—the wives and girlfriends looked on with friendly indulgence.

"You should have brought what's-her-name," Billy said.

"Who do you mean?"

"You know."

Billy mentioned a woman.

"I don't go out with her anymore."

Billy, dangling on a strap, swung with the train. The roar and screech made conversation difficult.

"That girl at Penelope's party," he said. "Nice, didn't you think?"

"Good writer, or was, anyway."

"Kind of quiet and strange, nice body."

"No one knows why she left New York."

"What do you think, should I take her out?"

"Writes some pretty critical stuff."

"What?"

He shouted. "Critical, critical writer."

Jennings did not want to give Billy advice. Women were not supposed to trouble Billy, whom the *Daily News* and the *Times* had each identified as one of the city's twenty most eligible bachelors under forty; if Kelly troubled him, perhaps Billy would learn something. Nor did Jennings want to tell Billy about his own afternoon with Kelly. Keeping him in the dark made this connection seem more vivid, more lively with danger and complication. He did not wonder why.

"The Red Sox are doomed," Jennings said, as they left the subway.

"Typical Yankee—but you may be right."

"What? You of all people—"

"I've read the papers. The Red Sox have been selling their good players to make money, and the Yankees have been buying good players."

"Also to make money."

"Yes."

Billy did not seem interested in playing the traditional Red Sox fan, who specialized in moral victories. Times had changed, and facts were facts.

At the ticket booth they dickered about where to sit. "Bleachers?" said Jennings.

"I don't think so, but if you want—"

"Well, what do you want?"

"This a welfare line?" shouted someone behind them.

They bought tickets for the second tier, then wound upward on the ramp. Inside the great generous space they found thousands of people milling and chattering. The organ played and vendors trotted up and down the steps, swinging under the straps of their beer and ice-cream trays. At the railing several twelve-year-olds tried to spit on the bat boys. Because the game had not begun, the power of the crowd seemed haphazard—all potential.

Bill paused. "So many people."

They shooed some kids out of their seats, bought beer and

66

peanuts, and rose for the national anthem. During the first two innings they said nothing. It became difficult, as a result, to say anything during the next two innings; the voice of the crowd filled the gap. In the sixth inning the Yankees put men on base. A good batter came up, the organ began its primitive singsong, people started to stamp their feet and hoot.

Billy asked, "Could I borrow the binoculars?"

He took the binoculars and focused on the distant batter. He looked for a long time. Although the Yankees scored, the Red Sox tied it up in the next inning.

"You see," said Jennings, "there you go. It's not so bad."

Billy nodded.

Jennings asked for the binoculars. Between batters he looked around the stadium. Behind him a pair of drunk fans began to talk loudly.

"Our shortstop isn't worth shit on a barstool," one said. "You've read in the papers where he's in church groups, kisses orphans, famous sweet guy, you know what I'm saying? And you know what?" He leaned toward Billy, so a woman nearby wouldn't hear. "Sleeps with his baseball mitt."

The pair collapsed in laughter.

Billy took off his cap. Then he turned around and said, "I think the shortstop's pretty good."

"My ass."

"We need to figure out who to interview next Thursday," Billy told Jennings. Then he turned toward the fan. "Best shortstop in the American League."

"That's like saying—hey, wait a second. Do I know you?"

"I don't think so."

The fan nudged his buddy. "Wait a minute, you're, you know, that guy. My wife turns you on sometimes."

"She does!"

The fan blushed.

Jennings, raising the binoculars, watched an adolescent couple buy a Coke hundreds of yards away. Billy signed a program, which the fan said was "for my kids."

The game was close. In a late inning a Yankee hit a home run, and the crowd as one jumped to its feet. Behind Billy the loud fan hugged and punched his buddy and shouted "Hallelujah damn" over and over again. Then, blissful, he circled in front of his seat like a dog settling into a spot of sun. Billy and Jennings also stood up. Around them, however, the cheering inside the stadium was merging into a hollow roar—a giant conch held to the ear—very much like silence.

CHAPTER

FOUR

I

Kelly invited Jennings to afternoon tea. She could tell he found the idea funny and quaint. So did she: tea parties were for old ladies and Englishmen. Tea was also for talk, however, and talk was what she wanted from him—not movies or bars or plays or discos. She also preferred a daytime meeting, since at night a decision about sex would have to be made; and she wanted to know him a little, first. She looked forward to showing off her new furniture: "And this is the bed."

The morning of their date she went shopping, planning to buy tea and some outrageous pastry. She wore cutoffs and a pale-blue blouse and hardly brushed her hair; it was part of the pleasure she took in a Saturday morning to stay sloppy. On Broadway she joined the frowzy couples who paused at the windows, bought newspapers or pinched the early peaches at the Korean fruit stands. Far above a soprano practiced her scales in one of the apartment palaces. It did not take Kelly long, not as long as she had hoped, to find what she was looking for—Earl Grey tea and a Russian coffee cake. The cake, she thought, peeking into the box, was serious about sugar: earnest, a good Russian.

She glanced at a bank clock, then remembered—how could she have forgotten?—her dinner date that night with Billy. He had called the week before. "Damn," she muttered. Suppose she wanted to spend the evening with Jennings? She almost canceled the date with Billy, but then decided to go. Billy represented a seductive side of New York. He had won the fame game. She wanted to test herself with him, for she was determined not to cast this game in a romantic or glamorous light, but to regard it as the ordinary thing it was—an often pathetic striving, in which the winners rarely did anything of true value.

She brushed the hair from her eyes. It was extraordinary how fast the West Side was changing. Most of the people on the street were young white professionals, and they had brought their tastes with them: stores for exotic coffee or dollar cones; countless restaurants; not many children. She was sorry to see the old Jewish butcher shops and hardware stores yielding to boutiques and the SRO hotels transformed into elegant cooperatives. Once she had written about people who were pickled in white wine, but she had subsequently modified her view, having acknowledged her own membership in the same group. She liked to shop in the stores that made her uncomfortable. It was naïve to expect neighborhoods to remain unchanged, she thought, especially before the weight of a generation as large as hers, and dimwitted to call the old days good.

But the character of the new stores—the glinting elegance of stainless steel, the hard joy of high-tech color—disturbed her. In this new kind of neighborhood the eye spun off surfaces, nothing held, days did not stick. She wondered whether the people on the street, when they were fifty, would still inhabit brownstone studios. She wondered if she herself . . . but that was a gloomy line of thought, and she refused to indulge in it. In any case, some of the old people who remained on the West Side dumbfounded her. Imagine sitting on a bench for hours in the middle of Broadway! No doubt peace and quiet were oversold, especially for the elderly.

She remembered the old people perched like pigeons on the benches along Riverside Drive and decided to read in the park for a couple of hours. The bank clock said 12:54—still an hour and a half—and the temperature was seventy-four. Not too hot, she thought, for tea. She smiled with affectionate pique: he did not have to sound so surprised. She dropped off her packages at the apartment and walked down the promenade that ran along the slow, tug-plowed river. She did not mind the tarry summer smell of the water; nor its dead fish, old tires, and gasoline rainbows. She thought they gave the river a sad proletarian charm. Or was that another sentimental conceit, on a par with babbling brooks? When the wind was right, she could smell the breath of the ocean on the old water.

She read her book—a history text on colonial America—on a park bench. She turned to the short section on Henry Hudson and occasionally glanced at the river, imagining what it had looked like four hundred years ago. She had no trouble picturing the water's edge, where the crabs crept toward the shore, or the Manhattan forest on a summer day; and then, the glide of a sail up the river. Nor was it difficult to replace this image with a vision of the jackhammer city. Yet she could not keep both equally in mind: as she stared into the water she grew dizzy among the slow, curling eddies. She looked abruptly at her watch. What would Jennings think of the river? He would probably have no reaction. That bothered her. So she thought back to the moment at Prendergast's when, as she turned her back, he stared at her figure. She had posed.

It was not easy to read on the park bench. Joggers cut sharply around the edge of her seat; divorced fathers played softball with tiny sons; a lone black man, performing a karate dance, chopped the air. Some park vendors now sold the same fancy food found on Columbus or Broadway—and their carts gave off the same gleam as the stores on those avenues. She looked away, toward two bare-chested men who were playing Frisbee. She liked watching them lope over the grass to intercept the flying arc. She liked it very much: the outstretched arm, the snare, the twirl away. Then the long soft float—and again, and again.

2

She found Jennings in the lobby, trying to describe her to the doorman. She stole up behind him, wishing there had been time to change, and touched him on the ribs. He jumped, to her satisfaction. Then he kissed her on the cheek and apologized for being early. "But I was in the neighborhood." He wore trousers with one torn cuff, a yellow shirt stained with white paint, and sneakers that were gray with age—preppier than usual, she thought.

Upstairs, he studied the view out her window. He ran a finger along a new table. He asked where she had found a chair with so many legs. His admiration for the bed he made comical. "Let's see, bedsprings . . . Hmmm . . . bedsprings!" She smiled at the ingenuity it took to say something about bedsprings. "It's their proportions," he joked, "their hint of the classical." His mood seemed better than at Prendergast's, though he was no less awkward. "So it's really tea," he said, when she put on the water.

"Yes, tea," she called from the kitchen.

"I love tea."

"You do not."

"Well, tea is mud."

"Thank you, James."

"All wrong. You have it—me—all wrong."

"I do?"

She sat on the couch, curling around to face him. It was fairly muggy, and his hair was damp. She remembered the film of warmth around him when he kissed her hello, and, shivering suddenly, she took a pillow in her arms. "Did you love James Bond when you were young? The boys I knew all read the books during math class."

"I read them all, but it's hard for me to remember. *Dr. No* I think I liked best."

"A mountain of birdshit!"

She was not certain . . . was he taken aback by her use of the word "birdshit"?

"Excuse me," she teased.

"What's that word?"

"Oregano?"

"No!"

"Guano!"

There was a pause.

She asked, "Were you a great reader?"

She did not care if this sounded like an interrogation. It could not make their conversation more forced. And she would never learn anything about him unless she asked—he was that reticent.

72

"Not really. Oh, I suppose I was, but I read mostly junk back then, mysteries, adventure tales, James Bond, the things people left around my parents' summer place. I guess I'm supposed to say that Proust changed my life at the age of nine." He paused, but she did not speak. "The only books I really went out and bought because I wanted to—aside from the Hardy Boys when I was seven or eight—were the C. S. Forester books about Hornblower." He smiled. "A sad sea captain."

"An antihero?"

"A hero in spite of himself, before that line was fashionable. I haven't read those things in so long. Boys' books."

"I think I'm going to read them."

"Come on."

"Something you liked must be—"

"I take no responsibility. Or yes, I do. I loved them then, it's true." He glanced at her. "My mother wrote children's books."

She was surprised at the confidence.

"Books for children up to the age of ten or so. She has one classic still in print—it's called *Penguins for Peter*—and she was always trying them out on me, even when I was fifteen. I think I built up a certain resistance—"

She laughed. "*Penguins for Peter.*"

"She would come into my bedroom when I was twelve, you know, when I had a shoplifted *Playboy* under my pillow, and she'd pull up a chair by the pillow and begin reading about the princess who loved chocolate."

She was laughing.

"Was—is—your mother very corny?"

"Hard-boiled. She's a very tough scholar, but I don't really know how good. Her field is medieval religious ritual, and she writes children's books on the side for extra money. They always have a moral."

"And your father? I don't mean to grill you."

"My father? A lawyer. A rich lawyer."

There was a pause.

"That's all?"

"He's a Democrat."

"Jennings . . ."

"Yes?"

"No—I was just thinking it's an unusual first name."

"My father's idea. I think he thought it sounded Western—he likes the West, like you."

"Not like me."

Jennings looked surprised.

"Why not?"

"Does he like cowboys?"

"Yes."

"I bet he likes a different kind of cowboy than I like."

"What's your kind?"

"Not John Wayne."

"Even in the movies?"

"I like him in the movies."

The kettle whistled. Kelly brought out the cake, then a ceramic tea service. She began to clatter around with the plates and spoons. "Hot water?"

"But you didn't answer my question. What kind of cowboy do you like?"

"One or two lumps?"

"Really."

She handed him his tea. "I don't know . . ."

She withheld the sugar, in obedience to his shaking head. "But I'm not old-fashioned about the people there, not at all." She felt embarrassed, so she said, "I don't think of them as"—her voice deepened—" 'upholders of traditional values' any more than I think of them as those New West macho types. I even got bored pretty easily."

She was angry at the disappointment in her voice.

"I didn't mean that," he said. "They could be no worse—"

"—than here. They're the same in the end. Only the subjects are different."

"Cows!"

"Bulls, more likely."

"I'm over my head."

She laughed, saying, "Have some of this." She cut him a piece of cake, touched that he had told her the truth about himself and surprised that he had questioned her too. It was ridiculous: she was on the verge of tears. "So what is your life like in New York—what do you actually do?"

"Oh, wine, women, and song."

She looked up.

74

"You don't believe it?"

She was prepared to tease him. But his expression, despite the flip smile, was not funny. What a strange man!

"Wine, women, and song," she repeated slowly.

There was too much slickness in his smile—a kind of ice. Then he softened: "Such a big question." He hesitated. "I'm not really like that."

"I wonder," she said, "if I would like working in television."

"No."

"No?"

He took a large bite of cake. "Fabulous." He took another bite and sipped his tea. "No, you wouldn't like it. It's as bad as everything you've heard, and worse. You're not serious, are you? Not really thinking of television?"

"No, but if you hate it so much—"

"Then why?" He finished his tea. She poured him more. He began a joky reply. "Hell, if I knew what to do— I wish I could *think* of something to do . . ." Under her gaze, however, he seemed to waver and bend. "Actually, the truth is that there are some things I like about working in television. Not what appears, but the actual work."

"Why not movies?"

He shook off this suggestion. "I don't want to live in California, and you pretty much have to. Television"—he seemed to think hard about what he liked, then began to speak rapidly—"I guess I like all that idiotic machinery, those dials and needles and mikes, and the taxi-driver kind of guys, you know, who lug around all that incredibly expensive equipment. I really like"—he appeared embarrassed—"getting Billy at the right angle, presenting him. I do."

He looked up cautiously. She took a bite of cake from his plate, while cutting him another piece. "You've got to have some more."

"Also the deadlines—I actually like deadlines. The craziness makes you click, but it also makes you calm. You become the eye of the storm, you get things done. Am I making sense? It's a bit like sleep. You seal out the world, only letting in what you have to. Very strange." He hesitated. "Even if it's Billy, I like presenting things, getting the image right. When I read your sketches I liked them because I could *see* what you were talking about."

75

The telephone rang. "Damn," said Kelly. She did not get up to answer it.

"But in general," he said, becoming vague, "I don't like TV, I really don't—it's crass, manipulative, obvious."

"Damn." She answered the phone. It was Billy, to confirm their date. "Yes . . . eight o'clock. No, I'll meet you there . . . Where? No, that's okay . . . eight o'clock. If you really want, but I can meet you . . . Okay . . . eight o'clock."

3

Why had he told her so much? He was not even certain of its truth, especially the part about television. He changed his position on the couch, wondering how she drew him out. It was dusky in the living room, and the air was pleasantly warm. Something about the way she tucked herself into the couch and then, facing him, looking straight ahead, eyes shining, not always speaking . . . coaxed him into talk.

"Is the water still warm?" she asked, after hanging up. She pressed her palm against the pot. "No." She brushed past him to heat more water, and he smelled her perfume. He loved the way she held herself. These things were not, however, the whole of his desire. Their conversation also appealed to him. The sharing of histories, the sweat-excited talk, reminded him of many years before, when revealing his thoughts to a girl seemed as important as revealing his body.

"That was Billy," she said from the kitchen.

"What did he want?"

"I'm having dinner with him tonight—he's been after me for quite a few days, so I couldn't turn him down."

"I think I told you—you have an admirer."

"I hope not."

He was pleased. When she brought in the fresh pot, he announced "More tea!" in a foolish stentorian voice, to make her smile. As before she followed ritual in serving; and he realized that the tea itself, working in tandem with Kelly, had led him to talk too much. Tea quickened his wit and loosened his tongue.

It gladdened his senses. And the way it was served—Kelly was formal but not prissy—was reassuring. The progression of steps put him in a comfortable trance.

They were silent. Then they looked at each other and looked away.

"But," she said, "you told me Billy likes Penelope."

"He does."

"You don't?"

"She's pretty."

"Why don't you? You wouldn't tell me the other day."

He shrugged.

"Not your type?"

He shrugged again.

"I'll bet you *do* like her. Wine, women, and song."

"Penelope terrifies me."

"So what do you like?"

Over an upraised teacup her eyes stared at him.

"Oh, darker hair."

"Yes?"

"Bluer eyes."

"Yes?"

He was almost led to separate, slowly, the cup from her right hand, the saucer from her left, and—but he was not impulsive. Behind a simple kiss lay so much else. He remembered his foreboding after their date at Prendergast's.

"Well?"

"A cowgirl."

"Yes?"

"Enough!"

They stared at each other for a moment.

"Now it's only fair," he said. "You have to tell me about your parents."

"Rather big question."

"Didn't faze me."

She leaned back into the pillows. "Well, my father died when I was very young. I have a much older brother who I don't see much—he lives in Idaho, and he's very woodsy—and my mother still lives in a suburb outside Chicago."

"I'm sorry about your father."

"I never knew him."

She looked at Jennings.

"I have a remarkable mother, too. She's a great Yankee. She is very tough, sort of wiry like an old vine. I only remember her sounding sad about my father once, long ago, when she was talking to somebody on the phone. I don't know who. Practical! She's very practical, willful—she mostly works for charities, a great organizer. Nothing can embarrass her. Professionally cheerful, no crying over spilt milk. Oh, I've made her sound terrible, but she's really not. Better than I am."

"Maybe we should get our mothers together."

Kelly smiled, then toyed with a spoon. He marveled at how gracefully her mood had changed. One moment found her warm and teasing. Then the light in her eyes deepened, like an imperceptible change of weather. And she kept her humor, whenever she did startle him, to take the edge off his discomfort. "My mother would die if she heard me describe her that way."

"And mine too."

There was a pause.

The distraction of tea and cake was gone.

Her words about her mother, as she stared at him from one end of the couch, had not been casually imparted. They were a gift of intimacy, and he felt placed under some obligation. Part of him wished to retreat, part to advance. So he moved ahead, resisting.

"You've never done a sketch of your mother, have you?"

"Oh no!"

He almost asked her, then, why she'd left New York. But it still seemed too soon, so he asked why she stopped writing the sketches. She continued to stare at him. He was a little frightened by the evenness of her stare; it seemed to measure something in him. At last she asked, "Why did you like them?"

"I'm not a critic!"

She smiled. He did not have to answer.

"I like them," he continued, "I liked them because . . . I liked their anger."

"Anger's not hard."

"But to express anger well? Calmly, with elegance and a certain kind of coolness . . ."

"Coldness."

78

"Coldness then."

There was a pause.

"I liked what you did with opinions, all those fashionable opinions."

"So your opinion," she said, "is that all opinions are foolish?"

"No, but you—"

His words caught on the barb in her remark: he felt like the subject of one of her sketches. "Obviously no one opinion is right," he said. "Partially right, maybe."

"You have to say something."

"You can say nothing."

"That's old."

"It doesn't have an age."

She paused. "Yes, you may be right."

He blushed. She should not hold that view, although he might. She should continue the argument. He tried to say something to make her persist, but nothing came to mind. For the first time ever he believed that he could not keep up. He knew too little to carry on the discussion. She had taken him to a place where ideas took their life naturally, inevitably, from the entwining of thought and feeling; to a place where ideas were felt, and were not the less for it. Anxious to speak, he touched her hand.

She moved closer, hot-blooded now. "Don't you see the easy pride in satire, in everything I wrote? Or the self-pity? It's sickening. You write, and you admire your singularity, your cleverness, your isolation. You take no risks, because you despise everything. You look things up and down, and you say 'no.' There's only one note, or at most two or three. It leaves out so much. Small, small, small! Or at most—good at small things."

"You could write differently."

"I don't like to write, not unless I'm angry. But don't you see"—she would not leave the subject—"how sentimental that sort of satire is, though the writers all pretend to be so hard-nosed? Really they're all so disappointed. They feel so abandoned. Their disappointment is so acute because their expectations are so high, so cornily high. They're spoiled, poisonous."

"What's wrong with a little revenge?"

"Yes, there's that."

There was a pause.

79

Then she was running ahead again. "The revenge is wonderful. Hitting back against all those idiots, all those offensive things. This world. You read and you know someone knows what you know. It's such a relief, a tantrum really, even when it's beautifully polished, even when it's full of"—she teased out the syllables—"el-e-gant el-lip-sis. But violence all the same, just revenge. Important but not something very grand or difficult. Just revenge. Small again, a small freedom. Like clever writing or puns. Puns! Do you like puns?"

"Sort of."

"They're wonderful little liberators, finger-snaps of freedom. Inside all that"—her voice deepened—"structure and dignity and grammar. Wonderfully perverse, like farting in church."

"You don't like them."

"Small."

"Some people don't sound as poisonous as you say," Jennings said. "They parody but—"

"They're warm. That's something else."

She rattled the crockery onto a tray. Jennings followed her into the kitchen, hoping to be useful. Soon he said he had to meet someone downtown, since her outburst made further conversation seem dull and stilted. At the door he took her hand in his, for a moment only. More would have been less.

4

Kelly had agreed to meet Billy at Mama's, a place on Third Avenue that resembled the informal bars in New York where people with a little money went to crowd out an evening. She had been to what seemed like hundreds. Usually the name was friendly: Ken's, or Scotty's, or Chaps. Inside there was a polished bar, behind which bottles and glasses glittered against a mirror. The tablecloths were checked; the waiters behaved like actors to whom life had been unfair. Mama's was different because Mama's was fashionable. Gossip columnists often mentioned it, and anyone famous was welcome. Of first importance were the more serious forms of reputation, rather than the slick snobbery of the designer group or the sudsy glitter of L.A. Well-known writers, actors, and directors, with the members of their world, felt especially at home. They liked its clubby camaraderie and the touch of camp in its name. They also liked the owner, Mama, a fat black blues singer who had once lived in France. She was a voluble woman who greeted her famous regulars with a hug. An old joke was that some of the scrawnier intellectuals had not survived.

Kelly had been to Mama's with the black turtleneck. It would make her uncomfortable to return, she thought, since her circumstances were now different. A year ago she would have visited Mama's armed with irony, the more cutting the better. She would have noted the hovering pilot fish and the basking great. Her irony would have been supported by her right to be there as an attractive young woman with a *succès d'estime*; her position would have been the secure one of attacking her own class. But now . . . She remembered her promise earlier in the day to recognize the shabbiness of the longing and the falseness of the achievement. She also remembered her determination to observe those failings in herself—she must not become pious!—and to find room for generosity. There were people she admired who went to Mama's.

In the taxi she thought about Jennings. Her outburst embarrassed her, but she did not regret it. She was proud to have asserted such things to someone that cynical. She wanted him to know what she was like. Despite her subsequent melancholy, his reaction gratified her: he seemed to take her seriously. He did not dabble with what she said only to flirt, though that was there of course. In the darkness she smiled. He had looked startled. She liked to startle him. And she was touched by his gentle departure. She believed, fondly, that his aloofness stemmed not from laziness but from bad luck, from having failed to find some worthy direction for his energy. In the taxi she decided that their tea was promising. And perhaps she wasn't crazy if Jennings—in some ways like her former self—did not think she was.

A crowd jammed the entrance, mostly stargazers and hangers-on looking for a glimpse or a table. Kelly pushed to the front, where Mama stood near an old lectern. An open book lay on this lectern, upon which were written hieroglyphs—reservations. Mama hugged someone Kelly could not quite place. Kelly disliked Mama for not forgetting names or faces. She also disliked her excessive tact. Mama knew how long to sit down with a favored guest (not longer than one good story) and how to season the evening with gossip suited to his taste; she knew who not to place near whom; and the famous could charge anything. Mama recognized Kelly, but did not smile until Kelly declared her intentions. Then, with a friendly pat on the arm—her usual greeting to women who belonged to important men—she said, "He's waiting for you, honey, he's waiting."

Mama, pointing to Billy's raised arm, accompanied Kelly to a table for two. Black mirrors lined the walls and the lighting was subtle: bright toward the center, shaded in the corners. Kelly did not glance around since the trick was to look while not appearing to look. Billy stood to kiss Kelly's cheek and then, having accepted Mama's compliment on his taste in women, he began to apologize. "I didn't want to foist this place on you," he said, as Mama left. "But it's convenient for me because there are some journalists I ought to talk to, and I told someone before we made our plans I'd see him here. A lot of my job—as you can well imagine—is pure hokum . . ." He dropped his hand on the table. "Anyway! . . . It's nice to see you." He looked very clean-shaven. "What can we get you for a drink?" He motioned to a waiter.

The day before she had watched his show. She found him more relaxed on the air than in person. "Oh, white wine, I guess."

"Some cassis for a kir? It's very good."

"No, just white wine, thanks."

"Have you been here before? I've about had it, the food's so bad. It's strange, isn't it, that in a place like this, or Elaine's, or '21,' or Sardi's, they don't pay much attention to their food."

His bullying good cheer made her uneasy. So she said, "Food's not what they serve."

"What?"

She could not help herself: she began to set him up. "If the food were good," she said, in a matter-of-fact voice, "it would get in the way."

"I don't follow—"

"Of what they really serve."

"What's that?"

"Well, they serve you your importance."

"I read some of your sketches."

"And?"

"Fabulous."

"I'm glad you liked them."

"Yes," Billy said, looking to one side. "I've almost had it with Mama's."

"I don't think it's so bad."

"No?"

"No—there've always been places like this, always will be. Nothing wrong with them."

"Have you been before?"

"A few times—a man I used to know came here quite a lot."

She defended Mama's because Billy criticized it. Mama's was made for Billy, so he should not apologize for being there.

"Penelope loves to come here," he said. "So I've taken her a few times. You probably met her like I did, being photographed—"

"Actually she was a friend of the man who used to take me here."

"Strange woman."

"What makes you say so?"

"Very ambitious. Sour in a way."

"She's been very kind to me—found me my apartment."

"I agree she's nice. An old friend. But you can't deny that she's a *little* peculiar. Come on now, you're covering up."

Once more Kelly was led to make a defense that did not come naturally to her. She enjoyed good honest malicious gossip as much as anyone else, but there was only effort in Billy's expression— as though he must, without fail, draw her into a shared dismissal of Penelope. It also annoyed her that he tried to anticipate her view of things, and spoke to that. Where was his legendary polish? She looked into the transparent eyes and experienced her earlier falling sensation. What did he want from her?

"But why am I going on about all these things?" Billy said. "I called you to talk about education. Just a moment, I'd like you to meet Ken Sarris—runs the city parks, poor guy. This is Kelly Martin." Billy, stretching out an arm, presented her as if she had won an Academy Award. "A great comic writer."

"I think we've met," said Ken Sarris, who then asked Billy if he would be at the office tomorrow. "I have a few thoughts I'd like to run by you."

She hated the introduction. The exaggerated compliment was patronizing. It was also coercive, for Billy had displayed her as an image for Ken Sarris to admire. And she had never met Ken Sarris.

"Now, education," Billy said, turning back to her. What should I be doing on the show?"

"You've already asked me."

"But at Penelope's—well, let's order first. Mama always puts a soul-food dish on the menu as the specialty, but she never recommends it. Really, the thing to do is get something ordinary that can't be ruined, and then a good wine . . ." As he spoke—with continued condescension, she thought—Kelly glanced at the other tables. She recognized no one. Suppose she saw the black turtleneck? How would she react? He would come up to say hello to Billy—he would want to be asked onto the show—and then, surprised and charmed, he would notice her. She'd be all right.

"I'll have the chicken, then," she said. "Any wine you want is fine with me." In an effort to be friendly, she asked, "How long have you known Jennings?"

"Since our first year in college."

They ordered.

"Jennings is my right hand. We've always—well it's happened that we've always worked together. I owe him a lot, and you know he is *good* at what he does. You shouldn't let his sloppiness fool you."

She was pleased to hear Billy compliment Jennings.

Then he added, "There's a . . . stubbornness about him, though, which is getting worse. Sometimes I think he might be more trouble that he's worth."

"Oh, that's just an act."

"He was on good behavior at Penelope's."

"Well, he can be generous. He went to a lot of trouble, I think, to work out a discount for me at Prendergast's."

"When was that?"

"Just the other day."

There was a pause.

"You can't let that sloppiness fool you," Billy said, looking away. "He's pretty sharp behind it."

"I just had tea with him today," she said. "He's not stubborn, just a little waspish."

"He's my best friend."

They were interrupted again. "Your interview of old Gargle was fine stuff," said a man whom she knew. He was about ten years older than she, a former correspondent for the New York *Times* who had written a sensitive book about police brutality in the late 1960s, followed a few years later by an unsentimental, sometimes humorous novel about the breakup of his marriage. His name was Theodore Oatis, and he was a friend of the black turtleneck. "Ted, this is Kelly, a beautiful and brilliant comrade of yours."

"I'm a schoolteacher."

"Oh, I know Kelly." He looked at her, as if for the first time. "Schoolteacher?"

"For the moment."

She despised herself for the retreat, but Oatis could do that to her. He had soft features, like cake; his superior air led people to defend their reputations when no attack was forthcoming. Oatis said, "Maybe we'll have a nightcap later," and returned to his table. Kelly smiled at Billy: better Billy than Oatis. Once again, however, she had the impression that Billy did not see her. She could not imagine what his gray eyes did see—certainly not a "beautiful and brilliant comrade" of Oatis.

"Did you ever read his books?" asked Billy. "I didn't finish the police one, though I meant to. Put it aside and then it was two months later."

"No, I never read it."

"You must be writing one."

"No."

"You will—"

"I don't know."

She caught herself. She must be friendlier. She must talk to Billy, not merely exchange words. "Oh, I suppose I might write something again," she said. "But right now I'm busy reading all these history books for my class—that's a program you could do, on how bad the textbooks are for high school students."

"That's a thought."

"But for pleasure—"

"Yes, what should we read?"

85

"I don't read much contemporary stuff. There always seems to be some excellent old book I haven't read. There's not enough time, I have to make a choice and"—she spread her hands, as if to say *tant pis*—"also I think I like to buy old books in the second-hand bookstores. All that wonderful dust! There's this one place—"

Billy's eyes began to slide.

She stopped.

Billy said, "There's Sir John Stanley."

She looked across the room at the great British director, who now lived in Malibu. Around his table Mama was directing a number of waiters; they behaved, Kelly thought, like beetles distressed by light. At surrounding tables people were studiously indifferent. A telephone was brought forward, a beat-up black phone not meant to be ostentatious.

Billy said, "I didn't know he was in New York."

She gave up. The eyes were too slippery at Mama's; she remembered, years before, trying to catch frogs at the bottom of a pail. "Who cares about Sir-John-Stanley?" she said. "He's just another person with a Rolls-Royce. There are millions in L.A."

"He was on my show a couple of years ago."

As if on cue, Sir John walked over to say hello to Billy. In fact, Kelly admired the movies of Sir John Stanley, and she welcomed the chance to see him in person. The old face, bruised by drink, was lovely. Her spirits improved. Billy said, "Sir John, this is Kelly Martin."

"My dear," said Sir John, bowing.

She was charmed.

When he left, however, she felt isolated. She wondered, was her pleasure in meeting Sir John any different from Billy's? Were her eyes just as slippery? Perhaps Billy was friendly and Oatis affectionate. Perhaps she was making up her problems, beginning to exaggerate everything again. Billy's introduction had been straightforward—for that she could be grateful. And here was their dinner, as Mama applauded their choice of wine. With the food served, the wine opened, the silence maturing, Billy said, "You know, the truth is I'm bored with my show. I need a new challenge, something fresh, more important. That's why I'm looking into politics." His manner had changed. He was now a tired friend confessing to a kind ear. He looked toward the director. "What a great old guy."

"I like his nose," she said. "It looks like you could plant it and grow a flower."

"I probably ought to ask him on the show. But I don't know, to be repeating myself already." He shook his head. "My mother was a great fan of his, incidentally. Of course, most of L.A. is."

Did I really say that? She wondered. Plant Sir John's Nose? How could I have said that? A jumpy impulse, she decided, to startle Billy's pretty face. But he didn't even notice the remark—which, now that she thought about it, she liked. She took a deep breath. She had also wanted to change the subject, for she always knew when a man was winding up to talk about his past. She did not know if she could bear it, not on the same day she had learned something about Jennings. She told herself not to think so much. It was foolish to get upset over an evening at Mama's with a man who meant nothing to her. But she rarely took her own advice: her curiosity was greater than her caution.

". . . She never thought I would go into journalism or show biz. Well, part of her might have suspected, but I think she saw me as a lawyer or doctor. Anything so I wouldn't be like my father." He smiled. "You can't imagine what I had to go through. The fights—"

"Seems to have come out all right in the end."

"Well, you see, both my parents are utter failures, though you wouldn't think so. Not when they start talking. My father owns a string of furniture stores, some of them pretty fancy, and every year on his birthday he opens a new one. Works himself to death for furniture! And my mother, always yammering for money to buy antiques. But she never does, not really."

She looked up. What Billy said interested her.

"Utter failures, both. I just flew the coop, and when I was young, too. Did you know they had boarding schools in California?"

She looked down. Interesting perhaps, but she did not believe the feeling he put behind his facts. She supposed there was a kind of symmetry at work. If he would not see her, she must not see him, or not as he really was. For her benefit he was playing a movie, one in which he was the star: benighted child makes good against the odds. Most people did that, of course, and some private movies were good. But she was not in the mood for one.

"You don't seem very interested."

"I'm sorry. Moving, getting readjusted—takes a while."

There was an awkward moment.

"Well, let's have another bottle of that wine, to help you relax in style. Mama! Let's have another of those."

"Not too much for me, Billy."

"Don't worry. Jim, pull up a chair. Do you know Kelly Martin? This is Jim Stanislau of the *Daily News*."

"When are you going to announce?" the reporter asked. "And for what?"

Billy smiled in answer. The Cheshire cat, thought Kelly.

In the next hour there began what Kelly, in one of her sketches, had called "the dance of the dominoes." In this dance an after-supper crowd, fresh from somewhere else—the theater, dinner parties—would arrive for a nightcap. Someone would want to join someone else's table. To make room one table would be joined, or matched, to another. A third, fourth, and fifth would be added, often at cockeyed angles. Sometimes the people at one table did not know those at another down the line; the third and fifth link might not match, for example, except with the fourth link, which connected them. In her sketch Kelly treated the dance of the dominoes as a curious sexual rite, whose purpose was the cross-fertilization of ideas, gossip, and personalities. Its offspring was the fashionable view.

This particular dance started when the *Daily News* reporter pulled up a chair. At Mama's, journalists were often busy keeping abreast, and if one fell into a serious, newsy conversation others would soon happen by: experienced subjects took advantage of this instinct of journalists to clump. When Billy began to discuss his political future several journalists joined the *News* man; others, not journalists, became curious and drew up chairs. As he spoke Billy gave a little, took back a little, but said nothing that could be published. There was something seductive, however, in the tease of the give and take, and something nourishing in the chewing-over of opinion and fact. Sometimes Billy glanced at Kelly, but he did not speak to her.

At first she was relieved not to talk and observed the dance with professional interest. She admired his handling of journalists. He was so intimate. Surely something like lovemaking was at work. She shut her eyes. His occasional glance—studied and non-

88

chalant—suggested the performance was for her. Or rather, as she came to think, against her. He was attempting to impress her with his power; he might have been making love to another woman. She opened her eyes. She told herself she should not be upset—offended at his rudeness, perhaps, but that was all. Besides, she had not been very nice to him.

Her detachment collapsed when two large men squeezed beside her. She was pinned against the wall, since her bench was only intended for two at most. No one knew who she was until Theodore Oatis sat down across from her and began to talk about old times. He told her how the black turtleneck was doing, how sorry everyone was to hear of their breakup and—was Montana interesting? Was she writing a book? Was Billy Bell really a *serious* journalist? Whenever she caught Billy's eye, in an effort to escape, she found nothing there; his attention would soon pass to a story being told by the journalists. She began to feel weak. Was Oatis pressing his leg against hers or was it merely the leg of the table? She noticed the smudged rims of the glasses, the dandruff inches away, and suddenly stood up.

It made a clatter, which pleased her. "Excuse me," she said—passing legs like logs. "Excuse me. Excuse me." She assumed she was searching for the bathroom. She thought it was somewhere back and to the left. When she did not immediately find it, her flutter began to tighten into panic. The black mirrors rustled with dim reflections, the familiar faces bobbed up here, there. Did she know that one, or just his picture? The low murmurings, the conspiring eyes—

"Looking for the loo, honey?"

It was Mama.

"Yes."

"Just to your left."

She recognized herself in the mirror.

Outside, she found Mama reshuffling some tables near Sir John. She studied the woman's face—few looked directly at Mama—and saw only midnight fatigue. The bar crowd was beginning to thin out, but there were still three hours to go. A departing couple let in a warm breath of night air. She heard the traffic. She decided to go. Why put up with it? She should have remembered. She considered telephoning Billy from the street: the ancient black telephone would be brought to his table. But that was too melodramatic. She smiled to herself. A wonderful old word had come to her. "Mama," she said, opening the door, "would you tell Mr. Bell that I'm indisposed?"

5

The whispered message came at a moment of exhilaration. He was talking to people who mattered. Their interest in him confirmed how promising his political prospects were. He nodded his thanks to Mama, then completed a story he was telling. The waiters, pouring and taking orders, slipped in and out of the seams between people.

The message stung. It reminded him of earlier, when he thought Kelly was baiting him. Had anyone heard the message or noticed his reaction? He looked down his table. No. It was not necessary to participate in the talk, not for a while, since a reporter had begun a long joke. He could rest. He glanced at Sir John, who was chatting to a lovely young woman Billy did not recognize, and remembered his mother's behavior whenever, in Los Angeles, they came within throwing distance of someone famous: her hand would fly to her hair.

Sir John's charm seemed invincible. He said the right thing on all occasions, in an accent as soft as old leather. His Hollywood circle, Billy was certain, contained no men who wore gold chains or unbuttoned silk shirts; or, if it did, they were there only for Sir John's amusement. What was more, he was a man of genuine achievement, about whom serious critics had written whole books. When Sir John walked into Mama's Billy felt insignificant; and Kelly intensified this feeling through her obvious disregard for them both. Billy recalled a high school expression, ice princess, and took a moment's pleasure in his freedom to be unfair. He murmured, "Cold bitch."

The punch line of the joke brought general laughter. Then the conversation began to lose its line. Billy did not notice, but thought with quick remorse, No, she's not a cold bitch. How could I have felt that? Her coolness became a soft remembrance, a kind of gentle refreshment, and he recalled her marvelous coloring: the brown and blue. Then the scrape of a chair startled him, and with a shock he remembered. She had walked out on him in front of these people. His anger returned, and he thought: She's trying to snare me. Someone next to him got up to leave. Well, he thought, he wasn't going to fall into any damn net. He nodded at Sir John a few tables away and Sir John nodded back, then returned to his lovely companion. Billy smiled. Hadn't Sir John stopped by to say hello? And then, suddenly, Billy relaxed.

After all, he was backstage. The backstage feeling, loosening every muscle, gentling every thought, came to him often. It was not a feeling confined to the theater. It could settle over a dinner party or a tennis court. It was prevalent at Mama's. Billy first knew it at the age of eight, when his mother let him join the live audience of a children's show. Off the air the casual behavior of the stars was wonderful beyond measure. To watch Wyatt Earp drink coffee from a Styrofoam cup! To hear him discuss the Dodgers! A privilege. Backstage meant membership in a club, the possession of a secret. Once again Billy looked in Sir John's direction. He thought, What a nice portly old guy. A call might be in order, to ask him onto the show.

Mama added a table to Sir John's. Only the parties of Sir John and himself, Billy noticed, required extra tables; yes, their respective chains touched. His sudden sense of power made Kelly seem like a moment's foolishness. "No—don't go." He stopped a departing couple. "One more drink, on me." He ordered fresh drinks all round. He teased some waverers into a nightcap. He mused about the mistress of a local Republican and told a lengthy joke of Gargola's about the difference between a New York politician and a nest of crows. The conversation warmed up again. Billy, who had been at Mama's for several hours, became a little drunk. He was a smart drinker, however, who drank only halfway down the glass. He knew the ways in which alcohol helped him, adding shine to his natural charm, and easing the play of his thought.

Earlier, while drinking with a couple of reporters, he had coaxed the notebook from a pocket. When other notebooks had appeared, however, he had retreated, since he did not want to say anything for publication. Reporters were never much of a problem. He knew when to assume an air of brotherly cynicism or deliver a few deft compliments. He knew how to provide a lead, use the word "new," or coin a phrase that called for quotation marks. Nonetheless, a few smart and bitter journalists resisted Billy. There was one sitting at the table, a friend of Oatis whose name Billy had forgotten. It became important to Billy, as things became important when he drank too much, to win over this man. That would put the right cap on the evening. And so he began to talk politics to the table at large. His sixth sense told him that the man's reactions were in keeping with what was known of his life. He had gone to Harvard and been a correspondent in Vietnam. He disliked the institutions of power, considering them corrupt, and regarded himself as an intellectual with the soul of a populist. He received large advances for his books. No doubt, thought Billy, he considers Billy Bell a lightweight.

It was not a question of talking directly to this journalist, who was muttering to Oatis. Nor was it a matter of staring at him: that would have seemed like begging. Billy simply discussed his misgivings about politics. His tone was sincere but not naïve; now and then he met the man's eyes. "I mean," Billy said, "let me tell you a story that Gargola told me, seriously now— no, on second thought I won't tell it, too long, but the substance is that the members of the city administration, in particular the ones involved with the construction industry, are *already* involved in kickbacks, pension fund schemes and so on." This did not work well enough— something was wrong about the way the glasses rested on the man's nose.

"As if that were not bad enough," he continued, "it is almost impossible to control events from the top, to really shape matters, especially with the power Washington now has. I was talking to Alfred Teitelman the other day . . ." Repeating a confidence from Teitelman made him uneasy, but he was willing to invest in this conversation; and the wry mention of Teitelman, a figure of consequence and suspicion, improved the position of the glasses. "He was telling me that once, recently, he was in the mayor's office and the mayor was crying, blubbering like a child, he was so frustrated—" The improvement continued, which prompted Billy to give the event more of a beginning and end. He turned it into an anecdote. "If the mayor and Teitelman, and Teitelman is as smart as they come, can't run the city, then who can?" The position of the glasses worsened. "Of course, God knows what would happen if they really had their way." The position improved.

Billy let someone else have the floor.

Then he took it back. "Why should I want to get involved in all that? Except"—he smiled modestly—"that I work in the one area that's more absurd than politics." The glasses vibrated gently. "The other day we made some news about handicapped children, so that we could have an angle for the show—*made* some news. You have to do that, or the ratings go down. Some system," he said. The position of the glasses improved. "Yesterday I was told that Trilby, who filled in at anchor on the local news, had never heard of Nathaniel Hawthorne."

Several people at the table feigned disbelief.

Billy declared himself disappointed, personally, in both politics and television. In neither had he found, over the years, much to respect. Some bitterness, the bitterness of the view from the inside, came into his voice. He hung an image of disappointment in front of them, a portrait in black tones that he occasionally enlivened with black humor. Then he changed everything: he began to talk about his parents. He described how hard they had worked, how badly they had failed, and how alienating—the word sounded pleasantly nostalgic when he used it—he had found Los Angeles as a boy. He remembered his immigrant grandfather . . . What he said was moving. If the world of politics was black, the world of his past was white—the lush white of dreams that could only disappoint. The transition was astonishing but not abrupt. The position of the glasses was excellent.

"I'm sounding like an idiot," Billy said, smiling. "Too much to drink." He knew that he had been talking more than was customary. That was all right, once he acknowledged it. Indeed, it became important to do so, for the long recounting of his past forced an awareness upon the table that he was different, that his future need not be ordinary. "The really odd thing," he said, "is that I love New York. I want to see it work better. It sounds corny, but I want to see it remain a great city." He stopped short. His tone was not in the least maudlin. He was revealed as a person who, in addition to sharing the cynicism of those present, had room for another dimension—hope. This was rare at Mama's. It increased Billy's stature. "Maybe I'll go ahead and give it a try. I don't know." He stopped short. "I just don't know." He was certain: the glasses were at rest.

*

Billy woke at 4:00 A.M. This was not unusual. When he drank too much, the hangover often woke him two hours into his sleep. He sat up in bed shaking with anger. The word "indisposed" swung in his head like the clapper of a bell. He reached for the phone and punched out Kelly's number, intending to ask her what she meant. It was already ringing when he realized what he was doing. He decided to hang up but did not. The phone rang and rang and at last a voice whispered, "Hello?" Not knowing what to say, Billy said nothing. "Hello? . . . Hello? . . . Who is this?" He shivered, half with fear, half with pleasure. "Who is this?"

He could not speak. He hung up and said, "Too much to drink." Then took three aspirin and some B vitamins. In the morning he was not certain he had called her.

CHAPTER

FIVE

I

Late on a Wednesday afternoon Jennings walked to a Chelsea church of uncertain denomination. Attached to one side of the church was a day-care center. Next Sunday's sermon, posted on a box, was entitled "*You* Are God's Poetry." Inside Jennings found Penelope talking to a red-bearded minister who palpitated, gently, with enthusiasm. He looked into Jennings' eyes and shook his hand for too long, reminding Jennings of those ministers who possess a master's degree in psychology and warn against the danger of role-playing. Jennings did not believe such ministers really existed, although they were often parodied, and he was surprised to find one in New York. The minister had just completed a sign in fancy script:

> *All Welcome*
> *It's Free!*
> *"Heart Murmurs"*
> *A Reading of Selections*
> *From the Diary of the Noted*
> *Artist Penelope Lamb*
> *8 P.M.*

Jennings smiled, but he felt listless.

"No rush," said Penelope. "Let's have a leisurely cup of coffee, then buckle down."

The air inside was musty, so Jennings led her to the church steps. He assumed Penelope wanted to ask him something. Why else order him to come early? He was not friend enough to set up chairs. While she mused about her nervousness, he stared out at the afternoon. The air ached with mugginess, the light seemed sluggish. Young couples—about to make supper, then damp love—passed by arm in arm, and the blue-jeaned walkers—lawyers and actors out of work—looked solemn: weighing their futures, no doubt. So many homosexuals . . . and, he thought irritably, why did they wear those little jackets that skirted the waist like that? There were few old people. In the South Village, he thought, it was still possible to find an old Italian. They were the local scenery, like churches or vegetable markets in Europe.

"You don't have to be nervous," he said. "It's your friends that are coming—imagine two hundred friends."

"I call that reason to be nervous."

"I'm sure they'll love it."

"Hits pretty hard."

"Hit them as hard as possible."

"Oh, *you're* impossible."

There was a pause.

"But," she asked, "why can't Billy come?"

This, then, was what she wanted.

"You know how busy he is."

"*But.*"

"Penelope, I honestly don't know."

Since the baseball game, he had only discussed business with Billy. "I think," he lied, "that Billy had a dinner invitation from the president of the station that he couldn't turn down."

"Well, I'm going to have to have you all out to the country," she said. Her eyes did not blink: she meant to get to the bottom of something. "Kelly Martin, you, and Billy. A replay. It was such a good dinner party I thought a weekend together would be even better. Are you free?"

"Yes."

"Would you find out when Billy is free for me?"

Jennings hoped Kelly was coming to the reading. It was several days since their last meeting, and the prospect of arranging another made him strangely apprehensive. If she came, something would necessarily happen.

"This is going to be very difficult for me," Penelope said, with an air of reflection. "To open myself in this way. But women *must* be willing, for the sake of men above all. You know, I was going to hold the reading in my loft, but some friends of mine said that was too humble. Typical. Women should *not* keep their emotions in the home."

"Where are the chairs?"

"This way."

The auditorium reminded Jennings of poetry readings and existential dramas in one act. Two spotlights were aimed at a solitary stool, and the little stage smelled of sneakers. When the chairs were unfolded, Penelope told Jennings to help prepare punch for the reception. That done, Jennings spent the last few minutes looking over the bulletin board, which was peeling with notices: one-bedroom sublet, $700; The Emotion Workshop, Sundays, 3:00 p.m.; Mature Singles Wine-tasting, Tuesdays, 8:00 p.m.; Yoga classes, 6:00 p.m. Mon.-Wed.-Fri. He was astonished by the number of people who came. He guessed two hundred. He found a seat to one side and looked for Kelly.

"Could someone please turn up the lights?" asked Penelope, taking center stage. She curled around her stool like a cat claiming its spot. Her dress was rippling black, and she held a book loosely in her hands. The light brightened.

"Thank you."

She tapped the microphone.

"Can you hear me?"

A few people nodded.

"Good."

She cleared her throat, and was silent.

At last she murmured, in a modified English accent, "Thank you all for coming. I would like to read several excerpts from my diary and afterwards, if you wish, discuss some of the issues that it does, and I suppose does not, raise." She hesitated. "I have been writing for as long as I can remember, but I shall spare you"—she smiled wanly—"the juvenilia. I have selected, more or less at random, excerpts from the last couple of years. I think of each entry as a kind of verbal photograph, one of whose dimensions is time. You are free to think of them as you wish."

She paused. "I never thought anyone but myself would be interested in my diary, but certain friends insisted otherwise. Consider this then . . . Well, I wanted to make you a gift of my . . . self."

"Oh no!" moaned Jennings, not quite under his breath.

"To present the text . . . of my life."

"No!"

"Hush!" said a woman behind him.

Jennings leaned back. It was dark except for the light aimed at Penelope. He could shut his eyes and just let her words roll past him. An hour or two—it could not last longer.

"This first entry," said Penelope wryly, "has to do with a friend of all of us. I am talking, of course, about despair. The piece is called 'February Fruit.' It's fairly . . . Kierkegaardian, although I came to understand this only later." She took a deep breath and began to read.

> February twentieth. Snowfall. Today, children in fresh snow. Children who, with each step, step older. Fresh snow, today. Streets dusted white. Tomorrow, tomorrow, tomorrow—black snow. And once we were virgins. Once, once, once it was morning. But this morning, today's *mourning*, I know I too will die . . .

Jennings felt his toes curl.

> . . . the mirror draws me like a lover. Save that, like no lover, it rests always in the same place. Cold reflections. The graven image? The icon of the self? The heart—quaint conceit—turns to a different kind of love . . .

In back a door opened, slanting light across the auditorium. Then the light winked out. His eyes narrowed: it was Kelly. Whispering "Excuse me," she found a chair across from him. Since each row of chairs, one higher than the next, formed a horseshoe around the stage, their line of sight ran over the top of Penelope's head.

Kelly looked warm from hurrying, and water streamed down her face. The weather had broken. He waited for her to see him—for rescue. When he waved at her, however, beads rattled behind him and someone said "Shhhhhhh."

". . . The urine of old men has wounded the snow . . ."

Jennings twisted in his chair. He crossed and uncrossed his legs. He leaned forward and back. He implored—but no luck.

". . . And I stare through my window at dusk."

Penelope raised her eyes.

Uncertain whether she had finished that entry, the audience clapped tentatively—so tentatively that, when it became obvious that Penelope had completed "February Fruit," the audience, not wanting to appear stingy, rebounded with vociferous applause. Penelope smiled modestly. Maybe now, thought Jennings. The light directed at the stage placed Kelly in soft shadow.

But no.

"Thank you. Thank you very much. On this next, fortunate day I had *two* epiphanies. I happened to be in the Caribbean, and I chose to write one of them down. I think it's very much about the response of art to our use-it-once-and-throw-it-away culture . . . our disintegrating world. But of course you must draw your own conclusions. It's about the way nothing connects, chance, entropy, dissolves, the deeper connections."

She paused. "I suppose that here Yeats, among others, is my master." She said this kindly, resolved to pay honor where honor was due. "The center cannot hold . . ." She let the line rest in the ear of the audience.

Kelly would not look up.

"Anyway this is not meant to be understood in a purely literal way. It should enter the mind on many different levels. *Infiltrate* is a word I like." She paused. Jennings longed to scissor his legs. He calculated that, to leave, he would have to pass fourteen knees and five umbrellas.

"To capture this second epiphany, I have scrambled a hymn from my childhood. Incidentally, I first wrote this in sand." She looked up significantly. "It concerns, I think, the use of chance as a way to structure experience. Reverend Peter, I hope you don't mind. It's based upon the deepest respect." From somewhere in back a husky voice said, "No problem in God's corner."

99

Penelope began:

> Part Two. From . . . To . . . Hope . . . Help . . .
> For . . . Eternal . . . Sufficient . . . Ages . . .
> Home . . . Stormy . . . God . . . Years . . . O . . .
> Blast . . . The . . . Past . . . Come . . . Our . . .
> Our . . . And.

The audience applauded, and Jennings gave up hope. He did what he had learned to do in high school: shut his eyes, sit very still, then swallow his energy. It would end; they would meet. He said, "This is purgatory"—but under his breath, so the beads wouldn't rattle.

"I know how difficult these early entries have been," said Penelope. "They've been concerned more with states of being than narrative. Not all of my diary is like that, so I'm going to move on to other aspects now. My next entries concern the relationship between men and women, as seen through the prism of my personality. The following is addressed to the women in the audience only."

2

Kelly thought: "To me?"

"I am sure my views are not so different," continued Penelope, "from all of yours." She paused to smile. "But I'm also sure everyone will agree we need a little open discussion about these matters."

"Hear, hear!" boomed the voice in the back.

"Thank you. Last May twenty-fourth, it was midafternoon as I recall, I was doing some cleaning up around the house. And suddenly, who knows why, I was struck by a severe apprehension . . ."

Kelly wiped a last trickle from her cheek. A thunderstorm had broken over the city during her rush to the reading. This put her in an excellent mood, since she loved few things as much as a thunderstorm. The congested air, the enfolding gloom, then glorious release. A revelation! And best of all, not theater. She loved the sweet aftermath too, when the world attained a clarity otherwise withheld. She settled into her chair, which was too rickety for her high spirits. Then she peered at Penelope, reviewed the earnest audience, sucked in the dead air, failed to find Jennings, decided everything was funny. She listened to what was said, but often jumped off into her own thoughts. "A deep, deep concern," Penelope was saying "that after years of progress the women's movement would lose its momentum." Kelly sighed, thinking "Protect feminism from its friends!" She considered herself a feminist, she supposed, and the horrible complacency of men around issues of importance to women offended her. She would ferociously defend the women's movement before any man, particularly in Montana, where men were not yet practised with feminists. But the truth, which made her feel guilty, was that feminism bored her.

"—a way to seize our situation!"

Oh, Penelope! Of all people, Penelope was warming up! Could this be the Penelope who, moments before, whispered her despair, who sounded so weak the audience wanted to help her with its applause? Kelly smiled. For a while she did not listen to what was said about feminism, but simply watched Penelope herself—understood and savored the slight flutter of conviction she had not known Penelope possessed. For a moment she envied her. What joy to find a source of warmth, to assign all of the blame, to sweat with an army of opinions. She herself would be sorry to think her pain had only one source.

"—and not be trapped in the kitchen. The wonder is not that women accomplished so little—"

Yes, yes, but to have stayed close to the great cycles of birth and death, to have become stuck in the glue and stuff of feeling, to have put what art there could be of food and comfort into the dailiness of life, was something more than martyrdom. It was the hidden history, portrayed only by a few artists.

"—the mere physical difference—"

She held out for some deeper distinction between men and women. She would be sorry to lose her profound sense of otherness, of there being another continent unknown yet at hand.

"—control of our own bodies—"

101

Oh damn, she thought, now becoming irritable. "These boring lectures." She looked around, hoping to find Jennings. Few faces showed any sign of thought; they listened like mules. And so she began to play a private game. She was a saboteur who stood apart and against. She would listen carefully—then suddenly answer Penelope. That way she stayed in a good mood.

Penelope promised to read an excerpt from the "intimate cycle" of her diary and Kelly noticed that the audience, as one, pricked up its ear. "Those who may be offended by the following I hope will, at least, appreciate my candor. If you cannot be candid to your diary . . . then *who* and *where* are you? I have selected two entries, which I believe will complement each other. The first concerns the breakup of a relationship. I will not reveal his name, although I have left instructions that, upon his death, the name may be revealed. There are *many* entries on him—"

That'll kill him, Kelly thought.

"I have lent him some initials—a kind of fig leaf." Penelope paused to let the audience titter. "The second entry is somewhat more . . . pleasant. To put it frankly, it's about a *series* of flings I had over the course of a single weekend in Connecticut." Penelope smiled. "Not something, I assure you, that I do every weekend." She took a deep breath.

August twenty-seventh. Tonight LM and I dine at Frederickson's. Cheerful tinkle of silverware. Babble of voices. We walk home. We do not speak. LM tosses his jacket onto the chair. In the bedroom I observe his toothbrush. Socks. A dead leaf on the windowsill. The wind beats against the pane. I notice the wrapper of a Big Mac."

Such dreary drizzle, Kelly thought. It was the preferred style in writing—that, or the cartwheeling or the macho or the camp or the whimsical styles; or the academic, which tasted like ashes in the mouth. She disliked the drizzle most. Thin, whiny voices, sickly secretions, and a gray pall highlighted by a pale rose-colored epiphany. And often, such a rhythm! Short, declarative sentences to suggest one's fine disconnection. Like sentences falling step by step down the stairs:

Bump . . .

Sigh, I'm sensitive.

Bump . . .

Sigh, I cut my wrists.

Bump . . .

All this red stuff.

Bump . . .

Bump . . .

Bump . . .

And so much talk of "relationships." In the window of every restaurant, women picked relationships apart—the word itself, Kelly thought, sounded like something in need of a cure. Yet she liked the talk of women.

"—Suddenly I have a flashback. As we walked along the beach—"

It seemed impossible, nowadays, to escape that personal tone. A leaky tap: the ooze of the self.

> Beside me, on the bed, he grabbed me. I said, "No, LM." He said "What's wrong?" I said, "You know." He said, "Know what?" I said, "You know." He said, "Know what?" I said "No." I saw he knew . . .

Penelope stopped. Then, like a minister who has completed a moment of silence, she looked up. For some time she said nothing. Then she permitted a sigh to escape. It sounded, Kelly thought, like the sigh of an owl that has dined on a fat mouse.

"Well!" said Penelope, reviving. "So relationships end. As I have said, my next excerpt is more joyful. It took me several years—"

Kelly wondered what time it was. Where was Jennings?

"—and, I confess, some therapy, but I can now tell you, without embarrassment, that I have come to terms with my body, despite the efforts of society to make me ashamed of my physical self. I do not, for example, feel guilty about satisfying my sexual needs." She paused, about to say something clever. "The problem is finding capable men."

The audience laughed.

That much was true, Kelly thought.

"In any case I spent a weekend in a house up in Connecticut, a huge weekend party, a sort of conference given by a rich and famous person. I cannot reveal his name. Where, to let the cat out of the bag, I had sex with, if you can believe it, a pianist, a painter, and a writer. Not at once, I should add. But I'm getting ahead of myself. Let the diary do it.

> July twenty-fourth. Arrived at the mansion. Leafy trees. Two guest cottages. All around pale artistic men. Or rough artistic men."

A painter, a pianist, and a writer! No doubt it was fashionable sex, Kelly thought, but probably not very good sex. Artists were usually too aware of their performance, even if they played well, and you could never be sure they weren't taking notes. She wondered how explicit Penelope would be. That was the only interesting question, since the main point would be the usual one: women, too, could play the rake. Merry fucking, bittersweet parting, merry fucking, bittersweet parting. And so on. It was odd that, despite this conception of the good life, she had known almost no women who were happy to sleep around. Those who did—she knew lots— did so to express their pain through their pleasure. Or because no man would stay.

". . . We both knew. No words were necessary. Odd how one knows. We wandered down toward the river . . ."

A fling was another matter. To yield to impulse could be wonderful, if only men weren't so crude about handling a one- night stand. They could not manage the mood of distant tender- ness necessary both before and after. They lied, "I love you," or they treated you like a boot. She smiled, remembering an ordinary graduate student in Paris with a terrific twinkle in his eye.

"With the painter," continued Penelope, "I'll confess it, he was entirely the aggressor."

But why hadn't Jennings come?

"He pursued me without . . . cease. I could not open a book without having him stand in my light. The gift of pleasure is . . ."

Penelope knew only one pleasure, Kelly thought, satisfaction; and satisfaction, sadly, was the killing of desire. She wondered if art had become pale and feverish because the pulse of desire, and of the dreams that were the overflow of desire, was growing weak.

"The only trouble with this painter," said Penelope—and then she paused. "The ladies are going to know what I mean . . . Pre- ma-ture . . . e-jac-u-la-tion."

Kelly laughed.

Perhaps the Europeans were better about sex. In books and films she had often come upon the wonderful figure of the wise European woman, about forty-five, who retains a wry detachment, a lovely quizzical humor; she can be wounded but not seriously; she regards love as a bittersweet chocolate. Were there really such women? And if so, did they pay a price? In hardness perhaps, or a certain shallowness of spirit? She looked around the room.

"Of course," said Penelope, "after that . . . disappointment . . . I had, to put it mildly, grown horns . . ." She looked up. "Wonderful, magnificent—I *ain't* apologizing—lust. So I set my eyes on a pianist."

Was lust to Penelope only sexual desire? But desire, Kelly thought, had object, direction, particularity. Lust was painfully vague. It was fire without fuel, the body's dream of itself.

"Let me be frank," said Penelope, looking up from her diary. "None of that high-flown sentimental stuff, those imprisoning stereotypes. Fucking—"

At last, Kelly thought, the word "fuck." An excellent word, now sadly worn with use. Its sound conveyed its meaning, said things that "making love" did not. It was best used when respect was paid to its years underground. It should suggest some brutality or toughness, she thought, the joyful moment, for example, when two bodies leapt at each other—*fuck*. The people who used the word with the most pleasure, Kelly had noticed, were at least ten years older than she was, the ones who had rediscovered that "fuck" was part of love. Now smart people used "fuck" indiscriminately, she thought, to avoid engaging the other dimensions of love. And they thought they were free!

Was that Jennings?

Her eyes dropped. And her thoughts slipped away.

"When we found ourselves in his bedroom," Penelope said, "we did not, to put it mildly, mess around."

She looked up. Yes.

"I tasted salt on his lips, and I placed my hand . . ."

Their eyes met and fell away. Kelly waved, a little.

"He grabbed every part of me. He was pinching and moaning and licking . . ."

Jennings, lost in a shadow, waved back.

". . . He ran his tongue . . . Yes, *Thanks*giving . . ."

Their eyes brushed, and they waved at the same time.

"Let me tell you," Penelope said, "we practically brought down the rafters of the house in Connecticut. . . ."

This time their eyes held; and, when Penelope completed this section of her diary, they smiled. The shadows softened the play of their expression. The presence of two hundred people, all of whom were watching Penelope, made them feel like two. During Penelope's next excerpt—concerning her disappointment in the American political system, as personified by a friend—they began a game. Neither actually started this game, which developed naturally out of their exchange of glances.

Kelly would arch an eyebrow.

And Jennings would cock a knee.

Jennings would lean forward.

And Kelly would lean back.

Kelly would shift one shoulder.

And Jennings would shift the other.

Kelly would stroke her cheek—

And so on, throughout Penelope's delivery. Their eyes during this game kept perfectly still. They sat, except for their small movements, absolutely motionless.

"In my final reading"—it was the "final" that roused them from their trance—"I hope you will find something heartening . . ."

Kelly sat up straight.

"One day I found myself walking down the street adding up the qualities that I believe artists have and should cultivate."

Kelly added on her fingers.

"This is called 'Untitled, June thirteenth.' "

Jennings pretended to sleep, but his acting seemed half-hearted.

"We who try to capture the essential nature of this civilization. And how hard it is, for we are offered no encouragement—"

So Jennings no longer wanted to act foolish? A plan came to her, a plan full of mischief. In this stuffy auditorium, among these earnest people—

"Have you noticed how many artists and writers are alcoholics. Or take too many drugs? How they are, in short, self-destructive?"

Kelly, looking silly, held a pistol to her head.

"Artists often feel compelled to poison themselves. And I thought, walking down Madison, that artists take upon themselves the burdens, the poisons—all the poisons of the society at large."

Kelly assumed a look of drunken nobility.

"I certainly do not mean to sound religious—that died for our sins stuff—sorry, Reverend, but I must be frank . . . yet we artists *do* take the sins of society into our systems."

Kelly groaned under the weight of society. Jennings' smile began to change character.

"I believe that what artists do is assume the burdens of society and *transform* them. To borrow a metaphor Reverend Peter will appreciate: they take the poisonous bread and wine and transform them into something pure, into *art*."

Kelly, astonished, pulled a rabbit out of a hat.

"This accounts, I believe, for the sense of *difference* that is the burden all artists must bear. They are singled out, touched by some higher thing."

Kelly blessed herself with her shoe—and Jennings' cheeks began to redden.

"Which creates the terrible solitariness, the sublime loneliness of the modern artist."

Kelly looked ravaged—and Jennings' cheeks began to swell.

"It is something I would never, ever wish upon any of you. Do not, I repeat, *do not* be an artist unless you must. You will see too clearly, possess the gift of sight not given to others. You will see with the sophistication of an old civilization, yet the innocence of a child."

Kelly stuck out her tongue.

And Jennings burst.

It was an implosive snort, ghastly and half smothered, like the death rattle of a giant. There was a moment of silence, then a few giggles. Penelope let the audience collect itself.

"I shall always consider artists—and I think of myself, frankly, as aspiring to that condition—the moral agents of society. They are free as others are not. In this world the artist must be an anarchist, of course, for in that way he or she will be available for the greater order of art." Penelope smiled, and softly closed the book on her lap. The audience applauded. "Now if there are any questions . . ."

Jennings jammed a hitchhiker's thumb in the air. Kelly nodded and, disregarding the audience, they made for the exit, leaving the questions behind.

3

Jennings, sputtering with joy, rode her mercilessly down the street. "You witch! I thought I was going to explode—that noise I made! Do you think Penelope knows who it was? I'm going to blame it all on you. You should have seen the people around me. This woman with beads!" On the sidewalk, carousers, four and five abreast, parted to let them pass. "What on earth am I going to say? I don't think anyone near me knew who I was. Except maybe that awful minister saw me!"

Kelly walked very fast, looking straight ahead, like a woman trying to outpace a lunatic.

"And everyone was so quiet! The whole place looked at me! I wanted to hide under the seat! Do you think Penelope knows it was a laugh? Maybe someone just sneezing? Do you think it sounded like a sneeze? That awful face you made. Where'd you learn to do that? You probably gave lessons when you were little. Come on, do you think it sounded like a sneeze?"

At last, to stop her, Jennings grabbed her shoulders. "Well?" he asked.

"Well?"

"Well," he said, after a pause, "where should we go for dinner?"

She cocked one eyebrow.

"Yes," he admitted, "that was pretty good, wasn't it? My transitions are not usually so suave. It just came to me . . . but it's possible I stole it from a movie."

She let up a little. "You sounded as if you'd just been hanged."

"Well, you did it!"

"It was good for you."

"Where are we?"

They found themselves on the edge of the West Village, some distance from most of the restaurants. They decided they didn't want to go to a proper restaurant anyway, not after sitting for so long. One of the loud informal places, where the food didn't matter, was good enough. Jennings had never felt better; he wanted to stay out late. With a mutual shrug they walked into the Wet Whistle, which had a sign Jennings liked—a green neon whistle. Just inside was a bar with people three or four deep; the men stood in half circles around the women. In back were booths and a small dance floor strewn with sawdust. It was early yet, and no one was dancing. The jukebox was loud.

"Okay?" he asked. She nodded. A waiter led them to a booth. Jennings, who did not like rum, ordered English gin in Hornblower's honor. She ordered a white wine spritzer. And then, because the waiter lingered, they also ordered hamburgers. "This is the sort of place I sometimes came to in the sixties," Jennings said. "There would be an imitation Bob Dylan tuning his guitar in the corner. Most of the people would be from New Jersey or underage—everyone had fake draft cards then—and just kind of hanging out in the Village."

She smiled.

"Now places like this—they don't know what to do with themselves. Of course, that doesn't mean they don't make money . . ."

He realized he was jabbering and his mood changed key. He lost none of his euphoria, but became more aware of the person across from him. To his overheated eye, she appeared fearfully complex. It seemed astonishing that she had put him through so much so soon, that she seemed to know more about him than he knew himself, that she should be sitting, right there, across from him. For a moment he stared at her as if they had never met; and the bottomless blue of her eyes started the hair prickling on the back of his neck. So he continued to jabber—more about what he and his friends used to do in the Village.

He might have calmed down at any time, but running slightly out of control was too rare to be quickly surrendered. He retained enough presence, however, to discuss only unimportant matters. They talked about the politics and demonstrations of the sixties. Then they spent half an hour over dinner picking apart the people at the bar. "Look at those fat old men," she whispered. "That circle of three around those women—old goats nibbling at girls." Even this chatter, however, possessed a certain weight. If he had known her somewhat more or less he could have talked lightly about nothing.

After dinner Jennings asked her to dance. He liked hearing himself ask. Then he withdrew the invitation.

"Oh no, you can't get out of it."

"I was crazed. You don't want to dance with me."

"Yes I do. I will."

"Please?"

"No."

"You trapped me."

She gaped, then looked sly. "You can't change the subject."

The jukebox played only the old music: Stones, Animals, Beatles. He thought, That was what tripped me up. And she would be an excellent dancer, he knew it, one of those girls with buttery hips that he remembered from high school; they liked dancing so much that, lacking a male partner, they danced with each other. Jennings looked at the dance floor. Several couples were dancing. They were very good. She warned, "You're going to hurt my feelings." Before his devil-may-care mood slipped away altogether, he finished his drink and said, "You'll be sorry."

He led her to the back of the dance floor.

The first number was fast—"Satisfaction." Her dancing, as he expected, was marvelous. His was a back-and-forth shuffle, in which it was understood the dancer was not trying. In the past he had been rather proud of this shuffle. It was a mark of intelligence. With Kelly, however, he could not maintain his superiority. The music was a wonderfully free thing denied him. He felt grotesque, like a beetle kicking in a bottle. At the same time, he loved watching her. Her dancing possessed rightness and joy; it looked like the simplest thing in the world. He wondered how she could yield to the music without reservation or dilution, how she could retain, still, her dignity.

When a slow dance started, Jennings, avoiding her smile, welcomed her close. This triggered a memory, a dreamy image that frightened him. He danced around its edge. He remembered the humor of the slow dances in ninth grade, the boys jockeying for the last dance and then . . . the soft crush against his chest, the breath of perfume, the magical complication of a brassiere strap. As they danced he left his memory behind for a moment, and let himself know Kelly in all her particularity. He lived what he remembered, except there was no brassiere strap, and he was conscious of so much that he had forgotten: the sweet confusion of leg, the salty damp around the neck. He was almost happy— almost, for being near her was also a kind of torment.

He edged deeper into his memory. What he had liked most about slow dancing, he remembered, was the tumble into reverie.

It represented something different from the usual approach to sex at that age; it was neither sweaty-fisted nor achingly romantic. Stepping into a slow dance brought him a strange peace, one in which his spine seemed to melt, as if he were easing into a warm bath. He lost his sense of self, in part because there was no immediate pressure toward lovemaking. His desire increased, and hung suspended. With Kelly in his arms he often drifted toward this bliss, only to be jerked back by her liveliness. She would not stay a dream. He felt a jab of nausea, like the sickening start awake when, on a train, his head nodded off. But he did not want to stop dancing.

Once, during a slow dance, he stepped back. Her eyes were smoky but no less blue: intelligence mixed with desire in equal proportion, with neither dimming the other. He loved the present moment, which left so much to come. He loved the keenness of longing, the melancholy of the detached view. He returned her to his arms, aware of her surprise that he gave her so many dances. Finally it was Kelly who pleaded fatigue. She wiped her face, then his, on a napkin. They ordered more to drink. Jennings wanted to return to the earlier, inconclusive talk. He thought of a topic—old rock-and-roll—but could not form the words into sentences. After a couple of moments, during which Jennings did not focus his eyes, Kelly took his hand in hers. He was startled.

"Jennings," she said. His own name cut him.

"Jennings," she repeated. She meant to speak, but instead drew him back onto the dance floor. It was another slow dance. When they were as close as before, but not looking at each other, she whispered in his ear "Jennings . . . let's not make love right away." Her legs continued to rustle between his; their pressure was neither more nor less than before she spoke. She whispered, "It's because of me, not you. It's something about the way you are too, maybe."

Jennings stepped back. He was about to be funny. "Aren't you assuming?" But her soft voice, her loving look—nothing was required of him. She had taken care of his vanity. So he said, "All right." Her words brought him extraordinary relief, so much so that tears filled his eyes. How could she know him so well? He was appalled and grateful. She was smoothing over the awkwardness by talking: ". . . so that it's not automatic," she was saying, "so that it evolves, if it evolves, according to our own sense of time, when the moment is right, and not anyone else's. Not a lightning bolt, I don't mean that—only that, if it should happen, it belongs to us. That's all I mean."

Did her voice tremble? He was not sure. Whatever it was that she had given him, however—and he realized that he had accepted a gift—he felt guilty. He owed her something, but he was not sure what.

"Don't you think so?" she asked. She appeared vulnerable to him for the first time.

"Yes."

"Tell me something you like," she said. "Please, you have to say something. Think."

"I don't understand—"

"Something you like." She smiled foolishly. "It can be anything, it's just that you're so . . . I don't know. I have to hear about something you like. Please." She took his hand once more. There *was* something he liked, some vague complicated gleaming thing, but he could not describe it to himself, let alone to Kelly. Not to speak to her, however, seemed a kind of betrayal. He looked into those eyes; and was suddenly lost there. He said, "You can't trust me, there's—"

She squeezed his hand. "Not now—tell me something you like."

"You."

"Something else."

He grabbed—trips to Europe?

"Monasteries."

"Yes?"

He did not know what he meant. Monasteries? But it was a word to hold on to, and she had said "yes." He could not imagine, in any case, how to explain himself out of it, not without making a joke of her question. Still headlong, he continued "Not religious, and not celibate, or it's not that part I like. I was in Greece once, the Greek islands, and you can't imagine how the light is there. You begin to understand about the ancient Greeks, Homer, when you see their light. I visited a monastery, part of the touristy thing to do—no, actually it wasn't, but there was a couple from St. Louis who had made a special appointment, and they said I could come too. Burros of course, and up a mountain overlooking the sea, but that's not what I liked so much. I got there, we made the tour, the monk was dumb, but there was a balcony—I don't know what I'm talking about."

"Go on."

"Of course it was beautiful. Light, rocks, sea. I'm not religious."

"I know."

"But that was part of the point. I did not think about religion once, that was very important. What was extraordinary to me, in that light, was not God, but the sacrifice the monks made, the sacrifice of a large part of the world. The giving up. People talk about the passivity of monks. How retiring they are. But can you imagine what an act that is, what a doing, to sacrifice so much of life? 'Sacrifice' is too elegant a word. Butcher. Just to achieve some greater clarity? Just to clear the eyes? You get rid of so much and—can you imagine what you can see in its stead?"

This last word, old and strange in his mouth, stopped him. "I sound like Reverend Peter."

"No."

"Forget it."

She shook her head.

He was dumbfounded by what he had said. It was a lie. He had been to Greece, but he had not visited a monastery with a couple from St. Louis. The balcony he remembered belonged to a hotel in southern Italy. He did not even believe the point of his speech. It was sentimental nonsense.

He said, "It's all a lie."

"I doubt it."

His embarrassment was so acute he shivered.

She said, "Even if it were religious, and I don't think it was, certainly not in the Reverend Peter's way, you shouldn't be embarrassed. I don't understand the condescension of educated people about religion, serious religion—it's stupid." Once again she seemed to be speaking to smooth over his awkwardness. "I sort of liked what you said."

The music continued, the waiter came by, they ordered another round. Couples continued to dance. "You seem so cold," she said. "Fearful."

"Not really."

"No?"

"No."

113

There was a pause.

"I left New York for many reasons," she said. Her voice was flat. "The last and most important was that I had an abortion. I don't feel very guilty about it, but I have a kind of horror at the memory, a pain that's not sharp but deadening, and always about ordinary things. How matter-of-fact my lover was, as if it was just a cold, or something womanish like cramps. He couldn't make it to the clinic until I was putting on my coat to leave. I remember the magazines on the table in the waiting room. Little mints. Muzak."

She stopped.

Once more something seemed expected from him. He did not know what it was.

"Lots of women have abortions," he said. "Certainly doesn't bother me."

"Bother," she said. "Bother."

It was not what was expected.

He tried again.

"It's grim to go through that."

"Not grim exactly."

What did she want? He became a little testy. Intimacy with her always entailed some obligation. He labored on nonetheless. "Obviously a man can't really know what it is," he said. "But I'm sure it's hard."

"Not for many people."

"For you."

"Oh, I don't know what I expect you to do." She waved it all away. His effort seemed to count for something, even if his words did not. "I'm strange in my own way—that's what you should know about me." Her eyes dropped. "You see, I love so many things so much it's easy for me to hate when—well, I sort of recoil . . . and then . . . well, I always know exactly what I'm doing, and I do it anyway."

She looked up.

For a moment he stopped thinking and became spontaneous and affectionate. The explosion at Penelope's, the decision to postpone lovemaking, the words between them—he was free. And with her he shut the world away. Saying little they played with each other's hands, spreading out the fingers or drawing designs on the palm, then asking for a guess at what was portrayed. Each moment was charged, each was light as a feather. Kelly did not let this interlude lose its magic—but, suddenly brightening, ended it. "One dance and let's go." She looked as eager as a child. "That monastery stuff was all made up," he said.

She raised a teasing finger. "Quiet."

He rose to dance with her. He remained awkward, but his compunction was less. At the end of the slow dance, when it was time to go, he kissed her good night.

4

In the taxi she refused to surrender to her demons, especially not to the pedestrian demon of loneliness. She recalled the glitter of his eyes before he kissed her and the play of his body when he chased her down the street. Sometimes he danced seductively, and he was marvelous when he relaxed. She tapped her hand, remembering their dandling fingers. And his strangeness interested her. He was not an ordinary eccentric, easily picked out, but one who passed in most respects as ordinary, with a sweet smile and a beguiling manner. Strange remote men had always attracted her, anyway— and she took some easy pride in her taste for difficulty.

Of course, she thought, nothing was resolved. The pressure between them, despite the one sweet moment, remained as great. What a ghastly noise! An internal explosion, followed by a spew of sound and a gagged rattle. Before that, she thought, his eyes looked dim and sunken in his body, like two lanterns in a cave. What kind of man was that to love? She knew very well: one of those complicated men for whom being simple was the hardest thing of all. One who despised the world too easily. And his dancing—many men were like that, but most did not realize or care that they were bad dancers. Some thought their bad dancing was cute: she remembered one who called himself an atonal dancer. But Jennings, looking trapped, did know and did care. Even during the slow dances, which required little skill, he was too tense; he could not yield anything. She was reminded of those boys in high school who were painfully shy or terrified the girls would notice their erections. Yet she did not consider Jennings shy or sexually frightened. His eyes told her it was not a sexual problem. Besides, she had run into an acquaintance whose closest friend had dated Jennings. He was impossible, but not in bed.

What bothered him then? She shuddered on the backseat, remembering his fevered march through the Village. He seemed either to sleep or to burn, with no time for the other things. Almost like Penelope, she thought, who celebrated the related styles of exhaustion and extravagance now fashionable in the arts. With Jennings, however, the style seemed more serious. She became angry. Perhaps he ought to retreat to his monastery, to a proud and selfish roost, vain in its holy remove. What a clichéd speech he had given—a Penelope epiphany! Then she remembered the fugitive warmth in his expression and hated monasteries with all her heart. And yet . . . perhaps the image of a monastery mattered less than the spontaneous feeling behind it: she liked the way the words ran away from him. And weren't all dreams of peace, refuge, and clarity sentimental? Even the great dreamed foolishly. It was what they made of their dreams, she thought, that mattered. To stare at such dreams through the dirty window of life, to state the simple from a position of intelligence—that was the courageous thing. But why monasteries, of all dreams?

She wondered for a moment what kind of lover Jennings would be. Probably skillful, considerate, somewhat reticent. The challenge would be to make him lose control. She smiled, then caught herself. She was right to postpone lovemaking: they would have hidden behind their sophistication. She looked through the window at the passing streets . . . All she had wanted, she thought, after their decision and his pretty speech, was some sign of affection, some touch or gesture. Why were men so stupid about women? She was tired of the way they used women to play out their little melodramas. Women did the same, of course; but her story still depended so much on the outcome of his. Why was that true so often? Perhaps she should become a firmer feminist. Or rid herself of the desire for dumb togetherness, stop investing so much of herself in others.

She paid the cabbie, remembering the whispered suggestion to Jennings. It was her favorite moment of the evening—odd, she thought, that she only recalled it now. Perhaps she had saved it for the ride alone up the elevator. It was the moment when she reached up to place her lips against his ear and felt his stubble against her cheek. He had stiffened and relaxed. And for a moment he seemed less strange to her. Then, when he stood back, she saw his humor, desire, wit, and intelligence. Her idea gave them time, some open space ahead. She unlocked her door. Turning on the light in an empty apartment let in the pedestrian demon, but she didn't mind. The demon was familiar, tame, worse at a distance. Turning on the light in her bedroom, however, made her shiver hard, whether from desire or a chill she didn't know.

CHAPTER

SIX

I

Without hanging up, Billy said goodbye to Teitelman, pushed a few buttons, and told his secretary to find Jennings. Then he stretched hard. The conversation had been good. Teitelman had initiated the call, to ask what Billy knew about a *Times* reporter who wanted to write a profile of the banker. This was the prelude to a discussion of city politics, during which each asked the other casual questions about what was really going on with so-and-so or about something or other. Billy stretched again. He was not a significant part of Teitelman's world, of course, for a talk-show host could not be of the first importance to a celebrated money man. But he was a part nonetheless. He wondered why. He had invited Teitelman to appear on the show, but the banker had not seemed anxious for the exposure. Teitelman had befriended him, Billy could only assume, because he thought Billy Bell might become powerful; and also, perhaps, because he liked Billy Bell.

His talks with Teitelman had prompted Billy to rearrange his affairs, which seemed too haphazard. Around Teitelman nothing drifted. Events did not shape Teitelman, Billy thought, Teitelman shaped events; at least, that was the impression he left. Billy was reminded of an old baseball coach who loved to say, "Okay, let's play hardball." What hardball meant for Teitelman was not quite clear, of course, but Billy guessed the banker hired and fired without qualm, invested large sums with confidence, wrote advantageous contracts. In all situations Teitelman knew who he was, where he was, and what was to be done.

Billy decided upon a number of steps. He would give as many speeches in New York as possible. He would cultivate the press. He would devote more time to serious issues, even at some cost to his ratings. And at the end of the year he would establish a fundraising committee. He would also relieve Jennings of most duties at the station, asking him to concentrate instead on advancing the political prospects of Billy Bell. Jennings might not approve, Billy thought, which was just too bad. Jennings was not only his closest friend, but also his most important employee.

After much thought, Billy had decided that he had outgrown Jennings. His friend was clever, his instincts were excellent, he was good with cameras. But his knowingness was immature, a kind of college smirk that no longer impressed Billy. Compared to Teitelman's savoir faire—there was no comparison. In the midst of another stretch, Jennings walked into the office. Billy's arms fell. It was as irritating, this loss of a moment's luxury, as an interrupted yawn. He became businesslike.

"Hi, Jennings. I wanted to talk over—"

"Sleepy?"

"No, no. Here, sit down."

Billy loathed the unkempt hair. It wasn't the disrespect—Jennings was always like that. It was the desultory manner. Jennings drifted. "I intend to move you out of your present duties," Billy began, noticing that Jennings was staring out the window. "Anyway, no more work on the regular show. Only on our special issues programs. I want you to begin thinking about the campaign. What office to aim at. What issues are coming up. I want you to set up speaking engagements with any kind of Democratic organization or group, even Republicans who might cross over. Anything political. Get to know the reporters. Research."

"Sure."

"What do you mean, 'Sure'?"

"I'll do it."

"Shouldn't you take some notes?"

119

"I'll remember."

"Come on, I know you don't like it. You don't think I should make a run." Billy smiled, but refused to work for Jennings' approval.

"You'll probably win on the first try."

Billy stood up. "Will the work bore you?"

"No."

"You're indifferent." Billy stepped around his desk. "Have you thought at all about the pornography issue?"

"Some."

"I want you to think about it."

Billy sat down on the couch.

"I've already told you what I think," Jennings said. "A great second issue, a wonderful attention grabber."

"Well, let's get going on the details. We can do one of our issue series on it, of course—maybe after Labor Day, when people will be back from vacation. Do some research about who to bring onto the show. It's a colorful issue, we'd need lots of color—"

"Smarmy color."

"Toward a good end."

"You probably want to interview a porn star, female I guess. Or maybe a typical topless dancer—the topless dancer next door."

"Great. Do some research."

"What do you mean 'research'?"

"Who to interview. The right topless dancer. And look into academic studies, things of that kind, to see if the issue is warm or if it just bothers a few Village feminists. How should we go about warming up the issues?"

"Pretty warm now. Those murders."

"There are always sex murders. Pornography's got to be . . ."

"A respectable issue."

Billy laughed. "That's right. A respectable issue. Come on, life's not as bad as all that."

Jennings glanced away.

Billy proposed a drink. "Come on, in honor of our despicable political future." He mixed two drinks at his office bar. He was delighted. Everything had worked. Jennings had not put up an argument, though he was hardly enthusiastic. There was just one other matter. He hesitated. Then he pushed ahead: he was not afraid of a man who worked for him. "You know what I'm going to do?" He bobbed the ice cubes in his drink with one finger. "Right now? On the spur of the moment? Go straight up to that girl's apartment. Kelly Martin. I'm not even going to telephone, I want to talk to her directly. You know why?" Billy told Jennings the story of Kelly's indisposition. "I'm going to ask her how she feels." And then, as promised, he called for a taxi.

2

Jennings interrupted Billy's story only once: when had this happened? He wondered why Kelly had not told him. He didn't mind. No doubt his own behavior had distracted her. He tried without success to telephone, in order to warn her of Billy's impending arrival. Then he spent some time leafing through the newspapers. At five o'clock, when the building began to empty, he decided to walk home. The change in Billy impressed him. For more than ten years Billy had been a friend—and now he was a boss. More dramatic still was the rush to visit Kelly without calling. Nothing that he knew of Billy could account for this infatuation, for Billy was not a passionate man. He was too conscious of his reputation.

That was accounting enough for Jennings. His evening with Kelly had left him numb with doubt, tangled into a knot of images and half-dead thoughts. Their one beguiling, childlike moment together, however marvelous, could not permanently relieve the pressures within him. It was only a respite—an intimation of what life could sometimes be—from his awful rooted reluctance. It even enhanced his unease, for nothing that passed between them could now seem insignificant. He had stayed up most of the night, after their evening together, then awoke in the afternoon hung over— and found his hangover a useful way to blunt his worry. Four aspirin turned his mood into pleasant mush. His earlier passivity increased, and he became stupid. He did not tell Billy about his friendship with Kelly. If there was to be some drama, all the better. Then matters might change.

He had not ceased to think, however, only to pay attention. Part of his mind was hard at work, and his passivity helped in

121

this work. Not having told Billy, for example, increased the pressure on his mind and imagination. He walked past the Plaza and admired the poor blinkered horses eating their oats from nosebags. He remembered that he was Billy's employee. All right, he would become an excellent employee. He saluted one of the horses. His new duties, he told himself, were political. He was supposed to do something about pornography. Well, that was simple. Hadn't he showered Billy with ideas? What they were he could not quite remember, but he decided to get to work anyway. Recently he had read about a place on Madison Avenue that a committee in the area was trying to close. It was called The Cat's Paw. It included peepshows along with pornographic books and gewgaws, but it did not resemble the sleazy shops on Forty-second Street. It was widely advertised as a fashionable place enjoyed by sophisticated people. It made much of a healthy, honest, open-minded approach to sex. To rebut accusations of "sexism," the shop featured occasional male, as well as female, strippers.

A fashionable place, Jennings thought, raised problems for Billy. There would be some danger of appearing puritanical. Better to attack Forty-second Street itself, which few people would defend. On the other hand, for the purposes of television, The Cat's Paw might be preferable. It would be hardcore—but cushioned by money and some taste. The women would be more attractive, the patrons more educated. The management of the store, having fought a suit and dealt with the press, would be accustomed to publicity. Besides, Jennings did not want to dig a story out of Forty-second Street.

From outside, The Cat's Paw resembled the boutiques on Madison Avenue. Its name, spelled out in swanky script, ran across the front. The letters were made of stainless steel; bands of red, green, and yellow added a European note of elegant zip. Moving shapes could be seen through the dark glass, but nothing indicated what was sold. Inside, Jennings first noticed the plush carpeting, which muffled the sound of the cash registers, and then all the contraptions. They hung on the walls like tack in a riding shop; a suede whip was on sale. To one side were racks of magazines, books and cassettes. Straight ahead were two low-slung circular counters, rimmed like condoms, that enclosed sales girls.

Jennings walked past the movie booths to where the live performers worked. In all essential respects, he decided, The Cat's Paw was no different from the Forty-second Street places. The store-front might be swanky, but it was no less blank; the light might be softer, but it was still neon; the dildos might be better plastic, but they were as mechanical as ever. By and large, the customers were the same rumpled businessmen, with the same proportion of gawkers, Japanese, and sophisticates. Perhaps the number of amused women, still very small, was greater. In college, Jennings had been attracted for a while to the then fashionable view of pornography among intellectuals. He'd expected to find in it some wonderful underbelly truth not apparent to bourgeois culture. He had hoped to mix desire and disgust. He had read the Marquis de Sade and a number of diaries. But it never worked. In a porn shop his desire always gave way to a disgust that, despite his con-scientious efforts, lacked any existential edge. It was just disgust. And pornography was just business.

Only the peep show interested him. At least the model was alive, however dead her circumstances; the books or films, un-touched by art, possessed no life at all. Jennings had not visited the live show for many years, so he did not know what to expect, but the format remained the same: a bank of doors, each of which led to a tiny booth. Inside a booth customers could view, for a quarter each half-minute, a naked woman on a stage. When the booth was occupied a red bulb glowed above the door. Jennings remembered the flat, stale air, which seemed to have been held too long in the lungs, He also remembered the cheap sweet smell, like perfumed toilet paper, that caught in his throat as he stepped into one of the booths. He dropped a quarter into a slot, raising a small electric curtain the size of a television screen. On a revolv-ing dias stood a naked girl, like a model in a life class.

He was shocked by her presence. He had forgotten that such an image possessed beauty. It was unlike any image found in tele-vision, film, or magazines—hardly an image at all, since the girl lived. Flesh framed by glass: something better, something worse, than ordinary nakedness. She stepped off the dais, and began to do some calisthenics. Jennings, unblinking, watched her. His desire came from the situation; the nakedness, the glass, the surprise. When the curtain came down, he was momentarily confused. Then he remembered his mission and was comfortable again. He put in a second quarter and studied the girl's face. She was young, perhaps only seventeen, with dark red hair cut short. She chewed gum, and she was heavily made up; it was strange to see a dressed-up face on a naked girl. Her eyes were expressionless. As she bicycled her legs above her head—she appeared slim and athletic—Jennings analyzed how she would look on television. The features were those of a cunning pixie, which would prove appealing if she was presented as a victim. Yes, she would do. That conclusion reached, Jennings examined her body. It was lovely. She was long of leg, with only a whisper of darkness between her legs, and breasts that were strangely wide apart.

During his next quarter, a ring interrupted the classical music. The girl picked up a phone and cradled the receiver under her ear. Then she lay back on the dais and, bored, studied her nails. Occasionally her lips moved. Jennings discovered a phone in his booth. Customers could, if they wished, call the girl. Amazing. He considered calling her, to determine if her voice was suitable for television, but he could not bring himself to do so. In any case, she was preparing to leave. Another girl—or, in this case, woman—came onstage. Jennings found her coarse. She bucked to disco music. Perhaps the management did not make the other girl do that, he thought, since her body looked so innocent. No, it couldn't be. How could there be enlightened management in a pornographer's shop, however chic?

For a few minutes Jennings lingered near the front of the store. He wanted to find out what the girl was like. When she walked past him, however, he was tongue-tied. She said "See you, Pablo" to a man at the cash register near the door. Jennings recognized him from the news reports about The Cat's Paw. He was young, bald, European, and dressed in an elegant gray suit. At regular intervals he pried open a pistachio nut with long pink-stained fingers and chewed it softly. She was gone! On the street Jennings overtook the girl, but once again could not speak. Instead he followed her. It was odd to see her dressed. She wore stiletto heels, extra-tight jeans, a violet blouse—tough-chic, not too expensive. Although pretty, her face displayed some Coke-and-pizza unhealthiness underneath the makeup; she resembled any one of the suburban girls that lined up for rock concerts at Radio City Music Hall. She led Jennings into Prendergast's, which was not far from The Cat's Paw. There, to his astonishment, she walked through a door marked "Employees Only."

124

He waited for her near the counter that sold sunglasses. Kelly edged across his mind: he remembered their afternoon in the bedding department. But he kept his eye on business. Soon the girl reappeared without her purse, and Jennings followed her to Counter 27, where she sold racy cosmetics—hence the painted face. He guessed that she worked part-time at Prendergast's, perhaps when the store stayed open late. Observing her from his new post at the bubble bath counter, he could hardly believe that half an hour before she was posing for customers at The Cat's Paw. He smiled: a good joke. In any case it would now be easy to talk to her, since he could pretend to buy some cosmetics for his girl friend. Yet he hung back, reluctant to give up his station.

When a middle-aged couple stopped at her counter, wanting to know how to rouge cheeks so they looked "very rouged," he walked closer. The girl began to talk. "You want blusher sort of *real* hot," she said. "I got it." A fleet of bottles appeared on the counter. "Okay, let's nobody panic, but I'm going to try a little on my cheek first, and if *I'm* not blown away we'll see where we are. Okay, here we go—and there it is." She looked in the round mirror on the counter. "Hey—I like it. Does he like it? Do you like it? Okay, now come here." She took the brush and opened a bright bloom on the woman's cheek. "Too much? *Un peu* softer?"

The voice was excellent. Uneducated, Jennings thought, but who wanted an educated stripper? More important, she was quick-witted and a natural performer. She would probably do well on television. She might even tell jokes.

The middle-aged couple, frightened, tried to escape. Very quickly the girl opened a second, lighter bloom on the woman's other cheek. Then she whispered, "Oh my God."

"What?" said the woman, dabbing fearfully at her cheek.

"Oh my God."

"What!"

"It's gorgeous. Nothing like me, I don't have the features to support it. Almost nobody has the features to support it. *You* have the features to support it. I swear to God."

"I don't know," said the woman, dabbing in front of the mirror.

"Don't buy it, I don't care, maybe you're a little mature for that kind of thing." She began putting the bottles back. "I was just glad to see it, that's all. One in a hundred."

125

"Well . . ."

"I'll take it off," she said, reaching for the sponge. "I wouldn't do it either, scares me to be one in a hundred."

"What do you think, Ben?"

"Depends how aggressive you're feeling."

The girl dropped a thumb in each pocket. "One in a hundred."

After the sale Jennings called Tom, hoping to see his old friend and get the girl's name. In his present mood, at once sleepy and arch, he could hardly get enough of Prendergast's. It was a marvelously mad kaleidoscope with which to awaken a jaded eye, a source of vast energy that made no serious demands on him; he found its force as soothing to his benumbed spirits as a frantic massage to a tired muscle. But Tom was too busy and asked Jennings to telephone later. And so Jennings, disappointed, went home and lay in bed. Then he telephoned Tom.

"Where the hell are you, oh shit, wait a minute, just have to get rid of these flashing lights, too many people, hold on—"

Jennings smiled. He imagined Tom seated at his console, where dozens of TV monitors displayed the behavior of customers in different departments. The way a thirty-year-old woman fingered a washcloth, Tom said, told you everything you needed to know about selling sheets, towels, and bathroom scales. One monitor, which Tom used for comic relief, surveyed the dressing rooms. Another provided a peek at Private Parts, the department Tom said taught him most about selling to women.

"Right." He was back on the line. "Now, how are you?"

"Fine."

"Well, we don't want—oh, sorry!"

Tom put Jennings on hold again. That simple question, "How are you," accompanied by a small smile, always preceded their conversations. Some of the old Tom was in the smile, along with his unabashed delight at having made himself over—at having invented himself. Then, as if a quarter had been dropped into a machine, the smile disappeared and he became an eccentric again.

"No more interruptions! Promise! I've cleared the lights. Why haven't you been trying to see me more? I have serious business to talk over with you. Lots of ideas and plots, because there's no way around it, I'm going to have to make lots of changes. And I'll even pay you. And there's one thing I have to talk to you about that's so serious I don't want to mention it on the phone—"

126

"Come on."

"Not on the phone, never on the phone." Tom spoke rapidly, like someone trying to outrun a stutter.

"Come on."

Tom whispered.

"What'd you say?"

The whisper became fainter: "The public is getting bored."

"The hermit bit?"

"Shhhh."

"People never get tired of hermits. They don't get a chance to."

"Shhhh."

"What do you mean, 'Shhhhh'?"

"Later. When are you coming?"

"Soon, but what I want to know is the name, something about your red-haired salesgirl on Counter Twenty-seven."

"Sex!"

"No, or not really," said Jennings, yanking back the phone from his ear, since Tom had shouted the word "sex." Although Tom was always fooling around like that, Jennings did not find him tiresome. Tom was without the beseeching expression, the begging for approval, of most people who constantly wisecracked. The antic manner was curiously impersonal. And the posturing seemed appropriate to his exaggerated persona and spirit of invention, as natural to Tom as ease and spontaneity were to someone else.

"Still there?" Tom demanded.

"You probably didn't know, but she's also a model in a new porn shop nearby, and we thought we'd interview her on the show—Billy wants to make an issue of pornography."

"How is Billy?" The voice, low again, confided, "What an ass."

"Okay."

"So you're going to make an employee a star." The voice toughened up: a hard-bitten lawyer. "So I'll have to pay her more. So whose side you on? But wait a minute, you're not just going to put her on the air raw, all of a sudden, and make her talk about pornography? I'm not sure Prendergast's should be involved in this." The voice dropped to a guilty whisper: "See what you've done."

"What?"

"We'll have to fire her."

"Come on."

Puritan style, the voice intoned: "Our employees are hard-working, honest, reliable. They support families. This would be bad for morals and morale. I'm sorry." Then Tom added, mockingly: "That was pretty good, wasn't it? Well, maybe it would be okay. I'll have to think about it. Depends if she's appealing. She a joker?"

"I think so."

"Good, but you can't just throw her on the air. You have to"—the voice became effete—"season her."

"That's why I want the information."

"Make her *delicious*. When you coming?"

"Soon."

Jennings, shaking his head, hung up. Tom's theatricality left him feeling peaceful. He could sit back, watch, play himself. The serious changes he was undergoing could be ignored, since the offstage life counted for little at Prendergast's. He was also genuinely fond of Tom. Like other hard-nosed people, Jennings was sentimental about the innocent and the roguish. If Billy no longer seemed so innocent, then Jennings would cultivate Tom the rogue. He liked having a male friend who was in the limelight through avoiding the limelight, one with whom relations, whatever the superficial kinks, remained easy.

It was a little past seven, bright and muggy. He turned on the air conditioner, pushed the books off the couch, and fell asleep. He was awakened by the phone. It was Kelly. He was not sure what time it was.

"No, you're not bothering me."

"It's just that Billy's been behaving so strangely. He left about an hour ago, I wasn't going to call you, but—it's okay if I call you?"

"Sure."

"Well, I forgot to tell you. The other night he'd asked me out to dinner, and he acted like a—I don't know, he just ignored me completely, talked to other people, and so I got up and left. It served him right. Then I didn't hear from him, and suddenly today the doorman rings and he's coming up in the elevator to see me. I opened the door, and he sort of looks at me and walks right past and stands there. I asked him what he wanted, and he said he was just in the neighborhood. Then he asked me how I was feeling. It was a little spooky. He wasn't like he usually is,

128

you know, talkative and charming. He was quiet . . . Why aren't you saying anything?"

"I'm listening."

"It was a little spooky. So I lied. I said I was feeling fine now, but that on the night I left him I was sick to my stomach. 'Let's go out tonight,' he said, and he doesn't look at me when he says this. Just standing there, in the middle of the room. I told him all right, but that he shouldn't expect too much, that—"

"Did you tell him about me?"

"No, why?"

"What happened?"

"Well, all of a sudden he said he was busy tonight. He thought that was funny. I couldn't think of anything to say, and he couldn't either, so I offered him something to drink. He said, 'It doesn't matter.' Then, and this was the first time he'd looked at me, suddenly he was walking through my apartment, talking. He would say, 'Yes, a good view, I like the way the streets crisscross up here, there's the park, the river, nice view, pretty good kitchen for New York.' He just walked through my apartment as if he might rent it. He pushed open my bedroom door with the tips of his fingers. He walked in, looked at the stuff on top of the bureau. He nudged open the door to the bathroom. I had things drying there—stockings, underwear—and then he said, 'Very nice, I'm glad you feel better.' Then he left."

There was a pause.

"Why aren't you saying anything?"

"I tried to call you several times. Billy is—well, I have no idea what to say about him nowadays. Very strange."

"Of course it's strange!"

"I'm thinking, would you do me a favor?"

"What?"

"This sounds strange too, but would you mind not telling Billy about me?"

"Are you embarrassed?"

"Of course not. But our friendship—Billy's and mine—is very strained now. He's been acting in a way I've never seen him act before. He's just changed my job all around. If he knew, well, I think, at the moment, it would end things between us."

"You want me to keep everything secret."

"If you don't mind."

There was a pause.

"Well, I do mind."

"Just for a while." This request increased the internal pressure. He said unexpectedly, "I have an idea."

"What?" Her voice brightened.

"Are you still reading those old history books?"

"Yes."

"You still don't want to do any writing?"

"No."

"I have a great idea, though."

"Yes?"

"About pornography."

"Photography?"

"A good woman's issue. Wait a minute, let me tell you, I'm just getting my thoughts together"—the internal pressure continued to build—"Billy may make pornography one of his issues, and I've been doing some research for him. We thought we ought to interview one of the women, and I've found this girl who works at a slick place called The Cat's Paw. She's hilarious. You could write a great profile—"

"Pornography? Why are you talking to me about pornography?"

"Not just pornography. You could bring out something fresh about it, the indirect touch. This girl is really—"

"You're flakking for him. Doing your job. Get Kelly Martin to write a story about pornography. Secrets, pornography, what—hell, no, I'm not going to write a story about pornography! You haven't even told me what you think about Billy's behavior."

"Bad. Worse—outrageous."

She was silent.

"Kelly?"

"You're not talking to me."

"Don't worry about Billy."

"I wasn't."

"He was probably drinking."

"He wasn't drunk."

"Well, in any case, don't worry, we're all having to put up with a new Billy."

There was a pause.

"I want to hang up but I don't want to hang up."

"What do you want to talk about?"

"Nothing," she said. "Just chatter."

"You're coming to the country, aren't you—Penelope said she was calling you."

"Are you?"

"Yes."

"Well, enough of this chatter."

"Hold on—"

"No, I'm being silly. I'm going to finish this book."

"I'll see you this weekend?"

"Yes."

Her businesslike tone made him uneasy. He lay back on the couch, and was soon asleep again.

3

Was it the middle of the night? Jennings stood up, groggy, then noticed the twilight between two buildings. He took some aspirin with the last gulp in a carton of orange juice, shielding his eyes from the refrigerator light. Then he turned on the radio and listened to the news and some songs and the same news. He took a shower and drank some coffee. He would have liked to go back to sleep, but a strange headache nagged him: he could feel the pulse of his heart inside his head. And so he sat on a stool aware, and not wanting to be aware, of his dim dissatisfaction. It was not the usual kind, for he was now dissatisfied with his dissatisfaction. He turned the lights on the sprawl of his apartment. He had made no attempt in six years to improve its appearance. The few decorative knickknacks put there by his mother highlighted the boxes of books, old magazines, empty cans, nondescript furniture, dust. The building itself was an anonymous white brick high-rise on Nineteenth Street, well east of Gramercy Park, in a neighborhood that appealed to him because it was without vulgar charm or identifiable style. He had once thought of himself as a person who liked border country, and in his neighborhood several regional styles met: Puerto Rican poor, Village chic, Gramercy class. He had been proud not to inhabit a SoHo loft, something cute in the Village, or a bookish apartment on the Upper West Side.

As he looked at his apartment, however, he recognized a style as strict as the others, a style as obvious as any author in a crooked garret—a style of disaffection. He felt its easy pride, its brag of living on the edge. He understood the moral cachet, which came from aping the poor, and the social cachet, which came from evoking Grub Street genius. He had been a prisoner of a cliché while declaring himself free. Still, what could he do? It was impossible to live without adopting some style. And the style of disaffection was surely better than that of the fat cats or the wicker-and-plants set. He was not proud of his apartment, but perhaps he should not be apologetic. He twisted on his stool: other, more important matters bothered him, but he could not summon the will to address them. Events might break through the crust of his stupidity, as at The Cat's Paw; sustained reflection could not. Conscious of his cowardice, he opened a window to let in the night air, then decided to go to a bar he liked on Canal Street.

He walked, hands in pockets, down the Bowery. Because of his earlier honesty, he felt entitled to a few of the old, stylish pleasures. He savored the hot disarray of the evening—the grit underfoot, the crumbling storefronts, the babble of Spanish, the broken glass. He passed others like himself, and also drunks and shouting children; their clothing, he knew, came from stalls on Fourteenth Street. For many years he had concentrated his sense of meaning in such things. They were his props, and he appreciated their beauty. He loved cold neon on a hot night. He liked buying a bag of egg rolls at a Chinese takeout place as sirens sounded nearby. Later he would ask one of the bartenders, Ernie, to warm up a sandwich in the microwave.

Mel's was an old-style workingman's bar, now patronized by some artists and intellectuals. It was said that Dylan Thomas had thrown up there. Jennings thought it should receive landmark status as an example of folk art, since few such bars were left in Manhattan. From the entrance he looked down a long line of muttering men, some of whom watched a foggy color television without sound. The back, where the tables were, was a cavernous hole lit only by the fluorescent gleam from the men's room. Throughout was a sour, pissy smell—a convivial smell, suited to the sharing of dour reflections. Jennings sat down at the scratched bar, full of nostalgic affection. He had often gone there for lunch, always marveling that anyone would ask for the corn on the cob, which was puckered, sticky, and taxi yellow. He glanced at the tables, but saw no one he knew. Even the sailor, a grizzled man who kept a mysterious trunk at his feet, was not there.

The sailor was one reason intellectuals liked Mel's. He never said a word until drunk. Then he stood up—groaned, shouted, snarled, proclaimed—and left. He was tolerated because the workingmen thought he was demented and therefore funny, while the intellectuals considered him a genius; his outbursts, which were sometimes taped, had inspired a novel and several epic poems. When Jennings asked the bartender what had happened to him, the bartender said the sailor had not been seen for some time. Jennings asked more questions not because he expected answers, but because he liked talking to the bartenders, who were old and from Brooklyn. They performed some of the duties of the old-fashioned wife. They were sympathetic when the customers wanted to talk, gabby when the customers wanted to listen; and their way with a dishtowel was relaxing.

When the bartenders moved away, however, questions tangled up his mind. How could he change enough to deserve Kelly? Why should this have happened to someone like him, who had already had several serious relationships with women? What was wrong with Billy? With working for Billy? More troubling still, his imagination kept cramping. It was now a clumsy business to wander with his thoughts, as awkward as learning how to walk after a mild stroke. He stared into his beer. At last some people he knew came into Mel's—a few artists and dealers, including a gallery owner he had once made love to. She had not come to the bar with anyone (her throaty laugh dismayed men) and he knew she would like to see him again. But he pretended not to have noticed her.

Soon he called to the bartender, hoping to coax him into more talk. But the bartender preferred a drinker at the other end of the bar, and paused only to draw a fresh draft for Jennings. Alone again, huddled away from the tables, Jennings became certain the woman he knew was watching him. His back began to itch. He tried once more, without success, to attract the bartender. Then, abruptly, he stopped waving. Something curious had happened.

The bartender was no longer "the bartender who works at Mel's." He was a person with hair in his ears who worked at a bar on Canal Street. A vision of the ordinary, hurtful in its precision, came to Jennings. He saw a brick row house with a geranium in the window, a posed photograph of the children, a wife whose hair shimmered with blue dye.

During the next hour the bar receded around him. He tried but failed to make out the conversation at the tables. Once he looked in the woman's direction; she was listening to someone else. He wanted to join them, but did not know how. How could he stand up, walk over, say hello, sit down, make conversation? Yet he also wanted sex—wanted it with a rare urgency. He tried to imagine making love to the dealer; and oddly enough, could not do so. "Oh, come on," he muttered, "what the hell is this?" He willed himself to have a sexual fantasy. Nothing happened. He tried thinking of the sexual parts, but he could not make an image jell. Then, suddenly, the pressure diminished. He had the queer impression that he had divided in two—that, from a position outside his body, he could watch himself hunched at the bar with the table of acquaintances behind and to the right. From the vantage of the second Jennings he could imagine making love to the woman. He could watch the first Jennings join her table, then begin the usual Jennings flirtation. Early on little was said. Then he smiled at her, looked interesting, ignored her. This centered her attention upon him. Then, toward the end, he used all his self-deprecatory charm so that, when everyone was preparing to leave, he could ask if she would like to go to another bar. It would seem too late to go elsewhere but too early to end the evening. So the question could be put, slyly—a drink at my place? Or yours? He loved the moment's hesitation, then the soft nod.

More talk, more charm, more humor—and behind it all the cool reserve of the first Jennings. The sex itself was a kind of intense forgetfulness, a kaleidoscope of parts; in the press of desire the first Jennings could resign his mind to his body, though this had become more difficult as he grew older. Then came the moment when something must be said. More charm, some humor, an overlay of sadness. Having connected they could not connect. And the first Jennings, distantly generous, realized that he had enjoyed himself.

Once again his imagination cramped. He was himself, and he did not know what to do. So he absorbed himself with a stupid game, similar to his private jokes. He kept asking himself, until the question filled his mind, "Was he or wasn't he?" He liked the sound of the question, because it reminded him of the old advertisement "Does she or doesn't she?" Was he or wasn't he going to say anything to her when she left the bar? He still wanted sex very much, but took pleasure in restraining himself—letting his desire back up, thereby increasing the internal pressure.

In the end he did not say hello. He decided instead to wait for the sailor. He drank slowly, so that he did not become drunk. At 3:00 A.M., when the call came for the last drinks, the sailor had still not come. "Might be he's dead," suggested the bartender. By then Jennings was too tired to think or not think. It was a tiredness he liked—a tiredness with a tradition, that of seeing a bar out. He kept repeating to the bartender, "Good time, yes, I had a very good time," having forgotten about the hair in the man's ears and the geranium in the pot.

CHAPTER

SEVEN

I

Penelope drove to Bridgehampton on a Thursday morning to prepare her house for weekend guests. On Friday the weather turned bad. There seemed to be some congestion at sea. Salt mists stole across the potato fields, shrouding the new tract housing; the crackers lost their snap. Penelope remained cheerful. The weather could disrupt sunbathing and tennis, and weekends were too expensive for bad weather. Yet there were cocktails at hand, dinner parties nearby, arugula and bluefish. After the city, the Hamptons beckoned with the charm of another place.

Penelope was proud of her house. To buy it she had spent her profit from some real estate investments in SoHo, along with a bequest from her grandfather. It was one of the old houses, with period details. Inside were a number of queerly shaped rooms, which she described as *naturally* odd rooms, with *natural* charm, not the sort of intentionally interesting rooms favored by the architects of the new houses—houses that, she was not afraid to say, she considered plain awful. The views were good: potato fields stretched flat to the sea, except for a few modern interruptions.

The weekend was planned with care. She brought in a cleaning woman to scrub; the furniture was rearranged. In the last two years she had not had enough time to decorate the house, but it didn't look too bad. She considered it informal, very much of the country: wicker, copper pots, flowers, a French country table. On one wall was an expensive painting called *Sea Study in Blue*, which she did not really like, though it was painted by a friend of hers, and beneath it was a superb kilim rug. This rug, woven in the desert air, smelled whenever the weather was damp—"of camel piss," said one acquaintance.

The best bedroom was hers. Jennings would have the crabbed back room, Kelly the airy room beside her, Billy the nondescript room down the hall. She did not mean to be obvious. Everything must be casual, with only a few events. That evening there would be a cozy dinner; and on Saturday cocktails for a number of friends. Her reading had been a great success, and many of her friends, she knew, wanted to ask her questions. Since the reading, in fact, she had composed a long entry on the problem of early success.

The weekend, she was confident, would reveal Billy's true feelings toward her. She looked at her watch, wondering if he had sat with the others on the train. Then she heard the whistle—on a gray day it was a sad sound, reminding her of foghorns. She roared the engine of her old BMW in answer, and set off down the road toward the station. Over the fields the sea mist was rolling in, past a man walking in a pair of beautiful red pants. Since Penelope was a little late, her three guests were talking amiably on the platform.

2

Although Penelope's dinner ended late, Kelly woke before seven. She remembered drinking too much wine, to add some sparkle to the evening. Most of the dinner had been spent in polite discussion of Penelope's reading, while there came from outside the delicious drip, drip, of a soft rain. She had wanted only to sleep or to walk. Billy, formal and polite, said nothing of his visit. Jennings was cheerful and distant—there was their secret to remember. She rolled over in her sheets, listening to the mad bird chatter. A sea-soaked wind blew through the window, and she slept for a few seconds more. Then she breathed in and sat up. It was before seven, she knew, because birds only racketed around like that very early in the morning. Not since Montana . . . The sky still hung heavily over the fields, though the rain had stopped. She enjoyed gray weather. She could read in a corner, then wet her face during a walk . . . but was that the ocean she heard? She stood still. She had not grown up on a coast. There it was—a hollow shhh that made her want to stretch.

She crept down the stairs, grimacing at each creak. For a moment she felt exhilarated (her childhood home, sold for something practical, had also creaked) and then, suddenly, saddened. Was anyone up? She poured herself a glass of orange juice, then turned to explore this new place. There had not been time last night. Outside, the grass was bearded in a wonderful white wetness, cool to the touch, and her sneakers quickly soaked through. On impulse she sat down against the hedge, showering her hair with drops. In the past she had often visited Long Island and always enjoyed the flat open landscape after the vertical jumpiness of New York. But she was snobbish about the social pressure and annoyed by the relentless chic. Especially disconcerting to her was the contrast between the countryside and its summer immigrants. The East End was a place of lambent light, potato dust, and old Yankee salt; it was honorably modest, like all flatlands by the sea. By contrast New York was an imperial city—brashly lit, sleek, pleasure-loving. It had made a colony of the hard, gentle place.

Yet she was pleased to escape the towers, for she had become too absorbed in New York. As she leaned against the wet, spiny branches she thought back to Montana—less to the details of the land, though she could call them to mind, than to the mood of acceptance that would sometimes come upon her unexpectedly, that came upon her now, before anyone was up and about. A cat glided along the hedge, then stopped to stare. A plane droned overhead. She returned to the house, her spirits restored. She reminded herself, as she had reminded herself hundreds of times before, to remember that she was capable of such moments. Not in the city, it seemed, but the country was never far away. She made herself some coffee and lay back on a sofa by the window.

In a few minutes Jennings appeared at the head of the stairs. He seemed to consider himself the first awake, for he stole down trying not to make a sound. He looked grim—snarled hair, puffy eyes, wrinkled shirt. She smiled.

"Good morning."

He started.

"What are you doing up so early!"

He peered out the window. "Terrible weather."

She smoothed back her hair.

"Where's the kitchen?"

She pointed, then followed him to the refrigerator. They made themselves toast and she refused to whisper.

"You're going to wake everyone up!"

"So what?"

"Anyway, I don't think I could stand Penelope so early in the morning."

"It would wake you up."

"Quiet!"

"No."

"Then let's go for a drive."

"With what?"

"Penelope said I could borrow the car. Come on, before they get up."

Driving fast down narrow roads, Jennings said, "I'll show you the places I used to go." His manner was tongue in cheek, and he turned on the radio.

"Isn't it too early for that?"

"Okay."

She flipped it off.

"First Bridgehampton," he said. He recited the names of the stores fifteen years ago—ordinary stores in an ordinary town. Now Bridgehampton was mostly boutiques or restaurants. It sold antiques, cookware from France, swimming and tennis gear.

"You didn't grow up out here?" she asked.

"Summers."

"Well, you can't complain too much. You have to consider yourself part of the problem."

"Yes, but we—well, there just weren't so many summer people then. It was smaller, the space was bigger, the New York people

139

were absorbed in the country. Bingo, it's gone. The balance tipped. Now it's just a nice resort. The money used to be quieter too—not less ostentatious, but the houses were shingle or stone. And surrounded by acres."

He pointed to the new houses, rising like mushrooms in a foggy field.

"Everywhere you look," he said, "there's hot fresh money."

"You're nostalgic."

"Not really." He pointed to some other new houses. "The architecture's like razor blades."

He drove past the Sagaponack cemetery, where headstones stood crooked with age, then to the road along the beach where his family used to go. It was once a dirt road, he said, that passed between a potato field and great dunes. Up the dunes and through the grass were trails where she would have burned the soles of her feet. You could somersault down the side of those dunes, he said, but now there was a city of razor-blade houses and no dune. They turned onto a road that ended in the sand and stopped for a moment. Kelly noticed the first white blossoms on the potato plants—a humble plant, if ever there was one. There were also whitecaps on the ocean. Although Jennings looked relaxed, she was saddened by the presence of something pallid between them—the result, perhaps, of their decision to postpone lovemaking.

"Do you love it out here?"

He shrugged.

It had been a mistake to use the word "love." Suddenly she was jealous of his love for this countryside; and afraid when he described its destruction. What did he mean to tell her—that his gentleness was located in the past? And did he really love Long Island, or did the contrast between then and now interest him most? She remembered to give him time.

He suggested a look at a few of the great houses. He drove her past some of the best in Southampton, fine in both proportion and fantasy. She liked the way he drove and how he looked in his old blue shirt; she liked his hands, too, which were beginning to weather well. Then he pointed to the court where, he said, he had learned to play tennis. "I can point to the exact one, because it's the pro's court, where I took endless lessons. Clip . . . clop . . . clip . . . clop."

"Are you good?"

"Steady, quick, imaginative—but no will to win. Don't draw any conclusions."

"Sounds like a report card."

"My parents played every day too," he said, "but they never actually played games. They just slugged it at each other for an hour, bang, bang, bang." Jennings, smiling, put an arm around her shoulder. "I had an odd sort of childhood," he said. "You ought to run like hell."

"I'll decide that."

3

They found Billy and Penelope in the kitchen. Jennings, handing Penelope the keys, told Billy, "I gave her the tour of my childhood. Very gloomy outside."

Penelope stretched, then rose from her coffee. "Well, I guess I should do the shopping for tonight."

The guests asked to be helpful. "The *men* want to carry packages? No, no. Come on, Kelly." And Penelope led Kelly back to the BMW.

"There's more coffee on the burner," Billy said. "Sit down. I don't know what else to do in the country, especially when the weather's like this. And it's only Saturday morning."

Jennings, waiting for the coffee to warm, wondered if Billy suspected anything. Surely it was fairly obvious, their having taken a drive together early in the morning. Or perhaps it wasn't. His drive with Kelly pleased him. It had been simple and unpressured, with the pain of his reawakened past eased in the telling. She had not challenged him, as she had before, yet appeared no less devoted to their future. And he took pride in having warned her about himself.

"Penelope is half mad," said Billy, smiling. "She was telling me about her reading and how angry she was I didn't come. You didn't tell me if it was good—it sounded good by her telling. Was Kelly there?"

"Yes. I don't know whether she liked it or not."

"Was she feeling well?"

"Seemed fine to me." Jennings hesitated. "How about when you dropped by?"

"Fine."

"In fact," Jennings said, "she seemed fine on our drive. I thought I'd show her around, since she hasn't been out here much."

"She's half mad too. Imagine, Penelope and Kelly. How'd we ever get hooked up with them?"

"Not me."

"No?"

Jennings shook his head.

"You don't like them?"

"Nothing special."

There was a pause.

"Is Teitelman out?" Jennings asked.

"He can't come tonight."

"Too bad."

"Kelly's arrogant, don't you think?"

"You've read her sketches. But I don't know if she's arrogant. Don't know her well enough. I guess she is."

"She was making eyes at me all last night. At dinner."

"Really?"

"Groupie eyes. The kind people on the air get. I'm used to it, but I wouldn't have thought it of her. Anyway it was strange— maybe it's her way of apologizing for the other night." Billy shook his head.

Jennings smiled.

There was a pause.

"You know what Teitelman wants to do?" Billy said. "I was talking to him on the phone, and he said something about using his house out here for a fund-raising party at the end of the summer."

"You'd attract a lot of money that way."

"It's not sure."

"Must be pretty sure, for him to mention it."

"You're probably right."

Billy slapped the table. "What are we going to do all day? Is it actually raining?"

"Just gray."

"Maybe I'll make some calls. Some people I should see."

Jennings offered him another cup of coffee, but Billy was already on the phone.

4

Half an hour before the cocktail party Penelope paused to take stock. Kelly was at work in the kitchen, spearing scallops with toothpicks; Billy would see to matters at the bar; Jennings, useless but underfoot, was looking through her record collection. Penelope put on a stack of Billie Holiday records, then straightened *Sea Study in Blue*. It seemed possible the sky would clear, in which case people might want to chat outdoors. She opened the back door, leaving the screen door closed to discourage the insects. Then, from outside, came boisterous voices.

An impressive assembly, a friend told Penelope, as they surveyed the guests sipping drinks, chewing carrots, and unspearing scallops. Successful poets, brokers, journalists, lawyers—and all of them, it seemed, had been to her reading. At least everyone mentioned it. When would the diary be published? How was her other work coming? She described her embarrassment at the attention. It began to be boring, she said, to have to repeat again and again the story of how nervous she had been: "It's a sinking feeling, not in but *toward* the pit of your stomach."

She spoke to each guest in turn. She also kept an eye on her houseguests. Jennings spent most of the party in a corner, trapped by a bore. He did not know how to mingle. Kelly moved now and then; she was talking, at present, to Theodore Oatis, whom Penelope considered an interesting writer she ought to photograph. Billy was the life of the party. She smiled: a little boy showing off. Not once had he spoken at length to Kelly. So confident was Penelope that, when Billy shook loose from a little group, she led him over to Kelly and Oatis. Conversation soon dried up. How foolish to have suspected something! For her sins Penelope decided to tend a forgotten poet.

143

5

Kelly was not pleased. Each time she met Billy he treated her differently. One moment she was an old friend, the next a flibbertigibbet. Oatis, telling her the story of his career, was problem enough. And Jennings—where was Jennings? He should not have left her undefended in this particular pack. She took a deep breath, sipped her wine, and tried to resign herself. Or to find it funny.

She listened to Oatis with renewed fortitude.

He asked her, "What do you think?"

Billy stole away, distracting her attention.

"I have to make up my mind very soon," Oatis continued. "It's not a bad subject. I've read all the Holocaust literature, and this is a relatively unexplored aspect. Grants and a fair advance would be available, sales would probably be all right. Maybe there'd be a movie prospect. And it would be useful—to keep the memory alive and all that."

"Go ahead."

"On the other hand—"

The weather was clearing. In the distant sky there was a faint crimson blush.

"A screenplay would be more fun, frankly, and I've already sold one, you know, so I think I have a kind of gift for it. Not that I respect that gift much"—his head dipped close—"but now and then I ought to take a vacation."

Moths beat against the screens. She became aware of the slow squeeze in her chest. How could she escape? There was no escape. She looked right at him, and a phrase came to her: the odious Oatis. She smiled. Oatis smiled back.

She asked, "Do you really like to snack on anchovies?"

Not long before the New York *Times* had investigated what snacks writers like—and why. Oatis, whose first book had been nominated for an award, was interviewed.

"Stupid article. But I really do. Believe it or not, it helps."

She studied him. He writes to be written about, she thought; his ambition is to be the subject of a biography. Perhaps there was no other kind of writer. No, no, she rebuked herself.

"I can probably get this screenplay done in a month. Then maybe I'll fly to Poland. You know, so much bad work has been done, I really think—"

She stopped listening, though she sometimes nodded her head. She wondered, Why do writers think they're so interesting? She took a deep breath; the clouds twisted in the sky. What would make a writer happy? She thought about it. To make a million dollars but appear indifferent to money; to be publicly recognized as a person who wants privacy; to win the Nobel Prize, at the youngest age; to have each fault, personal and professional, attributed to genius. And if male, to have women part their legs for your gift; if female, to be the first of your sex, et cetera, et cetera, to have surmounted terrible handicaps, et cetera, et cetera.

She smiled at Oatis.

He asked her about a book.

What a writer wants most, she thought, is for other writers to come to him on bended knee, offer up their puny pencils, and retire into silence. No, no, she rebuked herself again. But her scorn relieved her claustrophobia.

"It's simply superb stuff, and hardly anyone has heard of him."

Where was Jennings?

"Of course it's a special taste. I know that—"

She broke to refill her glass, but Oatis followed. In self-defense she continued to analyze, harshly. Oatis was praising an obscure English writer dead twenty years; this meant, Kelly thought, that he could seem generous without having to praise better, more threatening writers. Besides, it was smart to develop certain obscure enthusiasms. Add a little eccentric color to your views and people would believe you thought for yourself. Now Oatis was attacking a contemporary writer—affecting, she thought, a crotchety highbrow taste. He's a man of independent vision, of debunking intelligence, looking down his nose at the middlebrows. He's the last educated man—oh, really, she thought, this is unbearable. She put her hand on Oatis' arm. "Excuse me, Ted, but I've got to help Penelope—"

"Attention! Attention!" Penelope called to the room at large. "Look at this!" She threw open the French doors, to display the deep red of the clearing sky. There was a moment's silence. A voice said, "Someone call the Sierra Club."

There was laughter.

Penelope asked, "What do you *do* about something like that?"

"What's that line?" Oatis said, " 'a patient etherized . . .' "

Penelope declared, "I know!" She hurried to the stereo and thumbed through a stack of records. "Here we go," she said, holding up a record to read the label. "This should do it." She eased on the needle, spun the knobs all the way up, and Beethoven's "Pastoral" Symphony sailed forth.

"Perfect!"

Penelope, having presented the stereo speakers to the sunset, led the guests onto the rear deck. Kelly put some dishes into the kitchen sink, then continued out the front door. It was wonderful to fold herself into the evening. The party, bottled up behind her, drifted away and back. She walked hard. She stretched her muscles. It was unexpectedly dark in the direction of the ocean—only a few stars pricked the sky. She walked down to the water, stumbling once in the cold sand, then scooped a hand through the foam: not as cold as she expected. She shivered nonetheless, having dressed for a party.

She sat down facing the water, hugging her legs. Her first few weeks in New York, she thought, had not been very successful. She did not place much faith in Jennings, and the city itself and the people she knew—the people she would always know—acted upon her as they had in the past. Was it impossible, she wondered, to draw a circle of friends around yourself? Or to find a single person, with whom to form a small town in the big city? She had watched herself—with Oatis—edging toward her old sketchwriting, unable to contain her disgust. But when she thought back to her published sketches, she liked them no better than before: that way was not for her. Then, recalling her earlier feeling of acceptance, she dismissed it, too, as small, passive, and fleeting. The ocean's pulse, she thought, was not reassuring. And the figure of a man staring out to sea, besides being a cliché, did not mean much if no one was watching.

She hardened herself and sat very still for several minutes. Then she mocked her pessimism, but murmured "It's the way I am, sometimes." Oddly enough, she did not feel too bad. When the headlights of a jeep bobbed toward her, however, her instinct was to run to the dunes, or even into the water, to escape the light that cut through the darkness. Instead she held her ground until the lights glared up and passed, leaving behind two receding red dots.

146

6

When Kelly left the house Billy followed her. He wanted to apologize, to settle this business that demanded too much time and thought. His apology—he was uncertain for what—would make her smile. Then she would shrug, and he would be set free.

In the twilight, however, he could not find her. Was there a figure down the road? Could she have gone so far? The darkness unsettled his thoughts, already loose with drink. Then he gathered himself up and rushed ahead, humming a little. An apology, yes, he would have his apology.

Something flung across the road.

He stopped short: only a rabbit. But then the darkness dropped around him, and he became aware of the batting of insects and creep of shadow. He disliked the country, even the Hamptons sort of country, which was just New York by other means. He hoped Kelly was not going to the ocean. He remembered the Pacific—the exposure, the awful flatness, the way the sea released rather than focused its energy.

And yet, he thought, many of his close friends had come to the party. Not that it did him much good, since he'd behaved so clumsily. Had he lost his touch? He shook his head, full of the optimistic logic of Scotch. Not everything was wrong; Jennings and Kelly were just friends. He hesitated. Was that somebody? The wind stirred the trees. Somewhere, far off, a door slammed. A dog barked. He thought: it's spooky. And smiled at the word. Boyish feelings helped make the night ridiculous. He lopped off the top of a weed with a stick.

The road ended abruptly. Kelly was probably one of those people, he thought, who liked walking on the beach at night. He stared, but could hardly make out the ocean, only the flick of stars on the moving water. He decided not to walk down the beach. Sand would damage his shoes. And if he found her it might be suddenly, startlingly, which was not appropriate for apologies. He began to turn around—suppose she loomed up beside him—when a jeep bumped down the beach, lights winking. He watched as the beach became pocked, almost lunar, and the ocean turned a ghastly gray. The shaky lights drew up, then passed a woman near the water. He felt nauseous as the ocean sounded in his ears; and then, as the red lights bobbed away, jealous of the way the headlights centered her on the sand. He shivered: too much liquor.

He remembered this nausea. In ninth grade, at an awards dinner to which parents were invited, he walked onstage to present an award to a teacher and nearly vomited. His mother dabbed her hair, shining faces turned toward him. Then he fastened his eyes on a spot beyond the farthest table. He could no longer see the upturned faces, but instead watched himself speaking, by instinct, to some imagined audience. The nausea passed, and he was at ease. A natural speaker, the principal said.

Billy started: she would bump into him! He whirled around, then restrained himself. He walked with quick, measured steps. It seemed darker than before. As the sound of the ocean receded, another noise pressed upon him, some awful croaking from a pond. He stepped in puddles and tripped over a branch. Had he taken the wrong road? Again he repressed a desire to run. When he saw the lights of Penelope's house, he wondered at his absurd fear. The liquor.

Penelope was at the sink. The guests were gone.

"Where have you been?"

"Just needed a little air."

Jennings brought in some glasses.

"Where's Kelly?" she asked, picking something off a plate with her nail.

"Is she gone?"

"Everyone around here goes for a walk," Penelope said amiably, "while I do the dishes."

Billy took the sponge from her. He turned to Kelly, who was opening the door. "Nice outside?"

"Beautiful night. It's wonderful on the beach after a storm."

Later Penelope put on some Elvis, but not too loud. They had another drink and discussed the party. When it was time to go to bed, Billy said he would stay downstairs for a few minutes and read a magazine. He mixed himself a drink, sat on a couch, and reviewed his moment on the beach. He took pleasure in the memory of Kelly's figure framed in the light. He did not wonder at his abrupt change of feeling, but settled more deeply into the cushions and decided, as he sipped, that of course he was right from the start. She was impossibly arrogant—in her opinions, in her beauty, in her decision to go for a walk by herself.

Once upstairs, he noticed a shadow move under the crack of her door and let his hand play across the rattly brass knob. Then he opened the door to Penelope's room.

She asked, "That you?"

7

Penelope, in a generous and expansive mood, decided to serve brunch on the beach. Several bottles of wine and many hors d'oeuvre remained from the party. The weather had been miserable, but her guests would have at least a couple of hours on the beach. And she had bought a new bathing suit that, on her long, lanky figure . . . well, she didn't mean to brag, but it looked smashing. She smiled at Billy. "Are you going to get the Sunday papers, or am I?"

The telephone rang. It was Ted Oatis, who asked them to brunch. He agreed instead to come to theirs, in return for which he promised to bring two Sunday papers. "I can't stand it," Penelope said, "when someone has Arts and Leisure when I want Arts and Leisure." Now—was everything ready?

"Jennings, you load up the car.

"Kelly, sandwiches all ready?

"Billy, don't forget the ice."

8

It was hot and hazy. But on the beach, Kelly thought, everything's clean . . . nice and snappy and fresh. A discussion began around her. Should they sit near or back from the water? Would the tide go in or out? "Who cares?" she said, "but let's sit close." She set off toward the surf, trailed by Penelope's qualms. They staked out territory, organized hampers, spread out towels. It was surprising to find the ocean so mild, Kelly thought, after the upheaval of the night before. It sparkled in the haze, and each wave made a modest little sound as it pushed its foam up the sand.

Before baking she liked to get wet and salty. She dove under a small wave, then rolled and floated and dove, staying underwater as long as she could. She loved to feel the water on her scalp, fanning out her hair. Afterwards she dripped over the others, especially when they complained. The sand was already spreading over the towels and food and an occasional gust off the water tangled the pages of the paper. Penelope, telling everyone to help themselves to food, stretched out with Billy's leg as a headrest. Penelope's bathing suit, Kelly thought, was very revealing: and her figure was good enough to support the revelation.

Kelly examined her own suit. It was also revealing. Her figure was also good enough, she thought, if not quite as lean as Penelope's. Of course, no one demanded that men have flat stomachs. A small lip of fat hung over Oatis' trunks, and his color was pasty. Jennings was too plucked, she thought; he should be fattened up. Billy's body was pretty good. He wore a French bathing suit that, while conservative by European standards, was racy for Hamptons heterosexuals; some cocky display. She lay down and shut her eyes.

"Well, well, Billy," said Oatis, looking up from the paper. "I didn't know you were such a man about town."

"Why?"

"The gossips have put you and Kelly at Mama's, with Kelly Martin leaving early. I quote, 'Billy Bell, who knows how to charm the ladies, has also charmed some of the hardest noses in city politics.' "

Billy took the paper from Oatis.

Penelope rolled onto her stomach in order to tan her back. She asked Kelly to undo the strap of her bikini top.

"Ridiculous," Billy said.

His face was suddenly dark. Kelly noticed that, having read the item, he did not know what to do with his eyes. She expected a darting, accusatory look. Instead he asked for an apple.

"That's one more call I'll have to make tomorrow. Excuse me, *ladies*"—Billy's charm returned—"but that creature is a menace. Always wrong."

"Little attention never hurt," Oatis said. "Attention is money, power."

"Not wrong attention."

"What was wrong?" murmured Penelope into her towel.

"There's nothing between us," Kelly said softly.

"In gossip columns you're always guilty," said Oatis, amused. "Guilty until proven guilty. Boring if proved innocent."

"Shut up, Oatis," said Penelope.

They all laughed—Billy too. He said, "Maybe it would be worse to call."

"Send roses," said Oatis.

Penelope got up to get a sandwich. She did not refasten the top of her bikini. Everyone noticed, Kelly was certain, but conversation continued as before, with Oatis relating gossip about gossip columnists. Kelly pretended to nap. Then her mind began to toy with ideas . . . to sharpen phrases. Gossip columnists, she thought, are the gnats, no, the wasps—the yellow jackets of prose. Gossip columnists are the yellow jackets of prose. They hang around garbage and overripe fruit, with their dandy little stings.

"Maybe I'll get a bunch of them on the show," Billy said. "And bring up some of their more vulgar 'errors.' "

"It doesn't matter, ever, whether the news is right or wrong."

"Come on."

"I keep forgetting," Oatis said. "You might become a politician, so you have to act responsibly."

"Least I can do."

Kelly smiled to herself: Billy was not good at sarcasm. Oatis, one of those able to resist Billy, forced him off his customary ground.

"Least you won't do," Oatis said, "if you're lucky."

His conversation would not make Oatis popular, Kelly thought, but it could make him feared. Wit was the simplest way to a reputation. A cold, condescending wit was respected in New York, and Oatis was fairly good at it. The masters of the style, she thought, compressed their bile into diamond-hard aphorisms. Even then, however, it wasn't worth much. Again, smallness.

Conversation faltered. Then Oatis groaned. "Look at this headline—COLLEGE LIFESTYLES SHIFT IN ERA OF PINCHED PENNIES. What a grotesque word, 'lifestyles.' The *Times* should ban it."

Jennings asked him why.

151

"Awful neologism."

Kelly said, "That's not the problem."

"Well?"

"The meaning."

"Oh?"

"Oh!" she said, mimicking his tone. She rolled onto her back. She disliked too intimate a relation between those two words; some space, however small, should separate life and style. She glanced at Oatis. She was surprised: he looked hurt. She shut her eyes. In her heart there was a very small soft spot for Oatis and his kind—for all those pickled in their own vinegar. Better vinegar than something bland. In certain respects, Oatis even resembled Jennings. He was the more successful of the two, owing to the greater purity of his vinegar and the greater simplicity of his drive for fame. Jennings possessed an internal saboteur, which was why her soft spot for him was large.

But why, she asked herself, glancing his way, was he so damn passive?

The men went swimming, then returned to the papers. Soon Oatis began to attack a book reviewer. Kelly wondered why Oatis was talking so much. Was he trying to impress Billy? An unpleasant thought came to mind: was he trying to impress her? He was sitting on the towel next to hers.

"He's a coward," Oatis said of the reviewer. "I've known him for a long time, I like him, he has good taste, but he's scared to really do something, say something."

"How old is he now?" Penelope asked.

"Forty, and do you know what? He's never going to do a damned thing."

Kelly wondered if Oatis would do anything significant. It was not likely. His opinions seemed inherited rather than earned. They were made to measure, without the irregular weave of conviction. Opinions were so cheap . . . nothing could be cheaper.

Something moved against her calf.

"Even the subject of the book was hackneyed," Oatis said. "Leonard Woolf had almost nothing to do with—"

Was it a toe?

"It's fashionable," Penelope said. "He didn't need to do any real thinking."

152

"Hell, thinking is an unnatural act."

Oh damn, Kelly thought: it was Oatis' toe.

"A little extreme."

What was it Oatis said? Thinking is an unnatural act? But how loathsome, to press against her with his toe! She tried hard to ignore it, but refused to move her own leg. She would not retreat. She would not react. It was possible he did not know what he was doing.

"Somebody should write a parody of that fad," Penelope said.

"You, Penelope, you ought to do it!"

The toe twitched!

"Too busy," Penelope said. "Why don't you?"

The toe: she must move! Opinion, she thought, making up a story for herself, is a nasty vine that grows on the big trees.

The odious Oatis!

She concentrated on the rich dark red behind her closed eyes.

The toe twitched. The toe wiggled. Once the toe even scratched. She almost burst into giggles; and then Jennings, wonderful Jennings, teased Oatis into the water. She rushed after them, in order to wash off the toe. When they returned Penelope thought it was time to go home. Kelly made certain, in the car, not to sit next to Oatis. And in retrospect she found the episode funny. She asked Jennings, "How come you're so quiet?"

He shrugged.

"Sunstroke?"

At the house Oatis left to pack. The others went inside to change. Kelly sat down on a deck chair for a few minutes and listened to the whir of the cicadas. Then she noticed an enclosed outdoor shower, open to the sky. It was wonderful to peel off the sticky suit, wonderful to stand naked in the open air, wonderful to let the airy light of the earth play over the protected places. In Montana she often swam in a small stream, alone and naked. It was not erotic; or not in the way of skinny dipping with a lover, real or imaginary. It was a private pleasure.

9

Jennings, toweling himself dry, noticed something through the blinds. Looking down, he saw Kelly rinsing her hair in the gush of water. She was bent over, and he could not see much, only the sweet almond curve of her spine and the flash of brown and silver. His breathing stopped. Soon she would straighten up and—Flinging her hair behind her, she cocked back her head, smiling into the sky. Her eyes met his. He could not move: he was aware of the rich shimmer of her body, but only as something seen at a distance, for his eyes would not leave hers. Then with trembling relief he realized that her eyes were closed, that she was running water onto her face. He wrenched himself back and away—falling, shaking, onto the bed. He lay there until the sound of the water stopped. He met her coming up the stairs wrapped in a beach towel. When she smiled he touched her cheek with his palm.

Downstairs the fret had begun about returning to the city. The traffic would be terrible. The train would be worse. Better to leave now? Or wait until very late? Billy was on the phone to Teitelman, who sometimes hired a helicopter. This time Teitelman was going to drive, but he was leaving that very moment. Billy would have to hurry. Penelope ferried him to East Hampton. Oatis called to offer a ride. Jennings accepted; running upstairs, he asked Kelly through the door if she would come. But Kelly had promised to accompany Penelope. Later, in the lengthening light, Penelope decided to stay another day. So Kelly, to avoid the train, stayed too.

PART

TWO

CHAPTER
EIGHT

I

Jennings did not call Kelly for three weeks. He had meant to call her in three or four days, but his mind clicked off whenever he thought of her. After the first week, it became too awkward to explain why he had failed to call. Each passing hour then increased his dread, until he seemed to sleepwalk through his days. And yet he had never been so excited.

He was trying to change. His moments of sudden awakening, of vivid and unexpected feeling, no longer seemed enough. He knew instinctively that, having passed the age of fifteen, he should place those feelings into a richer context. But like an adolescent, he did not know how and retreated into torpor. At the same time, he was no longer sure he wanted a serious relationship with Kelly. A shared life with a woman of intelligent passion would demand the best part of his energy and determine most of the meaning he found in life. It would threaten his natural detachment, a perspective he now sensed could yield something important.

He always felt guilty, but hardly noticed the cruelty of his behavior, seeing little beyond his private, evolving picture of the world. His selfishness, however, served a purpose: by hurting Kelly he made it easier to hate—and change—himself; by denying what he wanted he felt its full value; by exaggerating his anomie he rendered it ridiculous. Behaving badly could teach him about goodness, in short, while doing nothing could quicken his desire. The sleepier he became the less he slept, and what sleep he did have was filled with sweat-soaked dreams.

Often he would telephone Billy instead of going to work. Afterwards he would call Tom. His feelings for Tom had changed from affection to a kind of awe. Tom the recluse was a hothouse genius, a man who loved bizarre change yet took nothing seriously; he was an artist, whose store was a work of art. Occasionally Jennings visited him, passing each time through the elaborate security system at Prendergast's. He liked to walk through door after door toward a great secret—that turned out to be only Tom, who opened the last door himself. Though rumored to be a place of great splendor, Tom's apartment looked like a furniture warehouse. Everything there had once been a floor model and nothing went with anything else. Jennings considered this an example of no taste, not bad taste —an important distinction. Before every third window was a powerful telescope, through which Tom spied on the street and nearby apartment buildings. In a back room were the TV monitors that surveyed the store.

"So how are you?" Tom asked during one visit.

"Fine."

The small smile looked more ironic than usual, but remained the fixed point of their friendship; it provided a license for whatever else they did. Tom himself, very plump, wore an undershirt, blue jeans, and Gucci loafers that did not match each other. Several deep creases in his forehead gave him a perpetual look of worry, like that of a juggler who must squint to keep an eye on the dancing balls.

"Sit down, sit down. Coke? Liquor?"

Tom reached into a Frigidaire next to the divan and broke off a couple of Cokes from a pack. This was not the ordinary manic Tom—but Jennings didn't mind. Though he preferred a perpetual-motion machine to complement his own listlessness, he enjoyed a good scoff almost as much. It served a similar purpose: it rendered absurdly dull anything sober, weighty, slow, or balanced, while celebrating cleverness, camp, and the lively surface of things. Besides, Tom might at any moment jump up: he required no transition of mood.

"I have a lot to tell you," Tom said, when the smile vanished. "So many problems that I want to talk about you first. Get it over with. I have to tell you that you look terrible."

The price tag was still on his chair.

"You look peaked," Tom said. "You're trying to make me feel sorry for you. Is that it? Okay, it worked. You have my ear. Speak. Would you like to lie down on the couch?"

"There's a girl I met—"

"Oh no! You mean . . . Oh, I'm disappointed. You mean you can't get a better problem than that?"

Jennings was startled. He had not intended to talk about Kelly, but was unable to resist doing so. It was exciting to translate her into Tom's tone of voice. It made worrying about her seem absurd, while increasing his guilt.

"I'm not being good to her," he said.

"Explain."

"I haven't called her in three weeks."

"Brilliant idea: call her."

"I can't."

"You want a dime?"

"I can't bring myself to call her."

"Don't call her."

"I haven't!"

"Listen to me." Tom became avuncular, a man of the world. "This is the approach you have to take. There is nothing more boring than problems with women. It could even be argued that there is nothing more boring than sex, except as a way to sell sheets. Boring! All you have to do is shrug. Now come on, stand up and shrug. That's Tom's therapy. It'll be cathartic. If you cry I won't tell."

Jennings smiled.

"Wait till you hear *my* problems. Make you cry for me. Certainly doesn't have anything to do with women. Nobody has to go through that anymore. We have lots of books on the subject in the book department if the condition persists . . ."

159

Jennings enjoyed this teasing, affected manner. The more artificial the manner, the more authentic the fancy. And the more
authentic the fancy, the more like a sham ordinary life seemed.

"What the hell did I have you over here for if you're going to
be silent? I hate silence. One drawback to my job here."

Tom sprang up, stared at Jennings. Then he clapped his hands
and began to pace. "Jennings," he said, the way a B-movie detec-
tive talks to his companion, "I've got to change my style. No—
wait a minute, hold on." A look of pain came into his face.
"Sylvia. That girl whose name you wanted. Sylvia Rogers from
Long Island, a good salesgirl; don't ruin her. Now . . ." He took
a deep breath, continued. "I've got to change my style. Things
are going too well. I know"—he raised his hand, before Jennings
could speak—"you're going to say 'stick with what made you
successful.' " Tom shook his head. He smiled. "No! I can smell
a cliché." He paused. "You have to change your formula while
you're ahead. Everyone's beginning to copy me."

He sat down.

"Which formula?"

"The essential one. But I'm getting ahead of myself. Save it
for last."

He stood up again.

"Whether or not I change the formula I've got to kick up some
excitement for fall. A new campaign on television is possible. The
ad agencies suck. So it's me who has to think of the angle—
me-me-me—then tell them what to do. You think the prices go
down when it's my idea? Hell no. Anyway, now tell me your
opinion, you're a television man, even if you never watch television.
Seems to me that the great ads are the ones that make you feel
like you're on the inside track. That make you think it's a *privilege*
to spend your money. You think you and the advertiser are in
cahoots."

"The 'home on the range in New York' ads are pretty good."

"Too old now. We sell change."

"So you think you need an ad that smirks, that's knowing, but
that doesn't insult the buyer—one that lets *him* smirk."

"Well, we ought to offend some people. Otherwise we won't
please anyone."

Jennings, thinking, felt less sluggish. He found that he could use his mind in Tom's way, turning things topsy-turvy. It was a way he could work.

"You want people to come to Prendergast's . . ."

He continued to think. He liked shaping Tom's image, like playing around with camp.

"How about a 'Don't come to—'"

"—Prendergast's' campaign!"

They looked at each other.

Tom said, "Fabulous. It'd work. You have some Anglo snob sitting there, and he says, 'Please don't come to Prendergast's. I beg you. You see, it's gotten *so* crowded—'"

"Then," said Jennings, "he takes a drink of something expensive, doesn't say anything for a while, he's considering, then he looks right into the camera and smiles a crooked smile. He says, 'Save it for me.'"

"Beautiful."

"The 'Don't Come to Prendie's' campaign."

Tom sat down. "Here, you deserve another Coke. I'll put you on the payroll too, for that one. You can be what they call a consultant around here."

"Me? Advertising?"

"You're not feeling snobbish about it? Hell, you're already in advertising."

"What do you mean?"

"Don't give me that."

"I don't follow."

"Tsk, tsk."

"Come on."

Tom assumed the role of pompous teacher. "Young man, on television the programs are advertisements for the commercials."

"Pop sociology."

"'Don't come to Prendie's,'" Tom said, sitting back. "Not bad at all. Let's let it stew awhile. What do you think—ethnic's over?"

"Yes."

"Unethnical. Sorry."

"Nostalgia over?" Tom asked.

"Never."

"Good. Best way to make money. Never, never, never. The baby boomers are getting older—oh, are we going to see nostalgia when they begin to wrinkle! Fabulous. They're already wrinkling."

"You already do lots of nostalgia."

"Except it's hard to keep up to date with what's nostalgic. Gets used up too quickly."

"What?"

"History."

"Nostalgia's not history."

Tom pretended to be shocked and Jennings smiled.

Tom said, teaching again, "Nostalgia equals history plus fashion."

"Plus fear—"

"Of what?"

"Death?"

"This is a department store!"

"I almost forgot."

It was very odd—the small smile passed across Tom's face again.

"You have to be reasonable," Jennings said. "People won't wear togas."

"Don't be sure. But yes, best to be nostalgic within the last one hundred years. Practical."

"Probably."

"No ideas? Okay, change subject. Dry well."

"Sorry."

"One idea a year is good enough. Here's a secret: almost nobody has ideas. Not even the smartest people."

There was a pause.

"All right," Tom said, springing up again. He took a slow look through one of the telescopes. "This is what I asked you here for. I have a confession to make. It is very pathetic, so I ask you not to laugh."

"Shrug."

"Don't make jokes."

Tom's tone of voice was almost straightforward, almost what it was in college.

"Well?"

"I've been having the strangest nightmare—I won't tell you."

"What!"

"Anyway, I think it's time to change the formula. Come out of the closet. Let everyone see me."

"But—"

"A major change."

"There's nothing left after that."

"I'm not so sure."

"You could do the television ad yourself."

"That's a thought! There could be an enormous buildup, all sorts of secrets and betrayals—'Wait for this or that program, you will see the living Tom Prendergast.' TV'd probably give us the ads for a song. Improve their ratings. Of course then the commercial would have to center on me. What could I say that's as good as the snob 'Don't come to Prendie's' theme?"

They thought.

"Maybe 'Make me richer,'" Tom said. "I already give a fortune to charity, so people can feel helpful about making me richer . . . No, somehow that doesn't work." The creases in his forehead deepened. "Shit."

Jennings said, "I can't think of anything."

"Oh, forget it. Another dry well. Must be other ways."

"The store's so successful now."

"Not only do I have a nightmare," Tom said, "also I'm bored. Also the climate is changing. Everything's been open and I've been a recluse. If there's a revival of privacy, maybe I should be outrageously open. Also I have a mountainous account in Switzerland, so if I go bankrupt what the hell?"

"You don't want to be caught off guard."

"That's it. I need a way to come out that's spectacular. That's *New York.*"

"It has to make money."

"Keep up a certain style. That's what makes money."

"Control the exposure, make it an event."

"That's it. Keep talking."

"A contest."

"A contest—maybe. Never go wrong with a contest. We have a contest. First person to photograph the mad recluse Tom Prendergast can spend $20,000 at Prendergast's. That way we keep the money at home. Yes, not bad, might work. Drum up the contest, get the papers interested. TV's always looking for good, upbeat, local color on the news programs."

"How would you get caught?"

"No one knows what I look like."

"Yearbook pictures."

"I never showed up for the picture. There's only juvenile things. I've changed. I hate being photographed, anyway. Those pygmies or whatever they are were right—rips off your shadow."

There was a pause.

"We'll plan it," Tom said. "Set it up. Yes, that would be better anyway."

"How?"

"We set up the photographer. Then everything can be arranged, right? We can even get a picture of the picture-taking for historical purposes. Fabulous. Don't say anything more!" Tom stood very still, as if the idea might shatter. Then he relaxed. "This should stew. Let it stew—then we'll meet, then the ideas will pop!"

He sat down on a divan.

"Anytime you want a job."

"My own hours?"

"All you have to do is have one genuine idea a year. No, a month."

Jennings smiled. The offer tempted him: another job would be useful if relations with Billy worsened. Besides, he might prefer to work with Tom—who in certain respects was not so different from Billy. Both men depended upon their public image, both had some narrative or shape to their lives. Tom at least knew it was all a game. Yet Jennings could not be certain, as a result, that Tom was serious about the job.

2

On his way out Jennings decided to visit Sylvia. He found her leaning against the cosmetics counter, filing her nails. Her thoughts seemed far away; then, with a start, she looked up. Her cheeks were rouged.

"Hello," said Jennings.

She gave a nail a couple of sharp strokes—like punching a needle through thick cloth. "Can I help you?"

164

"I want to talk to you about your work at The Cat's Paw."

"Excuse me," she said and moved several yards down the counter. She resumed filing her nails.

Jennings moved too. "I'm not trying to pick you up, I just want—"

"Get off my case."

Was this the girl who, a few weeks before, seemed promising material for television? "I'm interested in interviewing you. I work for television."

"Give me a break." One nail required particular attention.

"I will."

"You want some cosmetics? You—party to that? Some men are."

"Maybe not for television," he continued, smiling at her "party to." "That is, maybe just for an article, a feature about you" —the file worked more slowly—"your past, what you have to say about the world."

"What's it to you?"

"You're so suspicious!"

"I shouldn't be?"

Jennings smiled. "Yes, you should be. Can't you see how ferocious I am? Well, think about it for a while." She almost said something as he moved away. Then she looked down and continued with her nails. Jennings, pretending to browse, paused to look back. He wanted to see if she kept her eye on him. He was surprised: she did not. Her eyes, when she looked up, were on the middle distance.

3

At the revolving doors Jennings stopped. He slipped out of the crowd into a telephone booth, buckling the door shut behind him. Then he listened to his dime trickle through the machine. He dialed Kelly's number. He did not let himself think. The air in the booth smelled like the inside of a lady's purse, and the sound of the store was muffled. The crickets lay deep in the grass.

The connection went through and the phone rang. The same impulsive spirit almost made him hang up.

"Hello?"

For a moment he could not speak.

"Hi, it's Jennings."

There was a pause.

"Where are you?"

"At Prendergast's."

There was a pause.

"How've you been?" he asked in a cheerful voice.

"Fine."

"Good."

There was a pause.

"Why haven't you called?"

"You could have."

"I did."

"I haven't been answering the phone."

There was a pause.

"An odd mood," he said. "I told you that."

There was a pause.

"I was talking to a woman here who also works in a porn place," he said. "She would make a great story."

The phone clicked dead.

"She hung up," said Jennings, to keep talking. He unbuckled the door and let in the pleasant babble of the store. If he could not see her again, if the space between them simply went dead, everything else would also be lost. There must be some connection, however painful. He buckled the door shut and dialed her number again.

The phone rang and rang. Then, tentatively, "Hello?"

"You have to let me finish—that was just an idea. I was calling because I want to get together."

"No."

"Why not?"

"Don't be stupid."

There was a pause.

"I don't understand."

"No."

There was a pause.

"Why don't you hang up again?"

"All right"—and she did.

This time Jennings left the telephone booth. He did not know where to go. Not home, not yet. It made sense to ride the escalator, then happen upon Sylvia.

"You again."

"Me again. It's not a bad idea."

"No?"

"No."

She was no longer busy with her nails.

"What's in it for me?"

"I've heard that somewhere before."

"Funny guy!"

"Some people think so."

"I've heard *that* somewhere before."

"Funny girl!"

"Come on, what's in it for you?"

Jennings, lightheaded, pretended he was an actor. She played the hostile, flirtatious hatcheck girl. He had never seen anyone like that, except in the movies, but she probably saw the same movies. He himself was the fancy rake, with fistfuls of cash, who leans against the counter.

"I work in television."

"I caught that."

"We always need stories, human-interest stories."

"What's the human interest in me?"

She did not wear that creamy red lipstick before, he thought, suddenly forgetting his role—that's one difference.

"Lots of it. Lots of human interest."

"Like what?"

There was a pause.

She leaned on the counter. "Come on, like what?" She left her mouth open, as if he were supposed to put the answer inside.

"Your career."

"I'm a modern dancer."

Suddenly one long leg lay on the counter.

"See? I can stretch." The high heel twitched a customer away.

"You're perfect for a story."

"Could be."

The leg vanished. Then she turned to fidget with bottles on the shelf, looking as if she wanted to do her nails. She was very young.

"So you might be interested?"

"You could say that I have plans to consider it." She rearranged three bottles.

"It's possible?"

"*Might* be possible."

This pleased Jennings. On the way home he was able to think about Kelly, and he decided she would change her mind. As the evening spread over the city, however, he became less certain. In his apartment he flipped on the overhead light—adding a dull yellow varnish to the disarray. Gone was the warming numbness of the recent weeks, when he was certain something was happening to him. Something had happened all right. But it was too soon, it was wrong, it was a miscarriage. A coldness came over him, and with it a second sort of numbness, one without pain or anticipation, without any dimension at all. He went to bed early, hoping rest would help.

4

"Did I wake you?"

Jennings, startled from sleep, sat up in bed. It was eight o'clock in the morning. "No."

"You're so hard to find nowadays," Billy said. "I had to call you. Look, I have to know something. I have to know if you're still interested in working with me. The political thing—it's taking off. A reporter is due here any minute."

"What for?"

He got out of bed. He wasn't too sleepy.

"I don't know—just a feature on my apartment, I think. But I've decided something. We have to be frank. I really have to get things in order."

"Can't we talk about it at the office?"

"You never come in."

"I'll be in today."

"I mean it."

"I hear you."

Jennings made his coffee, then sat in a chair beside the window. He thought: Kelly must be angry. Of course, she had every right to be angry. But he had not been well, surely she could understand that. Lord knows, she had an imagination. She would forgive him in time, and then—he could remember the coldness of the day before, but less distinctly. The sun was hot on the window frame, and he heard from somewhere the soothing hum and drip of an air conditioner. The coldness was now no more than a slight deadness of tone, one that left him less sleepy than before and also more willing to go to the office; he could work more efficiently at this lower temperature. And so he arrived at the office before the secretaries, and cleaned up his desk.

Soon Billy buzzed. Jennings found him talking on the phone, signing letters, reading the newspapers, drinking coffee. He motioned Jennings to a chair. When the person on the line continued for too long Billy cupped the phone and asked, "We on?"

Billy returned to the conversation. "That's right."

Jennings did not know what was meant by "We on?"

"That's right."

Billy cupped the phone again. "We on?"

"Yes, that's right. Look, I know—"

Jennings leaned back in his chair. What the hell was this? Billy, standing up, turned idly around with the telephone cord stretched out behind him. "Let's talk some more later. I have a million things . . . sure . . . okay." He hung up—"We on?"

"What do you mean 'We on'?"

"Something strange has happened. You used to come in, now you don't. Something I did? I don't know. But I don't have time to think about it. These things happen." A secretary came in to ask a question. "Later," said Billy. "I don't want to know what's happened. All I want to know is if we're on."

"What is this game?"

"That's it! I-don't-want-to-talk-about-things-like-games." He stretched each word to an even length. "That's a morass. Either we're on or we're not. Either it's the way it was and we get to work or we have dinner once a month, we're great friends, we talk on the phone and, well, you do whatever you have to do somewhere else."

"Have to do?"

"That's what I can't stand: all this psychological garbage. I don't care. Oh, of course I care, but I don't have time. Over dinner maybe, but not—are we on?"

"Sure."

"You don't mean it."

"Sure I do."

"Why do you say 'sure' that way? *I'm* not going to talk like that. Sure, great, okay. We have to chart this pornography week for the end of the summer, a good wind-in for the fall, but first I want some help preparing this speech I have to give in a couple of weeks. Gargola's asked me to address some union convention—a big crowd, he said. I thought we'd try out pornography there, among other issues, to see if it's warm. But we have to approach it right. Will you think about it? We'll talk tomorrow?"

"Sure."

"Sure!" Billy dropped his hands on his desk. "Sure, okay." He buzzed his secretary.

To see if Billy's demeanor on the air had changed, Jennings watched him interview a Broadway star. If anything, he was better than usual. Jennings also loitered near Billy's office. The secretaries, distracted by the many buzzings, memos, and commands, hardly noticed him. Nearby the intern whose name he could not remember was discussing, importantly, the possibility of taking a year off from college. He turned away, wondering at his failure to notice this frenzied tempo earlier. It was true he rarely went to work; and he avoided Billy when he did. But so marked a change . . . He sat back in his chair—and Billy opened the door. "Let's have lunch."

"I haven't thought—"

"Not that, never mind." He waved it away as just business. "You free?"

He almost said "sure."

"Come on."

They went to Ryan's, at noon a lunch spot for businessmen, at night a West Side bistro. It was the sort of casual beer-and-hamburger place they liked. Billy, who began to talk the moment they left the building, was now amiable, even intimate. His intimacy was not that of an old friend, however, but that of someone who wants something—the barstool bonhomie of a salesman. His office gossip about sex and salaries obliged Jennings to speak intimately. But Jennings did not.

"How was the interview this morning?" Jennings hoped to turn the subject away from money.

"The *Times* interview? Oh, she was a young reporter—chic, hard-boiled, probably shops at Prendergast's. I don't know what she'll write. Imagine: she spent most of her time trying to determine what shade of white I used on the walls. She said it glistened but did not glare." He smiled. "Nice-looking woman, though. I'll tell you, I never used to do this so much, but for some reason I've been screwing around a hell of a lot recently. Not her, of course, just in general."

This also did not sound like Billy. It was too vulgar. In the past Billy would not have used an expression like "screwing around" without irony. He would not have left a brag unsoftened by a smile.

"And Penelope! My God, is Penelope on my back! Get that woman away! Penelope and her camera. Nice person but"—he shook his head, unable to find the word—"wasn't that an awful weekend? I just don't understand it. If you want to go so far, well, they go for the parties I guess."

There was poison in Billy's voice, which was also new.

"And this, that, and the next thing. No, I don't think I need another," he told the waiter. "Do you want another drink?" He waved the waiter away. "Where was I?" Jennings hated the difference in Billy. And so his own behavior was stiffer than usual. Was Kelly still rankling Billy? Billy, who rarely saw any woman more than a few weeks? Or was it just the puff of politics that disoriented him?

"Anyway, I'm going to go out there as little as possible. I've had it. I'm happy to stay in an air-conditioned apartment."

"I know what you mean."

There was a pause.

"Billy, I don't think politics is good for you."

"What do you mean by that?"

"You're acting strange."

"*I* am!" He laughed—in the old, controlled way. "If anyone is acting strange!"

It was the memory of their friendship that led Jennings to issue

171

this challenge. He wanted to shake Billy free of this odd behavior, since he bore some responsibility for it, having failed to help his old friend. At the same time, he took a cold interest in baiting Billy, just to see the full extent of the change. "That doesn't mean that politics hasn't gone to your head."

"I told you I don't like that kind of talk. I don't *buy* it. Look"— Billy's anger suddenly slipped away—"we've talked about this before. The world is not perfect. But now, isn't an honest politician a better thing to be than a talk-show host? Don't we need leaders with some hard-nosed idealism? I have a dream about what we can do with New York. When you think of the talent in the city! If only that talent could be brought to bear!"

"Billy, you're talking to a friend, not the voters."

"Just brought to bear!"

His eyes were open too wide.

What he said sounded absurd to Jennings. And he would not stop. Brushing aside Jennings' skepticism, he described his political future as nothing less than the quest of a white knight. He's trying to force me to agree, Jennings thought, using that wild eye and flowery talk. Once upon a time, he thought, Billy worked more subtly, seducing others by knowing what was wanted, by drawing on something like grace.

"Billy, you know that's garbage."

"Sometimes," said Billy after a moment, "I don't know what to do. What would happen if everyone had that attitude?"

"There's everyone and there's me."

"Penelope's cynicism. I'm not going to be a booster, but you have to get people to work and change. That means the backroom stuff, but it also means convincing people. *Leading.* The crowd at Penelope's—"

"All right, all right—" Jennings raised a hand in mock surrender.

There was a pause.

"Speaking of the Hamptons—I called up Kelly the other day," Jennings said.

"Oh?"

"I thought I'd ask her for a drink, but she turned me down. Not interested, I guess."

A moment passed and Billy said, "What does anyone see in her? She seems snobby, aloof." Then the bully left his voice. "I don't know. All those things."

172

Jennings was astonished at his own cruelty.

"What did you want to see her for?" Billy asked.

"Maybe get her to write something on pornography."

There was a pause.

"Politics . . ." said Billy, letting the word hang. Then he smiled, more like himself. "You're right. Mostly I hate it. You can't believe the idiots you have to be nice to. I haven't even really started. Those boring dinners, all the problems, so many favors to be done. I have to be an optimist, don't I?"

"I guess."

During the rest of their lunch Billy attacked the political life. Jennings, remembering the earlier manifesto of his friend, did not join in this attack. The appeal was too blatant, the surrender too disturbing; Billy in defeat seemed little better than Billy in victory. And Jennings himself was not what he had been.

5

Jennings thought off and on about his lunch with Billy during the next few days. It seemed absurd to feel guilty. Who had behaved badly? The answer—of course—was Billy. Nonetheless, the knowledge of what he must have meant to Billy, both as a friend and aide, began to trouble him. It was he, Jennings, who, during the whole course of Billy's public life, had designed Billy's image. Wouldn't Billy think he'd lost something essential, almost part of himself like his shadow? This fresh guilt increased the pressure on Jennings, but did not overwhelm him. He retained his cool temper. When Kelly called, however, he was thrown once more into flux. It needed only her questioning voice—"Jennings?"

He nearly dropped the phone.

"Hi."

"You're forgiven."

"I am?"

"Yes."

"For what?"

"Please—don't be stupid."

"I don't feel guilty."

"You should."

"I do."

"I shouldn't have hung up."

"Yes, you should have."

There was a pause.

He asked, "Shall we go out?"

"Yes."

"Where?"

"You say."

Her voice was small.

"Do you like jazz?" he asked.

"Anything's okay."

"Well, let's just go to Reno's one night."

"When?"

"A couple of days. Friday night? Let's meet there at eight."

Afterwards Jennings sat in his chair. The window was always open now, since his air conditioner did not work. Outside, the weather was windy and gray. Grateful for the turbulence, he shut his eyes, letting the moist wind gust across his face. He fell into a kind of rhythm. He would begin to relax, and his mind would open. And then he would see, swimming up in the dark, the image of one of his friends. And snap!—his mind squeezed shut, propelling the image away. He jerked from one image to the next: to Billy, to Kelly, to Tom, to Billy, to Penelope. Suddenly he stood up, slightly disoriented, like someone who rises before he knows he's awake. He was numb. He was warm. More so than before he called Kelly from Prendergast's—much more so, for now the stakes seemed still higher.

He sank back into his chair. He did not know what he wanted, and he hated himself for his uncertainty. Yet he also welcomed, as usual, the vague qualms, pressure, doubts; they were the detritus of change. After a while he stretched. He drank a glass of orange juice. Then he picked up the telephone, imagining Tom atop his castle of style.

"Tom!"

"So, we're meeting next week—you'll make me think of more ideas. I need them."

"Tom!"

"Stop shouting."

"You're a genius!"

"Heartfelt flattery. I have consultants full of heartfelt flattery. What I need from you is viciousness, to make me think. I want to pay you for getting me excited."

"I have an idea."

"Go."

"I know a photographer who would like to catch you in the act. We can set her up, set you up—it's even possible we wouldn't have to tell her."

"What's her name?"

"Penelope Lamb."

"Her real name?"

"I assume that's it, but I don't know."

"That's something you should always know."

6

Reno's was a decaying jazz club in the West Fifties. Although many of its regulars had died, and the Dixieland was a little tired, the flavor of the thirties was authentic. The waiters, gruff old guys, wore frayed tuxedoes and cheap white shirts without studs. The lights, which were crooked on the walls, glowed with cocky panache, and the smell was peculiar, like that of a cigar dropped in a drink at 3:00 A.M. Reno's remained what it had been, and Jennings—who arrived early and sat at the bar—admired its sour integrity. A touch fell upon his shoulder, a touch that men did not possess, except, perhaps, for the piano player, whose fingers dropped across a chord as softly as rain.

He met the brimming blue light of Kelly's eyes. Her head, poised, moved slightly. He shivered, and kissed her cheek. "Here, let me just pay for this drink and we'll get a table." He fumbled in his pockets and signaled to the owner, who led them, as he led all younger people, to a table near the kitchen—a small table with a marble top smudged by a thousand wet glasses.

"Here we are," said Jennings. "They serve dinner, which isn't great, but I wasn't thinking when we talked. Would you like to go somewhere else?"

"This is fine."

"Do you play the piano?"

"Not really. I had lessons as a child. My parents played."

"This guy just plays between sets."

There was a pause.

"The jazz isn't the best, but I sort of enjoy the place. I didn't even ask if you like jazz."

"I don't know much about it. I always thought it was something you had to learn, almost like classical music." She smiled for the first time. "Don't say you just have to feel it. I'm sure you have to know something."

"I guess."

"I like it, though—and I like this poor player no one seems to listen to. I wonder if he only plays for the check."

"Well, I got tired of rock music after a while. I still don't know too much about the newer stuff in jazz, but the older styles . . ."

"Maybe he considers the conversation and glasses and noise as part of the music—puts it in."

"The older styles are the best."

There was a pause.

"How've you been?" she asked.

"Not so well, obviously. I'm sorry I didn't call. I don't even think I could explain."

"Don't try."

"Tell me about you. Have you been reading all those history books?" He questioned her for several minutes about teaching, trying to make his voice sound more natural; it was familiar but hollow, a disembodied sound in an empty room. Her replies were perfunctory, without her usual quickness. When the Dixieland quartet began to play, she turned to listen. A pause in the conversation continued for too long and he said, "I should have called."

"It seems to bother you," she said, her focus restored. "That's twice now you've mentioned it."

"It does."

"Why?"

"I just . . ." He opened his palms.

"That's not an answer. But I don't want to nag."

"I knew I should call you, but I just couldn't. Each day got worse."

"Malaise?"

She said "malaise" the way the cigarette girl said "Cigars, cigarettes, Tiparillos?"

"Something like that."

"Still suffering?" She arched one eyebrow in question, but the sarcasm was less.

"You know I warned you—when we were in the country—that I'm not such a good fish."

"Fish?"

They smiled.

"Billy's even worse than I am . . ."

His voice was brotherly, but inside the pressure began to build.

"Why don't you quit?" she said, suddenly leaning forward. "Do something else. You'll feel better." She hung on the edge of her words. "Wait a second. I've told you that. Isn't that horrible? Two months since we met and I'm repeating advice to you . . ."

"You should see Billy. I went to lunch with him recently and in the beginning he told me how great politics could be, a noble dream and all that"—his own voice, with its unfamiliar timbre, excited Jennings—"and then he turned right around and told me he hated politics. I still think he might be stuck on you."

"What's that have to do with changing your—but how could he? I've only seen him twice."

"Seems like a thousand calls come into his office a day."

"Are we talking about the same thing?"

"Aren't we? Probably I shouldn't have said anything. I've never really understood his mind."

"He scares me."

"That's silly."

He noticed how she moved. She was never quite still, yet no single movement called attention to itself. She moved as leaves do in a small breeze; and her clothes seemed too stiff for this graceful shifting.

"He bothers me."

The pressure inside him built.

"He shouldn't."

"How—"

The band, swinging into a loud rendition of "Basin Street Blues," covered her reply. Not once during this number, in which

177

each musician took a long solo, did she look at him. At the end she applauded warmly. He asked, "How'd you like them?"

"Terrific . . . What'd you think?"

"They're pretty good—old-timers."

"Oh, they're better than that!"

The quiet pianist returned. Their plates were removed, a woman at a neighboring table laughed, and Kelly asked Jennings if Billy first suggested that she write the story about pornography. Jennings was taken aback. He had not intended to raise the subject.

"No, it was my idea," he said, aware of the pressure. "At least the idea of doing something about pornography was mine, to make it part of Billy's campaign. About you—well, I thought when I was looking into it that some aspect might interest you."

"Why?"

"Not all aspects. Just certain parts, about the character of the people who participate. Not only you, lots of writers. But you're the writer I know best."

"I'm not a writer."

"If you ever go back." He smiled. "I didn't know it was so easy to get over."

There was a pause.

"In doing research for Billy I've met this remarkable girl. She couldn't be more than eighteen, and, well, she's a wonderful study. Red hair, chews gum, talks sort of sassy, no education to speak of, probably she's run away from home. But she's not dumb, street smart I guess—I'm not a writer—and, well, she finishes her job at The Cat's Paw, walks over to her job at Prendergast's—and she wants to be a modern dancer. There's got to be something there."

"What's her name?"

"Sylvia."

"Sylvia."

There was a pause.

"I might be interested."

Jennings tightened.

"Do you want to go over there?" he asked, blushing. "The set's finished, and they won't be back forever. I think she might be on. I found out her schedule."

"Okay."

After the noise of Reno's, which was becoming crowded, the taxi seemed too quiet. And so Jennings joked about how absurd

178

she would find The Cat's Paw. Once, when he turned toward her, she looked so lovely that he glanced away.

Outside the taxi he took her arm.

She said, "I've never been inside one of these places."

It was surprisingly busy. Single men, alone on a Friday night, browsed in the stalls; a few couples, on their way home after dinner, laughed together. He dropped her arm, and she looked around with casual curiosity. Her expression turned vague. She said, "I don't like it here."

"Demeaning?"

"That's only one word."

She repeated, "I don't like it here."

"Do you want to go?"

"This awful music!"

"Let's go."

"No." She continued to look at him. "Let's see if she's here."

They walked toward the back.

"No one ever looks up," she said.

Then, a bit later, "These sad men!"

And, when they came to the booths, she restrained him with one hand. "Do you like this? I mean, seriously, don't say anything smart, but—do you get some . . . charge from it? Obviously lots of men do." In her eyes and voice there was no judgment, only disinterested curiosity. The question unsettled him.

"For a couple of minutes. Then I get bored."

This sounded honest, and she appeared relieved. Her shoulders dipped. She smiled. She looked around with more freedom. Nearby were the movie booths, covered with glossy pictures. "A couple of minutes is a long time," she said. "What are those doors?"

"That's the live show."

"Where Sylvia might be?"

"Do you want me to see if she's there first?"

"No—no."

It was obvious she did not want to be left alone. He opened the door, then followed her inside. There was hardly any room; they breathed as one. He dropped in the first of several quarters.

They were silent.

The pornography did not interest him. But—his eyes blinked, his mind cleared—he felt sick with gratitude. It was neither the framed image of Sylvia nor the living presence of Kelly that moved

179

him. It was their conjunction. It seemed just right, just so. He was thankful that a moment could hold so much, that he could feel at one and the same time the sensations of near and far, warm and cold, real and make-believe. He wanted her to look at him—to see his profile with one eye and Sylvia with the other. To turn her toward him, he asked, "What do you think?"

CHAPTER

NINE

I

"What do I think?" Kelly glanced at him, then turned toward the naked girl on the stage. She hated the narrow box, the dead air, the smudged glass. What did Jennings want?

"What do I think? Well . . ." She began to tap one foot softly against the floor. Then she started to hum and then she sang under her breath, "Well, the kneebone's connected to the thighbone, and the thighbone's connected to the hipbone, and the hipbone's connected—"

"Stop it!" He took her arm.

She stiffened. Then she wrenched around. "What the hell's wrong with you!"

The curtain came down.

"Nothing's wrong with me."

There was a pause.

"Let's go then."

He dropped her arm.

There was another pause.

He said, "You couldn't tell from that what she's like."

"I want to get out of here."

She led him down the dark passageway, past rows of movie booths, past the man who liked pistachio nuts. Outside she took a deep breath and shook her head. Jennings suggested a nightcap.

"I'm tired," she said. "Too much for one night."

"I don't think we should have come here."

Was he making light of their visit?

She said, "I'm glad we came."

"You are?"

"Yes."

He looked confused, which was fine with her. Let him wonder why she was glad. A taxi nearby discharged some people.

"I'm going to get this cab," she said, opening its door. "Thanks."

He looked hurt. "Call me if you like." She would do no more.

2

At home she sat in the dark, listening to the traffic. How could she love him? They had not spent one simple evening together. How could she even use the word? But why not? There was no other. She had dated two men in his absence, friends from before. They bored her. They reminded her of the past, and she wondered if her life would ever change. Was she sentimental to expect something different? Perhaps. And so she had dutifully read her history books, as the city's heat ironed each day flat. Only in the early evenings, when the air began to cool and Central Park was busy and the men jogged past with glistening backs, did she go outside to take a deep breath. And that was always the saddest part of the day.

His failure to call hurt her. The worst wound was the simplest: he did not want to be with her. But there was another. A person as perceptive as Jennings should not be insensitive and cruel. Knowing as much as he did, sharing her dislike for the usual practice of the world, he should lead a life she could respect— with or without her. If he did not lead such a life, then she herself found it hard to do so, for she was growing tired of her lonely ambition. She recognized the hope she placed in him, not only as a potential lover and friend, but also as a symbol of what was possible. Yet she became neither despondent nor lethargic. The hot and empty days made her, if anything, more efficient. She channeled the force of her disappointment into a determination to see clearly, whatever the outcome of her hopes. Nothing must blunt her senses or muddle her thoughts.

Sometimes this ability to marshal her own mind frightened her. The longing for clarity seemed almost eerie, and she worried that, despite her even mood, she was becoming too detached. She saw no alternative. During the weeks when Jennings did not call she had analyzed ways to fill his absence. It must be through her work, she decided, and teaching schoolgirls was not a lasting solution. Nor was writing satire, which she still considered easy and cheap. Reading history books reminded her that she had once considered becoming an academic, and one day when she was nostalgic she walked through the disheveled campus of Columbia. But it was too late to join that world, she thought, and she would dislike its small politicking anyway. Of course, she could work somewhere in the arts as an editor or writer, but she retained her strong bias against that field—against art itself, perhaps. She loved the power of art to focus, but disliked the self-importance of most art and artists. So much art seemed to her crude, thin, and vain. But her real objection to both the arts and the academy was more fundamental: they seemed ancillary business, part of a shadow life.

She wanted something more alive. And so, as the days passed, she thought about writing a profile of Sylvia. Pehaps she could tell the plain truth about something important; then do so a second and third time. Pornography was a serious issue, one she had not thought about, and Sylvia was a girl beginning a dangerous life. Perhaps she could teach something to herself. And to Sylvia, to her readers, even to Jennings. She smiled a little, wondering if he really liked pornography. Anyone would be curious, of course, but what could explain his stubborn repetition of the idea for the story, or his eagerness to take her to The Cat's Paw? Or his harsh "Stop it!" when she joked around?

She walked to the kitchen to defend herself against the pain and fixed some tea. In the late evenings, alone and with the day shut away, she liked to steep herself in tea and reflection. Certainly he did not seem to need pornography, she thought, or not as the other men did. He possessed neither the tousled furtiveness of the solitary nor the playful smirk of those who brought women to The Cat's Paw. It was something else. She wished she knew what. She herself had never been inside a porn shop, and when she thought back, the elegance of the accouterments surprised her. No doubt Times Square was different; but The Cat's Paw was well lighted, with no suggestion of the sneaky or furtive. That seemed strange. The only excitement she could imagine in pornography was the thrill of the illicit—the creak of back stairs, the slow parting of curtain and skirt.

She wondered if that was the point: to strip sex down to the ordinary. Bodies presented as facts. Faces, if shown, denuded of joy. No animal high spirits, no spontaneity, just the labor of hired hands. Pornography subtracted the spirit from sex, many people said—which was true, she thought, but a prissy way of putting it. The pleasure must lie in revenge. Violate the impossible dreams parents tuck into your head, demand the crude and the simple, cut the knot of contrary feelings. Best of all, shine a bright light into whatever is mysterious or dark. She remembered reading, astonished, that in pornographic movies the man must always come outside the woman. If anything were hidden or left to the imagination, she supposed, sex would seem like a con.

But perhaps she was being too harsh. Obviously pornography stirred the sluggish sexuality of the middle-aged, reminding them of their youth, when desire rose as spontaneously as a spring. And yet the excitement of pornography did not seem erotic to her; it was no marvelous and lush awakening, but a curiously icy heat that nurtured only the angry, demanding side of sex. The pornographic distortions—the mammoth cocks and breasts—must diminish the watching men, she thought, while puffing up their dreams of power. Virility was paired with impotence, a union whose result must be a mental violence that deadened everything. Perhaps they preferred the dead to the painfully alive, or maybe they really found in porn a liberating recognition of the hidden and per-verse. But she did not trust this freedom, which fenced out the other parts of love. Pornography must harden their hearts. Like a loveless art, it merely isolated, heightened, separated, exaggerated.

She remembered drawing close to him for protection. Jennings! And what, she demanded again, could his motive be? Her analysis of pornography did not fit him. He seemed too passionate to enjoy so coldblooded a pastime. In the narrow booth he had brushed against her; she had known he was watching her tenderly—or some part of him was, for he had also watched that lovely girl. She raised one hand to her eyes and sat very still. His behavior at Reno's seemed unchanged from before: the manner distant, the eyes beguiling. She loved his distance, if only he would sometimes reach toward her. Then the world at large would become smaller and more intimate. She continued to sit very still. She stopped thinking for a moment. Why, she wondered at last, didn't he tell her more of the truth about himself? Her curiosity demanded some satisfaction, a bit of revelatory tease. At Reno's he had seemed so stiff and she so thwarted. At Reno's—

But then, something had excited her about the group of musicians, especially the saxophonist who dipped his horn into the music like a cup into water. Three of the group were puckered old men and the fourth was a young drummer, who often shut his eyes and acted musical. The old men, open-eyed and businesslike, husbanded their energy: the saxophonist stared into space when not playing, keeping time with his little finger and acknowledging applause with a small nod. His face, like an old shoe that retains the shape of the foot, kept its grimace whenever he unmouthed the horn. What was so remarkable about him? What stirred her memory?

She thought back to the moment when, having given up on Jennings, she had turned to listen. The jazzmen as one had played a little tune—nothing much, a dee-dee-dum plucked from the air. It had a sweet-sassy toughness, as sentimental as a daisy in a railroad bed. Then, without wasting time on compliments, the group had begun to tease the melody apart. Each player took a solo, and her mind had sometimes wandered . . . until the saxophonist blew a little whisper, like a guttural promise. She was embarrassed by the intimacy of it. He blew some more low, throaty sounds— the air in the horn was a man's hot breath in her ear—until the back of her neck prickled. He seemed to laugh, a flutter of high tenor trills, then swooped to the ground, to go as low as you go. She smiled as women smile when watching favorites strut: a little disapproving, hardly fooled, smiling still. Then he stopped. Was something wrong? He began again, but louder, tougher, meaner, demanding by force what he had not won by guile. The horn slipped and dove, swooped and cried, with the discordant beauty of gulls quarreling.

Suddenly he stopped again, until the awful ordinary bar clatter

185

took center stage. Then he began to nudge the mike with the cup of his horn—a pathetic act, like the paw of a beggar's cup at a passing hand. Something hardly music spirited out, a series of grunts, squeals, and burps, without redeeming pattern. She was horrified and transfixed. He seemed so utterly honest and revealed and alone that she wanted to share in his ragged embarrassment. Her wanting emanated from the base of her spine, sending shivers through her body, until the hair rose again on the back of her neck. At last the drummer entered the music, leading the saxophonist back to the melody. But the old man added one dark whisper at the end.

Afterwards she had wanted to be kissed. The applause was as usual, however, and Jennings told her the saxophonist was stealing from younger players—"the bit toward the end is popular now, pushing jazz to the edge." She had watched the saxophonist break down his horn and put it into a small suitcase. And then she had asked Jennings about Sylvia . . . Kelly stood up and looked at her watch: ten past one. She walked to the window and raised it high to get some air. There wasn't much wind outside and the air, as warm outside as in, hardly moved into the room. Why blame Jennings for taking her to The Cat's Paw, she thought, since she herself had wanted to go? She smelled the river, and she steeled herself again. How strange, she thought, that a woman would submit to the fish eyes behind the glass. She had not even considered that part. What must it be like? Remembering her joke about the thighbone song, she murmured, "It was right to make a joke, wasn't it? It wasn't such a bad joke, was it? So why did he squeeze me so hard?" But she did not want to struggle with her questions or her hope; not then. Tomorrow she planned to talk to Sylvia.

3

The polite man who answered the phone the next morning at The Cat's Paw was not certain when Sylvia would be onstage. He promised to check. After a couple of minutes, he said Sylvia made her first appearance at 3:15. Kelly left early, so she could walk through the park. She stopped for charcoal-blackened shish kebab and watched the rowboats on the pond, enjoying the soft creak of oars over water. Other sounds flirted with the summer air: Puerto Rican reggae, a bird or two, distant laughter. She aimed at the calliope music of the carrousel, then smiled at the smaller children who were frozen by fear and wonder as they went round and round. Soon it was almost three, too late to watch the seals.

She was not afraid of The Cat's Paw. She assumed the comfortable perspective of the working reporter, making it necessary only to ask but not answer questions, to describe but not fathom mysteries. Nonetheless, she hesitated at the entrance. Would the customers be surprised to see a woman alone? She walked in. Yes, she thought, it's unpleasant. The man with the pistachio nuts watched her, the women in the sales booths watched her, everyone watched her. Or so she thought. But the daylight outside and the chic ambience within made the store less threatening. And she remembered her thoughts of the night before about pornography: what's functional about sex is presented as extraordinary, she thought, and what's extraordinary about sex is not presented at all.

She avoided the booth she and Jennings had shared, along with those on each side. Instead, she entered one on the very edge, then discovered she had no quarters. Hard as she tried, she could not look at the man who changed dollars into quarters; she hoped he did not notice her blush. When the metal curtain went up, she wondered if she was really looking at Sylvia. Then she remembered a tiny flaw in that fine figure, a flaw that made it easier to like the girl. Yes, her waist could be a little longer, she thought, just a *little* longer above the smashing legs. Yes, of course it was Sylvia.

The girl was dancing lazily to some disco music. Kelly decided that, behind the makeup, she was seventeen. With less makeup more subtly applied she would be pretty—not beautiful, for her features, though even, were not surprising. And perhaps, Kelly thought, the figure was *too* good, which would only encourage her to play it up too much. Yes, she decided, the legs were too lovely, the breasts—but oh, she hated how the metal curtain hummed down every minute, requiring more quarters! Then she noticed the telephone that hung on the partition beside her. Could that be a way to get in touch? She bought two of the five-dollar tokens, then dropped one in the slot. She was amazed to see the naked girl

187

walk over to the phone—to hear her say hello. She sounded like a bored adolescent.

"Hello, honey, what can I do you for?"

"Hi."

"What?"

"Hi."

"This a joke?"

"No."

"You . . . ah . . . What are you, female, queer?"

"Can't you see me?"

The girl squinted, then looked flustered. She seemed to want to cover herself. "What do you mean 'see you'? But wait a minute, what is this? I believe in women for friends, but I don't like to fool around with them, you know what I mean? If you want to be laid or something you've called the wrong operator." She edged away from Kelly's window.

"Sylvia?"

"Yeah?"

"I just wanted—"

"Hey, slow . . . it . . . down. How do you know my name? You're not supposed to know my name."

"Well—"

"You're not my sister!"

"What?"

"My sister likes practical jokes."

The phone went dead. The girl resumed dancing.

Kelly put in a second slug.

"Hello, honey, what can I do you for?"

"Me again."

"If you're a cop, there's nothing on me, I bet my bed is cleaner than yours."

"I want to interview you."

"Jesus, another one."

"No, you probably met someone who asked you about it, Jennings, he said he spoke to you."

"Sort of short, messy kind of guy?"

"Yes."

The girl sat down and crossed one leg over the other. "So I'll tell you what I told him, namely, to make a long story short, what's in it for me? I'm talking cash."

The phone went dead again. Kelly purchased more tokens. This time, however, her token was returned: someone had beat her to Sylvia. When the girl hung up Kelly tried again.

"Hello, hon—"

"It's not paying you for a service, I just want to talk to you."

"For free?"

"There'd be an article."

"So what do you want?"

"Anything, everything. About you."

"I don't get it."

"Just what . . . you think about things."

"Nosy!"

"No, I—"

"What I think about life and stuff? I don't even *know* you. I don't talk to anybody, I've got my privacy. I'm not supposed to insult the customers, unless that's what they like, but are you, you know—" An idea hit her. "Oh my God! Shit, you are probably *religious*. You probably want to shave my head. Let me tell you something, 'Thanks but no thanks.' "

"For an article, let me take you to lunch."

The girl considered.

"You probably want dirty pictures."

"Just an article."

"For free?"

"Yes."

"Why do I do you a favor?"

"You don't have to."

Sylvia agreed to meet Kelly for lunch in a couple of days.

4

Kelly planned a portrait that was not satirical. That would be a challenge, since Sylvia lent herself to satire, but also a pleasure, since Kelly liked brightly colored subjects. Sylvia reminded her of a suspicious parrot—yet Kelly was moved by the girl. She did not seem stupid, though her eyes often clouded over with the moodiness of late adolescence. She was roughly the age of the girls who would be in Kelly's class, but with such a different life—such new-minted cynicism! What led Sylvia to turn herself into an image of that kind? What had Jennings said about modern dance? And then, what magazine would buy the article? She did not know the free-lance market that well, so she called Theodore Oatis, to avoid asking Jennings for advice. This made her somewhat uneasy, since Oatis reminded her of her past. But the article excited her and she felt businesslike being on the phone.

"How've you been?" Oatis asked. "You know, I've been meaning to call you. But all this work, and then I had to go to California. Madness."

They chatted about his problems: he had postponed his decision about the Holocaust book. Then Kelly said she wanted to write an article about a girl in the pornography business.

"Terrific. I'll look it over for you if you want."

She ignored his condescension and told him more about the subject. Would there be any problem publishing the piece?

"Simple." After it was written, he said, he would put her in touch with the right people. "And by the way—" He asked her out. She could not say no, but she put him off with a story about going home to visit her mother. He himself had to return to California. They gossiped for a couple of minutes about Penelope, and Oatis told her that the black turtleneck was writing a Broadway show with two collaborators, who often lost their tempers. "What'd you think of the article about Billy?"

"What article?"

"In the *Times* this morning."

"I missed the *Times* today."

"Usual thing. Well, I have to be on my way—"

"Thanks."

"We'll be in touch."

In her mail Kelly found an invitation to a speech that Billy was to give at the Waldorf. On it was penciled a note from Billy, who said he hoped very much to see her there "since I know you don't own a television." Beside the garbage chute she found a discarded *Times*. The article covered half the front page of an interior section called Home. She shook her head in wonder: if you had to be told what home was, you didn't have one. The story, entitled "Making It Personal," included a large picture of Billy

190

smiling in his living room. Behind him were plants, bookshelves, low-slung furniture. She read:

Billy Bell, the television personality, spends his days talking to and worrying about 1.7 million people—the estimated audience for his afternoon news and interview show. At night he prefers to worry about himself or a few old friends. "I need that sense of difference in my life," he says. "I wanted a quiet apartment with an ample sense of space—remember, I'm originally from California."

The problem for the design firm of Apple, Ltd. was to open up Mr. Bell's Village floor-through—"to give it," says Murray Wilder, the president of Apple, "some California light. Mr. Bell wanted to avoid an overly 'designed' look, but he didn't own many of those quirky individual things that add accent to an apartment. He told us what he liked, gave us what he had, and told us to make it personal."

For Mr. Wilder that meant knocking down the walls between . . .

Kelly began to skim.

Mr. Bell is one celebrity who takes his privacy seriously . . . He likes romantic candlelight dinners ("I'm old-fashioned that way") . . . Because his client was adamant about retaining a beat-up reading chair from college, Mr. Wilder added some old blue-and-white homespun to the furniture . . . "More and more I find myself returning to the classics," says Mr. Bell, who thinks nothing looks better than a roomful of books. "Right now I'm tackling Dostoevsky . . ." He likes to cook vegetables in a wok, so counter space was at a premium . . . Leading politicians (who are finding Mr. Bell an increasingly attractive candidate) sometimes gather in the window alcove . . . "But I never let it spoil our dinner, and we never talk about politics after the first glass of wine" . . .

She tossed the paper aside. Her own apartment was not much of a home, she thought, how could she criticize Billy's? She remembered his walk through her two barren rooms—"Very nice, very nice." What an unpredictable man. How he looked at her in Bridgehampton! How he ignored her! She stiffened. He had not forgiven her; and there was nothing amusing, she thought, in the way he had walked through her apartment. She realized, suddenly, that he was more important to her than he should be. He stood in her mind for a kind of shining blindness. He refused, again and again, to see her for herself. He seemed to have turned her into an enemy, she thought, to be conciliated or scorned. Even that note—"since I know you don't own a television"—had edge.

Look at the men she knew! Jennings—distracted. Oatis—perfumed. Billy—blind. She thought some more about her article, then decided to go to Billy's speech: she wanted to understand everything around her.

5

When she saw Sylvia outside The Cat's Paw, Kelly smiled to herself—"parrot" was a good description. The girl, bra-less of course, wore a flaming red blouse and green trousers that skinned her hips. Her lipstick was crimson and her sunglasses, ballooning goggles, were violet. "Sylvia?"

"You who I'm supposed to meet?"

"Yes."

She chewed her gum thoughtfully. "Aren't you too young to be a writer?"

"I'm almost thirty."

"I thought writers were *real* old. You have proof?"

"Of what?"

"Being a writer."

Kelly smiled. "No proof—will you take my word for it?"

There was a pause.

Kelly took Sylvia's arm and led her down the street. The girl, suddenly trusting, said, "You can't be too careful."

It was Kelly's plan to postpone difficult questions until later meetings. With that in mind, she asked Sylvia to name her favorite restaurant. A sly look, poorly concealed, came into Sylvia's face.

She took Kelly to The Artful Dodger, a chic and overpriced restaurant where famous athletes were sometimes spotted. Kelly placed a tiny tape recorder next to a tulip-stemmed glass. Then she began to explain her intentions. It would be best, she thought, to meet several times—

"What's that for?" Sylvia stared at the tape recorder as if it were a dentist's drill.

"It's a cassette recorder."

"I know what it *is*, but what's it *for*?"

"To remember what you said."

"I thought reporters used pads, all the reporters I've seen use pads. Keep a pencil, you know, in the ear."

"You can use a tape recorder. It's better—I'll check all quotations with you."

"What do you mean, 'quotations'?"

"What you say."

Wonder lit her face.

"I talk in quotations?"

The waiter opened the oversized menus like a pair of fans. He departed with an order of Tom Collins for Sylvia and wine spritzer for Kelly. Sylvia palmed her gum. Then, getting down to business, she asked Kelly her reasons for writing the story.

"I'm not sure," Kelly said. "I think it's because—"

"I know what you want to do. You want to write a story about a girl who strips for men. I saw a TV special on that once."

"No, that's not quite right. I want to know more about you—"

"On this TV special they interviewed the parents, you saw the houses—you know, all that kind of stuff."

"Better than that. I want to find out what you're like."

The girl stared into space. Then she looked at Kelly. "I don't strip for men. I perform modern dance."

"You do?"

She nodded and looked away. She seemed to go in and out of focus, like someone whose duty requires politeness but whose desire is to nurse some large and tender dream that will not bear discussion.

"The strip part is just to make money. A friend told me about it. I take lessons in modern dance. Teacher tells me I'm doing pretty good, too. So I get up there, do some patterns, exercises, and things." She stared into space again, then came back into focus. "That's what you want to write about, right?"

"Modern dance?"

"Yeah."

"That and other parts of your life."

"Who cares?"

"Me."

"Shit."

"You're wrong."

"Yeah, well . . ."

Whenever Sylvia stared into space she hummed a song of no discernible tune. Sometimes she half whistled between her teeth —and then, stopping abruptly, turned her attention to Kelly. It was disconcerting. Kelly thought she must bore Sylvia. Even so, she found her sympathetic. The tough-girl manner fit Sylvia little better than her clothes, and the awkwardness hinted at another sort of character.

"We don't have to do the story if you don't want. I told you that. It might be better for me anyway—you see, I don't really like to write. I only came back to New York a couple of months ago . . ." Kelly told her about the year she had spent in Montana. She did not know how to make a friend of Sylvia, but thought it might be reassuring to talk about herself first. Besides, it did not seem wise to press Sylvia about The Cat's Paw, not yet, although what she had said about modern dance intrigued Kelly.

She told the girl, "I'm not sure I want to be a teacher."

"You're a teacher that doesn't want to teach?" The idea struck Sylvia as hilarious. "I'm a student that don't want to study!" She reached into her purse for a cigarette, which she smoked in the covert but ostentatious fashion of high school students. "That's all right," she said, blowing a couple of smoke rings. "A teacher-that-don't-want-to-teach." Having drinks, lunch, and a cigarette at The Artful Dodger with a teacher that didn't want to teach seemed to suit her. The Tom Collins loosened her up even more. She ordered another, and when the waiter returned she asked for a shrimp cocktail and filet mignon, two of the most expensive things on the menu. This put her in an expansive mood. She became overly nice, like a con-man to a sucker.

"How did you hear about me again?"

"Through Jennings, who met you at Prendergast's."

"That guy . . ." She thought for a moment. "You like him, huh?"

Kelly was taken aback. "Sometimes. What made you say that?"

"I could tell."

Her respect for Sylvia increased.

"So what's he do?"

"He works for Billy Bell."

"The TV guy?"

"Yes."

Sylvia could not speak. Then she said, "Do *you* know Billy Bell?"

"Yes, a bit."

Her self-possession vanished. "Who else do you know?"

"I know a lot—"

"Famous, I mean."

"Well—"

"Rock stars? I've seen lots at the doors. You ever met—" She repeated the names of half a dozen rock stars, most of whom became famous after 1975, when Kelly began to fall out of touch.

"No—I don't."

Sylvia grabbed Kelly's hand. "Is that Stan Turner?" Her eyes, afraid to look, darted toward a tall man dressed in a peach suit. Kelly had never heard of Stan Turner. Sylvia fell back in her seat. "No, it's not. Me and my friends get bent out of shape about Stan Turner. I read where he has a house with a swimming pool in the front *and* back yard. Not that that's what I really like about him."

"What else do you like about him?"

She stared into space—if you didn't know you couldn't be told. Then she took a long, studied sip of her drink. "So what's this Billy Bell like? I see his show sometimes."

"Oh, he's smart, good-looking, quick. I don't know, what do you want to hear?"

"Well, you know"—she looked away—"the personal stuff."

Sylvia seemed both disappointed and relieved. If Kelly did not know celebrities well, if she was normal, it would be simpler to talk to her. She turned to her food and ate voraciously. She drank three Tom Collinses. For dessert she ordered cheese cake. Kelly wondered how she kept her figure.

"Who you writing this article for?"

Kelly mentioned three or four good magazines.

"How many people do you figure would read the article?"

"Depends where it was published." Kelly thought she should exaggerate. "Might be as many as a million."

"Million!" An expression of cunning—a little loopy with drink—glinted in Sylvia's face. "There'd be pictures?"

"Might—depends."

"Not cheesy, you know what I mean."

"Probably not."

"In my leotards?"

"Maybe."

Sylvia lit a cigarette as another burned in the ashtray. Then she bestowed a smile on Kelly—a rock star being kind to a fan.

Kelly asked her where she grew up.

"On the wrong side of the tracks."

"What town?"

Sylvia took a long drag on her cigarette and tapped off the ash with care. "You want to know about my roots," she said, exhaling. "I grew up in a town called Hempstead." She paused. "Which is not far from Mineola. My parents were, how should I say it? good people, hard-working." She paused again. "But I always knew I had to get away." She pulled on the cigarette until the tip sparkled.

"What does your father do?"

She inhaled deeply.

"He always wanted the best for me."

"But what does he do?"

"Sure we fought, but that was"—she tapped the cigarette—"that was because"—she tapped the cigarette again—"let's leave it that my father was a good man. Someday I'm going to buy him a big house."

Kelly put little faith in what Sylvia said. The girl, who was drunk, described her life as famous lives were described in magazines, movies, and on television. Nonetheless, Kelly paid close attention. She noticed how Sylvia moved, how she tried to elevate her language, which clichés she loved. They left the restaurant friends.

6

Kelly went to Billy's speech because she did not want to go. Her uneasiness, she told herself, must not master her. She also wanted to observe Jennings at a distance and see how Billy behaved in public. She did not intend to say hello. Billy's speech, which capped an afternoon of seminars and talks arranged by a confederation of city unions, was entitled "Labor and the Media"—which meant, she assumed, he could talk about anything he wanted. That would explain why a man with a flair for publicity would choose such a boring title. She found an excellent crowd scattered around the conference room of the Waldorf, a much larger one than she had anticipated: many workers in the area, alerted by their union representatives, had come to see the television personality.

She took a seat near the back, then watched Billy and Jennings, flanked by bobbing photographers and men with manila envelopes, walk to the front of the hall. Billy sat behind a conference table, while a small man with a balding head tapped the microphone, saying "Testing . . . testing . . . testing . . . one—two—three." He identified himself as Pete Gargola, leader of the sanitationmen, and began to introduce Billy in political singsong: It was his great, his important, his honored task to introduce not just one of the up-and-coming leaders of the greatest city in the world . . . Kelly studied the audience. It was composed largely of middle-aged men, some of whom wore ties. Those with ties had the slightly worn look, the blindness to fashion, typical of bureaucrats who have worked in the same place for a long time. The few professionals, probably lawyers, sat bored and whispering near the front; they acted as if they knew what was going to happen. Kelly assumed they were reporters or union officials. Most of the audience, however, was made up of people she saw every day but rarely met—those who didn't read the New York *Times*.

"In fact, I only have one problem with this young fellow," said Gargola, removing his glasses, "he's too damn good-looking!"

Kelly laughed with everyone else. Gargola was very good at warming up a crowd. What he said mattered less than his joy in saying it: the singsong, corny jokes and podium-thumping were so genuine that the audience joined in his pleasure. And everyone liked to watch an old man tease a young man of promise. As Gargola waggled his finger at Billy, the younger man pointed at himself as if to ask, "Who, me?"

"Now where was I?" Gargola demanded. He returned his glasses, which were enormous and black-rimmed, to his nose. "Got to keep our mind on business here." He paused. "Ladies and gents, I would like you to give a big hand, a hand from the heart"—he paused again, with his hand over his heart, as in the Oath of Allegiance—"to a young man, ladies and gentlemen, not just a good-looking young man, but a young man with one helluva big future. Billy Bell."

In the swelling applause Billy stood to thank Gargola and shake his hand. Then he took comfortable possession of the podium. He did not immediately look up, but appeared to be composing his thoughts. It was apparent, as always, that Billy belonged to a different class from Gargola. It was not merely his dapper clothes or youthful looks. His seriousness and his judgment were also of a different order. He did not work with favors, sweat, and the slap on the back, but with images and neatly typed memoranda. He understood the new, complicated things.

"Thank you, Mr. Gargola," he said, still composing himself. Then, without having looked at the audience, he turned to the old man and said, "Someday I hope I'm as good-looking as you." The audience roared—but stopped laughing too soon. Billy had made a mistake, Kelly thought, a serious and uncharacteristic mistake: the young should not rib the old about age. Only the old were allowed to make that joke. Was Billy aware of his mistake? She thought so, because he flattered Gargola with stories and jokes for longer than necessary. Billy closed this portion of his speech by recalling that, when Gargola was a guest on his show, the old man had caught him off guard several times. "You know what?" Billy asked. "Right there on the air he taught me some important lessons in city politics, which I don't mean to forget." That was better. The contrast between the men was no less sharp, but the young had nonetheless learned from the old.

"My topic today," said Billy, turning to business, "is labor and the media, but I'm going to stretch that a bit and try to talk about how the issues that are important to working people—I mean jobs, crime, benefits . . . even the pursuit of happiness—are addressed today. Who listens to the working man and woman? The media? The politicians? That's what I want to talk about."

Kelly stopped analyzing. She forgot to. She was led to listen and watch. Billy spoke simply, in a smooth and rounded voice. He edged an occasional word with anger, which kept him from appearing too soft or earnest, and his eyes looked in all directions, as if all opinions were sought. He might be good at images and memoranda, but he was no less warm than Gargola. What he said, moreover, sounded significant; the cadence of his argument commanded assent. One after another he addressed the issues, each in the same way. First he demonstrated the depth of the problem: five hundred reported rapes in such-and-such a period. Next he demonstrated the sluggish response of the politicians and the media. He did not excuse himself from blame, but sometimes added, by way of example, "On my show I recently invited—" He was trying to do something. No one would forget that Pete Gargola was his regular guest.

In concluding his discussion of each issue, Billy quietly asked: "Is that right?" A pause followed. Then he said in a louder voice: "My answer is . . . 'No.'"

In this way the speech gathered momentum.

It was wonderfully seductive to join the others in support of the man out front. Then, abruptly, Kelly came to herself. The issue was pornography. She was astonished that, given her relations with Billy, she had entered into the mood of the audience. This was not her Billy Bell, the one whose character seemed so vague. Or was her private view mistaken? The man onstage, like the man in the Home section, seemed genuine, warm, and unaffected; he spoke to the issues and his speech had a shape. What was more, he appeared passionate, full of quiet but righteous anger— an appealing anger, which frightened her.

She began to distance herself. The people nearby, who nodded with Billy, heightened her sense of estrangement. She looked for Jennings and found his head—a small, far-off island. He sat with the lawyers. When he whispered to the person beside him, she felt keenly that the whisper was not to her; and she could picture him, for the first time, as an employee of Billy Bell. Perhaps, she thought, Jennings had written the speech that turned the Billy she didn't like into the one she did. She continued to distance herself until Billy and the audience could be seen in a cool light. Friends were strangers, strangers friends; sometimes she clapped with the others, sometimes not. Once, when Billy asked "Is that right?" everyone else cried "No!" She waited to answer with Billy, as he said "My answer is 'No.'" But she was just humming along with the tune. She could also have said yes.

CHAPTER

TEN

I

Billy meant "Is that right?" to be a rhetorical question. He was surprised when, a few minutes into the speech, hundreds of people began to answer him, each time with a more resounding "No!" Their heat both pleased and dismayed him. He was not experienced at controlling crowds and had never intended to whip this one up. Yet he did not change his approach. After each ragged chorus he paused. And then, as if his were the only finger left in the dike, he repeated in a firm voice, "My answer is . . . No."

In the silence that followed each "No," he stared for several seconds into the face of the crowd. He was disappointed not to find Kelly. She would have been impressed, he thought, with his success. The jab of disappointment led Billy to stare into the audience for longer and longer periods of time, searching.

He repeated, "My answer is . . . No."

He found some relief from disappointment in the approval of the audience. These good people were with him. And so, early in the speech, he took a chance. He abandoned his text for a moment to talk about the fear of an elderly woman walking home alone. This was an extraordinary thing for him to do. When speaking to a live audience, he always followed the script. To throw himself into the arms of the audience was like falling into the sea. The same horrible floating, the same choking on a terror close at hand; the pop of the flashbulbs, when he looked up and out, resembled the swimming of the stars after a cuff to the head. Yet the risk exhilarated him, and the words carried themselves. He touched bottom by instinct: safe! And the audience loved his daring.

Soon he began to take the risk often, certain that a live audience —so volatile and impure compared to the invisible crowd of television—would never trouble him again. He retained the structure of taking issues in turn, ending with the rhetorical question, but he often added asides. He discussed the poor, the black, and the elderly—and then jumped into an account of his visit to the home for handicapped children in Queens. "I am not usually a sentimental man," he said, looking up from his speech. "I go to my office every day, as you do. I work on what's there. I try to do the best I can. Sometimes, though, when I go out on a story, something different happens. I'm caught off guard, and an ordinary day in my life becomes extraordinary. That happened not long ago when I visited a home for handicapped children." He asked, "How many of you have seen a handicapped child?"

He answered himself, "Oh, you've probably seen them, like me, on those charity programs on television, or walking down the street."

He paused.

"It's different when you *really* see them."

A tear formed in Billy's eye—and trembled there. This astonished him. He had not known himself to possess such intensity, not in so spontaneous a form. There was a sweet and seductive danger in this: a loss of control, a release, an end. But no, he would not weep in public. He focused all the power of his will upon this trembling at the back of his eyes, and let the words take care of themselves. His voice continued firm. He found that he could control, if not stop, this small upwelling. He came to like the trembling in his eyes and throat. It was a kind of harnessed power, which lent energy to his speech.

"I wonder who among us has held a handicapped child in his lap. Not many I think. It's easy to make a few public pronouncements, but to really do something—"

Billy did not describe the children. They formed too vivid a picture in his mind, and instinct told him he might weep on the podium. This was not necessarily dangerous, if the subject was right and control maintained.

But no, he must not.

"I ask you, Is that right?"

The audience shouted "No!"

"My answer is . . . No."

During the pause Billy searched the upturned faces. And then, with the tear still trembling in his eye, his disappointment turned to anger. The wetness glinted; his throat tightened. "There is one further issue I want to talk to you about," he said with conviction. "Pornography." The word settled over the room, and he continued parenthetically: "I've often wondered what happens to children who are abused in pornographic films. They are also handicapped."

He took a deep breath. "I want to know," he said, "what our politicians have done to clean up Times Square. I want to know what our politicians have done to clean up the Times Square that was once the heart of our city. I should say diseased heart. We read all the time in the papers that something will be done. But has it? Has something been done? Ever?"

Some people in the audience shouted "No!"

"No, it has not," Billy said. "And what has the media done? Aside from an occasional feature story, the answer is equally clear . . . nothing." He paused. "Of course pornography is a complicated issue. It has some bearing on freedom of speech. We don't want censorship. Nor do most people today oppose the free and healthy expression of love. And yet when so many decent people feel so strongly about an issue—something can be done. Something must be done. _I_ want something done."

The audience burst into applause. Jennings' hunch was right: pornography could be a useful issue.

"I plan to spend a full week on that issue alone next fall, but that is the effort of only one man. Nothing will be done without broad political action. Pornography, culturally sanctioned, is an expression of . . . social rot." He paused. "It is a cancer . . . threatening the health of our city." At the word "cancer" the audience quickened, then drew close to Billy—Dr. Bell.

"Is that right?"

"No!"

"My answer is . . . No."

Billy never raised his voice. He depended for drama on pacing, in particular the dramatic use of pauses and the repetition of "Is that right? My answer is . . . No." He knew that if he were to raise his voice, the audience would become even warmer, the applause still more frequent. He did not want to be considered an orator, however, or a conservative who took advantage of the fears of the lower middle class. Nothing he said would prevent him from wooing liberal Democrats. His speech to them would be different, but not duplicitous in its difference.

During his attack on pornography the trembling had moderated. When the time came to end the speech, however, his sense of kinship with the audience again raised a tear. Unlike tears of sadness or rage, this feeling was easy to control. He played it with pleasure. First he gently weaned the crowd of its anger. "We've been doing a lot of talking about 'no,'" Billy said. "I wouldn't want to leave without a few words about 'yes.' To look at an audience like this, to accept the podium from a man like that"— he held out his hand to Gargola—"gives me a sense of confidence, even of optimism, about the future of our city . . ." He continued in this vein for several minutes. He complimented the audience on its hard work. He praised New York City for its energy and leadership. He drew a picture of safe streets, comfortable families, and ready work. He ended by asking, "Is that right?"

He paused. "My answer is . . . Yes."

Billy received a standing ovation. By then he was already wanting to be alone.

2

Billy, who had the use of a limousine, dropped off Jennings and a couple of officials. He considered asking the driver to take him to the office or to a bar that he liked on the Upper East Side. In the end he just went home, where he put on the soundtrack of a cheerful Broadway musical—a present from an ebullient actress. He made himself a drink and sat in an expensive chair. He read over the article about Billy Bell in the Home section. The reporter had made several mistakes. Billy Bell had not referred to "tackling Dostoevsky." Nor did Billy Bell cook with the wok that hung on the kitchen wall. Nonetheless, he decided to write the reporter a note of thanks. He had never known a reporter to dislike a note of thanks.

When the record player shut off, the apartment hummed with silence. He strained to hear—a distant siren, a muted conversation moving past on the street. Normally, in the period of mourning after a performance, he took comfort in the memory of success; he relived his moment of connection. This was no longer possible. Kelly, a kind of static between himself and others, interfered with his remembering. The intrusion of politics, the falling away of Jennings, the arrival of Kelly—for a moment he sat quietly, not knowing what to do or think. These problems together were beginning to destroy his poise, as a few small flaws will destroy the performance of a delicately tuned machine before that of a rougher instrument. He seemed to spin up, up and away, unable to find the necessary mesh in his relation to others. He was losing his sense of proportion: small and large problems bothered him equally. It did not matter, for example, that he hardly knew Kelly. His vague unease found its necessary concentration in his obsession with her. He blamed her with a conviction so certain that he never considered its unfairness. Blamed with love—for her brown and blue expression held out the promise of peace, even as her indifference tormented him.

He slapped the side of his chair, protesting the tyranny of this crowd of one. He thought back to his speech and stood himself above the ovation. He delivered the keynote speech to the Democratic National Convention and shook hands with the Russian premier at a summit conference. This dreaming only made matters worse. The higher he rose the further he fell; the kinder the dream, the crueler the jerk back into anger—until at last this strange seesawing led him to ask himself what he was doing. He could not answer. Billy did not possess the habit of curiosity. He reacted and he fought.

3

He woke whispering the word "indisposed." That word, her excuse for leaving him at Mama's—who used that word today? It made him feel like a footman. A shower improved his spirits. He fetched the morning papers and read about the Mideast, browsed through the sports, glanced at the gossip. This daylight dose of the ordinary enabled him, after a while, to scoff at his behavior the night before. It was a phase: everyone went through phases, said the psychologists who appeared on his show. That the *Times* failed to cover his speech did not disappoint him. The paper had sent a reporter, but Billy knew beforehand that a story would be published only if he announced his political plans. With a sense of personal importance he reminded himself that he planned to take his own sweet time. Let the newspapers send reporters.

At the office, Billy confirmed his lunch date with Teitelman, then asked his secretary to call Jennings. He was surprised: the man had actually come to work. Jennings even dropped by the office to say, "I thought the speech went extremely well." His voice, however, was not enthusiastic enough.

"Now what do you really think?"

"I never saw you handle a live audience that way. You left the text, and, well . . ." Jennings peered at him. "What were you doing? A little more and those people would have—I don't know —started doing jumping jacks."

"It wasn't such a dumb crowd."

"There's no such thing as a smart crowd."

"What about the pornography? I didn't push it as hard as I could have. I was deliberately pretty straightforward."

"It went over great. Of course, if you ever got elected—well, I doubt you could do much."

"I know you think that."

There was a pause.

"The little sentence," Billy said. "The little sentence you put in—you know, 'Is that right?'—worked better than I expected. Did you know the crowd would answer?"

"Not at the time. In the hall, yes, I could see it might happen."

"Brilliant idea."

He sounded like a boss complimenting a junior, which he knew irritated Jennings. At the same time, he was truly grateful. And suddenly sentimental: think of Jennings' role in his career! "Brilliant," he repeated. "I'm not just saying that. The success of that speech owes everything to you."

"No."

"Yes it does."

"No."

"Come on."

"It's in the way you speak, how you look, the way you smile at the audience. I'm a mechanic."

Why wouldn't Jennings accept praise? Did he think working for Billy Bell didn't matter? Jennings now seemed like an offensive intrusion, an unpleasant reminder of the past. He knew Billy from other years and guises. He did not treat Billy the way people treated Billy Bell.

"Oh, come on," Billy said. "Take some credit."

Jennings shrugged, smiled.

Billy did not press the point, suddenly afraid he owed all his success to Jennings. Perhaps Jennings' way with ideas, images, drama—the little phrase, the clips on the show, the suggestion about pornography—brought success to Billy Bell.

"Well, if you're not going to take any credit for yourself," Billy said, "I'm going to give you some." He smiled. "And leave it at that."

"Whatever you say."

There was a pause.

Billy laughed, his mood now one of paternal indulgence. Perhaps Jennings was eccentric, but that was his right. So long as he came through when it mattered—and he had always done that. What nonsense, in any case, to give the credit to Jennings. However good his ideas, they were useless until Billy Bell put them into practice. He stood up. "I made some promises in the speech that I'm going to have to deliver on. Particularly about pornography." He sat on his couch. Jennings, he thought, does not contribute all the ideas. I wrote the speech . . . except for that little phrase.

"You mean the week-long series on porn?"

Billy nodded.

"Well, I've been working on that, as you asked. I'm not altogether sure, but I think I've found a girl—about seventeen or eighteen, probably telegenic—who strips for a living. She's not dumb, wouldn't be trashy on the air, at least I don't think she would be. Seems slightly vulnerable, maybe a little coarse. But that's the seasoning you want. Coarse but vulnerable."

"A princess in the rough!"

Jennings smiled—as if, Billy thought, the boss should take pride in his rare display of wit.

"Where'd you find her?"

"The Cat's Paw. Which is good, because it's the place that's been in the news. I haven't formally asked her to do anything, but I've talked to her. Opened negotiations."

"No mixing pleasure with business! Or, in her case, business with business." He stared the smile off Jennings' face, then said, "I think I ought to meet her sometime too, to see if we can talk effectively together—but not for a while. Meanwhile, you—"

"I don't need to talk to her anymore. Kelly will."

"She . . ."

"Well, remember, we talked about it. Thought it'd be a good idea to get some more fashionable thinking going about pornography, more widely based than just the feminists. Well, I think Kelly might write a profile of this stripper."

There was a pause.

"Unfortunately," Jennings said, "her article, if she writes one, probably won't come out till after the show. Still, I think it would build some strength among sophisticated people for your position."

"Yes, it might do that."

"I haven't done much else. I'm finding the names of the best psychologists in that area. I'll look into it today."

"Good."

Billy's secretary poked into the office. Mr. Gargola was on the line, wanting to thank Billy once again. Would Billy speak to him? Billy picked up the phone beside the couch. He talked to Gargola —in a charming, lighthearted manner—until Jennings left.

208

4

Teitelman suggested they meet at the Century Association. Billy planned to join the Century, which was reserved for men of accomplishment; perhaps Teitelman would sponsor him. Billy liked passing from the cramped energy of the city into the ample consequence of the club—a place where nothing had to happen in rooms with soaring ceilings. In such rooms sound itself seemed to pass on tiptoe: the occasional ring of a bell to summon a shuffling waiter or the mumbling of men here and there. Above all, Billy liked the studied indifference of the club's style. A wine-colored painting hung a little crooked. A chair, undistinguished and old, looked as worn as a well-thumbed book. The smell was of superior dust.

Billy arrived first. One of the waiters, a black man with white hair, indicated a pair of chairs where Teitelman would join him. There were only three other people in the room. Billy asked for a double Scotch. Of course he must join this club. The slightly seedy style was correct, just as it was correct for a brilliant professor to dress haphazardly. The affectation was not wealth or social standing but accomplishment. In a few minutes Billy had been a member of the club for years. His conversation with Jennings, to say nothing of the difficult night before, seemed the stuff of head-shaking reminiscence.

The floorboards squeaked. "Sorry I'm late," Teitelman said. "Damn traffic on Sixth."

Teitelman often came to the Century for lunch, Billy knew, though his office was on Wall Street. His connections were varied, ranging from actors and intellectuals to politicians, bankers, and heads of state. He was a broker not of stocks, but of favors, advice, and ideas. He helped shape the smart opinion. Billy had never examined Teitelman with detachment, having always been too concerned with his own behavior. This time, however, lulled by the chair and the Scotch, Billy noticed the trimness of his figure—the man was well past fifty—and the directness of his approach. There was nothing bland in Teitelman's appearance (he often wore a bow tie) but he was not easy to label. To Billy he looked like a college president who knew how to balance a budget.

How had the speech gone?

"Pretty well. Gargola seemed pleased."

"Wish I could have made it."

Teitelman ordered soda water. "Old Gargola. You know, someone really ought to write a long piece on him before he dies. The last of the classic city politicians—one of the true old-timers."

"He was wonderful on my show."

"Why'd he take such a shine to you?"

"The show, I suppose."

"No—he's too smart for that. He plays the clown sometimes, but he runs that union very tightly. I've always been impressed with him since he hires smart people who understand the new ways of doing things. He's a guy who builds a bridge to every potential source of power. Great instincts."

This flattered Billy.

"It was easier than I thought to talk to that audience."

"You better be good at talking to different kinds of people. Mind if we go in? They're so slow here."

Billy stood up quickly. Around Teitelman he was always too rushed or too relaxed. Teitelman would be charming, full of stories and information and digression; and then he would snap to the point or leave for a meeting. These abrupt changes, which did not seem harsh, kept conversation sprightly. On the way to their meal, members of the club repeatedly waylaid Teitelman. Brief discussions followed about the events in the morning news. A consensus was usually reached, some significance downplayed. Usually there was a joke or smile. Teitelman always introduced Billy, who was always recognized. "Sorry," said Teitelman, when they were seated. They selected a private table and ordered immediately, since the food was only fair. The Century presumed to serve good conversation.

Teitelman teased him. "You sure you want to get into politics?" He was referring to a corruption story, which a lawyer had asked him about. "To change anything is halfway to impossible. Not just changing, even controlling the city government is like turning an aircraft carrier."

"Unless things break well I'll get out."

"You're going to have to decide very soon which office you want."

"I know."

"Next couple of weeks, if you want to get the committee in position by early fall."

Billy liked listening to advice from the older man.

"Done anything about your staff?"

"I'll do that when I make up my mind."

Teitelman wanted him to run for Congress, Billy believed, though he refused to say so. Billy himself preferred a congressional seat to the other possibilities, though his chances of winning were slim. In Congress administrative skills were less important; campaigning and voting mattered more. On impulse, knowing the strangeness of the question, Billy asked Teitelman how he had spent his morning.

The banker smiled, as if he'd just been found out. "Yes, I've been plugging you with all these questions. Well, I've been trying for some time now to negotiate a merger between a couple of solid middle-sized companies. Makes sense in a thousand different ways."

Billy loved this way of talking. Complex matters yielded to common sense for those in the know.

"It's a medieval problem of precedence with these executives, though they rarely admit it. You have to make sure enough of them feel properly respected in the final settlement." He smiled again. "There have to be some broken eggshells. But not too many. So I've spent all morning on the telephone talking to one person and another."

They discussed the best way to organize time. Then Billy said, "You know, I'll probably aim for Congress."

"Bad odds, and people like Gargola wouldn't be so useful, but I don't think you'd go wrong. The next time you might win—hell, you might win on the first go. You probably know how to run a media campaign, and if you can raise the money—well, I told you, I might be able to help a little with that."

"That's very generous."

Teitelman shrugged. "The man in there now is terrible for a city that depends so much on federal aid, that has been double-crossed so often by the feds. A city with our kind of welfare problem."

"He's popular, though."

"Republicans are always vulnerable in Manhattan. You'd lose in the primary, not against him. Anyway, if you want to hold a fund raiser at the end of the summer, or just a party to announce something, you'll have to decide pretty soon in order to get everything organized. I'm not going to actively support anyone, but you could use my lawn, since you're a friend, for a cocktail party. A couple of others are also going to be held there. But you ought to let me know. In any case I can introduce you to some contributors."

"I'm very grateful."

"Politics."

It seemed important, once this business was concluded, to discuss something less serious. They chose the club itself. Billy did not mention his desire to join, nor did Teitelman suggest it; enough debt had been contracted over lunch. Instead they chatted about whether or not women would be admitted. This served as a kind of dessert—soon finished, since Teitelman was running late.

5

That afternoon Billy put together a list of people who might join a "Committee to Elect Billy Bell to Congress." Then he called several people on this list, most of whom had appeared on his show. He was gratified when they agreed to join the committee. None of them would be asked to do any work; they were meant to provide money or noticeable support. In a few days he intended to ask Teitelman for advice about campaign managers: no doubt several were looking for slots. Everyone he called was told to keep the candidacy secret until a formal announcement was made. This flattered his supporters and ensured that someone would leak the news. Rumors and speculation, far from being a problem, were politically useful. Depending upon the reaction to a leak, he planned to use Teitelman's lawn to announce either his candidacy or the formation of a committee to explore a possible candidacy.

He also taped two shows and questioned Jennings about the psychologists who had something to say about pornography. He did not inform Jennings of his decision. At 6:00 p.m., as most of the office staff was leaving, he shut himself in his office. Rather than ask Jennings to dinner, he ordered in food from a Chinese restaurant. He did not want to stop working. At 9:00 p.m., still

212

reluctant to go home, he began to tire of work. He fixed himself a drink at his bar; and another. Then, not knowing what to do next, he went for a short walk down a hallway. He wanted to be among known things, to wrap himself in the familiarity of the office. But he found only covered typewriters, black corridors, and bulletin boards that were peeling with the photographs of lovers and children. At 9:30 the air conditioning shut down; a single phone, in the middle of a long row of desks, rang and blinked. The familiar became strange—and seemed stranger than an unknown place, without the echo of familiarity, could ever be.

He returned to his office, but spun around when he heard the babble of far-off voices. He saw a light and figures darting down a long corridor. Who? What? He waited. They drew closer—the cleaning women. They spoke a queer language and wore bandannas and rolled down the hall emptying and dusting. He stopped them at his office, but they laughed or were embarrassed and soon passed on. Their chatter, unimpeded, grew faint. For a moment Billy considered going to a psychiatrist, then dismissed the idea as politically dangerous. He made himself another drink and sat down, shaking his head. Even before his lunch with Teitelman, he knew this would happen. Once he learned Kelly was writing an article about pornography, he knew it would be a bad night. He stroked the ice cubes in his drink, and thought how unfair it was to be overtaken this way, just when his career was accelerating. He dreamed, as he sipped, of a vacation. Someplace cool, where he would be free to do what he wanted. And spontaneously, with hardly a suggestion of the particular or precise, just the whisper of forest or girl.

Damn Jennings! He imagined Kelly turning her cool eye—she's very sophisticated, he thought, she would take pride in her objectivity—on the cunts and the pricks of one of those places. He hated the thought. So he made himself another drink, then tried to think of her in another way. Soon he fell into his usual pattern. Angry that she ignored him, he flattened her into caricature. Then, forgetting himself, he raised her in reverie—until once again he remembered her rejection. He was half aware of this circling pattern, but did not try to escape it. Its power increased with repetition, like the line of a circle that is penciled around and around until the paper tears.

213

Billy, drunk, stood up from the couch. He demanded out loud, "Why the hell won't she think about me?"

The sound of his voice surprised him. When the silence re-formed, he broke it again: "I spend all this time thinking about *her*."

He paused.

"And hell, I'm a busy man."

He raised a finger in the air.

"Why won't she look at me?"

He poked the air.

"In the country she wouldn't even look at me."

He poked the air hard. The gesture had the right jaggedness—a kind of rough letting go.

"Wouldn't even look at me."

He smiled. The sound of his voice made him feel witty.

"Or rather, I should say looked *through* me. Snob, might not even be there for all she knows, for Christ's sake."

His jabbering told him he was drunk. He took hold of himself. Stopping the jabber made him feel sane and sober again. He judged himself a great wit. Indisposed, was she? Well, he had an idea about that. He would write her a letter—ask how she was. He laughed. Brilliant! Indisposed, was she? He pulled his typewriter close. Writing a letter was just the thing. Old-fashioned. He rolled a sheet of paper into the typewriter, flipped on the current—but could not think of anything to write. Of course! He slapped himself on the forehead. One did not *type* a personal letter to an indisposed lady. He unrolled the paper, flipped off the current, found a pen. He wrote the date and "Dear Kelly . . ." Then he stood up from his desk. What should he say? Composing a letter was difficult, not like using the telephone. He sat down again. The paper was wrong. One did not write a personal letter on business stationery. One simply did *not*. He fussed inside several desks until he found something blank and creamy. Just passable. Should he write his full name and address in the upper right?

Billy aimed his attention at the letter as if it would solve every-thing. He cleared away every other thought: there was freedom to be found in making himself the servant of his purpose. Pen, pen, pen, pen—there had to be a better pen around, he thought, something finer than a cheap ball point. He found a better pen.

214

Was it all right for the ink to be blue? Probably. He composed the piece of paper into a rectangle perfectly centered on the rectangle of his desk. He supported his forehead with one hand. He poised his pen.

He leaned back. It seemed excellent to write a letter. Old-fashioned and correct. He was put in mind of something important and half forgotten. Richly woven rugs, a certain elegant condescension. "My dear Kelly, I was so sorry to hear that you have been indisposed . . ." A hundred years ago she would have liked to receive such a letter, he thought, but he must not be ridiculous. A certain formality was wanted, but nothing as pompous as that. He stared into the whiteness—a terrible swimming whiteness. A word must be found to anchor the page, but he could not decide on his tone of voice. He fixed himself another drink. Certainly the principal point, he thought, regaining some sense of wit and balance, was the lady's indisposition. It was the critical thing. He wrote, "I would like to say, in all sincerity, if you will pardon the oddity of writing a letter (but it seemed the appropriate thing)"—and then crumpled up the paper. He reminded himself that, however much he might *want* to write in such a way, he had decided that he simply could not, must not, send her such an artificial, contrived, and rococo sentence. And so he wrote draft after draft, crossing out words, writing sideways notes, trying on different styles. He laughed at his cleverness and despaired at his stupidity until he came up with something that, while far from satisfactory, did not totally displease him. Then it became a question of arriving at a suitable handwriting. His "t" would seem too bold, his "s" too scrawny. He wrote and rewrote his message until it didn't look too bad.

He dispensed with dates, writing only "Wednesday" in the upper-right-hand corner. This seemed rather splendidly offhand. "Dear Kelly," he wrote, taking half an hour to decide that a colon was too bureaucratic and a comma not too personal. "I was sorry, Kelly, to hear of your indisposition. We must get together, once you feel better." Short and to the point—that was the best approach, he thought. One cares, but not beyond a sentence or two. He took pride in some of his finer touches. He liked, for example, posing Kelly between two commas. Then he spent an hour deciding how to close. "Love" was out of the question; other words

215

seemed too formal or informal. He decided, in the end, to sign it "Lve"—love, but brisk and abbreviated, like a kiss to the cheek of another man's wife.

*

In the morning he could not remember which words had been sent. He recalled their substance, however, and was overcome with shame. Nothing was worse in his mind than to appear the fool; no doubt she would read the letter aloud to her friends, and smile. He called in sick. All day he watched television or listened to music, but thought only of the progress of the letter. He imagined it wending through the sorting machines, lying in a greasy mail sack, adhering to a yachting magazine. Perhaps the post office would lose it! Perhaps he could steal the letter from her doorstep or bribe the doorman not to deliver it! His powerlessness before the passage of the letter made him feel weak: others ruled his life. Oddly enough, he thought less often of Kelly herself as he concentrated more and more on his embarrassment.

He could not stay home a second day; there was an interview to tape with a real estate tycoon. So he worked feverishly, hardly able to speak without losing his temper. He assumed the letter had been delivered that morning, which relieved him of the anticipation if not the embarrassment of its arrival. The show went smoothly enough. Afterwards he called in Jennings to discuss the list of psychologists for the final time. They settled on one. Billy did not look at Jennings, for fear of losing control—and was soon left alone. He canceled dinner with Penelope, telling her he was sick. Then he read the folder that Jennings had prepared on the psychologist. At six o'clock he looked at his watch. If she had been out all day she might, at that moment, be reading his letter. Billy stood up: he did not plan to spend another evening at the office.

There was something else to do, investigate work. Since he could not trust Jennings, he should visit The Cat's Paw himself to gain a proper understanding of pornography. He went home and changed into dark sloppy clothing and put on sunglasses. Even so, he suffered a moment of stage fright at the entrance. Would everyone at The Cat's Paw gape when he opened the door? The ordinary elegance of the interior reassured him—but there were so many people! Where was the strip show? He followed the flow of traffic past the little movie booths—how could she look at such pictures?—to the semicircle of doors in back. Inside one of the cramped cabins he hurried to raise the screen with a coin, if only to lighten the space. Then he walked out; instantly another man ducked into his cabin, to take advantage of the free screening.

Billy returned to a second cabin. It was not her nakedness that shocked him, for he had seen many prettier girls at first hand, but the unusual intimacy of the view—an intimacy without consequences. He put in more coins. Here he could watch in the darkness, without having to perform. He relaxed, and from his privileged position dreamed a little. It was not a dream of the night, with character and crazy plot, but a dimming of the day—a tender twilight. Then his mood changed again. From a sweet refuge the booth turned into an invincible position, from which he could judge her performance. He delighted in this perspective, this singular chance to assume the power of the audience. He analyzed the wobble of the breast, studied the slimness of the leg. His breath began to catch. And then, suddenly, a surge of pride swept through him. So that was what it came down to: tits and ass. He relished his power and certainty until, unexpectedly, he became aware that he was just standing there, in a cramped booth, behind glass smudged with the palms of other men. He fidgeted. He stamped one foot. He disliked being trapped. He envied her the caressing spotlight—then hated his glassy isolation, despised his enforced impotence, resented the protected position from which she could ignore him. Words began to jerk in his head: cunt, tits, prick. This time, however, reducing her to her parts did not satisfy him. The booth became suffocating and he was about to burst out when he noticed that the girl was talking on the phone.

He remembered Billy Bell: in a place like this! He retreated into his terrible vagueness of mind as the booth tightened around him. He stood in darkness before the image of a naked girl who stretched indifferently. He bought a token and picked up the phone.

"Hello, sweetheart," said a voice.

He was put on the spot. The booth squeezed and the open stage taunted.

217

"Hello, sweetheart," repeated the voice.

He stiffened. He relaxed. Then, much as the empty air contracts into a flash of lightning, he spat out: "Hello, bitch."

There was a moment of silence. Then, with an obscure happiness —she could not see him—he began to gush words. They came without order or meaning: "cock, shit, fuck, cunt, goddamn, mother-fucking."

Afterwards Billy was gentle with himself. The Cat's Paw was so awful that anything that happened there was too good for it. No one had seen him; he took care on the way out to remain unobserved, and he slept soundly that night. But in the morning he couldn't shake the curiously sweet smell of the place from his clothes.

CHAPTER
ELEVEN

I

At a surprise party for Theodore Oatis, given on his fortieth birthday, Penelope, who hatched the plot, decided that the guests were not having a good enough time. They looked too "self-involved," she told Kelly. It was time for a little action, she declared, time to "juggle the deck." She jerked Billy from one corner and planted him beside Kelly. She stole Jennings from another corner. Then she ordered the three of them into the kitchen to light the candles on an enormous birthday cake. At the proper time she said, "Kelly, you take in the cake"—but relented when everyone protested that she should do the honors.

They followed her into the living room, then stood together as the party sang "Happy Birthday." Once the song ended, conversation became necessary. "How are you?" Billy asked Kelly.

"Fine—thank you for the letter."

She turned toward Jennings. "How's work?"

Jennings turned toward Billy. "We're busy, aren't we?"

And Penelope cried: "Quick! Plates! Plates!"

2

Kelly left early. She was worried that Oatis would ask her out, and it was too crowded to talk to Jennings. On the way home she criticized herself for being mercurial. She had gone to the party in order to circulate more, and she had enjoyed herself at first, sipping and chatting and teasing and smiling; she had also looked pretty, she thought, earning a sidelong glance from Penelope and several men. But Jennings was ill at ease with Billy there. And Oatis used the prerogative of birthday boy to kiss her twice. And Billy himself frightened her. His anger no longer seemed directed into the air, as it had during his speech, but at her.

The anguish in his letter, which she had recently received, astonished her. It seemed crazily disproportionate to her crime. What was that crime after all, but a bit of impulsive rudeness? Why should he care? She regretted hurting him, but she did not deserve the cold fury of a letter mailed so long after the event, with the two clipped sentences, the sarcasm passing as concern, the contraction of the word "love." She felt arraigned before an obscure and indiscriminate anger, a kind of hard white glittering, as eerily insubstantial as a mirror she could pass her hand through. At the party he had treated her coolly, while remaining close by. Each glance turned her into someone she was not, as if to steal her from herself, until she had the strange impression that the New York she had spurned was turning against her in revenge.

She told herself this was self-centered nonsense, but did not listen. No friend was there to agree. Nor could she easily dismiss Billy as a pest, having never acquired the knack of ignoring others. And so she felt more and more isolated. From a private outpost she examined the decoration of the apartment, where money had done the work of imagination, and studied the guests feeding on hors d'oeuvre: their fingers, she thought, plucked like minnows at the carcass of a salmon. She imagined suddenly leaping onto the food-strewn table, causing a great clatter of silver. In the distant rooms, as she tapped her spoon against a crystal glass, the babble would subside. "I regret to tell you," she would say, collecting eyes, "that each and every one of you—yes, one and all, each and every one of you is a . . . gargoyle." Then she would pause. "Yes, you too . . . Yes, I'm afraid so, you too . . . Yes . . . Yes, I wish I had better news . . . Yes, sorry. And Jennings, alas—"

It was soon after this fantasy that Kelly departed, walking west on Fifty-ninth Street alongside the park. The soft and muggy evening, like a warm felt cloth, brought a gleam into her face. Her hair, damp and dark, fell around her eyes, which shone too brightly. She walked, and a couple divided to let her pass. She walked, and the colors of night blurred before her, the white of onrushing headlights merging with the red of receding cars. She remembered Oatis, she remembered Billy, she remembered the fingers that plucked like minnows; and she shivered hard. She remembered Jennings, and blushed. Hot flashes alternated with cold. Disgust quarreled with hope. She walked and she walked. And then she couldn't put up with it anymore.

She increased her sense of control, yielding to neither her disgust nor her hope. Then she squeezed out the last drop of self-pity and, as the city trembled, tightened up still more until she suddenly gave way to something different, a kind of madness. It came as a relief, like the parting of a taut rope, which leaves behind a feeling of lightness and airy power. The exact moment of giving way also had a particular sweetness. It resembled one of her favorite parts of lovemaking, the time of coming together when, as the man eased into her, she relaxed into a moment of peace before the tumble toward bliss. She was able, for a minute or two, to walk down the street without thinking. Then she glanced up sharply. Her mood, one of intensified detachment, was fine, hard, and clear.

There was nothing outlandish in this madness, last experienced the year before. The bumpy world simply receded behind her, as behind an ascending plane, until she stared into a focused landscape, one clarified by a blue light that was severe but not unpleasant, like the glint off the best steel. In that light she could study everyone at the party, including herself, and care about each from afar. She could do the same with New York. She did not dismiss the energy or messy menace of the city, but she herself now culled the images from her surroundings, rather than letting the city present them to her. She arranged these images into her own messages. A lit telephone booth recalled a lunatic who once howled into a pay phone next to hers; he leapt into the air to propel his outrage into the receiver. A teenage boy, walking toward her armed with a radio—and she let him walk directly, indolently, at her. His radio might blare, she might step aside. But it was not necessary to do so.

She liked playing with such images. They seemed a little small-minded, however, in the severe blue light. She dreamed of doing something herself, something extraordinary. She longed to make a resounding objection against things as they were, a gesture of grace, perhaps. There would be no whimpering, no teary accommodation, no coming of age. Nothing self-pitying or indulgent or wounding to others, like suicide. Nothing vain or malicious, like the usual blistering article. No, it would be an action that was clean, general, abstract; one that rose above the sticky particular. A disinterested act of the private will, set in the severe blue light—what could be more beautiful?

3

Because Sylvia liked expensive restaurants, Kelly took her to Ma Tante for the second interview, hoping to bill the meal to whatever magazine bought the article. She selected the restaurant partly for its name, to tease herself for taking an almost familial interest in Sylvia. She also knew Sylvia would be impressed. At Ma Tante the cuisine was *nouvelle*, the style was peasant chic—stone walls, wood tables, oversized tableware, bright accents of blue and white —and the maître d' was young, handsome, and French. His charm was made of crushed velvet, and his brother was the chef.

This time Kelly planned to ask riskier questions. She wanted to learn more about Sylvia's private feelings, though she did not intend to ask about The Cat's Paw unless Sylvia herself wanted to talk about it. That Sylvia would lie, as she had before, did not concern Kelly. Lies possessed their own kind of truth.

"There you are!" She waved to Sylvia across the street.

"I'm late?"

"No, but look at you!"

Kelly spread her arms, in appreciation of Sylvia's outfit. She wore a red silk bandanna, an electric-green blouse and baby-blue designer jeans. It was obvious the clothes were bought for this meeting.

"You like it?"

"Love it."

"I thought it might clash a little."

"What's wrong with a little clashing?"

"That's what *I* said."

"It looks—"

"You can do whatever you want today. Be creative."

"Why not?"

"Today everyone's an individual."

Sylvia spoke with certainty, as if she had just read an article.

"Today everyone's an individual," Kelly repeated slowly. Then she laughed—a kind laugh.

"What's so funny?"

"You."

"I thought you liked them."

"I do."

"You're weird. I mean, I don't want to insult you or anything—"

The maître d' gave them a better table than Kelly expected. Would mesdames like a cocktail? Kelly asked for the wine list. She wanted her subject tipsy but not drunk; a drunken Sylvia would put on too many airs. In any case, despite her clothing, Sylvia seemed more nervous than before. She had decided, it seemed, to proceed with the article.

"Did you come from Prendergast's?"

"I'm off today. Anyway I only work there part-time, so I can do my dancing."

Kelly turned on the tape recorder: Sylvia brushed her hair.

"What's it like working at Prendergast's?"

"I enjoy it, yes."

"Talk naturally. You sound fine. Anyway I told you you can see anything I use."

"Yes, I enjoy it."

"I'm glad you do."

It took two glasses of wine to help Sylvia forget the tape recorder. She would forget, remember, then forget again, jerking from the pompous to the colloquial. At last Kelly coaxed out her real opinion of Prendergast's.

"It's all right, I guess . . . boring, though, know what I mean? All these old bags, I mean Jesus Christ. Sorry."

"But you like cosmetics? At least, you wear a lot."

223

"I like to put it on *me*, not on them. They do this, they do that, they do this." She mimicked a woman in front of a mirror. "Gives me a pain."

"Why do you like putting it on yourself?"

"Why, why, why! Like my dad says, 'Why's the sky blue?' " Her eyes turned vague, then darted toward Kelly. "How come you don't wear more? It's fun. How come?"

"I do wear some—but I guess I don't like to paint myself up for men."

"Might help a couple of your features. But look, let's be frank. Are we being frank?"

Kelly nodded.

"Okay. This is what the deal is." Sylvia sipped her wine, lit a cigarette, inhaled, exhaled, considered. "You have good eyes. You could have great eyes. You understand the difference? You have good cheekbones. You could have great cheekbones. Put a little highlight here, little blush there." Her fingers played across Kelly's face. "So we're being frank, right?"

"What kind of highlight?"

Sylvia told her the best brands. "You got good eyes so you don't need to overdo it, you don't need to *pretend*. You understand what I'm saying?"

Kelly sent away the waiter, then asked, "Now, where does this highlight go?" For ten minutes they discussed a makeup strategy for Kelly. They also finished the bottle of wine, and ordered another. To talk to a woman about things of interest only to women—the actual topic did not matter much—gave Kelly intense pleasure. There was some danger, however, of forgetting the business at hand. "I'll try it," she said, referring to the highlight.

"Understand I'm not pushing it, just if you want some advice."

There was a pause.

"Modern dance must be very interesting."

"I enjoy it, yes."

"I mean—Well, I never understood what people *do* in a modern dance class."

"It's like this," said Sylvia, becoming serious. "Art requires effort."

"Kneebends?"

"*Splits*. Can you do a split?"

"No."

"Technique. Let me say that again. *Technique*."

Sylvia lit another cigarette. "Technique is everything. And technique is nothing." She paused. "Technique is just the floor, you understand what I'm saying? It's the floor on which you raise the . . . art. Or it's the soil . . . of the soul." She hesitated. "Actually I didn't make that up myself. That's my teacher."

"What kind of art do you want to raise?"

"That's the thing you're not allowed to ask."

"What?"

"Artists don't like to talk about it. I know that for a fact."

"How come?"

She shrugged.

"You just want to express yourself," Kelly suggested.

"That's it. Express myself." She ground out the cigarette. "You see, art can't be described. It's something beyond, out there." She waved her hand. "I won't say cosmic or anything, but, well, it's like another language." She hesitated. "I didn't make that up either."

"You seem to like your teacher."

"She's okay."

"Just okay?"

"Well, okay."

Kelly asked for the teacher's name, to find out her reputation. She wondered how Sylvia got along with the college girls, who received allowances from their parents. "How long have you been taking classes?"

"We started in school—gym class. I was pretty good at it. No, I was the best. So I don't know. I thought that's what I ought to do."

"You didn't graduate, did you?"

"What do I need to graduate for? My friend, she just graduated and she hasn't done anything. Sits around all day."

"It's pretty hard to get a job in modern dance."

"Like I said, art requires effort."

The distant look came into her eyes.

"But—"

She looked up. "Sure, I know. It's a bitch. But I have prospects. The teacher says so." She lit a fresh cigarette and stared at the tape recorder. "I'm going to tell you what I'm really good at, okay? Here goes. What I'm good at is flowing *with* the music or *against*

225

the music, all depending on my—you know. After that, well, I *combine* them in a single piece."

Kelly teased her, "Thesis, antithesis, synthesis."

"How'd you guess? . . . I forgot, you're a teacher too."

The waiter brought their meal. Once again Sylvia had ordered filet mignon, though she planned to become a vegetarian—under the influence, Kelly guessed, of some other dancers. For a few minutes, between bites, they discussed the practical side of her dancing lessons: their cost and length, the music, the exercises, the number of students in the class. "Have you made friends?"

Sylvia shrugged. "Some."

Kelly took a chance.

"You haven't really made friends, have you?"

Behind the circles of paint Sylvia's eyes began to cloud over. That was all Kelly needed to know. She would definitely drop in at the dance studio, to determine how snobbish it was. She imagined the instructress—graying hair pulled tightly back, something English in the accent, a story on occasion about her friendship with Martha Graham, presented to the students as a gift.

Sylvia said, "Some people are nice."

"But?"

The words began to tumble. "Sometimes I think they just want my money, but they do really well placing people and sometimes famous dancers, you know, they come and give guest lessons —but I don't, you know, go out with the girls afterwards."

Kelly remembered that Sylvia was seventeen. Alone in New York, without parents or friends, she seemed willing to defer to Kelly. Kelly reminded herself that Sylvia was at the age when social standing was of vast importance, when it was possible to talk about the meaning of life without irony or shading or embarrassment. She had led Sylvia to do exactly these things; now, unexpectedly, she began to feel some responsibility for her. "And men?" she asked. "Any nice boys in the class?"

"I got plenty of boyfriends." Her eyes became saucy. "How about you?" The big sister was being teased.

"I don't really have any."

"I know what you mean."

"You just said you had lots of boyfriends!"

The expert in makeup lit another cigarette, then said, "We still being frank?"

Kelly smiled. "Sure."

"I have lots of boyfriends, but I don't have *a* boyfriend."

"Not a steady boyfriend?"

"Just kids."

Suddenly Sylvia brightened. "You ever made it with Billy Bell?"

"No."

"Oh, sorry."

"I don't *want* to!"

"You don't like sex?"

"Sure I like sex."

"Well, *lady*, I don't understand you. You'd turn down, I mean, I could see it maybe if you had this heavy other thing, but—"

"Well, do you mess around a lot?"

"It's natural, right?"

"Sure."

"Zippers unzip: it's organic."

Kelly tightened.

"You don't—"

"Tricks? No. 'Course I could if I wanted."

"And no steady boyfriend?"

"I had a steady boyfriend on the Island but that's over I guess." She paused—and smiled shyly. "I tell you, if I ever see that mother again I'm going to cut off his prick."

"What'd he do?"

"Wouldn't call, other girls, heavy into drugs, things like that."

"Good riddance."

"That's what I say. Anyway, just kids."

"There's nothing wrong with seeing people your own age."

"I got plenty of boyfriends, I told you that. But next to, you know, I'm not saying Billy Bell—"

"You shouldn't think like that!" Kelly leaned forward, speaking with some heat. "You're thinking there's men with a little 'm', the 'kids' that you see, and then there's"—her voice assumed an exaggerated deepness—"MEN. Some mystical MAN out there. If you think like that, you'll be miserable. Billy Bell's just a screwed-up male who happens to be famous, not so different from—"

"I've had two abortions."

"What!"

"So you see, I've got plenty of experience. I don't need anyone to tell me where to get on, where to get off."

There was a pause.

"How did it happen?"

Sylvia mimicked the voice of a teacher. "Well, *first* he stuck his you-know-what into—"

"Why didn't you use birth control?"

She shrugged.

"So the abortions were no problem?"

The vague look. "No sweat."

"There ought to be some sweat."

Sylvia looked directly at her. "No sweat."

Kelly finished her meal. After a while Sylvia said, "You're mad at me. What did I do?" She did not appear disappointed. Making Kelly angry was an accomplishment.

"I'm not angry."

"Yes you are."

"No I'm not."

"So much wine, Jesus Christ we've drunk so much wine!"

"You've drunk it."

"Hey, listen, you did okay."

Kelly smiled. She could not help it. She asked Sylvia if she wanted dessert. The girl, studying the pastry tray, selected strawberry shortcake and flirted with the maître d' for an extra portion of whipped cream. Then Kelly, not wanting to ask more questions, told her about Montana. She knew Sylvia would be impressed to learn that some of the men still wore cowboy hats, though the truth was that fewer and fewer of the real cowboys did.

4

At home, Kelly, still tipsy, called Jennings at the office. There was transferring, clicking, "one moment, please." Then Jennings said, "Hello?"

"It's me."

"Hi."

"Well, I'm glad you made me do this story. She's nice—I actually like her. Really, I'm not kidding, and she's not dumb either, though her head is filled with all kinds of junk, especially about famous men. Billy, I told her I knew Billy and her eyes almost fell out. Anyway I haven't asked her the hardest questions yet—next time—but she's already told me some interesting things. Once I see the place she lives and the modern dance studio, where she goes several times a week, I may take a trip to the Island, actually just to see the house where she grew up. But I like her, that's the main point."

"I never heard you say so many words in a row."

"Well, we drank almost two bottles of wine. But what I'm calling about, I said I'd call you, so here I am. Would you like to come over to my place for dinner?"

"All right."

"Don't sound so enthusiastic."

"Well—"

"Is there someone with you?"

"Yes."

"Who?"

There was a pause.

"You can't say. Well, next Friday evening all right?"

"I have to go to a speech. My job."

" 'Someone there.' Well, when would you like?"

"Saturday's good."

"Eight o'clock?"

"See you then."

There was a pause.

"Was that Kelly?" Billy asked.

"Yes."

"How is she?"

"Fine."

"It was nice to see her the other day."

There was a pause.

"How's her story coming?"

"She says very well—sounds enthusiastic."

"What's the girl's name?"

"Sylvia Rogers."

"Sylvia Rogers."

There was a pause.

"She's the subject of the profile?"

"Yes."

"She works at Prendergast's too?"

Jennings nodded.

"Amazing."

There was a pause.

Billy smiled. "We done?"

"Guess so."

5

Jennings stopped outside the room where he once edited tape, wondering who now did that work. The room was empty. Seating himself behind the monitor, he ran back some recent clips. They were mediocre, but he was not critical. He believed he could not have improved them even if he had wanted to. His skills remained the same, but his outlook had changed. He no longer knew how to make the right decisions for Billy.

Outside the room he heard several voices pass by. The silence they left behind seemed oddly private—all his. He began to fool around. He ran tapes this way or that, juxtaposed the images, experimented with length. He lost himself in play. This eased the pressure on him and refreshed his imagination. When the door opened, he did not notice—then whirled around, expecting Billy.

"I was just going to get an old tape," said the intern whose name he did not know. "Are you still doing this? I thought—"

"I'm not any more."

She looked curious. So he told her to sit down. "What are you doing for Billy these days?"

She sat on the edge of the chair, to indicate she only had a moment. "Just errands, but I actually did one of the tapes myself . . . You weren't here."

"Did you like doing it?"

"Very much."

Jennings glanced at the monitor. "I was playing. Seriously, I like to play with these gadgets, just to see what I can do now that I never did before."

She nodded. To humor me, Jennings thought. She would not

understand what he meant, so he simply said "I hope you stay happy."

"Yes, well . . ." She stood up. "I better give this to Mr. Bell."

6

Billy told the intern that no, he did not have time right now. Kelly and Jennings were no doubt on the phone—perhaps right then, at that very second. He would have called her back, and she would read and reread the letter to him. Perhaps she had already sent a Xerox to Oatis, who would release the letter to the papers. Billy's embarrassment, honed at the cocktail party, sharpened still more. He assumed her remark acknowledging the letter—"Thank you for the letter"—was sarcastic. Or worse than sarcastic, because delivered in a deadpan voice: condescending.

He forced himself to work. He dictated a long letter to the attorney whom he wanted to head the campaign, and he composed a model fund-raising letter. He skimmed the book of a writer to be interviewed the next day. By six o'clock he had decided to write Kelly a second letter. He made himself two drinks. He remembered enough about the circumstances of the first letter, however, to drink with care. There was no way he would write her a drunken letter at 3:00 A.M.

He sat quietly. It was odd, but he could not remember what she looked like.

This letter came easily:

Dear Kelly,
I hope you will forgive me for the letter I wrote you the other day. I have recently been under considerable strain. There are some important decisions to be made. Perhaps Jennings has told you about them—in any case, I won't bore you with the details. Again, please accept my apologies, and I hope your work is progressing to your satisfaction.
Yours sincerely,
Billy Bell

7

In the morning Billy regretted having sent this letter, too. At least, he told himself, the second was less offensive than the first. Later in the morning, however, his concern increased. He had forgotten to make a copy of the letter, and he could not remember his exact words. Perhaps he had been drunker than he thought. Perhaps something unintended had slipped in. The phrasing might have been awkward, the tone wrong. Assaulted by doubt, he felt his confidence erode until he lost all idea of what he had written. The two letters, he thought, made a mad pair. She would never want to see him again. She would show the letters to more and more people, especially when his political prospects improved. Even if the letter was harmless, wouldn't she think it strange that he felt obligated to write a second time? Wouldn't she consider him ridiculous?

It was a relief to tape his show. He found the red eye relaxing, though he was somewhat less certain of his touch. His ratings, however, had never been better. What mattered, he reminded himself, was his professional ability. This business with Kelly—so what? Soon after the taping, as he was unwinding at his desk, Teitelman called to ask him to breakfast at an uptown hotel. He wanted to discuss strategy. Billy's sense of power increased until he was able, almost, to excise Kelly from his thoughts. He buzzed his secretary: "Do I have a lunch today?"

He did—Jennings.

"Oh damn!"

Should she cancel it?

He thought for a moment. "No."

He buzzed Jennings. "Let's go somewhere expensive."

He selected SoHo's most fashionable restaurant, a rich and punky place called, with tongue in cheek, Dressage. Show-biz celebrities liked Dressage, which was designed to look like a Parisian brasserie, but with an added touch of art deco swank. At Dressage it was best to be known—less as a regular customer than as a personality. Billy pushed past the crowd at the bar until he found the maître d', an elegant homosexual who always wore an

232

expensive scarf, the sort that would look good snapping behind the driver of an open MG. The maître d' refused to fawn over the famous; it was understood he was part of whatever the best crowd was doing. Despite his silken indifference, however, he was at hand for the right people. To help Jennings slide onto a banquette, he turned back a table with elegant concision—and like a good bullfighter turning a lazy bull disdained such an easy effect. Then, leaving, he glanced over his shoulder. "We have truffles today."

Billy called him back. "How are you serving them?"

The maître d' recited a list of dishes, and Billy dismissed him. Then Billy informed Jennings of his decision to hire an attorney, recommended by Teitelman, to run the campaign.

"Good idea. I've heard he's excellent."

"He won't get in the way of anything at the station. I'll have one life at the station and another in politics."

"You'll have to leave the station to run."

"The producer said he'd welcome me back anytime."

Jennings could not care less, Billy thought, whether I succeed or fail. Look at him: without fizz. It was a miracle they were allowed in the restaurant.

"The Yankees are doing well this summer," Jennings said. "You must be miserable."

"I haven't been following too closely. Haven't had time."

"They murdered the Orioles last week. And the Dodgers are playing like they're still in spring training. You *must* be miserable."

"I just don't have the time."

"Not only are they dominating the league, they're also lucky. The other teams are hurt by all kinds of injuries. The Yankees hardly have a sore arm."

Billy thought Jennings looked smug with gossip, as if he might mention the letter at any moment. Jennings shouldn't treat me like this, Billy thought, not after so many years, not when Jennings was the employee. "If the Yankees win it's only because of money. What kind of victory is that?"

"Still victory."

"Some victory."

Billy asked for a very good bottle of wine. He ordered the truffles. "That what you're ordering too?"

233

"I don't think so."

"You ought to."

"Well, I just—"

Billy waved the maître d' over and together they talked Jennings into a shrug—okay, he would have the truffles.

Then, like someone settling down to business, Billy said, "I've decided I want you to look for another job."

Jennings smiled.

Billy, shocked, looked away. He had wanted surprise, hurt, anger. "In other words," he said, "you're fired."

Jennings smiled.

Billy's fingers trembled.

It soon became an issue who would speak first. Then, suddenly, they both laughed. "I wanted to have this lunch," Billy said, "so we could discuss finding you another job. I might be able to help, if we pinpoint what it is that you'd like to do."

"I'll be fine. No help necessary."

"It was clear you'd lost all interest in the job at the station."

"Yes I had."

"You can take as long as you like to leave."

"Couple of days is all I need."

They passed the rest of the meal in silence, broken only by the occasional exclamation over truffles. Once, having called over the maître d', Billy began to compliment the chef at such length that, in the end, the maître d' walked away. And so, over coffee, Billy daydreamed about his future political power. This did not, however, lessen his bitterness: he could not feel powerful anymore without feeling weak. When Jennings wished him good luck in politics, Billy thought, "I just fired you."

8

Jennings, impressed by his own power, welcomed the firing. Billy could take his job, but not shake his confidence. Who then was the stronger? He owed his new power to that intense compression of force, that deepening guilt and passivity, which came from his stingy treatment of others. This internal pressure gave him the strength to wrench free of Billy and deadened his fear of change, the way an anesthetic deadens the nerves. It helped to destroy a job, a friendship, and one shape assumed by his character. He could not work comfortably through another any more.

He continued, nonetheless, to worry about Billy. His old friend seemed so different! Once upon a time Billy had moved through life in a straight line; or relaxed, seemingly without a care. Now he appeared maundering and lost. He would toy with a glass, look up, glance away, put down a fork. Jennings did not worry too much, however, since he was so struck by his own behavior. Shucking part of his past had left him lightheaded. Suddenly, despite his passivity, he wanted to float on impulse, to talk, to act, to do. And Prendergast's still seemed to be the right mirror, as flattering to his exuberance as to his torpor. He called Tom, who told him to come by in an hour. In the meantime, he said, Jennings should visit Home Furnishings, where he would find a surprise. Jennings shook his head with pleasure. He meant to enjoy this surprise, whatever it was. Since their last meeting, Tom, promising to walk in public once a day, had offered $10,000 to the person who first photographed him. Feature writers and television reporters played up the contest, and a clever *Times* reporter noted that the contest, while enlivening a dull summer, advertised Tom's business. People came to Prendergast's hoping to win $10,000, said the writer, but left owing the store money.

Prendergast's was full of teenagers with cameras. They did not have much money, Jennings guessed, and they probably stole things. He wondered how good the summer figures would be. He took the escalator up several flights, then watched the store dance below him, mad with color and hooting with noise. He told himself, as usual, that it was wonderful. And then, for the first time, he felt disappointed. This lasted only a moment. It was not fair, having just won his freedom, to admit new doubts. He rode up another flight and examined the store with ferocious gaiety. He relished its oddities, lost himself in its twirling powers, admired Tom's shaping of style. The arrangement of the Crescent was brilliant.

At Home Furnishings he found nothing unusual. He recognized the spidery salesman who sold Kelly her bed and remembered how she had jumped up and down on the mattress, indifferent to the looks of passers-by.

Then he saw Tom.

He looked again.

Tom winked.

"T——."

"Shhhh."

Tom, standing near the sheet and towel department, wore scuffed shoes, old green trousers, and a T-shirt. He often dressed that way, but in public the clothes made him look like a man from the maintenance department.

Jennings said, "Here?"

"Did you think I was lying about the walks?"

"Yes."

Tom's head shook—in sadness, it seemed, over mankind's incurable mistrust. "Sometimes I walk around like this, and no one would ever think *that's* Tom Prendergast. Other times I dress up a little and strap a camera on my shoulder. Then they think I'm looking for Tom Prendergast."

There was a pause.

"So how are you?"

In Tom's expression, lit by the small smile, Jennings noticed for the first time a glimmering that he could not quite understand, almost a look of worry. And once again he felt disappointed. The trick was good, but it bored him. Tom's kind of fun, the right kind of fun, seemed almost as stale as working for Billy. Still, he refused to let his spirits sag. That small smile—Tom was the master of the private joke, he thought, a person who pulled strings to make the world dance! Jennings, also experienced in working behind the scenes, saw in Tom's approach a much more powerful, worldly, and artful expression of his own ways. As he looked at the disheveled little man, worth millions, he told himself he loved the tricks of Prendergast's. They were examples of superior honesty. Wasn't there some mean motive at the bottom of even the fanciest virtues? Wasn't the truth always vulgar?

As Jennings boosted his spirits, he began to tease Tom with threats. "Fabulous!" he shouted. "Ladies and gentlemen, with me I have here—"

Several people turned round. Tom, his face wrinkling with unscheduled worry, hurried away.

"Excuse me, ladies and gentlemen, I've simply had a little too much to *imbibe*."

A salesman, prepared to summon a guard, watched Jennings and Tom scoot from Home Furnishings. "Got to get out of here," mumbled Tom. "Goddamn maniac on my tail." Once out of danger, Tom said, "Hard to know where to do the deed. Hard to know where to get caught. Well, not up here obviously. Either on the main floor where there will be lots of witnesses. Or"—he winked at Jennings—"intimate apparel?"

"Intimate apparel!"

"Shhhh."

"Intimate apparel!"

"Awfully corny, I know. Trashy. I don't know, perhaps another idea . . ."

"Intimate apparel it is! You have to. As your adviser I insist. Intimate apparel!"

Jennings pumped more and more air into his mood, until he could hardly speak without exclaiming. The volume of his voice became the measure of his happiness.

Tom stopped. "You really think it's okay? Perhaps there's a better plan. I might have one. Must stew over it, though."

"What plan! What! Omtay Endergastpray, what is your plan?"

"Don't worry. You've earned your money. But . . ."

"Yes?"

"Could you lead your friend to a certain spot of Ladies' Underwear—Private Parts? Not the main floor intimate apparel."

"My man!"

"Have to stew over it."

"But no men are allowed there!"

"We'll take care of that."

"My man!"

Tom, thoughtful, decided to return home. He waved Jennings into a service tunnel, at the end of which was a locked door that led to more tunnels and locked doors, then at last to the private entrance to the apartment. Tom said little. Jennings, who kept up a constant patter, sounded more like Tom than Tom. "And now," Tom said, letting Jennings help himself from the Frigidaire, "you have to telephone this Lamb."

"Love to."

Tom held up a telephone receiver.

237

"Remember, it's a secret between you two. Offer to split the money. She gets the credit. And she can't know the game comes from me."

Jennings hushed Tom.

"Penelope, my lady, I have a proposition for you." He looked at Tom. "She's gone to the other phone."

"You can reveal it in a few years," Tom said. "It'll just make me look like a clever scoundrel. Any sooner and the teenagers will lynch me."

Jennings hushed him again.

"Penelope, my lady—what?—oh, don't be so touchy." Her irritation set off his outlandish manner. "Listen, old girl," he said, glancing at Tom, "would you like to be the person who photographs Tom Prendergast? You know the contest? . . ."

The more manic Jennings became, the quieter Tom seemed.

"So it's all right . . . I'll call you later to settle the details." He looked at Tom again. "Done."

"Bravo."

"You're not kidding, bravo. Don't you have anything to celebrate with around here? Just beer, Coke—"

"I never saw you in such a good mood."

"Me?"

"You must have worked it out with the girl."

Jennings sat down. He did not want to tell Tom anything serious about Kelly or the firing. He did not want to translate those things into Tom's tone of voice. It seemed worse, however, to yield to his vague disappointment; and worse still to admit to a desire to nurse in private his feelings about Billy and Kelly. So he said, "No problem, all worked out." And then, because this sounded defensive, he dragged her into the open. "I took your advice—just sort of *eased* out of the situation with the lady, it's the best way with women, never fails, just kind of *ease* away . . . Hold on!" He stood up. "Not only that, but today I was fired. I've been daring him to fire me, can you imagine that. Fired and free, that's the way to be."

"Could've just quit."

"Fired and free, the way to be! Change everything around, little razzle here, dazzle there. I should write one of those self-help books, you mentioned that once. I could call it 'Fired and Free.'"

"King for a Day."

"President Me."

Tom, unable to best President Me, fell silent. Then he said, "I'm exhausted. I'm sick of coming up with ideas. I don't know what I'll do when I come out."

"You're not allowed to be depressed, not you of all people. Come on, rich as hell, going to get richer, not only the best in the business, not only a great merchandiser but inspired, do you hear, inspired! Someday sociologists will write books about you and your store."

"Thanks a lot."

"You're scared of your little ploy? Tom Prendergast is chicken?"

"I don't know if it'll do me any good. These stupid night-mares—"

"You're sounding sorry for yourself."

"What's wrong with that?"

"You have plenty of energy."

"I'll lose my sight. You don't know it, but right now, by reading every magazine and newspaper, I can guess, ninety percent of the time, what people think they want. If I have to go outside, walk around, talk to people"—he opened his hands—"mud in my eye."

"Don't the designers always say they get their ideas from mar-velous girls walking on the streets of Paris or Milan or New York? Come on, the street, actual life—"

"Garbage. People on the street usually look terrible. That's the fact. I'm surprised at you, bad consulting there. 'Actual life,' what a phrase, 'actual life,' no wonder you were fired. 'Actual life,' as you put it, makes bad boring business. Anyway, I have to think this through. I'm tired—all those goddamn ideas, everyone needs ideas from me, picks me clean. A Labor Day display for shoes."

"Just a little work. You have a great touch."

"I guess so. Right. Okay, I come out." Tom stood up, began to pace. "I'm a star, give fancy parties, maybe you're right, people will love the great rich star. Maybe it'll work. Hell, it's not hard to be stylish. Actual life, what an idea—the trick is to live a certain way, in a certain style. I can arrange that. Sure, Tom Prendergast can arrange that."

"Deep down you'll be the same anyway."

"Deep down!" roared Tom.

Jennings wondered why, after trying to help Tom, he had said something so obviously provoking. But it served in the end to upset

239

Tom into better spirits. "Deep down!" Tom shouted. "Who wants to know what's deep down?" He assumed a fey English accent. "My dear fellow, isn't a spot of class, a touch of style, a bit of elegant, how should I put it, *hipfaking* . . ." Then his voice changed to the supplication of a vulgar aunt: "The dear good Lord above help us!"

CHAPTER

TWELVE

I

Without a job Jennings spent almost all his time in his apartment. His passivity became practiced. He did not block every thought, only those that seemed important. This was like stopping part of a well. Fresh impressions, damp and unexpected, surfaced in corners of his mind; long lost things bobbed up. He passed whole days among junked memories—and not just those from his adolescence. He would remember his old dented bicycle, a worn carpet in a Village apartment, the salt on a Long Island breeze. These memories emerged without shape, and he found nothing remarkable in them. It was not the images that were important, but his ability to reach them. As his mind grew more vivid, he possessed fresh access, developed broader reach.

At times, when he wanted rest, he watched the worst possible television with utter belief, like a child. Soap opera was best. He enjoyed the evenness of the tone, the sameness of the sets, the liquid eyes. What attracted him most, however, was the strong narrative. He loved gliding from one event to the next without an end in view. It was as restful as being led by the hand. At other times, when he tired of his apartment, he let Kelly lead him, following her at a distance wherever she went. One hot morning he waited for her in a greasy spoon, drinking coffee until his nerves hummed; and then, surprisingly, she appeared, walking past the glass front. He followed her to Central Park, where he spent the morning dangling on her whim. She walked with determination across the Sheep's Meadow or sat on a rock glittering with mica. She studied the defeated lions in their cages and smiled as the children spun on the carrousel. A noisy softball game stopped her. And then there was time to skirt the Reflecting Pond.

He observed her with care: the white of her blouse, startling against the grass, the soft ripple of her figure. She often drew back her hair from her eyes and sometimes she slapped her side with one hand, in accompaniment to a thought. Jennings, keenly aware of the space between them, kept himself back. Distance let him nurture his desire, a strange fresh desire that was not narrowly focused, but more like an erotic apprehension of the world at large. This new kind of desire was still weak. Satisfaction could kill it, the way a candle is guttered by its own wax.

She led him to Central Park West, where the tarry heat rolled up from the pavement, then crossed to Columbus Avenue. She stopped in front of a restaurant. He stopped too, a block and a half away. Someone arrived, perhaps Sylvia. Then Kelly disappeared behind the door. She left behind in Jennings a trembling like the shiver of candlelight when a door is closed. Subsequently he became aware of another kind of beauty—of things glimpsed but not seen.

2

The restaurant was a West Side place with quiche like any other quiche—the sort of restaurant, Kelly thought, where the girls who left out Sylvia would go for an impromptu lunch. She selected it because she wanted Sylvia to attach less importance to expensive restaurants; she ought to abandon, or at least modify, some of her romantic conceptions about money, celebrity, and style. Otherwise she would suffer too much.

This time Kelly meant to ask Sylvia about her love for celebrities.

She also wanted to know what Sylvia thought about when she posed at The Cat's Paw. It was Kelly's intuition that the two were related. As part of a fawning audience the girl surrendered her own significance to the idealized figure; then, onstage and idealized herself, she yielded to the male dream of a woman's body. Both as a fantasizer and as an object of fantasy, in short, she gave herself over to somebody else. Kelly could conceptualize this, but she wanted to do more: she wanted to feel as Sylvia felt, to know what she knew. This desire was stimulated in part by her experience with Billy, whose second letter she found more polite but no less strange than the first. Why did he turn her into a kind of mannequin, an image to suit his own purposes? She herself saw him as little more than a mannequin, since he changed so radically depending upon his circumstances.

She began slowly, asking Sylvia for facts about her parents and school. The girl replied with a flurry of her own questions. What had Kelly learned? So how many interviews would there be? So what magazine would publish it? Sylvia, with a plan of her own, looked determined to defend herself and offended by the choice of restaurant. It was not long, however, before the wine and Kelly's straightforward replies reassured her. Soon she became as pliable as ever, and then almost anxious to talk. Kelly noticed that Sylvia's clothes were less outrageous this time—perhaps she did not feel she could wear the same thing twice or was copying Kelly's quieter style. She wore more makeup than usual, though: her eyes were two black stars.

Kelly mentioned, as if it were nothing, that she'd recently seen Billy Bell.

"Again!" Sylvia squinted. "So anything nice happen?"

"No, we just chatted briefly."

"Too bad."

"I don't understand what you see in him."

"He's good-looking."

"Less so, off TV."

"Still."

"What do you think about when you see him on TV?"

Sylvia shrugged. "He's good-looking."

Kelly, prompting, said, "You imagine him in your arms?"

"Getting heavy here." Sylvia picked apart a book of matches. "I never really *imagined* it . . . or, that's not true, yes I did."

"And why's it so wonderful?"

There was a pause.

"Come on, you can tell me."

She arranged the loose matches into a circle. "I like to be held."

"Anybody can hold you."

The vagueness entered her eyes. "But to be held by someone like that . . ."

"Anyone like that?"

"Someone like that, you know."

"Lots of them?"

"Lots of good-looking actors, musicians. Some better than others."

"Someone like that would be . . ."

"It'd be unbelievable. It'd be, I don't know, it'd be different. I'd feel . . ."

"Yes?"

"Special. I'd do anything for him, and then I'd have maids too you know."

Sylvia, unable to describe what she meant more clearly, lit a match. In her face Kelly saw a remoteness, very sad, that was eloquent enough, and for which she meant to find words in her article. Wasn't it strange, she thought, how well the sentimental and the hard-boiled went together? Then she remembered her desire to help. She set out to mar Sylvia's fantasy. She said, "Billy Bell just fucks his way through girls."

"I know, I read that. They all do."

"Doesn't that bother you?"

"Movie stars."

"Like boys will be boys?"

"*Not* boys."

"Where'd you read it?"

"Magazines."

This time Sylvia ordered a hamburger, too obviously Kelly thought. Then the girl became unexpectedly surly, as if Kelly's attack on Billy had been directed at her. "Look at that old bag!" she said, pointing to an old woman who sat alone. The woman, twenty years older than anyone else in the restaurant, wore heavy, expensive clothes and costly jewelry.

"Not an old bag."

"An old bag!"

"You might look like that someday."

"Never. I'd commit suicide."

Sylvia repeated, "Goddamn old bag. You see how she dresses? I'd commit suicide." Sylvia, not looking at Kelly, seemed personally offended.

"There must be a lot of baggy old men that try to pick you up at The Cat's Paw."

"Sure, I can handle those guys. I tell them to—"

"But you take off your clothes for them."

"Nothing to be embarrassed about."

"It must be difficult to do."

Sylvia, about to speak, looked away. The violence in her manner subsided. "Not so hard, really."

"Why?"

She rearranged the matches.

"Easier to strip in front of strangers than friends."

"Maybe so but—" Kelly stopped. "But you must feel embarrassed."

"Yeah, well . . ." Sylvia kept time to the rock Muzak with one finger, lightly clicking her lips.

"Bored?"

"I'm not bored."

Kelly, who remembered doing the same thing to her mother, persisted with the questions. She needed to know.

"Can you see the men when you're standing up there?"

Sylvia finished tapping out a rhythm. "Not at the place I work. Lights are too bright in your eyes. Anyway I don't care about the men. I'm doing my dances or resting or exercising. Sometimes on the phone. Pablo doesn't mind, since my body's so good."

"Doesn't mind what?"

"That I practice my exercises, you know, instead of grinding like the other girls."

There was a pause.

"I know it's just a job," Kelly said. "It's good money, it becomes ordinary after a while. But when you started . . . Sylvia, please, tell me what it feels like. To stand up there."

There was a pause.

"Tickles."

245

"What?"

"Feels kind of funny, since you're used to having clothes on. Right?"

"Right."

"All these eyes on you, right?"

"Right."

"Tickles."

Kelly laughed. "Tickles."

"Anybody likes to be admired, right?"

"When you're up there—well, what do you think about?"

"I don't know."

Kelly waited. "Do you think about your dancing?"

"Sometimes."

"Or . . . do you really like it? Standing up there, naked but no touching, intimate and apart. Turn everything inside out, be admired and hated, free and trapped, sort of publicly alone. Feeling clean . . ."

Kelly waited.

"You must think of something."

"My paycheck."

"What else?"

Sylvia shrugged.

"You must think of something else."

"England."

There was a pause.

"You know," Sylvia continued, "on television there's all those shows from England. I like it there. Everything's just right, even when they're unhappy."

"England?"

"You been there?"

"You think about England?"

"Is it like the shows?"

"Not really."

"I don't believe you."

"You should go."

"My friend went and she said they have all the same things as on the shows—you know, tea and palaces and how they talk. They didn't make it all up."

"The phone must interrupt your thinking about England!"

"I don't think about England all the time."

"What else?"

"Sometimes nothing."

"Does the phone surprise you?"

"I know when they turn it on. There's a signal."

"You like talking on the phone?"

"No, but sometimes—well, sometimes I like telling them off. Only it's kind of frustrating, because the meaner you are the more they seem to like it."

Kelly smiled.

"Pablo says I have room for improvement."

"In what?"

"The phone business. I mean, it's boring and besides I'm not a hooker or any of those things."

"Can I see your apartment sometime?"

"I guess being nosy is your job, right?"

Kelly smiled again.

"It's not much of an apartment."

"Neither's mine."

"I don't get how you know Billy Bell."

Kelly described her own apartment, then learned that Sylvia lived in a walkup off Second Avenue on the Upper East Side. Kelly knew those places—roach-infested brownstones with gates on the windows. "Live alone?"

"Yes."

"Must be lonely sometimes."

"I told you. I can take care of myself."

There was a pause.

"Look at that!" Sylvia whispered, nodding toward the old woman. Kelly had been watching her all along. After a salad she ate an ice cream sundae. Then she prepared, with great deliberation, to devour the cherry.

"Like a giant spider!"

"Shhhh."

"I'd rather commit suicide."

The woman noticed that she was being watched. Her pleasure in the cherry, Kelly thought, will now be less. The fat fingers, glittering with diamonds, picked up a knife and fork. Then they slowly sliced the cherry in half. Kelly shivered with disgust and

247

Sylvia, convulsed with giggles, choked on her dessert. Kelly, confused, did not know what was on her mind. To steady herself she wrote some notes when Sylvia left to find a bathroom.

The interview was a success. Something in Sylvia, Kelly wrote, would never give up the obsession with celebrity. It was too important, since it gave her a direction in which to dream. Something in Sylvia also enjoyed walking naked onto the stage. She liked the tickle of recognition; and some recognition was better than none. Onstage was also a good place for fantasy. In the haze Sylvia could imagine a difference—modern dance, England, celebrity. Of course, to someone with her small sense of personal importance the posing also represented considerable aggression. The girl said, "Look at me," then told them to go to hell on the phone. And of course the men could not touch.

Kelly put aside her pencil. Why save the cherry till last? Why wear heavy jewelry, when nothing was lovelier than a delicate gold chain? Why come alone to a restaurant for the young? Perhaps the hard, heavy jewels were a memorial to youth—a sparkling diversion to lure the eyes away from decay. She loved her own youth too much, Kelly thought, I'll never do that. I'll never retire behind jewels. I'll never add as I become less. She dreamed rather of a subtraction like freedom, of an emptying out that brought peace. She left Sylvia at the door to Prendergast's.

3

Soon after she began work, Sylvia learned that a man had come by to see her. Jennings? No name had been left, but the man had said he would return. It was a slow afternoon and Sylvia was talking to a woman at the lipstick counter when someone stopped nearby. She whirled around.

"Hello," he said. "My name is—"

"Billy Bell."

He smiled in a good-natured way.

She blushed, then made sure her mouth was closed.

"I thought I'd stop by to introduce myself. I think my colleague has already spoken to you."

248

He was shorter than she expected.

"As you probably know, we're thinking of doing a series of programs about places like The Cat's Paw—"

She sat down. "You talk . . . just like on television."

He smiled in the good-natured way.

"And," he continued, "I would like to get to know something about you, with a view to asking you onto the show. Perhaps in a group, perhaps singly."

She could not quite look at him. He was a holy glare in the corner of her eye.

"Touch me," he said.

Her eyes would not blink.

He took her hand and ran it down his arm.

"You see," he said, "I don't bite."

"Never said you were going to bite."

She tried a smile.

"I think we ought to have lunch—maybe at the private dining room over at the station—to talk this over."

"Lunch, lunch, lunch."

"I don't understand."

"You all"—she tried a laugh—"have a lot of lunch."

He smiled in the good-natured way.

"Don't you?"

"Sure I go to lunch."

She laughed again. Witty conversation.

"So it's settled then. I'll call you."

But he did not leave. Then, when she did not know where to look, he said, "Have you seen much of Jennings?"

"Comes around here sometimes."

"You go out to lunch with him?"

"Oh no."

"What sort of things does he say about me?"

"He doesn't say anything."

She pulled at her fingers. "I don't mean that. I mean everybody knows who you are."

"He didn't talk about me?"

"I don't see him too often."

Billy stared at her until she blushed. Then, still looking at her, he said, "I fired him. Too bad."

He smiled in the good-natured way.

She nodded—as if to say, I can keep a secret, I know these things happen.

"Too unreliable."

She nodded.

There was a pause.

"See much of Kelly Martin?"

She shrugged.

"You have."

She looked down. "Well, yeah."

"Lunch."

She nodded.

"What sort of things do you talk about?"

"Oh you know, we just talk about life."

"What else?"

"Well, I don't know, all kinds of stuff."

She tried to smile, as if to divert him with a joke. "You name it, we talk about it."

"You tell her about The Cat's Paw . . . Everything she wants to know . . . all the details? Ev-er-y detail?"

He smiled in the good-natured way.

There was a pause.

"I don't think much of her," he said. "Do you?"

She shrugged,

"Sort of snobbish," he said. "Or didn't you find that? You might disagree."

She balanced a smile, a shrug, and a frown.

Billy stiffened.

"Don't tell her I was asking about her."

"Oh no, never. Height of secrecy."

He smiled in the good-natured way.

"We're old friends," he explained in a confidential voice. "I'm always teasing her about every damn thing, but she can get a little touchy."

"Sure."

"Here, let me buy something."

He was all movement.

"You don't have to."

"I insist."

"What do you—"

"I'll take that." He pointed to a mysterious nest that contained bottles. His hands played around his wallet.

"For your girlfriend, right?"

"For my girlfriend."

When Billy left, the woman from Lipstick strolled over. Sylvia, doing her nails, hardly looked up. "Well, there's one thing I'll say," Sylvia told the woman. "You can tell he's out of the ordinary. You can just *feel* the power."

4

Billy met Teitelman for breakfast at an elegant uptown hotel. The men in the dining room wore expensive suits and there were few women. Some men sat singly, reading a newspaper folded to an article of interest. Others, in pairs, conversed quietly. Their newspapers, already read, lay on the extra chairs. Teitelman always ate breakfast here, often with a client. His table never varied, and his order did not change. The waiter tapped his pencil as Billy asked Teitelman for a recommendation. Teitelman looked up from his newspaper. "Whatever fruit they have that's good, usually melons this time of year, peaches are good too, one soft-boiled egg"—he glanced at his paper—"decaffeinated coffee."

"The same," Billy said, "but regular coffee."

Teitelman shook his head over a bankruptcy that, with foresight, could have been prevented. "Such a waste," he said. Then, dismissing that problem, he addressed himself to Billy. How was everything coming? The waiter brought sliced peaches in a bowl resting on a bed of ice.

"All right. I've spent too much time on staff problems."

"Always true."

"I finally fired Jennings—my long-time assistant. Very tough. He was an old college friend."

"It *is* hard. One of those things you just have to get used to. You'll have to do a lot more firing before you're through."

"It's usually best, anyway, for the person fired."

"Not always."

251

To say "I finally fired Jennings" gave Billy confidence. It did not last, however, since he could not find a comfortable way to talk to Teitelman. His discussion of the firing, casual but hard-nosed in the Teitelman way, sounded false. To keep talking, he mentioned that the attorney had not yet agreed to handle the campaign.

"He'll come around. If not, there are other good ones. He just doesn't want you to think he's eager."

"Why should he be? There's not much chance."

"You can think that, but you shouldn't believe it. Anyway, I wouldn't push him for an answer until after Labor Day. No one really focuses sharply enough before then—not enough to make a decision."

Dishes disappeared, eggs arrived. The one waitress among so many red-jacketed waiters filled their coffee cups to the brim. "Have you framed a strategy for your campaign? Of course you'd change any strategy in the thick of things, but usually it helps to have a plan."

"I've been researching some issues. The *Times* will be impressed if I demonstrate that I know them. Later the *Times* won't matter so much, but to get attention in the beginning—"

"I wouldn't box yourself in too tight."

Teitelman was holding something back, Billy thought, something he would have suggested if Billy had not spoken with such confidence about his approach. "I'll give myself some room, but—you don't seem to think it's a good idea."

"I do, I do."

Teitelman scraped an eggshell clean.

Billy was silent.

"I would only suggest that you aim your campaign, early on, at your opponents in the Democratic primary." He sipped. "Stress your youth, don't run from it. Fresh face, new ideas. It might also help to set up a pattern of endorsements, not all at once, but over time, to develop a sense of momentum. And from people with some experience in New York politics. Not just the stray celebrity. I might be able to help you with that."

Billy wondered once again, What does he do? The banker's confidence, hard as crystal, weakened Billy's faith that he could succeed in politics. It was not his world, and no one seemed impressed with his political savvy. And soon, perhaps, he would have to leave television. Billy was sorry for himself—but then mounted a small rebellion.

"I'd be grateful for any help of that kind, of course. But I do think in the early going I have to stress the issues rather hard, particularly since my background is television, where people are not supposed to know a damn thing."

"I agree one hundred percent."

Billy pressed on. If Teitelman wanted to force favors on him, he would do the same to Teitelman. "And I really want you on the show. People should get to know you better. And I have a slot open in ten days."

"What day is that?"

"Friday."

"I'll have to look at my calendar."

Each sipped coffee.

"Sometimes I have to travel unexpectedly to Washington or Los Angeles," Teitelman said. "Can you handle cancellations? It's not too likely, but—"

"Of course."

At the limousine door Teitelman offered to drop Billy at the station. Then he read deeper into the paper as Billy stared through the tinted glass, remembering his conversation with Sylvia.

CHAPTER

THIRTEEN

I

After the food was prepared, but before taking her bath, Kelly telephoned her mother. She did so on impulse. "Hello? . . . Yes it's nice to hear from you, too . . . Things are going pretty well. School starts in a few weeks . . . Yes, I know more history than I ever expected . . . Please don't start about that—I know plenty of people. Every time I call . . . I know, I know . . . Well, I promise I'll try to get back before school starts . . . That's too bad . . . No, I don't remember him . . . Everything's fine . . . Yes . . . Yes . . . I love you too . . . 'Bye."

For a moment she was still. Then she wondered what remained to be done. The cucumber soup tasted fresh, the Mexican dish was ready. The salad awaited its dressing and the bread could be warmed up anytime. Dessert, wait until he saw the dessert! She smiled and unbuttoned her blouse. Her bath was a great pleasure; also a great solace. She never rushed it. There were many different kinds of bath, from the businesslike to the hour-long soak, and each had its rituals. The most serious bath included the washing, drying, and combing of her hair. That morning, to put the world into perspective, she had washed her hair. Her present bath, as a result, had no particular purpose. It was a serious indulgence.

She considered: no, she did not want bubble bath. She tuned the stream of water to the right temperature, then slowly undressed while the tub filled. Articles of clothing were placed one by one into the hamper; at a certain level the water was tested again for temperature. Then she turned off the tap, disturbing the sudden silence with a splash as her foot touched water that was always too hot. There followed the easing under, sending shivers rising like sap up her legs, and the final surrender, when the water touched where it would. A moment's reluctance, a long relaxing, and then she lay composed under the surface. She did not hide from uncomfortable thoughts, once her mind began to work, but she could dream her difficulty into stillness with the help of the warm water. Jennings was everywhere in her mind, yet she did not think directly about him. What could be done had been done. It was her mother, so exasperating in her no-nonsense way, who disturbed her. Not once in fifteen years had Kelly discussed anything important with her mother. It was impossible. While loving Kelly, she was deaf to everything but her own conviction. Now and then, on impulse, Kelly had tried to establish a truer connection, but invariably gave up. Only a shout could penetrate her mother's certainty. And Kelly dared not make such a penetration, for without certainty her mother would have nothing.

This was nonetheless a familiar sadness, skillfully borne. Far more difficult was her love for her father. She sat up to wash her face, then sank back under the water. It was the oldest fact of her family life that she did not know the circumstances of his death. "Quickly," "unexpectedly," her mother informed the little girl. And Kelly remembered her objection: "He's a doctor." It still seemed wrong to her that a doctor should die young and unexpectedly. Over the years the facts of his death had grown to disproportionate size, since her mother did not volunteer the information; and Kelly, when young, never demanded it. She had worried that her mother had her reasons, that she might become violently upset if asked. Now, when Kelly had every right to the knowledge, part of her did not want to know. Suicide? That was rather romantic; but also cowardly in a man of steady mind. A car crash or heart attack, however, seemed too ordinary an end to the years of not knowing. She wanted more from her father.

She began to weep. Her face did not contort and she did not make any noise. Water simply ran down her cheeks into the bath. She teased herself gently—it was amazing that this could still happen to her—and wondered if everyone, at bottom, was so sentimental. She hoped not, and reminded herself that she was sentimental about very few things. The tears, which came in waves every half-minute or so, continued for some time. She muttered "Damn, damn, damn" into the steam. Perhaps she should find a psychologist to rinse out her sorrow and hang it up on the line to dry. No, her sorrow was too important. It had become a place to locate meaning if other things failed.

She shut her eyes and sank deeper into the water, wetting her hair. There was no photograph of her father in the apartment. His picture always seemed wrong to her. He was a stranger stamped with the look of the 1950s, someone seen in an old *Life* magazine. An image of that kind could not sustain the weight of her feelings, and so she retained her own impressions and images, which possessed greater talismanic power than any photograph. She recalled his smell: rich, sweet, and heavy. She remembered his rough, grainy cheek—her legs stirred lazily. Her favorite image, told to no one, not even to the black turtleneck, was of her game of hide-and-seek as her father read the newspaper: she played over and around and under his chair. The strongest image, however, was of the upstairs closet in their old house. After her mother gave his clothes to charity the closet was left empty—except for heavy wooden hangers, which clattered quietly at the opening of the door. This image brought on her final wave of tears. Then, calmer, she let the water rise like a blanket to her chin.

Her calm never lasted long, not with her relations to her father so incomplete. It had a way of slowly going flat, then of emptying into despair. Often she tried to imagine him, in an attempt to counter this despair—and failed. On those occasions he became a yawing absence in her mind, and she would feel on the verge of falling off balance. In this edgy spirit she wrote some of her best sketches, honing her wit to withstand the sharp images that came to her from unexpected directions. In the bath, however, the soft enfolding water cushioned the force of her despair. The memory of her childhood, the comfort of her tears, the caress of the bath aroused instead a sense of play. She became aware of the float in her arms and the lift in her legs. She stirred up a wave, enjoying the browse of the water, and made a bowl of her hands to catch a drop from the faucet. Then she smiled: bodies were blessedly foolish.

She remembered the baths of childhood, when a nipple might be an island or a toe a mountain. She wiggled a toe, let a nipple poke the surface. And then, hardly noticing, she began to dream of making love. Her dreams were not very specific, at least not at the start: just a few hints about the build of a man's shoulder or the curve of his hip. Each image came into her mind, then disappeared; and her desire rose to fill the space left behind, like the water that seeps into a footfall. Sometimes she stirred her legs to send small kisses up her thighs. Or shifted an arm to caress her ribs. Slowly her dreaming, while no more specific, became rougher. She was pushed around by her memory of the angularity of a man's body; by his unexpected hardness where she was soft; by the bristle of his cheek, the boniness of his thigh, the grip of his arm and leg. His chest, so wonderfully ungenerous! To move, to move more than the bath allowed, that was what—she stopped. She sat up when dreaming was no longer enough, when life itself was wanted. She scrubbed herself. She made a lot of noise. Then, once again, she eased back and let the water, slick with soap, become still. Her desire subsided into a glow. Did she sleep for a moment? Without deciding to stand up she did so—rising to receive the chilly kiss of the air.

2

Kelly decided against the blue blouse. It was ash blue, the color of butterflies in a potato field—but something plainer was called for. She selected a simple white shift, which brought out her dark coloring. She added a light gold necklace. Perfume? Well, she shouldn't be too plain, and perfume enhanced a severe dress. Then she took a walk around the apartment. Nothing expensive had been purchased, but her mother had sent some furniture from home, and she herself had bought some things in the stores on upper Amsterdam. Her taste, neither expensive nor showy, was elegant; she liked to please, even surprise the eye, without the mind having to notice. General lines were simple and clean, and the furniture was energetically positioned. She also had a sense of humor. On one table she put a chipped china plate of fussy integrity, bought because it suited her notion of what an eccentric aunt would choose in 1900.

She rearranged the flowers. Then there was nothing to do. To her eye the room now looked stiff and prepared—embalmed. With sudden fury she changed everything around; and still nothing looked natural. She took up a knife to shorten the stems of the flowers, but the chop, chop, chop did not help. Then she became calmer, knowing what to do. She sat by her window with a drink and began to argue, with the cold conviction of someone who clear-burns a field in an effort to restore its strength, against her hope. "I always pick wrong," she murmured. "Why bother?" This search for love! This old game! By thirty, she thought, the heart has lost its springiness. The newness has gone. One is left, if one wishes, with nuance. That was if *one*—she used the pretentious "one" with grim glee—could find a nuance worth noting, in what was always the same game. The repetition! The meeting, the batting of eyes, the exchange of stories, aren't we interesting?, the nodding, the smiling, let's agree to disagree!, bed. The same old record with the needle stuck: fuck, fuck, fuck.

Oh, tenderness could be expected. Didn't cattle rub together on a cold night? And pleasure taken in lust. Didn't an itch relish a scratch? Peaceful anniversaries by the hearth . . . boredom had its rewards. For others the bleeding away of love, divorce by a thousand cuts. And in the end, of course, you never knew anyone. She stared toward the glass buildings downtown—fool's glass, she thought, you can look out but not in. The right kind of glass, for who would want to look in? She remembered the polished behavior of friends, wonderfully polished behavior, with the shine of the glass downtown. Inside, she knew, was the usual cluttered room, crossed by a few dim paths, like the trails of mice. She stared at the windowsill. Her thinking slipped away until she saw only what was in front of her—things. Then she looked sharply up, refreshed.

3

Jennings, kissing her hello, gave her a bottle of wine. His eyes were warm but guarded; his smile was in place. She was disappointed that he wore nondescript trousers and a shirt with faded stripes. "Sit down, sit down," she said. "Or make yourself a drink." She stepped into the kitchen. The wine was very good.

He called out his admiration for her apartment.

"I've had plenty of time," she said, "since you were here last."

He joined her in the kitchen. By unspoken agreement each decided on a stiff drink. "You look nice, too," he said, and began to uncork the bottle of Bordeaux.

His manners were also in place. That was all right—from Jennings she welcomed any compliment.

"So," he said, moving to the couch, "what's new with you?" They chatted about her article, though she told him nothing important, and gossiped about the party for Oatis, where they had last met. Then Kelly said in a teasing voice, "So, what's new with you?" She took a sip, keeping her eyes on him.

"I've been fired. Billy fired me."

"You're smiling!"

"I'm glad he fired me."

"But that's wonderful!" She touched his arm. "I don't mean wonderful, but now just think, you can—" His smile stopped her. She dropped her fingers. There were many sides to this firing. Then she looked up again, confused and angry. She did not deserve the condescension in his smile. So: she was willing to begin right away.

"Well, tell me what happened."

"We went out to lunch, and Billy obviously was nursing a grudge. I don't really blame him, since I wasn't showing up for work the way I should have, but it was unbelievable the way he did it. All this politics, it's turned his head. Can you imagine having to run for office every two years? Anyway, he might have been firing his secretary. He was compassionate—you know, this hurts me more than it hurts you, in the long run it's for the best."

"It *is* sad."

"Come on."

"I think it's sad."

He adjusted.

"Of course it's sad, I suppose. But we've both changed. It probably *was* for the best."

"I think it's sad."

"Okay," he said, with an air of tolerance. "Tell me why it's sad."

"It's harder to make friends as you grow older. Your time fills up with acquaintances—and he was your oldest friend."

"He's gotten all important."

"Maybe so, but you go back with him. Don't you see? Just think of the time you've spent together. All that dead time lives again when you see him. It's as though"—she chopped at his arm—"you've lost a branch."

He smiled. "Very pretty."

She colored with anger.

"The fact is," he said, "Billy Bell is an ambitious, not very pleasant man, who is becoming more ambitious daily. Not very nice at all."

"Maybe so, but you should feel—well, not cold and righteous."

He shrugged, waiting.

"Tell me the truth," she said. "You don't feel any loss at all?"

A timer sounded in the kitchen.

"It's too bad," she continued, "because I don't like Billy Bell either, and I know men don't like to be sad, especially about other men, but tears are wonderful, lots of storminess to distract you, and all that water to soften the sting." Her heightened tone, she knew, was a little crazy—out of proportion to the subject at hand. It was a relief, however, to be reckless. "The worst is to be cool, calm, collected."

She rose to answer the timer.

He applauded, and had she not glimpsed something in his eyes, she would have slapped him. "Well, come make me another drink," she said. In the kitchen, as she spooned sauce into a pan, she remembered the onions, which she had forgotten to chop. She smiled wickedly. "Jennings," she said, "I have a job for you."

"I don't like the sound of this."

"While I fuss around over here you have to cut up these onions. Chop them *very* fine."

They worked in silence for a few minutes. Then she turned toward him too quickly. "Come on," she said, handing him a Kleenex, "better get it off your chest." She trembled—on the verge of giggles. And Jennings, through his onion tears, laughed too. She took a deep breath. "Half an hour," she said, pushing the onions into the pot and returning with her drink to the other room. "Let's put on some music. What do you like?"

"Anything."

"Yes, I like that too."

She rustled through her stack. She decided to play her one jazz record. "Duke Ellington?"

"Sure."

"Sure, sure."

Something frisky started up. She almost asked him to dance, but decided he had been teased enough. They ought to relax a bit. He asked her about school, and she said the history texts were beginning to bore her—"too bland, too careful."

"Are you going to back out?"

"Not for a year. The texts don't matter much to high school teachers anyway. Or at least I can't imagine they would, especially after a few years. It's the back and forth with the class."

"Aren't the kids sort of nasty at that age?"

"Yes." She remembered Sylvia. "But not much nastier than later."

There was a pause.

She leaned toward him. "But what I sort of look forward to—you can't imagine the baroque politics of the teachers and administration. I've just glimpsed the edge of it. The headmistress, my God, she's this la-di-da lady, too good to be a teacher you'd think, and she has an English accent." Kelly spoke with odd enthusiasm. She felt open, able to say anything. She described the condescension directed at young teachers, the warfare between different groups, the eccentric sexual tastes of the music teacher, the dismal quarrels about pay. Then, over the soup, she asked him how he planned to spend the next few months—and stared at him until he spoke.

"I'm not sure yet."

There was a pause.

"I'm getting an enormous severance check from the station, and I'm doing a little work for Tom Prendergast."

261

"Tom Prendergast!"

"What's wrong with that? Consulting. Ideas for advertising. That kind of thing. So all of a sudden, now that I've been fired, I'm richer than I ever was before."

"But what are you going to do?"

The slight smile stole into his face.

"Any suggestions?"

"Well," she said, angry again, "it's too bad you've broken with Billy. But come on, you're free, you're not even under pressure to take a job for the money. Nothing to hold you. You can do whatever you want."

"How do you find out what you want?"

"You're free!"

"To do what?"

"Stop it!"

She spread her hands open. "Do something worthwhile. Get out of television, maybe. Just start. Just try something. Maybe it won't work, but most people don't even get the chance. They're trapped at an early age. You have all that experience. So work for some independent production group. Or make your own something or other. Or go into the movies."

"Where do you find so much energy?"

"Where do you lose yours?"

" I think I just want to take it easy for a while."

"Well, get excited about that—make plans, read long books, fix up your apartment." This reminded her that she had never seen his apartment, and for a moment she lost her way. "Completely redo your apartment, take a trip, go to some different place. You can go sit in a bar that has 'Blue Suede Shoes' on the jukebox."

It was not working. She felt like a cheerleader.

He repeated after her, "Blue suede shoes."

When she exerted herself most, his eyes brightened like a spark under her breath. But the spark never seemed to take. She thought, He was that way when I met him, too. At times, when she leaned forward to upbraid him, she was exhilarated; at others, exhausted, so tired she wanted him to leave. Soon these two sensations, exhaustion and exhilaration, became almost the same to her. They gusted together like the winds of a dying storm.

She retreated to the kitchen with the soup bowls, waving him

back when he offered to help. She wondered if he found her behavior peculiar. This was supposed, after all, to be a friendly dinner.
Or was he also disoriented? She was not even certain what she
wanted from him. Sex? Not really, or not just. Sex alone would
not release the tension in her body and mind. She wanted him to
do something, to stop just being and become. So much of life
seemed merely imagined, hardly there. She wanted a person like
him to put his imagination at risk.

She checked the main course. It seemed ready. She called out,
"Change the record, will you?"

"What do you want to hear?"

She did not like music during dinner, but she wanted him to
choose something. "Not jazz this time." After a long silence she
heard in the other room the peculiar wheeze and bang of early
Renaissance music. It was a record her mother had given her, after
an early music group had played a concert at the local museum.
"I didn't know you liked that!"

"I'm not sure I do."

She set the excellent bottle of wine between them, then brought
out the main dish. As she expected, compliments soon followed:
it was just spicy enough, the sauce was excellent, very subtle too.
Where did she learn how to do it? She said "instinct," knowing
he'd seen the Mexican cookbook. For a time they ate in silence.
Then they discussed Mexico. Each had made a trip there. Then
they discussed—but no topic of conversation lasted long. She
noticed, during one pause, how candlelight brought the rose to his
cheek and picked up the distant dance in his eye. She waited. She
waited as the wine caressed her tongue. But he would not speak.
Suddenly she blushed—then turned cold. She spoke softly, without
inflection.

"I wonder," she said, "if you'll be like those old men who talk
to themselves, those people who have spent their lives shut up in
a closet and then when they're old and the hinges begin to rust
the words jump out unexpectedly like cats. You see them on the
street muttering. They sort of shout and then subside. Or maybe
when you're old you'll become artistic. Would you like to be
artistic? I remember what you said about the monastery. It shows
you have some sentimental notions about being alone. But you
know, that wouldn't be so bad for you, to become artistic. You
could find some sort of solace in dim, pale poetry—you know the

263

kind I mean, there's hardly any other now—that seems to have grown in too thin a light, a library light, that smells very faintly of confessionals and those horrible damp corners in churches. The subject doesn't have to be religious, of course."

She saw that she had shocked him. So she simply asked, "Why?"

He didn't answer. She asked again, "Why do you behave like this?"

There was a pause.

"You're one of the people who can see," she said. "Who knows about the important things. I can tell. So you don't have any excuse for being small."

He looked stunned—unyielding and dumb, like an animal in a trap.

"Can you say a simple sentence?"

"I don't know what you mean."

"Something direct, without the smile . . . anything."

There was a pause.

"Coward."

There was another pause.

"If you don't try, I'll do something dramatic."

She lifted her glass.

"I promise, something dramatic."

"Not that cliché."

She flung her wine into his face.

There was a moment of shocked silence, then nervous laughter. He mopped his face. She cleaned up the puddles. They continued to laugh intermittently. Then she said, "I have a couple of old shirts, men's shirts—I'll get you one." She closed the door behind her into the bedroom. She intended to find him a shirt, but she also wanted a moment to lie down.

4

Jennings could not rinse the stickiness from his hands or the burning from his eyes. In the kitchen he cleaned himself as well as he could with water from the tap. Now and then he gasped. He could hardly believe it. Done it! She'd really done it! Uncertain what to do with himself, he cleared the plates and turned over the record. Then he sat down again, too surprised to think. When she did not immediately return, he poured himself a fresh glass of wine. Really done it! So extraordinary did her act seem that he began to disbelieve it. Such an act was pure theater, just a night at the opera.

"This might help."

Her voice startled him. She held up a large work shirt splotched with red paint. She looked paler; some hair grazed her forehead and cheek. He remembered her expression just before she flung the wine. It was her most beautiful: taut, still, brimful. He remembered, too, her moment of silence—when she shuddered like a bell that cannot sound.

"This is ridiculous," he said. "I'm sorry for—"

"Take yours off. I'll put it in the sink."

He became a little afraid.

She held out her hand.

He began to unfasten his shirt. He met her eyes, and could not find the buttons. It was the blue of her eye that stopped him—a flat anonymous blue, like the sea around a ship; a blue so open he could have sailed into her mind, a blue so indifferent he would have left hardly a ripple. They stood that way for a moment. Then he gave her the shirt and she went into the kitchen.

Jennings pressed his palms to his face. Something terrible had happened. A delicate membrane—of hope, possibility, trust—had been torn, irreparably. He had never intended it, never known he had that power, never believed he could not correct past errors. He hurried into the kitchen determined to make amends. Each time he tried, however, her expression—cool and polite—made serious discussion impossible. Nor would she let him touch her. Over dessert she was friendly, but her thoughts were elsewhere. She seemed to be receding. At midnight, when it was time to go, Jennings tried again. There was no question of making love, but he wanted to be affectionate and kind.

"I don't want to go," he said.

"Don't then."

"I don't mean, I'm not trying to—"

"We don't have to fuck."

265

Her small smile, chilly and ironic, reminded him of himself.
"Kelly—"

"I don't really want to talk to you."

She took the cake into the kitchen. Then, returning, she said,
"You can sleep anywhere you want. The couch is pretty comfortable or you can use the bedroom." She went away and came
back in her bathrobe. She found sheets for the couch, helped him
make it up, then turned off the light. "Good night."

5

Jennings replayed their evening in his mind. Though full of self-
recrimination, his thinking was straightforward and clear—more
so than in months. The reason was simple. He had exorcised his
particular ghosts. He had forced certain traits of his character,
certain values in his life, to their natural conclusion. He had exposed their impotence and capacity to harm. And he had done so
publicly, before someone he admired. In doing this, he had
destroyed one side of his character—as surely as he had destroyed,
in his break with Billy, one of his ways of working. He had touched
bottom. Now he could rise.

He did not put this change into words. He simply knew (his
happiness flared up) that he would never be the same. He also
knew (his happiness flared against a dark sky) that he had used
Kelly to make this change. It was his callous behavior, along with
his concern for her, that kept him awake. How could he have
been so cruel? So stupid? So blind? Perhaps he did not realize,
he thought, how self-absorbed he had been. Perhaps he had never
believed she could love him or take his behavior seriously. Perhaps he had thought he was cruel only to himself. Perhaps he
could not take responsibility for the person who clicked off in
conversation. During their dinner, he remembered, he was almost
siding with her, cheering against himself.

He disliked self-disgust, but he did not avoid it. It seemed
right that he should pay that penalty and fitting that he should
suffer this painful isolation. He might even come to love a

secondary life, his face pressed to the glass, if what he saw had worth. The memory of her vivid character warmed him; her decision to fling the wine gave him strength. It was the intimation that she was not all right, that he could not make her all right . . .

He woke before seven, blinking under a window without curtains. He felt alert but unrested. He made himself coffee, folded his sheets, sat on the couch. In the morning light their behavior of the night before seemed exaggerated. He studied his wine-stained shirt in the sink: it looked a little foolish, he thought, like a theater prop in the sun. He asked himself, "Why not put matters right?" He pushed open her door, full of the good sense of morning. He planned to wake her, apologize, perhaps make love.

She stirred but still slept. Her body was curled to one side, the naked shoulders twisted back, one arm flung across the bed. Hair lay strewn over the pillows; her fingers jogged now and then against drawn-up covers. He studied her face, magically dark against the cascading sheet; and serene too, amid the hair. For the first time he saw her clearly, without her eyes turning him back on himself, and he was touched by her simple and plain humanity . . . a young woman asleep in a bed. He watched her— and then, suddenly, startlingly, her eyes opened. They looked right at him without sight. He tightened with terror; and then remembered everything.

Her eyes focused. She breathed in and sat up, holding the sheet to her breast. Morning seemed to age her. "What time is it?"

His briskness returned. "Almost eight—beautiful day."

She shielded her eyes from the light. Jennings said, "Thanks for the dinner." She appeared amused by something. Then she turned her head, still protected by her arm. "I think I'd like to sleep for another hour."

"I don't blame you."

There was a pause.

Jennings said, "We'll be in touch." He shut the door softly. Later, he thought, I'll make it up to her later. Once outside, he could not help but enjoy the morning, though his concern for her remained strong. The sun was burning off the haze and New York, on an early Sunday morning in August, seemed curiously gentle: clean and uncrowded, new and precise. There were only a few cars, and the air carried a hint of forest and ocean. He felt free of many things, and free to look at many others. Why had he never noticed how much yellow there was in the gray city—the taxis, the storefronts, every traffic light along Broadway? It was good to work for himself, he thought, right to mend his friendship with Billy. Tom was amusing, but forgettable. Later.

CHAPTER

FOURTEEN

I

After firing Jennings, Billy began to tape most of his interviews in the late afternoon. That made it easy to have a few drinks first. He did not consider himself an alcoholic: the drinking had begun too recently, and he knew the warning signs, having been informed of them many times by psychologists who appeared on the show. Liquor merely eased him over a rough spot, he thought, and he made a firm promise, often repeated, to cut back on his drinking once the campaign was established. Anyway, no one noticed.

In the last few weeks it had become increasingly difficult to recognize himself in the eyes of others. Often he had the impression he did not register; sometimes he forgot what he was saying, even on the air. More recently he had found himself disliking the red eye, which he had once considered soothing. His timing felt off, and he was frequently caught by surprise. A few drinks always restored his touch. He could pretend he was what he had been. Sometimes the liquor prompted him to take chances, to speak before he thought, as he had when addressing the unions. This was always charming. It lent his manner the spontaneity that had been lost.

Drinking also became a friend, to help him over the loss of Jennings. Although he actively disliked the man, he missed the friendship, since there was no one else with whom he could talk frankly. No one provided perspective on his problems or told him he was being silly. And Billy, lacking detachment, could not do so himself; he was unable to examine his own nature, being one who saw himself only in relation to others. At work he could not find anyone with whom to discuss politics, and he dared not make an error or sound stupid in front of Teitelman. He hardly knew the attorney who might run the campaign. Who was there to give him ideas, as Jennings had, or to help him shape each show?

He drank heavily on the day he was to interview Teitelman. He had wanted Teitelman to come early, to discuss the interview, but Teitelman was too busy. On the telephone they agreed to begin with local politics (making a reference to Billy's campaign), then to advance to national issues. Billy planned to ask Teitelman for the "thoughtful" analysis—the best thinking about how to renew America. This analysis would be presented as dispassionate. Teitelman was not a politician. He was beholden to no constituency. Five minutes before air time, Billy shook Teitelman's hand and explained a few things about appearing on a talk show. "I remember this from last time," Teitelman said, nodding at a cameraman he recognized. Billy indicated the chair Teitelman was to take, then introduced him to the red eye as a "leader of Wall Street, a man who has already had the ear of several presidents and who will, I'm sure, help shape American policy in the future. If that sounds a little awesome, well, it is." Billy paused, then smiled. "This banker, I want you to know, is also a warm man who plays a mean game of tennis. We'll get to the tennis later. But now, Mr. Teitelman," Billy said, turning to his guest, "how are we doing?"

"In what?"

Teitelman smiled comfortably.

"I could say, 'almost anything.' But let's start with New York. I know you take some hand in city politics."

"Oh, no more than many people."

"We've been reading that financial ruin is around the corner if the mayor . . ." Billy lobbed several questions about the city at Teitelman, whose answers suggested that, although everyone did his best, the best was not good enough. He spoke pleasantly, but with a scientist's concern for precision. "Often the way we structure our political life is at fault," he explained, "so that it's literally impossible to arrive at the right solution." He told an anecdote—sharp and to the point—which demonstrated that the mayor had failed to solve the problems of a city hospital because of a state law.

There was a break for a commercial.

"Everything all right?" Billy asked.

Teitelman nodded, then asked if the attorney had agreed to run Billy's campaign.

"Sixty seconds!" someone announced.

"Not yet."

Billy, tightening, wondered what Teitelman was thinking. Had he, Billy, made a mistake? Was Billy Bell no longer someone in whom to take an avuncular interest?

Teitelman sipped some water and cleared his throat.

"Thirty seconds."

Billy continued to tighten.

"He's very busy," Teitelman said. "But there are others if he turns you down."

"Fifteen—"

The red eye glowed. Billy looked down at his pad. Although he rarely relied on written questions—they sounded canned—he read Teitelman a question about the future of city politics. A concerned expression, which suggested that certain problems were intractable, entered Teitelman's face. He brought his hands together in an open triangle, and gently jogged the fingertips together.

"What I would say is this . . ." He explained the difficult adjustment the city would have to make from an economy based upon local manufacturing to one based upon other sources of income, primarily services. "There will need to be some carefully managed shrinkage. And, if you'll forgive the awkward phrase, some patience of expectation."

Teitelman stopped talking—surprising Billy, who was not listen-

271

ing. It was the meeting of the fingertips that absorbed Billy, a meeting that suggested better than words the fineness of Teitelman's discrimination. Billy wondered if he had ever met the man who sat beside him. He must be a relative of Teitelman's, who, when he looked into the red eye, behaved somewhat differently from the familiar Teitelman.

Billy blinked. "We ought to elect you."

The fingers parted in friendly exasperation.

Billy knew he had made a mistake.

Teitelman said, "Preserve me from politics." He regarded Billy as a father regards a wayward son. "We've had enough of everyone going into politics. This country, we're coming to realize, has been over-politicized. *Some* people ought to offer advice from the side-lines. That's not to say"—Teitelman paused, like a father indulging his son, then opened his hand as if to introduce Billy to the audience—"that Billy Bell shouldn't enter politics." He paused again. His indulgence appeared to best his discretion. "We've all been hearing a lot about that, Mr. Bell. I know politicians are cagey, and journalists are even cagier. But you must have something to do with all this talk. What do you have to say, if I may turn the tables for a moment?"

Billy did not hear the question. He was more interested in Teitelman's indulgence. He looked into Teitelman's eyes, then into the red eye. He became bewildered. When the silence began to lengthen, Billy back-pedaled: he must answer a question, which hung before him like the question mark found in comic books. He grabbed at some words. "Getting ready, maybe."

This was unsatisfactory. Teitelman did not reply.

The silence began, once again, to lengthen. There were shuffling sounds from the crew; he saw some shadowy shapes beyond the lights. And he was overcome, suddenly, with weariness. He wanted to be done with cameras and crews. He wanted Teitelman to be a pal. He drew his chair closer to his guest. "Tell me," he said, "how do you spend the day?"

Teitelman was taken aback—but exaggerated his surprise until it all seemed like good fun. He clasped his hands around one knee. "How do I spend a day?" he repeated. "No day should be like any other day, though I do have certain routines. I usually have break-fast, as you know . . ."

Billy recovered, aghast. His awkwardness and banal questioning were diminishing Teitelman's importance. Teitelman, having reached midafternoon, gave him a quizzical look—and Billy lost control again. He feared above all else the moment when Teitelman would stop talking. And so he boxed himself into the present, without a sense of what went before or should come after. Between each second was a locked door.

"In the evening," Teitelman said, "I like an old movie or a good biography. Unfortunately, I often have to dine out . . ."

Billy forced himself to think. What came to mind, however, only worsened his predicament. He remembered his two letters to Kelly, the firing of Jennings, his future in politics. And yet—it was very odd—something in this predicament promised relief.

Teitelman stopped.

The silence began to unreel.

Billy made a second grab for words. This time, in the middle of the grab, he balked. "What"—he began—and stopped. "What?" he repeated, and realized he was about to ask, "What do you do?" He stopped too fast—and sailed into a ghastly skid, in which the passing time seemed made of air. He was aware, dimly, of the tiny red eye.

His expression did not give him away. At worst he was trying to phrase a question correctly. At best he was almost as thoughtful as Teitelman.

Billy said, "What do—"

He said again, "What do—"

Then Teitelman, stepping into the silence, mentioned that he needed very little sleep. It was time for a commercial. "A little rocky there," Teitelman said.

"Sorry—a doctor gave me some antibiotics and . . ." He shook his head in friendly surprise. He was able, now, to resume control of the show. He exerted all his charm. They discussed national issues: the problems of energy, poverty, regional decay. They composed an ideal national agenda. Then, with a couple of minutes left, Billy joked with Teitelman about tennis. Serving was the strongest point of his game, Teitelman said. When Billy asked for his weakness, Teitelman, laughing, wouldn't say. "That," he said, "I keep to myself." Afterwards Teitelman appeared pleased. He thanked Billy for inviting him onto the show. He would be in touch, he said, about the fund raiser.

2

In his office Billy busied himself at the bar. There was some threat of sobering up. He thought Teitelman was offended, and he was reminded of his letter to Kelly. As always she served as the counterpoint to his political dreaming: she was the mistake that could bring down everything. By six o'clock he was drunk. He decided to discuss the Yankees. He flagged a taxi and talked baseball to the driver. Once home, he fell asleep with the radio on, then woke up woozy at eight-thirty in the evening. His empty apartment—which left him too full of thought—disgusted him. He made reservations at five or six expensive restaurants, and mixed himself a drink.

To some extent, he could control his drunkenness. He could put on a good front, which made it hard to tell he had had more than one or two, and he could make himself feel drunker than he was, which let him do whatever he wanted. Drinking was a way to coil and uncoil his internal spring. "The *hell*," he said out loud, "with restaurants." He decided instead to return to The Cat's Paw. It was to be, he informed himself, another research mission. He stood himself up. No one could say, no one could say for a moment, that Billy Bell did not work hard. He dressed himself in his darkest clothes, parted his hair in the opposite direction, put on a pair of sunglasses. During the ride uptown, he fancied himself an undercover agent: it would be exciting to recognize someone else at The Cat's Paw. Probably a lot of respectable people loved pornography. He knocked on the screen behind the taxi driver. When the cabbie opened it, Billy shouted, "An awful lot of respectable people are perverts."

Once inside The Cat's Paw, he bought a roll of quarters and stepped into a booth. A shadow crossed his mind—the memory of his last visit. He ignored it. Why get complicated? He was a free man; he liked or didn't like, dammit. He raised the screen and he liked. "This," he said loudly, relishing the vulgar break in his voice, "is an adequate piece of ass." He watched the girl as she walked, stretched, and answered the phone. "Hold your horses," he whispered—and his whisper inside the booth sounded very loud.

Did he know this girl? It was hard to tell. The light was too bright. It altered the play of her expression, but yes, that was the girl he had seen at Prendergast's. What was going on here? Was this a trick of Kelly's? Anyway, what was her name? He slapped on the glass with the flat of his hand: the girl ignored him. He slapped the glass harder: still nothing. He put in more quarters. A second shadow crossed his mind, and he slapped the glass a third time. Now the girl looked in his direction, but she could not see him. Hell no!—she shouldn't be posing for those other men.

Billy bought tokens and jammed them into the telephone machine until he heard her voice. "Hello, honey, what can I do you for?" Because he did not answer, she hung up. In a fury he got her on the line again. "This is Billy Bell."

"Give me a break."

He saw her laugh. He heard her laugh.

"Look, I'm Billy Bell."

"And I'm Cleopatra."

"I was talking to you at Prendergast's, at your cosmetics counter. I bought some pink thing."

She sat down on the divan.

"You're . . ."

"Billy Bell."

Her hands fluttered helplessly over her body. Then she ran off-stage. Billy waited outside until Sylvia walked past, dressed to go home. He said, "Here I am."

She ignored him. He caught up.

"Here I am."

"You're not Billy Bell."

"Of course I'm Billy Bell."

She stopped to look.

"Jesus Christ, why're you dressed like that?"

"Shhh."

"I get it. You don't want to be recognized. Fans'd tear you to pieces."

"That's it. Fans'd tear me to pieces."

She blushed.

Billy said, "Let's have a date."

She could not look at him.

275

"Don't you want to have a date with me?"

"Sure."

He flagged a taxi. His first thought, to take her back to his apartment, did not satisfy him. He wanted to make a night of it with this girl who could not meet his eye—this girl who, moments before, paraded naked before him. Mama's? He would have liked to take her to Mama's, guiding her eye to various celebrities. But instinct warned him away. He was too drunk, she was too common. He took her instead to a piano bar, where he made himself known. He tipped the captain for a good table—flamboyantly, so Sylvia saw the money. When she ordered a Tom Collins, he said "No champagne?" Sylvia nodded, shook her head, nodded. "Drinks as a main course," he told the waiter. "Champagne as dessert." Then he ignored her. He pretended to be a man of mystery, with an ear for the nuance of the post-prandial piano. Sometimes he smiled at her between drinks.

In fact, he hardly listened to the music. He savored her stolen glances and, when the champagne came, insisted that she drink most of it. He refused to accept more than a glass himself—for fear he might fall down when he stood up. At last, with great indulgence, he turned in his seat to study her and said, "I would like to ask you, and it is your right to refuse, there are girls, pardon me, *women*, or pardon me once more, you are a *lady*, anyway there are girls who refuse, and it is their privilege, so to make a long story short, will you, I was going to say, but I shall not be so crude, will you accompany me back to my abode?"

Sylvia nodded, as if it were her patriotic duty to accept. She seemed too drunk and scared to speak. In the fresh air, however, her curiosity overcame her awe and, observing Billy rumpled against the taxi seat, she quickly asked, "Hard day at the office?"

Billy stretched out the words. "Hard . . . day . . . at . . . the . . . office."

"I've heard that's what it's like. Behind the wining and dining there's a hard day's work."

"Work!"

"We don't know the half of it, thinking it's just glamour and parties and stuff. There's the behind the scenes, right?"

"Right!"

She considered. "You probably live hard and play hard, right?"

"Right!"

"Thought so."

There was a pause.

"Got everything organized," she said. "I bet down to the last minute, the *last* minute. And then, all of a sudden, you fly to London or Paris. Just time to pack a bag, right?"

"London! Paris!"

"Thought so."

There was a pause.

"Lots of beautiful models and actresses, I bet, but you're not ready to settle down yet, right?"

"Right!"

"Thought so. Your privacy's vital, right?"

"Right!"

"Thought so."

"Probably got some pet peeves too. Like eccentricities. I read where you all have these eccentricities, right?"

"Ecc—" Billy stumbled on the word. "Hobbies," he declared. "I have hobbies."

"Hobbies! That's right, I almost forgot that." She tapped her head. "Probably got some favorite charities, too. Don't want to forget that."

"Charity!"

"Even a few nobody knows about."

"My heart!"

"Like an orphan or somebody dying in South America."

"Thousands!"

"You got a Rolls-Royce?"

"Never."

"Modest, right? I should have known." She paused. "That's it! All dressed like that. Can't believe I forgot. You've got a style all your own, right?"

"Right!"

"Thought so."

"You have a golden retriever or anything?"

"What?"

"That's just something small. Like to go for walks on the beach, right?"

"The beach?"

"Thought so."

There was a pause.

"'Course there's me," she said, puzzled. "Where do I fit in?"

"Whirled you off your feet!"

"That's it! Shows how you got to be where you are." She looked impressed. "Probably a whirlwind romance."

"Whirl!"

Her eyes softened. "A storybook romance?"

"*Mais oui.*"

"What?"

"French."

"You speak French!"

There was a pause.

"A gift for languages." She shook her head in admiration. "But back to this storybook romance . . ."

"A princess!"

"And you're the prince. Of course, then you would had to have been a frog first."

"What!"

She blushed. "I'm getting mixed up."

"A frog?"

"You know, kiss the prince he turns into a frog, no, wait, the other way—but who'd want to kiss a frog?"

"Frogs? Kissing frogs? I hate frogs."

"We've got something in common!"

"Frogs?"

"You're not a frog, it's the prince and the pauper—"

"Not a frog?"

"I meant the prince and the pauper. You're the prince, I'm the pauper."

"Papa?"

"I'm getting screwed up again. The prince and the pauper are the same thing. Or are they? Shit, I can't remember—"

"Papa?"

"You're the prince, but you're really the pauper. Or the other way around."

"Papa prince?"

"That's it!" She jumped around in her seat. "See, here you are dressed undercover so you won't be recognized. Right now you're the pauper but you're really a prince!" A look of religious respect entered her face: the word was made flesh.

"What happened to the frog?"

"Forget the frog."

"The three little pigs? Maybe you're talking about the three little pigs. There's also something about a pumpkin." Billy's eyes focused; he was about to be mischievous. "I'm the big bad wolf, I'm going to huff and puff and—"

"Wait a minute."

"Blow your house down!"

"Wait a minute."

"Stop!" Billy told the cabbie.

"No, I didn't mean that!"

The taxi continued.

"I have my pride," Sylvia said. "Even if you *are* Billy Bell I don't want to be one of the little pigs, just like you don't want to be a frog."

"Frog?"

"I want to be a princess."

"My little princess . . ."

"That's right."

"My little Cinderella . . ."

"I forgot about her!"

"Pumpkins!"

Billy pounced, and almost missed. He retreated woozily to his side of the taxi.

Sylvia said, "This is our carriage."

"Going to ball!"

"Except—what about glass slippers. I'm supposed to have a glass slipper."

Billy pounced again. This time he yanked off one of her shoes and proudly displayed it. "A glass slipper!"

Sylvia smiled: fun with the famous.

"A glass slipper!" Billy shouted—and then dropped it out the window.

Sylvia took a deep breath. This was something more than fun with the famous. This was glamorous enough to read about in a magazine or see in a movie. Only someone very, very glamorous would drop your shoe out the window.

"What do I do now?" she asked, when the taxi pulled up to Billy's building.

"Out you go."

"But—"

"Princess in distress!"

He picked her up in his arms, like a bridegroom taking his bride across the threshold. He almost fell.

"You do this every day?" she asked.

"Play hard."

He waved her into his apartment. "What do you want, pumpkin?"

"Everything's so new!"

"Not homey enough for you?"

"But I like it new!"

"Antiques for the princess." His expression became less friendly. "Princess!"

"Wine."

"Wine in a glass slipper." He poured two glasses of wine. He would have preferred Scotch, but instinct warned him away. With a bow he presented the wine to Sylvia, who was examining his shelf of photographs. Then he put on the soundtrack to something. He intended to dance Sylvia into his arms and take her to bed. But he was too drunk to dance. He sat down on a couch—furious, suddenly, that he could not perform as he wished.

He said, "What shall we discuss?"

"I never know what to discuss. You say."

Women, he decided, always put you on the spot.

She sat down on the same couch, but not too close.

Women: very cagey.

He said, "We've already discussed the glass slipper."

Her voice lost its accent. "That we have."

"Princess of porn!"

She smiled again: the wit of the famous, after hours.

"Do your act for me."

"You like modern dance?"

"Modern dance. Frogs."

"I'll do a dance called 'Spaces.' "

"You know what I mean."

"Well—"

"The Paw. Do your act at The Paw." He did not sound drunk.

"Combined—that would be creative."

She stood up nervously. It was sometimes difficult to remember that Billy was famous.

"What are we waiting for!"

She relaxed: They probably did this on yachts.

"What are we waiting for!"

She looked at him with sympathy. Perhaps he'd had several wives who divorced him for the alimony. Perhaps the only wife he loved had died of cancer.

"Come on!"

She began to unbutton her blouse.

"Stand on the table!"

Billy indicated a glass coffee table.

"But—"

"Don't worry about all this junk." He swept the ashtrays and magazines onto the carpet.

"What are we waiting for!"

She stepped onto the table, then continued to unbutton her blouse.

"Too slow!"

She sped up.

"Too fast!"

She rebuttoned.

"No!"

She did not know what to do.

"What's wrong?" he asked.

"Nothing."

"Indisposed?"

"No."

She began to unbutton.

"No!

". . . Yes.

"No!

". . . Yes.

"No!"

Then she stood still. Billy smiled. "Poor girl," he said. "I'm not letting you get on with your work. What was your name?"

"Sylvia."

"Sylvia."

"Want me to dance?"

He shut his eyes, and the world turned.

"Mr. Bell?"

There was a pause.

"Mr. Bell?"

The eyelids flew up. "Keep going!"

She removed her blouse and unbuckled her trousers.

"No, no, not like that. No elegance." He forced himself to stand. This was very, very important. This must be done right. "Continue," he said, "with elegance."

She tried to curtsy down her zipper.

"No, no, not right. Here . . ." He stepped onto the table beside her. "Elegant, you see, this way." He unbuttoned his shirt with flicks of the wrist, like a boy skipping stones. "What do you say to that?"

She smiled.

"Magnificent?" he suggested.

"Magnificent."

"Mais oui."

He had forgotten to take off his tie. He did so. "What do you say to that?"

"Magnificent."

"With conviction."

"Magnificent!"

"Mais oui."

Each sock drew a "magnificent." *Mais oui.* To remove his trousers, however, was a feat of impossible daring. The maneuver in itself was complex, and there was not much room on the table. He announced, "I will do what I must do." He ordered her off the table. This was no place for women and children. Then, summoning his courage, he reached for his belt. He made it. Lowering his eyes, however, made everything more difficult. He was very high in the air, and the glass below twisted over the carpet. He did not remember falling, but found himself sprawled on the couch. It was quite comfortable; and so, conscious of having done his duty, certain of his heroism, he did not open his eyes.

"Mr. Bell?"

She rebuttoned her blouse.

"Mr. Bell?"

He did not wake up. She looked around. Then she folded his shirt, tie, and socks. She picked up the things swept onto the floor. It was very quiet.

"Hard day at the office," she murmured.

He did not stir.

"Not yourself today."

He sputtered a little.

"Play hard, sure do."

He was very rumpled.

"You can do anything! Like drink so much! And all that money . . . and kinky . . ." She smiled. "I read about that on yachts . . . Wouldn't believe what goes on."

He began to snore.

She studied his photographs. Many showed Billy laughing with celebrities. In one Billy Bell and a famous actress took a ride in a balloon. "A balloon!" she said. She peered at Billy's smiling face, then glanced at the couch. Billy continued to snore.

"A bad cold. Working so hard, playing so hard, his defenses get down. I should've known." With the dispatch of a nurse, she wrapped a blanket around him, then tucked it under his chin. "Poor boy." She wiped the drool away.

"Guess I should go home," she said.

She stood up straight.

"Wonder what time it is?"

She walked to the other end of the living room and stared at the plants, the stainless steel, the rows of books. Then she walked through the rest of the apartment, looking at and often touching everything in turn. In the kitchen she opened the door to the refrigerator.

"Milk! . . .

"Eggs! . . .

"Beer! . . ."

It was the same kind of orange juice she bought. She opened the top of the carton for a swig—but reconsidered and poured some into a glass. Then she carefully washed the glass. She patted the pillow on Billy's bed and looked out his window. It was two-thirty, time to go. She turned off every light, except the one that lit the shelf of photographs. The smallest photograph, the one half hidden behind the picture of the balloon—he would never notice. She dropped it into her purse, glanced toward the couch, and put the picture back. Then, seating herself on the edge of the coffee table, she put his glass into her purse. For a moment she watched him sleep. Then, very softly, she kissed him. Amazed, frightened, exhilarated (suppose his eyes opened, suppose he leapt up?), she slipped out the door. And barefoot caught a cab.

3

Billy, hung over, met Penelope for brunch.

"This is going to make you angry, I know," she said. "But it's my opinion that you've been working too hard." She raised one hand to halt an objection that was not forthcoming, then used this hand to brush some lint from his white jacket. "You're still the most handsome man on television. You are, to use that awful expression, real, not like all those blow-drieds. But you do look a little—I have to be honest—the worse for wear."

They ordered Bloody Marys.

She continued, "I know how it is. I haven't given myself a break in months. Work is my tyrant. I can't sleep at night because I get so worried about my piece on time. I think about its implications. But that's not to say *you* should be that way. If you ask me, both of us need a vacation."

The waiter provided menus.

They ordered.

"Of course, I know a vacation is out of the question. I can't leave my work until January, when the time piece reaches its conclusion. Did I tell you, by the way, about the ramifications for women I've discovered in the piece? Ideas keep unfolding, I keep *learning*."

Billy shook his head.

"Well, women, of course, have always been the prisoners of time. They are terrified of losing their looks. Then there's the monthly cycle. And the famous nine months, of course, about which I mean to do something. *Nine*. What a resonant number! I'll tell you the rest later. Let's stay on more optimistic subjects."

She smiled.

"I couldn't take a vacation, and I know *you* couldn't take a vacation, now that you've decided to become Abraham Lincoln." She took a long sip. "Billy," she said, "I had my doubts about you going into politics, but I was wrong. I'll admit it. You would be wonderful. I've been watching your way of interviewing carefully in the last couple of weeks—"

Billy ordered another Bloody Mary.

"And I won't say I don't have a few minor qualifications, but it seems to me, well, I'll say it outright, it's the best television being done today. Better than public television. It doesn't even *seem*"— she smiled at the irony—"like television, it's so good. It's not just me. I've always been an incorrigible fan. It's my friends too. You talk about serious issues seriously and lighthearted things lightly."

Their food came.

"You know the old expression 'form and content'? Well, your form suits your content, which doesn't mean you don't sometimes use one as a foil for the other." She smiled, as if to say, "You can't fool me." "So you'd be perfect in politics. Good-looking, serious, with a sense of humor, a great speaker. You could be one of our political form-givers."

She passed a fork through her omelet.

"But I have to say, even if you decide against politics or for some ridiculous reason—and politics, well you must know this better than anyone else, is often the art of the ridiculous"—she paused, to let this observation ripen—"even if it doesn't work out for you, you're ahead. Your TV show will become better known. You'll probably be syndicated by one of the networks. When you think of all the Yahoos in Congress it might be better to stay where you are. Anything that happens is just fine."

Billy ordered a third Bloody Mary.

"All I'm saying is that once you get settled into one thing or another, maybe in the fall or winter before the campaign really starts up—do you want to stay with me, by the way, for the fund raiser?"

Billy nodded.

"Wonderful! Once you're settled, then you *have* to take some time off. In the end it's a good investment. I promise. There are all kinds of places we could go—do you have any preference? No? Well, given how hard we've been working, we should be able to

285

go anywhere in the world. *Anywhere.* Someplace where we won't be recognized. It'd be heaven. And I also don't think we should spare expense, for once. Both of us are too frugal. At this point in our lives, after so much work, we deserve some extravagance. It's *cheaper* in the end. Besides, you're an important man."

Billy ordered a cup of coffee.

"I have in mind some place that hasn't been discovered. Or possibly a place that's only been discovered by people who like undiscovered places. Don't worry, I see the irony in that. But you really don't want a completely primitive place—what a romantic cliché that is, spare me from tents. Someplace that's almost like it was. It's getting hard to find something like that, but I can't believe it's beyond us . . . Yes, I'll have some more coffee too, please."

4

At Prendergast's, Penelope was met by Jennings—who found her rather cool. Perhaps she'd heard about the firing. "You look very well," she said, "but I can't say the same for Billy. He looks badly overworked to me."

"He likes to work hard."

"So do we all. Or almost all. *But* . . . Well, I don't have to tell you about it. How is Kelly?"

"Why do you ask?"

"So touchy."

"Have you seen her?"

"Not since the surprise party for Theodore Oatis—and *everyone* was so strange there."

"Ready for a dry run?"

"Rush-rush-rush."

He took her to the lingerie department. "Now, I know that around eleven o'clock next Tuesday Tom Prendergast is going to walk into that place. I'm almost certain. He wants to get noticed by someone, since no one's been able to catch him. If you just poke around near the side door all the way on the other side"—he gave Penelope a map that had been drawn by Tom—"he should appear. You'll recognize him, since he'll be the only man in the place. You take his picture. It'd probably be good to get some crowd reaction if you can."

Penelope listened. "Jennings . . ."

"Yes?"

"Is this moral?"

"Moral? Who said anything about morals? This is business."

"I mean, betraying your friend."

"Look, Billy and I—"

"I mean Tom Prendergast."

"Tom *wants* to be betrayed!"

"Do you have the right to be his psychiatrist?"

"Penelope?"

"We'll split the money?"

"It's all yours."

"Is your word worth *anything*?"

"You don't have to do it. I'll get someone else."

"Of course I don't have to do it." She withdrew a pocket watch from her vest.

"Billy's not too bad, is he?"

"Could be better."

Jennings, leaving Penelope on the ground floor, walked to Central Park. He tried to call Kelly. He had telephoned several times already, without success. Receding—she was receding. He remembered the moment when he left her apartment, that moment when, for the first time, no current connected them. Better that they quarrel, he thought, than that the connection go dead. He stayed near the center of the park, to avoid the Maine Memorial. He asked himself what he wanted. Friendship certainly and love perhaps. Right now, however, what he wanted most was some reassurance that she was all right. Some connection, even if brief. And so, at a pay phone, he tried again. He let it ring.

*

The ring . . . ring . . . ring . . . awakened her to the moaning. "Let's not get it," Oatis said, and continued. She resumed, but was now of two minds. The first moaned under Oatis; the second, more quizzical, listened to the ringing phone, wondered what time it was, noticed the mole on his shoulder. Who was calling? She

287

was not overly fond of Oatis, but he was pretty good . . . practiced. The ringing stopped.

The more quizzical mind annoyed her. Well then, she could shut certain doors. She rode hard with Oatis, intent upon nothing but release and relief. Soon she did not know who or where she was. Oatis, in admiration, muttered, "Un-fucking-believable." When the phone rang again, her moans became louder, until the ringing was hardly heard.

*

Jennings hung up. Why couldn't he reach her? School hadn't begun yet, had it? He continued to walk through the park. He had no destination in mind, but his aimlessness was not what it had been. His thinking had direction: he worried about his work, he worried about her. He did not know yet what sort of job he wanted, only that it must seriously employ his imagination. Over the weeks, as he blocked his desire for Kelly, his habitual musing had strengthened; his dreaming became the overflow of his desire. Whether or not he worked as an artist, however, mattered less to him than that his warmest energy find some significant end.

Where was she? He stopped by her apartment, but the doorman had not seen her; and so, tired of walking and calling, he went to a double feature in a revival house on the Upper West Side. The star was Jean Harlow, in two obscure movies from the 1920s. He liked the oldness of the movies and was attracted to the stories, though he did not surrender his intelligence to them, as he had to the soap operas. Most of all, however, he just liked the movies for what they were, without thinking about it too much. Now and then he also looked at the audience: homosexuals savoring camp, lovers laughing together, old people remembering. When something onscreen outraged contemporary taste—when, for example, a woman described the joys of keeping house—the audience crowed like a bunch of sports fans.

The movies put him in a good mood. He did not overlook their vulgar sentimentality, but he liked their sweet, life-affirming spirit. He felt robust. It did not seem necessary any more—not since his dinner with Kelly—to restrain his desire or smother his life. The night seemed wonderfully dark as he walked, and the breeze was silky. Downtown, the great towers shimmered inside bracelets of light. He blushed. He blinked. And around him the colors deepened, the lights came up, the air itself seemed full of touch. He took a deep breath; and, as he breathed out, two women across the street became marvelous. It had been a long time since he had known desire of the fine, foolish kind.

He continued his walk, aware of a catch. He could not forget Kelly. He sped up to outpace his thoughts and soon his soft longings hardened into a lawyer's logic. Hadn't he tried to call? He couldn't spend all his time worrying: this was a woman, he must not forget, whom he had not slept with, lived with, or married. His night stirrings clarified and he appraised each woman who passed. What was thought, next to this wanting? He took the subway to Canal Street, where he planned to order dinner at Mel's and pick somebody up. He did not like the bar anymore, but he understood how it worked, so his chances of finding someone were good. He soon joined a table—pretending to recognize a friend—with an opportunity. She had come with a couple. She was about his age, a quiet person, not unattractive, with a bored look that Jennings knew was affected. Around her neck hung something large and Indian.

He stared at her for a long time, endowing everything about her with a sexual charge. The slight resistance he saw in her eyes—that affected quality—stimulated his sense of unbounded freedom. The cheap, pretentious clothing, which suggested a careful budget, aroused his feelings of power. He loved the press of the nipple against her blouse and he relished the faint sheen on her naked arm—fine soft fuzz. He honed his desire until he almost trembled. Only then did he speak. He pretended to be in awe of the Indian something around her neck. He discussed his ongoing interest in the vanishing culture of the American Indians and told her of his personal outrage at their plight. He paid no attention to what he said, but spoke with great energy and flair, going round and round, looking for a way in. When the time came to be more intimate he described his disgust with the phoniness of New York intellectuals. This put them alone together on an island of integrity. "You know what a conservative is?" he asked her, waving his hand. "A conservative is a fashion-conscious person who takes pride in resisting radical chic. A radical is a fashion-conscious person who takes pride in resisting conservative chic."

She smiled wryly. "Indeed?"

Jennings had never before heard the word "indeed" used in conversation. It made everything easy. He touched up his performance of the disillusioned intellectual. It was a simple role, in which he had had plenty of experience, and she approved: her body began to soften under the dress. Despite her quiet manner, he coaxed free some flirtatious behavior—fluttering fingers on his sleeve, teasing arguments about whether or not to order another drink. He was not interested in what she had to say, unless it had a flirtatious undertone. Nor did he search out her character. Not until they were in a taxi on the way to her apartment did he learn that she was a doctor. This surprised him, until he discovered that what she doctored was plants.

In the taxi he tickled her arms and dallied with her fingers and licked her palm to make her giggle. He wanted nothing to interfere with his enjoyment; his freedom must expand to determine its extent. Any doubts that he felt only intensified the righteousness of his lust. In the old days, the situation would not have been as simple, though he might have picked up the same woman the same way; he would have had to admire his alienation, to savor the sadness of their mutual isolation. Not now. He did not care what she thought. He was wild for bed. Then he saw her studio apartment—and knew instantly that he had lost. He folded her into his arms, but could not avoid noticing the postcards she had taped on the refrigerator door: an Arcimboldo still life and a cute giraffe with a puzzled expression. He closed his eyes. He did not let her fix him a drink, for fear they would have a genuine conversation, and took her straight to bed. She complained with all the merriness she could muster, then leaned over to push a button on a cassette recorder: Bach.

He smothered himself in pleasure, but his eyes would not stay closed. He noticed, in addition to her body, the smudge of makeup on her pillow and the purple sheets that were not too clean. He smelled her old perfumes, creams, and soaps. Her eyes, staring back, were half closed. To see him the better, he wondered, or the worse? To turn him, perhaps, into someone else? It would probably not be very interesting, whatever it was, but he suddenly wanted to know. He kissed her—and for a moment he was reluctant to come. Then he gave in, knowing as he did so that it would not be what he had hoped, that the few seconds of forgetfulness would not equal the remembering. He sailed into a wild fantasy of possession. He imagined, she imagined. She came, he came.

Afterwards, he drew from her the story of an affair with a married man whom she still loved, though she would not admit it. It was the tired old story, as he had expected: she hoped (without much hope) to turn him, Jennings, into someone else. When she fell asleep he gently untangled himself and sat down by her bookcase. He thought, I'm free, but there's no escape. Whatever it was that liberated his desire also forced him to look. The blessing of blindness was denied him. For much of the night he sat in the chair, surprised and exasperated. No doubt he was free of his recent paralyzed behavior; free, too, of his earlier set pieces of alienation and despair. But he was not free, in his awakened condition, to do anything—not at all. Casual sex, for example, was no longer casual. He paid too much attention, his imagination was too fluent.

The difficult thing, he decided, the *truly* difficult thing, was to think in the round. It was hard enough to hold two contrary ideas, each true, in your mind. But to hold five, six, more—to understand what happens to a doctor of plants, while remaining aware of what is happening to yourself! He wished, ruefully, that he could be either a rake or a monk. One or the other. But he could not. Pair the two, cross their wires, juggle them: perhaps that made something more interesting than each alone. Yet there was always loss in such mixtures, loss of purity, conviction, direction; in the end, perhaps, you were left with nothing but mongrel smarts. He shut his eyes. You lost some edge if you thought in the round. He missed that edge. And he wondered, after a moment, what Kelly was like as a lover.

She could think in the round—he was certain—but was also a wonderful lover—he was equally certain—who gave herself up without qualification. She possessed a generosity he lacked; he, who always held something back. He stared at the sleeping woman, knowing he did not want any connection to her. What he had done, he thought, was little more than masturbation—that pleasant prison, in which there was no risk of connection. And yet he remained curious, very curious. As quietly as possible he began to poke around her apartment. He looked inside her medicine chest, examined all her books, noticed the pucker of her Cézanne poster on the bathroom door. Then he wondered whether he should leave quietly. That would be kinder. They could avoid the bonhomie over bitter coffee. She could wake up—and wonder whether she had really brought that guy home last night. But he decided to stay. He did not want to miss anything.

CHAPTER

FIFTEEN

1

Kelly called Jennings from Montana.

"Who?" The connection was poor. "Kelly! Where have you—I've been trying to reach you for days."

"I flew out here a while ago."

"Why?"

"To take a vacation."

"You didn't tell anyone?"

"No reason to."

"I've—been wondering where you were."

"Spur of the moment. Just went to the airport, got on the first plane."

"When are you coming back?"

"I have to do a little more research for the article on Sylvia."

There was a pause.

"How's it coming?"

"Pretty well."

"Can I do anything—get you anything?"

"I thought I should tell someone where I was. It was nice to talk—"

"Kelly!"

There was a pause.

"It must be beautiful out there now."

"Yes."

"What?"

"Yes."

"I'd love to see it. From photographs—"

"There was even a rainbow this afternoon, but I wouldn't call it beautiful."

"What, then?"

"I don't know."

"Well, it must have been something."

"A pretty cliché?"

"Rainbows," he repeated, to keep the conversation from ending. He continued stupidly. "Hard to imagine a rainbow in New York."

"No kidding."

"What?"

"I didn't look."

There was a pause.

"Were the colors clear?"

"Not in a rainbow—what are we doing talking about this?"

There was a pause.

"Well—" she said.

"Kelly?"

"Yes?"

"Call when you get back. First thing."

"Call. Yes. Call."

After hanging up, Jennings wanted to retrieve the conversation. He hated everything about it. If only he'd been prepared for her call! He tried to find her number, but he had never asked her, during their talks, the name of the town where she'd lived. Nor did he know her uncle's name. If it was Martin—even Montana would have too many Martins. There was nothing to be done.

2

On the day set for Tom's photograph, Jennings heard from Billy, who asked him to lunch. Jennings agreed. He hoped to reestablish cordial relations. Tom called soon after. "Where are you! Don't you know I'm terrified!" Jennings hurried to the store, which he found very crowded. There was a one-day sale, with ridiculously low prices, in the lingerie department. Tom had also doubled the sales force in Private Parts and broadcast hints that Prendergast's would offer something special. "Are you sure," he asked Jennings, "that your friend is a professional photographer? She *knows* about camera angles? She doesn't forget her film? God, I hope she's not an artiste. Is she an artiste? Tell me no."

Jennings lied.

"Even so—" Tom held up a small, very expensive camera. "I am giving this camera to you. I want you to take a few pictures. The film is in, everything is ready to go." His small eyes peered at Jennings. "This is an intelligent camera. It is probably more intelligent than your photographer. It is only necessary to point it in the general direction. No *fussing*. You understand? Snap a few, give me the film, and we'll print some copies for publicity in case she blows it."

Tom looked at his watch. "I'm terrified, I really am." He paused. "So how are you?" Behind the small smile, Jennings saw a chubby man who was losing his hair.

"You're not really scared."

"Did I ever tell you my nightmare? A kid from Kansas blows my cover."

"What?"

"A kid from Kansas!"

Jennings laughed with genuine good humor: the Wizard of Oz. Then he noticed the strange flirting shadow in Tom's eyes, a dark glimmering that resembled the shifting of a restless audience. "Well," said Jennings, "you're about to finesse the kid from Kansas."

"Couple hours till high noon. Plenty of time for the TV folks to get here for interviews."

He doesn't see me very well, Jennings thought, certainly not as well as he sees a crowd. And he sees himself best in the press clips.

"We've warned the TV bunch, of course. The reporters will talk to eyewitnesses in time for the evening news. You want to see my new suits?" He opened a walk-in closet, where he introduced Jennings to a long row of unworn suits in fashionable styles. In the breast pocket of each jacket was a handkerchief of appropriate color, rakishly pointed. Jennings, remembering the quiet, sluggish boy in college, wondered what first led him to become a recluse and now, probably, a socialite. The pressure on him must have been great.

"Pretty good, right?" said Tom. He pulled a suit from the rack, then tucked it back. "Let me ask you something. What would you think? I own the store, I get the cops to arrest me for causing a commotion. Imagine how crazy everyone will—but then even you don't know what's up."

"Tell me."

"Wait, wait, wait . . ."

Jennings was more interested in Tom's character. The relation between the usual and the unusual was so intimate! They seemed almost indistinguishable. That willed wildness, that efflorescence of the ordinary—for Tom, it was practical to be eccentric. The small smile had always been important, Jennings supposed, because it suggested what was human and centered under the surface of their dealings—under the surface of the store itself.

"The sad thing," Tom said, "is to lose all the rumors. Very very sad. Of course, others can be started that are just as good. Wait till you see how I redecorate this place, my private baronial pad, Tom's tower, top of the town. But still, one grows attached to the old ways . . ."

Tom was one of those, Jennings thought, who would never understand a certain kind of seriousness, considering it too boring and straightforward. He was also one who would never find much magic in life. To the magician, Jennings thought, there can be no magic. And he remembered the sad story of Houdini, who spent so much time at the Ouija board, hoping to discover that spirits exist.

Tom lay back on an older new sofa. "People will just have to learn that I don't have a hideous, defacing disease. Sad. They will have to learn that I am not better looking. Sad. They may find it hard to believe the rumor, now about, that I keep a harem in my closet. Sad."

Jennings' thoughts drifted elsewhere.

"I'm going for a walk."

"Remember what you see. It may be for the last time. That's it. Sayonara! Jesus, I'm terrified."

"You don't look it."

"Oh, I am."

"I don't think you are."

"Of course I am! Meet me here at eleven-fifteen sharp. I'd better remember to shave."

Jennings' new curiosity did not extend to his old enthusiasms. Prendergast's seemed dull to him now, despite the furious activity. Its energy lacked direction, substance, or weight. It was as boring as the circus; only children or lazy artists in love with dead symbols would find Prendergast's of more than passing interest. His earlier infatuation surprised him: had he really viewed the store as a fine, amusing model, the representative of an attractive attitude toward life? He was beginning to regard with skepticism anything that stood for something else, though his love for such symbols or private metaphors remained as strong as ever. Too often, though, they disguised rather than revealed the truth; they cut the world to their own shape. He smiled at the metaphor. It was right to be careful. Metaphors should be exact, deep, thrilling, obedient—or the facts were enough.

As he wandered he studied the store, a more comfortable way to pass time than brooding. He observed the customers and enjoyed the precision of his observation. Later there would be time for the tricksters; his eye, for the moment, was on the tricked. In half an hour he came to the cosmetics department, where he remembered Sylvia—and then, with a start, Kelly.

He found Sylvia, who pretended not to recognize him.

He asked, "What's the importance for?"

"Wouldn't you like to know?"

"Have you heard from Kelly?"

She shrugged.

"Tell me!"

She looked uncomfortable.

"Not for a few days."

"She's away. But if she calls you," he said—writing his name and telephone number on a scrap of paper—"find out her number. I have to get in touch. It's an emergency."

Once again Kelly seemed to be receding. And now he could no longer study the store. He left Sylvia not knowing what to do with himself. Then he stopped short—a present! He would buy her a present, a very, very good present. He would spend almost anything; Tom's check made him rich enough. He went to the jewelry counter, where he examined necklaces and rings without asking their price. This absorbed him until he realized he was not thinking about her. He was not imagining the subdued shimmer of gold against her neck or the sparkle between a jewel and her eyes. He had diverted his worry onto an object, letting a jewel stand for his concern, his apology, his hope that all would end well. He had, in short, devised the sort of symbol that moments before he had criticized. He paused, and the saleslady left.

And yet—he was good at such things. Couldn't he also summon her living presence before his mind's eye? Not lock her in a jewel? He had always loved jewelry, if well made and free of the brag of price or size. It seemed important, when the hand of a craftsman conspired with nature to make a third thing—a solid thing full of light. The saleslady returned, and he asked her to scatter her best rings across a piece of velvet. He liked a pale-blue opal, but shied away from that color. Instead he selected a small ruby set in an oval of granulated gold, then shrugged at the price: two thousand dollars. On the way to his rendezvous with Tom, he slipped it on and off his little finger.

In Tom's quarters Jennings found a fat man in Elizabethan costume, whom Tom called "the store's best Santa Claus. He plays the trumpet too." Tom himself wore a bathrobe. He told Jennings that Penelope was ready. A few other photographers would also be present, "to photograph Penelope getting the picture. We don't want to miss any history." Was Jennings prepared? Jennings nodded. Then Tom stared at him long and hard, like a sergeant in a war movie. "Let's go."

Jennings did not ask about the bathrobe or the fat man. He assumed it was part of the act. Tom led them through some back passages, then to the hallway outside the lingerie department.

Jennings noticed incongruous or debunking details, such as the plump fire hose or the sweet reek of marijuana—some employees, perhaps, taking a break. He remembered those times in Europe when a guide would point to the spot where, for example, Queen Mary lost her head and Jennings would think, "Here?" and notice the bubble-gum wrapper, the horn of a car, the sign "Gentlemen."

The fat man lit a Marlboro.

Tom stripped down to his underwear.

"Surprised you, eh? . . . I'd do it buck naked except I decided, hell, I don't want a citation, no way to start over. But damn, it's cold in here. What do we have, air conditioning in the hallways? Waste!" He hesitated. "So what do I say? I say 'Underwear to underwear.' " He paused. "Remember that." He paused again. "Look, I know it's stupid, but it's going to look great. Remind people I'm crazy, get the store noticed. So don't tell me you're scared. *I'm* the one that's got to do it."

Jennings said he was not scared.

"That's better."

Tom looked at his watch, about to take his men over the top. "Okay, Claus" . . . For a moment he forgot the war movie. "That's sort of cute isn't it, call a guy 'Claus.' Do you think I should have had him actually come as Santa? I thought that was too much. Besides the children's lobby might—"

"Would've been too much."

"Everyone loves Shakespeare. All right, Claus." He slapped the fat man on the back. The man threw away his Marlboro and shook his trumpet. "You know what you're supposed to do?" The fat man nodded, and the door flung open. In an operatic baritone he boomed "Hear ye! Hear ye!" and blew a blast on his trumpet.

Tom followed ten steps behind. He smiled, raising his arms over his head—a Roman consul on his victory parade.

A few people were in the area. They behaved correctly. Several squealed, principally saleswoman who, Jennings suspected, had been paid to do so. Everyone else was struck dumb. Then an eerie silence settled over that section of the store.

Cameras began to flash.

Penelope—photographing and being photographed.

Tom began to pose. He pointed to a respectable woman and

laughed maniacally. "You!" The woman was properly shocked; the photographers captured her expression. Tom smiled. The customers relaxed, laughed. Some tried to get in the pictures. People began to gather around from other parts of the store. The crickets chirped again. A couple of customers began to chatter. The word spread—"It's Tom Prendergast"—and a few women asked for his autograph. Jennings himself took some pictures: the scene looked very small through his viewfinder. He was reminded of Flemish paintings, in which the great event—Icarus falling, the crucifixion of Christ—is a detail in the vast panorama.

Now, Jennings thought, Tom will use the photographs of his eccentric behavior to elevate the walk into a magnificent advertisement. This depressed him. He slipped the ring on and off his finger. "Can't hang around too long," Tom said. "Magic will disappear. Let's beat it." He shooed Jennings through the service door, then locked it. He put on his bathrobe. "The newspapers won't want to show me in my underwear, so they'll have to use a head-and-shoulders shot—the rest will be left to the public's imagination. Perfect. This afternoon I'm sure the TV stations will be around to interview me. *Perfect.*" Tom rubbed his hands together. Then, suddenly, inexplicably, he stopped short.

"What's wrong?"

Tom shook his head.

"You okay?"

"Jennings?"

"Yes?"

"What now?"

Jennings smiled.

"What do I do now?"

Then Tom relaxed and slapped him on the back. "A table at Mama's!"

3

Billy stood up from the table to shake hands, like a Southern businessman greeting a customer. "Been too damn long," he told Jennings. "How the hell did we let that happen? Well, we're

300

going to do something about it." He had arranged to meet Jennings at Ricardo's, once a fashionable hole-in-the-wall that they liked. In recent years its reputation had declined, however, since the food was consistently mediocre and Ricardo himself was too amusing. The restaurant was now popular with people who had some money but no taste, particularly tourists who liked a sideshow. Billy selected it because he deeply regretted having snubbed Ricardo. Damn snobs, he thought. Here this man opens a place all by himself. It's one hell of a lot harder than what they do.

Billy motioned Jennings to a chair. He enjoyed the attention of Ricardo, who remembered him from the old days. Ricardo brought him the "best Scotch, Mr. Bell, on the *casa*. You may not be familiar with it, Mr. Bell, I want you to try and you tell me the truth." Billy sipped. "You know," he told Jennings, "I can't believe we haven't done this sooner. I mean, Christ, two people ought to be allowed to break off a business relationship and still remain friends. I want to have dinner with you, I want to have dinner"—he slapped the table too hard, as if making a New Year's resolution—"at least once every couple of weeks. And I don't want any backing out at the last minute."

Billy realized he had gone on too long.

"Good to see you too."

"Mr. Bell?" said Ricardo. "May I recommend—"

Jennings ordered a glass of wine.

"What were you going to recommend?" Billy asked and listened with interest to a description of the dish of the day.

"Remember?" Billy said. "We used to come to this place."

"When we were first in New York."

"Those were the days."

Jennings smiled, but said nothing. "Those were the days" might be a cliché, Billy thought angrily, but a good friend did not smirk when the subject of old times came up. And, Billy thought, Jennings' expression—the narrowing around his eyes—was too puzzled. Damn, Billy thought, can't you be natural with your best friend? He asked, "Something wrong?"

"No—nothing."

"Of course nothing's wrong."

Billy waved away the wrongness. Then, without transition, his anger turned into sorrow. "Hell, I'm sorry, something's wrong with me, I'm not trying to put it on you. It's just . . ." He looked at

Jennings. His sorrow became love and tears warmed his eyes. This friend would help. "Well," he continued, "I wanted to ask your advice about something. You know Teitelman? Well, he was on the show the other day, and it wasn't a bad show but it didn't go all that well either. I don't know whether this has anything to do with it or not." Billy thought: I'm not making myself clear. I used to be articulate. He looked at his oldest friend. "To make a long story short, I don't think Teitelman was too pleased and, well, he's canceled the fund raiser. At least, not exactly canceled it, but he's moved it down the road to somebody else's house. You'll go, right? Really, I want you there."

Jennings nodded.

"Anyway, Teitelman said something came up. His house could not be used. He's—I never know what he really wants, whether it's true or not. It could be nothing."

Jennings grasped Billy's wrist. "You take him too seriously. Believe me. I've told you. You don't need Teitelman. He's a stupid obsession with you. If he helps you, fine. If he doesn't, fine too. You can be sure he has his own interests at heart."

There was a pause.

Jennings continued, "I didn't know whether to tell you, but I think I should. Maybe you already know. I was reading the other day that Teitelman has a longstanding quarrel with a fairly liberal lawyer with good political connections"—Jennings mentioned a name—"who may also want that seat. He would have the same constituency as you. It struck me that Teitelman might be trying to fence this man out, or divide his vote. Maybe, maybe not—"

Billy thought: Jennings looks healthier than usual. He hated the concern in his friend's face and would have preferred, at that moment, the old indifference. Or a disdainful reference to Teitelman.

"Oh I know, I know," Billy said. "Politics."

Such concern . . . that was not the Jennings he knew. "Politics, I know it's just politics."

"I didn't say you didn't know."

Jennings believes I can't do it without him, Billy thought.

"If you think Teitelman is edging away," Jennings continued, "well, who cares? Teitelman is just—"

So Jennings did think Teitelman was edging away. Suddenly

302

Billy wished, fervently, that he had not told Jennings about his difficulty with Teitelman. Jennings would tell the press. And there were others, too, who knew damaging things. The list unfolded in his mind: Kelly . . . Sylvia . . .Teitelman . . . Jennings.

Someone laughed at a nearby table.

Jennings must resent me, Billy thought, he has every reason to spread damaging information. He will be on the phone.

The laughter continued.

Billy interrupted. "Funny joke?"

Jennings stopped talking.

"Ricardo and his jokes," Billy said. "Did you hear it? I only got the last part, something about a fat bride in Napoli. Hey, Ricardo!" Billy called Ricardo over to their table, and asked him to repeat the joke. Ricardo did so and added another. Then they ordered—slowly, for Ricardo, pinching the air between two fingers, described, intimately, the secrets of each spice in each sauce. Once Ricardo left, Billy began to analyze the pennant race, while staring past Jennings' shoulders.

Over the meal, however, Jennings interrupted him.

"Come on, the hell with all this stuff about the Yankees."

"Never thought I'd hear you say that."

"Neither of us cares about baseball."

"Speak for yourself."

"What is this jolly, good guy business?"

"I think," Billy said to Ricardo, "my friend here needs another drink."

"Ah, *signor*—"

Jennings dismissed Ricardo.

"I don't want a drink."

There was a pause.

"Billy, I didn't see it before. I just thought it was a mood you were in. But I don't think you're feeling well. This drinking—"

Billy waved his hand.

"This drinking. You never drank so much before, not at lunch anyway. Your voice is different, your manner is different, you're unpredictable . . ."

Billy began to feel swollen.

"I think you must be exhausted. Nervous exhaustion maybe. You need to relax, take a vacation. Even on the air—sometimes

303

I watch—and you're good, don't think I'm criticizing, but it's different. You're not as comfortable."

"It shows?"

Billy's voice thickened. Blood prickled under his skin.

"Not much . . . No one but me would notice."

"It shows."

Billy released his breath and wanted to confess something. He did not know what. To confess—or upset the table, throw a glass, shout.

"No one but me, Billy."

There was an unexpected softness in Jennings' voice. It brought the swollenness inside Billy to a head—until, slowly bursting, he was suffused with warmth. He murmured, "I watch myself on television, now, sometimes . . . as if it weren't me—the audience, they're so lucky, just able to sit back there. And you get so tired out there in front of them, working . . ."

Jennings was quiet.

"They're so lucky, like women . . .

"Sometimes," he said, "I wake up in the morning and for a moment I've forgotten everything that's happened . . . And I feel cleaner, like I used to. I wish—I wish I could be like that again, just regular day to day. Then I remember. And I think: When did this happen? What happened? I was fine and then . . ."

Jennings sat very still.

"I wake up and I remember and it's so . . . so inexplicable that I'm horrified, and it all comes back to me, all knotted up, and I jump out of bed and I'm not thinking about it, I'm just doing the regular things. But it's there, and I get used to it again . . . and I even sort of like it . . ."

Billy shook his head.

"No, I don't like it. But the way I am always seems to make sense right then, at the moment. Afterwards no, but right then there's always logic, real logic—I know it's logical for me right then. I know."

Billy looked up.

"I watch myself on television and I never used to. It got in my way. But now, I don't know, I can't resist. I try to remember what I'm going to say before I say it. Sometimes I can't remember what I said"—his tongue thickened—"I can't even recognize myself. I say, 'Who is that up there, this is me here, what's he saying, he's moving, he's alive, but I'm here.' Sometimes I think . . . I don't know, that I'm made of air."

He paused.

"Made of air. And I don't know where I am."

"Oh hell, Billy, none of us does."

There was a pause.

Billy's eyes shot up. He repeated to himself, "Oh hell, none of us does." That sounded like the old Jennings, who was wry and skeptical. But not now—no, he did not want the old Jennings back, not after what had been said. The old Jennings would make a joke. To be the butt of a joke . . . was happening too often. He felt tricked into exposure, trapped for all to see. He said, "None of us does, sure."

"Of course not."

Billy shut his eyes. Which Jennings—or was Jennings the same and he himself changed? And what impression did he make on Jennings? The swollenness was gone. It was replaced by a kind of rawness; and there, around this rawness, he began to harden, narrow, contract. He laughed. In his ears the laugh sounded like the rasp of a file on wood. He laughed again, and slapped the table with the palms of both hands. "Of course not!" he declared. "Sometimes I can't believe what I say. You're right, of course, I've got to cut down on my drinking." He shook his head. "I can tell you, I'm glad I don't talk that way on the air."

"You didn't sound bad. I promise. You worry too much."

Billy did not want to be contradicted.

"I don't worry enough," he said. "Now—how are you doing?"

"Fine, but Billy—"

"How's Kelly?"

"I haven't seen her. Billy, I know that's part of your problem—"

"I don't have any problem with that cunt."

It was too quiet.

She's showed him the letters, Billy thought.

Jennings was staring at him. "Oh, I didn't mean that, just that she's a little particular. We've said this before. You've told me how arrogant she is." He smiled, certain now of his charm. "No, she's wonderful . . . marvelous, smart as hell. Someday, well, I don't know where she's going, but we both know it will be far."

He paused. "I sound like a director of admissions."

"Not really."

"Don't tell me what I sound like."

There was a pause.

"I didn't mean—" Billy said.

But he was too tired, now. He did not want to talk. Why bother? He called for the check. He refused the zabaglione. This distressed Ricardo, who added anisette to their espresso and served them brandy on the *casa*. Billy, sitting back, let Jennings describe the antics of Tom Prendergast. He had rarely seen Jennings so animated, but he did not wonder why. He preferred to shelter the glass in his hands and let the brandy glaze his tongue.

4

It was time to go. Billy became furiously happy. "Hallelujah! Action! Lights!" He looked at Jennings. "Hey now, what's the rush away? Let's be reasonable about this." He punched Jennings lightly on the arm, with the aggressive good cheer of a college boy determined to stay out all night. "Where do you think you're going? You're coming with me. No ifs"—Billy stood up, to indicate that nothing must stop him—"no ifs, not even any buts. You hear me? Now I don't expect you to come to the station with me"—he smiled, as if their breakup were amusing—"but you can at least drop me at the door. Yes, sir." They walked out, with Billy stopping now and then to admire something in a window. Then he had an idea. "Come on," he said, "let's go to The Cat's Paw. Good for a laugh."

"Someone will recognize you."

"I'm working on a *story*."

"No."

"Come on."

The prospect of the visit dismayed Billy. He was delighted, however, with his dismay. He would brave any danger . . . climb any mountain . . . He began to hum . . . swim every sea.

"Don't tell me," he said, "that Jennings is embarrassed!"

"I don't know if it's smart."

Billy began to joke. "Isn't it unbelievable, those raincoat men lurking around the stalls? I hate to think what they do in the stalls, or those salesgirls, so blasé, inside those tubes." Then he remembered that, as far as Jennings knew, Billy Bell had never visited The Cat's Paw. He thought, Well, I blew that one. His spirits remained high, but he became more cautious once they entered the store. Carrying himself with elaborate dignity, like the drunken retainer of a bishop, he studied the man with the pistachio nuts beside the door, the one Sylvia called Pablo, and surveyed the extent of the crowd, which he judged sizable. As for Jennings—Billy decided he looked too damn bored. "Oh it isn't *that* boring," he told him. "You're just trying to show off." His own voice startled him: people rarely spoke inside The Cat's Paw. The rock music covered most incidental sound and heavy carpeting absorbed the rest.

"I've been here before," Jennings said. "Not much new for me."

"Not much new, you think . . ." Billy spoke with vast deliberation, trying to recognize his own voice. He chewed each word, he increased the volume, he forgot to be dignified. "Think of all the ladies for de-lec-ta-tion." From a rack he picked out a magazine. "Any and every kind of lady, for your very own. You name it, you got it."

Sylvia! He whirled around. My God, he thought, forgot about— suppose she walked through the shop, recognized him, kissed him! What would Jennings—

Behind him a voice, not Jennings', said, "Hello, Mr. Bell."

Heads turned.

It was a warm, honeyed baritone.

Billy twisted back.

The voice cleared: a sweet, honeyed rumble.

"Mr. Billy Bell," said Pablo, "it is our honor to have you in our shop."

To hear his name broadcast by that man, in that place—a hot poker entered his heart.

"We hope that if we may be of assistance, Mr. Bell—"

To fend off the voice Billy raised one hand. Then, skipping backwards, he bumped into a rack of magazines, which toppled into a counter. There was a smash and tinkle; and then nothing,

307

except the beat, beat, beat of the music. Billy stood too still. He was recognized.

"Mr. Bell, we will soon—"

"Shut up!"

Billy, striking out, overturned another magazine rack. Then a third and fourth, fifth, sixth. He paused and smiled. Then he grabbed an ax from a counter—no good, it was rubber—and flinging it aside picked up a gilded chain. He lashed it into a black mirror. There was a moment's quiet. Then from every direction came a scurrying. Men with downcast eyes—they seemed very short —hurried past like small animals escaping.

More splendid smash!

More!

Sometimes, from the corner of his eye, he saw Pablo—who hardly moved.

More, more, more!

It was a blessed relief. He strode from one end of the store to the other, swinging his chain. Now and then he smiled, and his cheeks ran with tears of happiness and despair. Then the music stopped. Billy continued to pace, lashing into the private movie booths with their stills of spread-eagled women. He smashed the glass around the stage. He tried to keep up the noise. But soon the silence began to strengthen, resurfacing whenever he lashed out like sand under a receding wave. He grew tired and almost stopped. He began to flail; the air seemed suffocating. Then he gave in. Everything was over, which was fine.

He refused to look up, until a hand pushed up his chin. Jennings, inches away, whispered, "Billy . . . Billy, listen to me . . . You did it on purpose. Do you understand? You did it on purpose."

5

Jennings seized him by the shoulders. "No, don't shake your head, listen to me. Do you understand? You did it on purpose!"

"Go away, please, I don't want to hear—"

"Listen to me."

"No, let me be."

"Do you understand?"

"Have to go home," Billy said, trying to move away. "I'm going to go home."

Jennings did not release him.

"Do you understand?"

The eyes began to clear—then went gray with exhaustion. "No, horrible, can't."

"Do you understand?"

"Please."

"Someone called the police. You can't go home."

"Have to go home."

"Billy! It could be all right. You did it on purpose. For show. Like La Guardia."

"I'm tired."

"But do you understand? If you understand and don't want to that's okay, but tell me. People will forget. You were working too hard. You could go away for a few weeks. Tell me."

He met Billy's eyes. What he saw there—furious resentment—shocked him.

Billy was smiling. "I did it on purpose."

"You don't have to. People will understand."

Billy laughed—the rasping laugh. He punched Jennings on the arm. "I did it on purpose." He waved at Pablo, who stared back with glassy indifference. Then, pretending to compose himself for a golf shot, Billy planted his feet, wriggled his rear, and slammed a magazine to a distant green.

"Billy, these people don't like publicity. I could talk to the guy. Probably nothing would happen. It wouldn't get out. But we've got to get out of here now."

Billy took a second shot.

Jennings turned away, tired of the violence. How little he knew of Billy! And how damning that he, Jennings, hadn't been friend enough to understand, anticipate, and perhaps prevent this breakdown. He marveled at his blindness. He walked some distance away—hardly able, suddenly, to control his strange exhilaration. As worried as he was about Billy, he felt immensely reassured by his outbreak, much as he had when Kelly had flung her wine in his face. Here was something spontaneous and truthful, which was not a matter of style, calculation, or pretense. Here was a heartfelt action—and Jennings had lived most of his life believing that that sort of thing only happened in the movies, not among old friends. He gently kicked some shattered glass. The ruse to save Billy's reputation, however, made him a little sick. He could not take pride in cleverness or pleasure in fooling a crowd.

"I did it on purpose!"

"Billy, we can go or stay."

"Tippecanoe and Tyler too."

The air prickled with static. "All right," announced a policeman, with a radio sputtering on his belt. "We've had a report." He scratched his cheek and looked at Pablo. "You the proprietor of this establishment?"

A customer had destroyed some property, Pablo said, but did not identify Billy.

The policeman, chewing on something, looked at Billy.

"You the perpetrator?"

Billy stepped forward. "Officer, my name is Billy Bell. I would like to identify myself as the instigator of this action. My purpose was symbolic. I plan to run for office in this city, and one of my intentions is to bring the spread of pornography under control. I'm willing to pay for all damages. And if the owners of The Cat's Paw wish to press charges, I am prepared to face—"

"Hey, hold on, aren't you Billy Bell?"

Billy smiled. "Yes."

"I saw you the other day talking to what's his name, I forget. My wife's always telling me I ought to take one of those courses in remembering."

Billy mentioned a name.

"Yeah, that's it."

Billy smiled. "I didn't do too well on that show, did I?"

"Hey now, don't get me wrong. I'm not an expert and maybe it wasn't the epitome or anything, but I thought you did all right. Who's this guy?"

"I'm a member of the press."

The policeman scratched his neck.

"Got credentials?"

"Rush job."

The policeman, upon consideration, let pass this once the failure to provide credentials. "I got to make sure I have this straight. What we have here is a symbolic action, so for all intents and purposes it didn't happen."

"Not exactly, but—"

"And the manager does not want to press charges against the perpetrator."

"I'll call the television stations and newspapers," Jennings told Billy. "Everyone to meet here."

"We'll march to Forty-second Street."

"I'll try to get an ax."

"No, officer," said Pablo. "I definitely do not want to press charges."

"Still got to make a report." The policeman, his brow wrinkled in concentration, spoke into the radio. "Ah, Officer Kip here, investigating report of, ah, destruction of property at, ah, place of pornography, name of Cat's Paw, repeat, Cat's Paw, on Madison Avenue Sixty-third Street. Porno place. We've had a, ah, symbolic action perpetrated by candidate for political office, name of Billy Bell, repeat, Billy Bell, television personality. Owner does not want to press charges. Also, ah, we have a quote unquote journalist here. More press expected."

The radio gurgled.

"Affirmative," said the policeman. "Billy Bell the celebrity. More press expected. Situation under control, but request reinforcement, repeat, reinforcement."

From a telephone booth Jennings notified the TV stations and called several reporters. By chance he found a shop for preppy backpackers across the street, where he bought an ax with a bright red handle. How amazing, he thought, that Billy moments before was incoherent, then with the policeman—perfect. Yet somehow it made sense.

Inside The Cat's Paw Jennings found the policeman lecturing Billy with great patience on the difficulties faced by the NYPD every day of the year in protecting the lives of famous people. Police reinforcements arrived and barricades were set up. Minutes later camera crews, reporters, photographers, and technicians rushed to the door. Then they stood around. They stubbed out cigarettes, sipped coffee from Styrofoam cups, flipped through the

311

magazines, and tried to get Billy to answer questions. Soon the journalists attracted a large crowd of onlookers, who jammed against the barricades. When the restlessness reached the right pitch, Billy stepped up to a microphone. "Today," he said, "I have struck a blow for decency in New York. In the spirit of Mayor Fiorello La Guardia, who many years ago sank a sledgehammer into the Mafia-run pinball empire, I today have taken an ax to pornography as part of my determination to *do* something about a problem about which we've had only words, not action. I do not mean to take the law into my own hands. I will personally pay for all damages and face any criminal charges. I have begun here, at The Cat's Paw, because this store is a symbol of the spread and proliferation of pornography into residential neighborhoods. Now, gentlemen, I am going for a walk to Forty-second Street. You are welcome to join me."

Surrounded by cameras, Billy marched toward Forty-second Street, looking like Paul Bunyan with his ax. The police, including mounted horsemen, cleared the way for him. Behind Billy and the press came a crowd, building of its own momentum. Most people did not know why they were there, so they sent a great onrushing murmur into the air—a seaswell of "What's going on? Who? What's going on? Who?" At Forty-second Street Billy selected a peep-show parlor with a large interior, which gave the TV crews enough room. Then, when the lights were adjusted, he drove his ax several times into one of the movie booths. Afterward he answered questions for half an hour, but refused to announce his candidacy. He promised, however, to continue his campaign against the proliferation of pornography. When some people in the crowd applauded, Billy led the cameras onto the street, where he spent an hour discussing the problem with New Yorkers.

Later, Jennings talked to Billy.

"You need rest."

"What do you mean?"

"You're not well, you know that."

"I'm fine."

"Billy!"

Jennings tried to hold Billy's eye.

"I've been known to drink too much. I'm going to stop."

"Goddamn it, you know you lost control of yourself! You're sick. You didn't do it on purpose."

"I did it on purpose."

6

By constantly changing the channels, Jennings, alone in his apartment, saw most of the television coverage. There was little difference among the reports, which were substantial. Two anchormen identified Billy Bell as a "television personality who made some news of his own today." All reminded viewers of La Guardia's famous attack on slot machines. Correspondents at the scene described the details of the march and narrated shots of Billy striding down the street, sinking his ax into the peep show, delivering his statement. A number of excited passers-by were interviewed; most supported Billy's action, but one witness on each program expressed opposition. The correspondents concluded their reports with speculation about Billy Bell's future. "If today's march is any indication," said one, "Billy Bell is off to the rousingest political start since Mayor Fiorello La Guardia attacked the pinballers."

All but one of the stations also broadcast a report on Tom Prendergast. This came, in each case, at the end of the show, where it was presented as a light note. There was a twinkle in the anchorman's eye when he described Tom's behavior, and some badinage with the weatherman about the boutique in Prendie's where it had taken place. A cropped photograph of Tom was displayed, and the prizewinner was identified as Penelope Lamb. Tom, explaining his motive for coming out of hiding, said "The suspense was killing me. I owed it to the store."

Jennings turned off the television. Then, restless, he turned it back on. For several hours he watched whatever appeared—several sitcoms and a special about corruption in college athletics. He did not turn on any other lights, but let the gray flicker possess the room. At ten-thirty he went out for the early edition of the morning papers, and read them in the television's light. Both the *Daily*

News and the *Times* put Billy's march on the front page. The *News* used a banner headline: "BILLYBASH!" Under the secondary headline, "TV Celeb Axes Porno," was a photograph of Billy swinging his ax. Inside was a feature story:

They unbolted their doors and spilled into the humid air cheering and talking and laughing. Not the hookers who patrol the no man's land of Eighth Avenue. Not the pimps who make Broadway the filthiest show on earth. Not the winos who were maybe once something but now paw you for a quarter. Yesterday the decent people, the ones who know how to smile through a locked window grate, reclaimed Forty-second Street.

I'm talking about the man who runs the deli on Eighth and Forty-fifth, the one who remembers how you take your coffee. I mean the widow from Puerto Rico who watches the kids from the stoop. The guys that deliver the mail. Yesterday they poured out of furnaces called apartments to watch a man who was fed up. A man who was willing this once to take the law into his own hands.

The man was Billy Bell. You know, the TV celebrity. The guy you thought hung out at Mama's, the guy who's maybe aiming at political office. Well, forget that for now. Because yesterday Billy Bell trashed a porno shop. And for once the law-abiding people of this city had something to cheer about . . .

Jennings skipped several paragraphs, then read:

Sam Fillipa is tough. Sam Fillipa has spent his life grinding a lathe. The eyes of Sam Fillipa get wet and sad when he describes what's happened to his neighborhood. Especially to the children.

"I can take it for me," he says. "But these kids. There was Suzy, you know, used to be the tomboy. She wouldn't take nothing from the boys, prettiest brown eyes you ever saw." Sam Fillipa does not like to tell this story. "Well, she got all grown up and . . ."

314

Jennings did not finish the column. The *Times* ran a news story with a picture below the cut. Also an editorial—quick work, Jennings thought—which read:

In a symbolic action that reminded many of Mayor Fiorello La Guardia's attack almost 50 years ago on slot machines, Billy Bell, the television interviewer, has swung a red-handled ax at the pornography business in New York. He attacked two pornography shops, one on Madison Avenue and another in the Times Square area, in an effort, he says, "to restore a sense of decency to this city." He did so fully prepared to foot the bill for damages and to face possibile criminal charges.

It is no secret that Mr. Bell harbors political ambitions. His action yesterday will probably advance his prospects by attracting the attention of those fed up with political dillydallying on this issue. Whether or not his action will help bring about a reasonable solution is more doubtful. However satisfying such inflammatory acts may be, they do not create a climate in which complex problems can be fairly considered. It will never be easy, as the best legal talent has demonstrated, to draw the line between the right of free speech and the understandable desire of both women and men not to see their sexuality degraded.

It is also disconcerting to many thoughtful people when a member of the press—especially a "celebrity" like Mr. Bell—enters politics. Certainly any citizen has the right to run for office, but there is something to be said for the separation of the fourth estate from government, for that difficult, often quarrelsome division between reporters and politicians that is one of the chief safeguards of a democracy. It is particularly important, when a member of the press does run for office, to avoid the sort of attention-grabbing showmanship that often tarnishes both our politics and our press.

Without question, however, Mr. Bell has displayed considerable imagination. As a way of winning arguments an axe may be little better than a gun, but great politicians—responsible leaders no less than demagogues—have often possessed an uncanny talent for the telling gesture. It is one, and only one, of the attributes of leadership. Mayor La Guardia did not drive the mobsters from New York with his ax, but he made a point remembered to this day. Billy Bell has not solved the problem of pornography, but we can reasonably hope he will have stimulated more fruitful forms of discussion—and of behavior.

Both papers also mentioned Tom's escapade. In the *News* Tom was the subject of a feature, and the gossip pages reported that he bought everyone at Mama's a drink. The *Times* ran a small story in the Metropolitan section, along with two paragraphs in the Topics section of the editorial page—a kind of prosy wink, like the twinkle in the anchorman's eye. New Yorkers didn't mind being had, the writer said, if they were had in style.

Jennings suddenly found the babble of the television intolerable. He turned it off, but that also seemed wrong. Leaving it on, he switched to a channel without a station. That was better: a snowy gray light absolved of images. He stared into this light. The empty blizzard was cleansing; he felt purged of the cheap images of the day. In time he began to ache—a vague ailment, almost a glow, that he could not place anywhere on his body. What was this ache? It was the pressure, he decided, between what had been presented to him and what he knew to be true. Then he thought: No, too easy. What did he expect? Of course the world was like that. It always had been. Nor were the images that Billy and Tom presented altogether false. They might violate the private truth, but they possessed some public worth; they plainly touched many people. How else to engage in public conversation but with a certain cheap flair?

He continued to stare into the dead eye of the television. Yet their way was also easy, too easy. And so, into the cold gray light, he drew up the small change of his happiness, the bits of solace and discovery that he had earned in the last few weeks. He remembered his exhilaration (and concern) when Billy went crazy—the excitement that he had now experienced several times of perceiving the living face behind the mask. Of course, how much did he really see? He hardly knew Kelly and he knew—after a decade—so little of Billy. As for himself, he knew himself perhaps least of all. And yet, when he stared into the light, he felt curiously confident. There was something centered in his mind, some obscure but strong idea of how to live: he had had his look. He began to slip the ring on and off his finger. And his awakened imagination? Could he sustain that while staring into the gray light? Was his dreaming, his way with revealing masks, worth more than a one-minute spot on television—a Tom trick or Billy ploy? The light glared off the surrounding walls. He pictured himself seated gray-faced in front of the empty screen. He sat very still. He knew his answers, but the ache worsened.

PART
THREE

CHAPTER

SIXTEEN

I

The house on the dune, where the party for Billy was to be held, had weatherbeaten charm. It was built rambling, stony, and odd in the 1920s, with a roof like a flattened fedora and rakish gables. Behind the dune was an ample lawn, where tough old trees put down shade, and flanking the entrance were two stone pineapples —objects that greatly amused the owner, a stockbroker in a torn Lacoste shirt who kept things casual, especially when celebrities were around. Doors opened and slammed, houseguests fixed their own sandwiches, splashes were heard from the pool. Near the hedge, goggle-eyed children gathered in clumps to watch tanless men from the city uncoil wires and slap around cameras.

Summer had made its turn. The light was longer now, a slanting light touched with the piercing tenderness of fall. The stockbroker, returning from tennis nicely sweated, shook Billy's hand with athletic good humor. Everything was proceeding smoothly, he said. There should be a good crowd, since it was Labor Day week-end. How many invitations had been sent? Almost a thousand? Pretty impressive invitation, the broker said, with those twenty-five names in alphabetical order, requesting the pleasure of your company. And you couldn't ask for a better day. The ocean murmured against the beach.

The broker clapped his hands. Sure you won't join us for a swim? He stopped a guest with plenty of towels—and a briny wind stirred the grass. Billy, alone, wandered past the television trucks. He studied the long tables, naked of bottles and ice. Soon three others joined him . . . Penelope, talking . . . then Jennings and Kelly, who hung back.

2

"We've been looking all over for you," Penelope said. "Now don't say anything, you've got to have lunch. Anyway, this doesn't start for a couple hours, and Jennings and Kelly are *starving*. Kelly said there wasn't any food on the train, only beer. Now that's something I don't understand. Beer in the morning."

She crooked her arm in Billy's.

"Seems like everything's under control. I had a long talk last night with the man who's responsible for all the little things, the kind of things that always go wrong, like the ice runs out, and I told him to bring *twice* as much ice as he planned, just in case."

She led the group to her car.

"Of course, I'm grossly insulted that you couldn't stay with me. Grossly." She smiled and ran her hand up under his shirt. "Still, I understand about politics. You have to stay with that dreary stockbroker since he's your host. You know, I'm even looking forward to this affair," she said, starting her car. "Just don't ask me to go to those rubber chicken things."

At the house they laid out the elegant fixings—French bread, exotic cheeses, a creamy salad—that Penelope had bought in East Hampton. Billy opened two bottles of wine, and Jennings pulled up the chairs. "I wanted to give you a piece of advice," Penelope said to Billy. "But I can't remember what it is right now. It was good, *solid* advice. Damn. What was it? I thought about it last night . . . oh, sit down everyone, it'll come to me. Anyway, it's the perfect weekend, absolutely perfect weather."

"There's some fall in the air," Jennings said.

"Perfect. The guests will have had their beach. They'll be relaxed. But going back to work will be exciting them too. They'll be *anticipating*." Penelope paused. "He's so quiet, rehearsing his speech I bet. Going to give us a preview?"

"That's right," Billy said. "Rehearsing."

"Well?"

"Just rehearsing."

Penelope rolled her eyes, then patted Billy on the arm. "*Anyway*," she said, changing the subject, "it's been a strange summer. That ridiculous business with Tom Prendergast . . . ." She shook her head. "Kelly, were you back for that?"

"Yes."

"Did you *read* all those articles, *see* all those clips on the tube?"

"Some of them."

"The television people even interviewed me, and for the first time I had some idea of what Billy goes through. Complete idiots. Billy, you're the exception of course."

She peered into the salad bowl. "Let's see—" She plucked out a leaf. "I love this arugula. But really"—she nibbled—"what a crazy man Tom Prendergast is." She selected a second leaf. "Except Theodore Oatis and I had lunch the other day—he *loves* you, Kelly—and we decided you have to make some distinctions about craziness. Between shallow craziness, just for show, and the real thing. Artistic madness. I sometimes think *I'm* really crazy. Mad as a hatter."

"You do?"

"As a matter of fact, Jennings, yes. Oatis and I had an argument about which of us was more crazy, I mean *serious* crazy."

"Who won?"

"Well, let me see if I can reconstruct . . ." She put down the leaf. "Both of us are artists—which makes us half crazy by definition, though I have some doubts about whether he's the real thing. He just says he is. I mean everybody today likes to *say* they're an artist. Then . . . well, he said he was impossibly absent-minded, and I said I had no head for money or figures . . . He said he goes on blind, despairing drunks, and I told him about my battle against drugs . . . we both agreed we were obsessive. Sometimes we do absurd things, jump in fountains, that kind of thing. We're loners, in private deeply anguished—yes, Jennings, you smile." She plucked out a fresh leaf. "We've both gone to the edge and come

323

back, part of the way." She smiled. "Not *all* wounds heal." She paused. "Who won? Artists don't think that way. We're lost. It's really true what they say. Lost in our own private worlds—intuitive, mystical, *mad.*"

She took up her knife and fork. "We decided that Kelly is the most sensible person we know. We both envied you. And Billy too, we thought you would make a great public servant because you're so sane."

Jennings said, "What about me?"

"You didn't come up."

"But—"

"Oh, you're level-headed too, nothing to be ashamed of. Billy! I remembered that piece of advice. I knew it'd come back to me. Don't talk too long. People want to sip their drinks, not listen to endless speeches. Short and snappy."

3

After lunch Jennings excused himself. He wanted to talk to Kelly, who had gone upstairs to work. He thought she looked all right—it was hard to tell—certainly better than Billy, who looked shuttered up. Billy would not meet anyone's eye, appeared to be drinking, and refused Jennings' attempts to draw him out. Sometimes when he spoke his face lit up with disconcerting charm, as if he were mimicking himself.

Jennings found Kelly seated at a desk with her back turned to him. He wanted to startle her—to spring free her true feeling. In a conversational voice he said, "Hello."

"Oh, Jennings, hi."

As she turned there was pleasure in her face, but only that of someone greeting a friend seen the day before.

"Penelope said you were here. I hope I'm not—"

"No, sit down."

"I haven't really had a chance to say hello with Penelope around. How was Montana?"

"Fine."

"Where exactly is it you go?"

She told him.

Her reticence seemed appropriate, the matching of the intimacy to the friend.

"How's the piece coming?"

"Oh, I don't know. I'm about done. Sylvia was not an easy subject."

"I'm sure."

He asked if she would like a cup of coffee. She refused, so he left to get one for himself. He was almost angry that she was this reticent. He almost wanted—like a stupid, determined child—to bull his way to the bottom of this bit of arithmetic. When he returned, she asked politely, "What have you done since quitting?"

"Not very much."

Perhaps honesty would prompt honesty.

"But I'm better too. I really am. I've been in a bad way, but—and this is the truth—thanks partly to you I had the courage to leave Billy, and I want to find something, I don't know, more significant to do." He hated his hackneyed phrases, despised his slushy thinking. They did not do justice to his experience. But her steady eyes made him nervous. And these were difficult matters, not easily described.

He pushed on. "It's amazing, isn't it, how you change. You remain the same person, made up of the same elements—except suddenly you've positioned the elements differently, like re-jiggering the muscles in your back. And that makes all the difference. I thought change . . . I thought it was a fantasy . . . I thought I would always—but not now. I'm the same, but—"

"Changed? Well, it's good you're pleased. Not everyone's so glad when they change."

"May I read your piece?" he asked unexpectedly. "I should have asked long ago how it went with Sylvia. Penelope said you visited her house."

"Her apartment too. I wanted to see where she lived."

"And?"

"Well, I went to her apartment last week, earlier than she expected, so she wouldn't clean up." Kelly drew the hair back from her eyes. Her tone was factual, and she seemed prepared, even pleased, to discuss subjects other than herself. "It's a railroad flat in the East Nineties, junky in a girlish way—hairspray cans, clothes strewn about, half-made bed with a cheap bedspread all rumpled, wrappers from McDonald's beside the stove, teddy bear in the corner. And celebrity magazines, television set, and posters of a rock star. What I expected."

She hesitated.

"I guess there were two things that struck me. There was a little ladies' makeup table in the corner, covered with standing photographs in expensive silver frames, all carefully arranged. A picture of her parents on their wedding day, her little brother, a framed postcard of a Coldstream guard in front of, probably, Buckingham Palace. Several rock stars and, believe it or not, a publicity photograph of Billy. It was a strange sort of table and a little spooky in the room of a teenage girl—morbid, like a private altar or the photographs on top of gravestones in Greece."

The description chilled Jennings.

"And the other thing?"

"There was only one window, which was barred. But that's not what struck me. Her little bit of daylight was soaked up by about twenty house plants, all of them fashionable-looking, with elegant feathery leaves or odd shapes. Not a single philodendron."

"Sad."

She repeated the word in a deadpan voice. "Sad." Did she find him sentimental? Was there scorn, barely concealed, in her expression? He must keep up his end of the conversation, he thought, and "Sad" was not good enough.

"I can imagine the house where she grew up. A house just like the house next door, ranch style and a little seedy. Levittown, with a one-car garage and a postage-stamp lawn."

"Better than you think. Very trim. Larger. Colonial and a two-car garage. I didn't go inside, and I never told her I was going to look at the house. I stayed around in my car until I saw her father. I wanted to see what he was like."

"And?"

"I pulled up pretending I was lost and asked him for instructions. He was pretty old, a building contractor who had made a little money. Not unfriendly, but"—she thought a minute—"well, he gave me instructions for a very long time, and he leaned on the windowsill of the car. He had a way of looking at me that was a bit of a leer, but not so I could say anything. I don't see how I can put that into the article, except perhaps I should find a way. If it's true, Sylvia would know it. Of course . . . maybe she doesn't recognize it. Anyway, it told me a lot about her life."

Jennings stared at the article.

"Well, here," she said. "Read it. I can't understand why you're so interested."

"I suggested it."

"I might not publish it."

"Why not?"

"That bother you?"

"No."

"I don't care about publishing it. I wanted to warn you."

"What did you care about, then?"

"Describing her in a certain way, not like before. Actually I just want her to read it. She doesn't have to like it. Just understand what I've said."

The article began, "I knew Sylvia's body, and also her voice, before I knew Sylvia. By dropping a quarter into a machine at The Cat's Paw I could raise a small screen and see the stage where she works, naked. The staff at The Cat's Paw usually aims several very hot lights at her to help customers inspect her body. The features that depend on some shading, such as her eyes or the hollow between her breasts, lose the most. Sylvia would like to be a modern dancer.

"She is only seventeen, still mostly a girl . . ."

Jennings, nervous, read quickly. Although he liked the article, he was disturbed by her tone of voice. He thought she sounded too strict. He did not mind her reserve, since some reserve was worth any amount of me-me-meing. Nor did he mind her severity, without which nothing hard or true could be exacted from the mush of feeling. What troubled him was her strictness with herself, with the Kelly he knew.

He told her, "I think it's wonderful."

"I'm glad you like it."

He pretended to reread a section. Before, in the sketches, she had written with cool disdain. There would always be something vivid or unexpected, however, a phrase of wicked charm or a paragraph of kind and forgiving reflection. He had expected to find,

327

when she did not write satirically, more of her warmth and teasing humor, traits easily developed, he would have thought, in an article about Sylvia. Instead, he found a style tense with the will to suppress. He was reminded of how she spoke to him—of the frankness that gave away little. She had straightened a part of her nature that he cherished, arranged a divorce that dismayed him. What energy it must have taken! Perhaps she even enjoyed her act of suppression—felt the pleasure of one who trims away much to live better on less. He could not let it pass.

"The style's not what I expected."

"I was hoping there wouldn't be a style."

He remembered their discussion weeks before about satire.

"I meant the difference with your other sketches. I thought this one would be more extravagant—brightly colored."

"At least I avoided that."

Was there bitterness in her voice? An uncaught tremble in her eye?

"What did you want the writing to be like?"

"Clean, straightforward. Nothing fancy. No tricks. Not that showy, plain-Jane understatement either. Or that elliptical style, dripping with meaningfulness."

"Why not some . . . panache?"

"What a word! No, no panache, no strut, no poetry. I'm tired of writers and writing."

"That sounds like a style."

She waved away his remark. "There'll be some style, you can't help that. I just don't want to call too much attention to the writing. I want to talk about other things. I want to look through the words."

There was a pause.

She continued, "Most of all I don't want to sound too sensitive. Or poetic. I hate that. Prose ought to feel a bit ordinary, even when it's not. Don't you think? It should hang around near home, which is plain old talking. Then it has a little dignity. When you fancy it up, push it around, give it smarts, it gets all embarrassed. It wants to be poetry. Do you like embarrassed prose?" Her question sounded pointed. There was no reason to lecture about writing, so her remarks must be addressed to him for a purpose he did not understand.

There was a long pause.

"You're so matter of fact," he said, the blood rising to his face. "I don't see why we can't be friendly, even if it's nothing more than that. I don't mean acquaintances. Something warmer, more spontaneous. I know it's my fault. I should explain. I was putting on an act for myself, no doubt I was using—"

"Jennings."

The name stopped him.

"Let's not start, all right? Things didn't work. There it is. I don't think either of us is altogether sorry, so let's not pick at it. It's boring, trite. So much . . . sloppiness. Okay? I came out here for one reason: because I want to talk to Billy right away, to get whatever bizarre business he's up to over and done with."

Downstairs he heard Penelope chattering.

He said, "I think we have to talk."

"Have to! What—"

The blue eyes trembled. She opened—quick as a shadow flying across water—and closed.

"Kelly—"

She raised a finger to her lips. "Shhhh."

Before he could speak she said, "You talked about using. Don't worry. I placed certain unfair burdens on you, for my own purposes. Using . . . well, that's not worth discussing. We're even."

She seemed so still he twisted around. Just a glimpse, and he could not be sure what he had seen. He grappled in his pocket. "Whatever you might say, here, I want you to have this." He handed her the ring. "You've given me a lot, and I want you to have it."

"I can't accept this."

"Yes—do."

She put the ring on the table and stared at it: a stone light, a drop of blood, a parrot's eye.

"Oh, don't look so forlorn," she said. "It's too melodramatic not to take it, so here—there." She glanced at her finger. "Very pretty, but you'll get it back later." Then, standing up, she shook her head. "Come on, we'll be late. I have to change."

329

4

The other two had gone ahead, so Jennings and Kelly walked to the party together. They did not say much; the crunch of their footsteps was sound enough. Soon they came to the cars, mostly foreign, parked in sloppy rows along the road bank. Beyond the stone pineapples, in the green place sheltered by house and dune, they saw a pastel crowd: peach and lavender blouses, chalk-white trousers, soft blue blazers. Men, pink from sun and tennis, steered elbows from one group to the next, and the air smelled of sea salt and barbecue smoke. They hesitated. Now and then, above the hollow roar of the ocean, a laugh kicked up—and died away, like spray over a rock. "Such an extravagant light," Kelly said quietly. Then she turned toward him, politely. "I guess Billy is not just an ordinary celebrity now. What do you call an important celebrity?"

"He hasn't been elected yet."

"Well, he's risen a notch. It's an incredible thing to have done," she continued. "Attacking those machines with an axe. Great theater."

Jennings did not tell her it was his idea. Nor did he mention the crack-up: he owed Billy some discretion. He said only, "The papers have been full of it."

They stood near the television trucks, among the children who rattled around the edge of the crowd. A miked voice began to echo over the party. "Testing . . . testing . . ."

Jennings said, "I guess we should—"

"Suppose so."

"Mingle."

He fetched two drinks. He wanted to be comfortable with her, which seemed a small enough hope. They chatted with Penelope, who could not talk for long, since she had business near the stage. They asked a film-maker about his film, and he talked at length. The party was not friendly, Jennings thought, just big and dull like most political gatherings. He wanted Kelly and himself to stand apart. And so, when the film-maker left, he said wryly, "Everybody who ever boycotted a grape."

"Testing . . . testing."

She said, "I wonder if Billy's so liberal."

330

"No one's so liberal now."

"I guess not."

"Testing . . . testing."

Jennings swirled his drink. He disliked the sound of his voice in idle conversation with her. He glanced at the drop of red on her finger. "Look at that," he said, pointing to a reporter who was trailed by a cameraman. Whenever the reporter indicated a person of interest, the cameraman took a picture. "That kind of reporter, all those people who are involved in the apparatus of celebrity"— he wanted to sound intelligent—"have a similar look or manner. I mean the reporters, photographers, flaks, that sort of person. They're unglamorous themselves, but—what is that look?—sort of bitter and brassy, and a little mangy too, tufts of fur here and there. Tough old hungry coyotes."

"Lots of those in Montana."

He glanced sharply at her. Was she listening to what he said?

"Testing . . . one–two–three–four."

"You usually hear them at night."

"I guess we should sit somewhere."

He did not want to force conversation, so he said nothing more —and wondered, as always, what she was thinking.

Again and again the voice testing the sound system cut across the cocktail talk. This prompted several couples to sit on the grass. Then more did so. Soon the few people who were left standing ducked down or hurried to the edges. Jennings found a spot against the dune, not far from the microphone. In the shade the sand felt as cool as the floor of a cave. He remembered his childhood summers: the salty air that got under his shirt, the swell of the ocean, the prickly dune grass.

"I'm pleased, very pleased," the host said, "to welcome each of you to my home on what is, I'm sure, a very important occasion." He smiled and complimented his guests on their intelligence in supporting a fresh face, then "without further ado" brought Teitelman to the microphone to introduce Billy.

Jennings turned to Kelly. "What are you thinking?"

"Nothing much."

"Doesn't look that way."

"I'm listening."

"Nothing more?"

"I'm tired."

331

"Billy Bell," said Teitelman, "has brought to television a distinction we have sorely missed in New York. And New Yorkers, almost all New Yorkers, have answered in kind. He is not simply a great popular success, in the tradition of Mayor La Guardia, he is also admired and respected . . ." Billy, not looking at the crowd, standing a little apart, appeared very modest as he listened to Teitelman. It was duty, rather than ambition, that called Billy Bell to public service. A faint nimbus of light surrounded him.

"I would like to tell this audience something strange. Billy Bell, deep down, doesn't want a job in politics. Others want him there. The committee established today is a compromise between *your* desire and *his* modesty . . ." Jennings dug his fingers into the sand. He hated what he saw and heard. The light around Billy was an illusion produced by the white suit. The appearance of modesty came from the easy posture, the half smile, the distance from the microphone. And Billy—but who could tell?—was almost drunk.

The crowd applauded, a timid sound under the sky.

Billy accepted the microphone. Photographers began to scurry, crouch, circle. TV cameramen, standing up to aim at him, blocked the view of many guests. "Thank you, thank you very much," Billy said. He pointed a finger at Teitelman in mock accusation. "The only reason I'm taking all of this seriously is because of *him*."

Jennings, remembering his resolve to help Billy, tried to watch. He gripped the sand with his hands, and looked away. What had she said—"such an extraordinary light"?

"This committee is modest in scope. I have had no direct experience in public affairs, and it may not be advisable for a member of the press to seek elective office. These are things we will investigate. So many friends have urged me to run . . ." Jennings struck the scene from his mind, and the grounds became almost quiet. What had she said? He stared into the raking afternoon light, an autumn light, slanted by the hour of the day and the tilt of the earth. It was a light in which time itself was refracted. He remembered many things, but nothing in particular.

"No doubt most of you have read about my response to the assault of pornography, that terrible assault to which we are daily subjected in midtown Manhattan. Well, the spread of pornography is certainly one of the things that is wrong with the city. But this afternoon, in this beautiful place, I would like to talk very briefly about some of the things that are *right* about New York." Billy smiled. "I want to throw a little corn in your direction . . ." Yes, such a light. It was distilled from the hot breath of summer, then polished by the sea. Jennings, enamored, loved this light as much as he loved anything. It would be easy to pay attention to little else, easy but not challenging enough, not quite right either.

"In the first place, *you* are what is great about New York. Think of the talent here in this audience . . ." Jennings looked at Billy, and his hands relaxed. The light was not only lovely, but cutting in its clarity: he could let many things go. "Talent in business, in the arts, in the professions. No other city in the world . . ." Let many things go, celebrate a light both lovely and exact. Yet Jennings did not rest there. Neither a moralist's nor a connoisseur's eye, nor the two working together, gave him a wide enough view.

Billy continued.

There was no need to look to know how she was. He could see the fall of hair across a smooth cheek and the drop of red on a finger. He saw her suffering too; and the space between them seemed a piece of madness. "Kelly," he whispered, then whispered again until she faced him. "I'm sorry. You have to let me say I'm sorry. Then we can go on from there—"

". . . New York is unique . . ."

"I'm not sure I like you enough."

". . . the Big Apple . . ."

"No pressure."

". . . extraordinary . . ."

"Maybe someday."

". . . if we pull together . . ."

Jennings kissed her to seal the small promise. He held the kiss for a moment, but she did not appear moved.

"This city . . .

"Needs . . .

"Can . . ."

Jennings became aware of the murmur of the ocean pushing in and pushing out; and then of the grinding of the cicadas and the squeal of the gulls; and then of the silence.

He looked down at the microphone.

Billy, staring up at them, would not speak. Jennings, trapped, would not look away.

"Billy?" said a voice.

The crowd began to stir.

"Billy?"

Jennings looked at Kelly. Her eyes were shut, her face tipped up. She might have been sunbathing, except for the flicker of her eyelids.

"Billy!"

The crowd began to jabber.

Reporters shouted questions. "Mr. Bell! Over here! Are you going to announce? Mr. Bell!" When he did not answer, they crowded around the microphone. "Billy—what? Are you all right?"

The TV cameras nosed close.

"Mr. Bell," said Teitelman through the microphone, "has been very ill. This morning he had a high temperature and at my insistence took some strong medication. He refused to cancel the party, though he was urged to do so. I think he just needs some rest. I'm sure we all wish him well—and thank you for coming."

The reporters began to shout questions at Teitelman.

"Not now, gentlemen."

Billy, smiling, walked through the crowd into the house. There was a movement beside Jennings—and Kelly was already up and over the dune. He walked to the top, but did not follow her down. Her pace was not that of a brisk constitutional or a sad brood or a convulsive upset; it was that of someone going from one place to another. Once, passing along the shoreline, she made a lobbing motion with her wrist, like a boy tossing stones into a pond. Perhaps, he thought, she has thrown the ring into the ocean: she wouldn't fear the expense or the cliché. He glanced at the clouds, touched with the first pink of evening, and restrained a desire to run after her. He respected her solitary form too much. And in that special light he could almost see and think and feel as she did. He could almost walk with her, from one place to the next, beside the humdrum sea.

5

As waiters clinked bottle after bottle into plastic sacks, as engines roared up and into life, the guests who wanted a last free drink gossiped about the debacle. Few believed Teitelman's explanation, but no better reason was advanced. Jennings, looking around the lawn, did not see his host, Teitelman, or Penelope. Inside the house, however, he found a small crowd of people putting the best face on things. He asked where Billy was. "Upstairs," said the stockbroker, who was polite. "But he prefers not to see anyone." Jennings walked briskly up the stairs, opening door after door. In a maid's room on the third floor he found Billy seated with his feet on the windowsill; he was rocking slowly, precariously, on the spindly legs of his chair. When Jennings knocked, Billy continued to stare out the window, without turning round.

"Billy," said Jennings, in a matter-of-fact voice. "Kelly and I are not lovers. I can truthfully say that. I only kissed her because—"

Billy raised his hand, so slowly he might have been holding up the sky. "I think," Billy said, "that the show hasn't had enough light personalities on a regular basis. I need to get some humor, life, funniness, back on. Don't you think? Of course, I'll never give up the serious stuff, after all that's my bread and butter, what makes me special on television. Just—the mix could be better."

Billy, smiling, turned round.

"In any case, I *better* think about the show." The smile edged wider. "Maybe more Broadway people. I think the audience likes it when stars sing a few show tunes. Takes some pressure off the interviewer, too. And comedians, I ought to get some more comedians, not the ones that are so bad they make you wince, but the good ones. The ones that make you really laugh out loud. You know the kind I mean. I bet they'd like to be on my show."

"Billy—"

This time the hand jerked up, as if another voice caused him pain. "I think," he continued, "that in addition to a more lighthearted approach I should work on the rhythm of the programs. I'll continue the special issue weeks, of course, but when it's not one of those weeks I should work hard on the rhythm. Rhythm. Many people watch every day, you know, so I don't want to have two bureaucrats in a row."

"Billy—"

"I want you to think about what I've been saying. Think about it."

6

When Jennings came downstairs Teitelman took him aside, saying, "He's drunk, isn't he?"

"Not drunk enough."

"What?"

"Think about it."

Jennings hesitated. "He doesn't want to see me, so you all are going to have to take care of him."

"And do what?"

"Call a doctor."

"He's refused to see a doctor. I asked a doctor I knew to come inside—a guest."

Billy came down the stairs. He nodded to each person in turn, like a Japanese businessman, and went out the door. Then he drove away in his car, so nothing more could be done.

CHAPTER

SEVENTEEN

I

Billy did not have a destination in mind. It was the driving itself that attracted him. He took pleasure in spurting along country lanes, then braking hard at stop signs. He wheeled the car around corners with his index finger and accelerated sharply coming out of curves. He turned the radio up loud. Whenever a car slowed him down he cursed the driver above the sound of the music. "Goddamn idiot!" Then, nosing his car within inches of the tailgate, he flicked his wrist, floored the pedal, and passed the offender. His rented car handled as sloppily as a boat, he thought, and its weak acceleration was disgusting—you might as well kick an old horse. But what could you do? Answer: nothing. In compensation, he took a sip from his pocket flask. He was careful, as usual, to stay on the right side of a vague but recognizable point of drunkenness. He was not out of control, he was not in control. He hung on the sweet edge.

His hope, after passing through East Hampton, was to leave the ocean behind. By turning at every chance in the direction that looked least desirable, he came to an area of piny woods near The Springs—thin, scrappy forest through which he could see vacation houses made of glass and board. On the sandy lawns were boats on top of trailers and plastic swimming pools connected to a house; and off the main highway were many new roads, built for half-sold developments, along which boys in helmets hot-rodded tiny motorbikes. These roads, which seemed to go nowhere, cut straight into the forest and then began to branch. Each branch —and the woods it defined—looked the same. Billy, losing himself on such roads, began to drive as if to float: wheeling and wheeling and wheeling. He loved being master of a machine, and lost.

He thought back to his speech only when he ended up on a more established road that led to the bay. What he remembered, for an awful moment, was the naked silence; and then the hiss of the sea. This, in turn, led him to play a game with himself. Upon sighting the water he would say with mock terror, "Something-tells-me-I-better-get-out-of-here!" He did not use his normal voice, but that of one of the Little Rascals, whom he had watched on television as a child. Then he would whirl the car around, thinking to himself, "Make tracks, buddy." And before long he would be lost again in the reassuring maze.

It was dark when he ran out of Scotch and decided to find a motel and bar. The motels near the shore were full, but inland he discovered a place with a lit vacancy sign. It was very small, in an area that was more than a stretch of road but less than a town; close by were a gas station, a 7–11, a body shop, and a bar with winking neon. Billy rang the bell to the office—and a cat scooted between his legs. He rang a second time and a fat woman, smelling of potato chips, admitted him to the parlor. From another room he heard the blare of the television and signed a false name in the register with keen pleasure. His room, just beyond the Coke machine, was exactly right. The doorknob was loose, the bedspread was orange, the television was chained to the floor. On the wall was a picture of Mount Fuji and the bathroom smelled of disinfectant. After changing into ordinary clothes, Billy walked over to the Tiptop Tavern. He was almost invisible.

He loved the place—loved the slightly sour air and the deep bar darkness. The clocks contributed by brewing companies glowed like lanterns; above the row of bottles was a mounted swordfish, nicknamed Ralph, with a busted bill. He ordered a beer. Then he ordered another, for the man two stools down.

This brought only mumbled thanks.

338

"You don't have to worry," Billy said, "I won the lottery the other day, that's all, nothing big, only a thousand bucks. Just seems like I ought to buy somebody a drink."

On the left arm of the man, who did not answer, was a green blur—a mermaid coiled around an anchor. His expression was not unfriendly, but it suggested that unscrupulous people had often taken advantage of his good and trusting nature. And brother, it wasn't going to happen again.

"You know what?" Billy said, not looking at the man. "Damnedest thing, but I win only a thousand dollars and everybody wants to know about it, even wants a piece of it. Christ. Aunts, uncles I haven't heard from in years. Newspaper calls me up."

The man glanced at him. Billy repeated "Everybody wants a piece!"

He loved talking this way, but he did not push too hard. The man two stools down eventually said, "Appreciate the drink. Except you can't be too careful these days."

"My sentiments exactly."

"Can't be too careful," the man said, shaking his head. "God almighty, but there's faggots everywhere now."

"Falling out of trees."

The man laughed.

"Falling out of trees," the man said. "That's rich."

On the big color television raised above the bar a football game was winding up and the local news followed. Something was wrong in South Africa, the president gave a speech in Denver. No one watched much, and the jukebox made it hard to hear what was said. His friend passed him a bowl of pretzels and the anchorman mentioned the name of Billy Bell.

Billy directed the attention of his friend to the screen. "Look at that."

"What?"

"That guy."

His friend looked. After displaying a still of Billy swinging the ax, the anchorman ran a clip of Billy's freeze at the microphone. Then a reporter told viewers, "No one can say for sure what happened to Mr. Bell. His aides tell me he has not been well in the last few weeks. At present he has gone into seclusion, refusing all comment. But a statement is promised for next week."

"Unbelievable," said Billy, passing the pretzels to his friend.

339

"Politicians is what's unbelievable."

"Rob you—"

"*Blind.*"

Billy's face burned. "All the goddamn same."

"Every last one of them."

"See that about that congressman?" Billy said. "Last week, the guy's been robbing some fund or something."

"Sure, but I'm not saying some of them aren't honest," his friend said, shaking his head. "Just the great majority, hell, proof's right before our eyes—in it for two things—money and sex. And that's a fact."

"What can you do?"

"Going to hell is what we're doing."

Billy laughed and ordered another round.

After a while his friend said, "Haven't seen you here before."

"Just passing through. Visiting relatives of my mother's."

"That time of year."

"Sure is."

"Married?"

"Divorced."

"Me too."

There was a pause.

"Ran off and left me," Billy said. "Damnedest thing."

"Happens to the best."

Billy's friend pushed him the pretzels and said, "Maybe you're better off without her."

"Can you believe it? Left me for a carpenter."

"You don't like carpenters?"

"This was an *artistic* carpenter."

"Oh, I'm following you."

"Sore of wavy hair, cute little smile."

"Faggot carpenter."

"That's it."

"I'm following you."

"Well, I get this guy in to do a little work around the house and you know he fusses here, he fusses there, and pretty soon he's fucking the wife."

"Rough."

Billy shuddered. How could he be so impolite? All this time, and he had not asked his friend what had happened to his wife. "How about you?"

The friend shrugged. "Got tired of her. Always whining, varicose veins. Got to be too much, you know what I'm saying? Up to here"—he raised a hand to his chin—"so one day she does a number on me so I did a number on her. No regrets."

"Lucky guy."

"Lucky! Took me to the cleaners is what she did."

Tears filled Billy's eyes. He patted his pal on the back and pushed him the bowl of pretzels. Barstool to barstool: that was friendship.

"So I enlisted," Billy said.

There was a respectful pause.

"You in the service?" Billy asked.

"Navy. Korea. Didn't do a damn thing except hang around the dock in Honolulu. Nice girls there, though. Asian types."

"Beautiful."

His friend asked when Billy joined up.

"Army. Vietnam."

There was a pause.

"Tough?"

Billy nodded. He could not speak.

His friend pushed him the pretzels.

"Still dream about it all the time."

Billy, suddenly busy, ordered another round.

He settled back. "Bloody," he said. "And nobody gives a damn."

"Tough."

"Most of my friends—blown away." He took a long pull of beer. "We're out on patrol one day, damn rice paddies, mud up to your ass, and we see this other patrol, except—" Again he could not speak.

"Tough."

"God's truth."

There was a pause.

"I don't need any more Fourth of Julys like that."

"Better believe it."

"My friend Roger got blown up—good guy, family and all. Bunch of other guys too." Billy smiled. " 'Course they got shot up pretty bad, too. I'd say worse."

There was a pause.

Billy took another long sip.

"Until there was just me and this other guy. Trouble was, he couldn't get his clip into his gun fast enough—so I just nailed him to this tree he was against."

Billy smiled.

"You think I'm kidding? I mean literally, I nailed him. Can't imagine what a burst'll do to you. Blew him away until there was just his trunk nailed to the *tree* trunk."

"Incredible."

"Nailed."

"Sure, nailed. Unbelievable. Trunk to trunk, that's rich."

"Over there," Billy said, "you didn't care about anything— nothing."

Billy chewed some pretzels.

"R and R, you didn't care about anything, just getting obliterated. Know what I'm saying?"

"Brother, do I!"

"Nice girls, Vietnamese."

"A-men."

Billy ordered another round; and several more, as the night progressed. When the bar closed, he wanted to take his buddy to another place. Told nothing was open, he tried to bribe the bartender not to close. Then he made his friend swear to meet him tomorrow night. "Cross your heart hope to die?"

2

In the morning his head was soaked through with pain. The slightest stirring, the softest whisper of a thought—impossible. He lay in bed hardly breathing, infinitely still, until his mind tightened into glass. Then he got up very slowly, carrying his head on his shoulders as if it might shatter. On the hotplate he made himself a cup of coffee, sweetened with Scotch. He did this twice more. He took several aspirin and began to feel better. Relief seemed all the more wonderful after the harsh hangover and soon he was almost euphoric. He celebrated with a drink and a shower. And then he went to work.

Driving the car was his sacred trust. He spent most of the day in the conscientious performance of duty, staying first on the back roads then pushing onto the highways. He did not notice where he was going and everything looked the same. Sometimes he stopped for a drink or pulled into a parking lot for a nip and a nap. Because the liquor stores were closed on Labor Day, he bribed a bartender fifty dollars to sell him several bottles, which he stashed under the seat. He liked their friendly clinking whenever he accelerated. He found his new duties somewhat disorienting— but also wonderful. He had often had too much to drink in the past, but never in the morning. And he had never been drunk for two days running.

It was like falling in love. Nothing mattered but the fine sweet bottle, which kept him up day and night. He was always too tired and too awake; and he was always very tender—but no more so than his lover, whose warm touch led him to relax and yield up. Over time, as the exhilaration of early love passed, he began to dote on his bottle, treating it with the familiarity accorded a spouse in a long, happy marriage. The bottle knew his moods, adjusted to his needs. It even told him when to lay off, in order to continue the performance of his sacred trust. The bottle made him feel like a great man, when he narrowed his eyes; or a kind man, when he smiled; or a powerful man, when he swung in and out of traffic; or a free man, since he did what he wanted. He ran through stop signs, he stopped for half a gallon of gas, he urinated beside the road. Afterwards there was always someone to talk to.

Liquor also brought him physical relief. If his eyes began to ache, he took a shot and the pain melted away like ice in warm water. If he began to tighten up, he took another shot—and relished the spongy sensation in his lips and the looseness around his belt. His greatest pleasure, however, came in the sequence of sensations that followed a good slug. First the gag in the throat, like a violent spasm; next the surge of nausea, full of disgust; and then the soft rewarding warmth, which radiated from his chest. His first day passed easily with the help of the bottle, and the police never stopped him. He was also able to find a motel after being thrown out of a bar at three in the morning. Two hours into his sleep, however, he began to drown. He was retching into his pillow. By turning over he found a place to pass out again. Two hours later he woke up blind with pain. To avoid subjecting his eyes to the light he groped on the floor for the bottle. At first the Scotch brought on fresh nausea. Then, with time, he felt a little better. He found a vending machine, and mixed his Scotch with Coke.

On this new day he also did his duty: he captained the car. It took more Scotch to kill his pain, however, and longer naps to restore his energy. The gagging became harsher, the nausea more virulent, the pleasure less soothing. In the middle of the day he began to feel fragile. Walls began to crack, and vague systems burst. He was surrounded by nasty little leaks. These impressions were not metaphorical. He heard walls shift. He saw stars when systems burst. And any liquid but alcohol disgusted him because it might leak; he deposited each drop of Scotch into his mouth with great care, lest it drip. Soon desperation—an old wolf banging against a door—began its assault. With it came fury that he should have to fight so hard.

In midafternoon he happened onto a road that led to the Long Island Expressway. He decided to go to New York—and became very brave. He gunned the car down the ramp, with the bottle between his legs, then angled with great flair around a truck. He took a swig: hot damn. He knew he was taking a chance, since the straightness of the road made him an easy target for enemy thoughts. Now he could no longer stop, reverse course, or make a sudden turn. He considered abandoning the expressway, but told his bottle that "of such stuff are cowards made," and bore on playing the hero. He imagined the steady progression of cars as a slow-moving wagon train, with himself as the courageous scout who spurs his horse up and down the line. Tractor-trailers were the damn oxen.

Unable to duck or turn, exhausted from his journey, pressed at every point, determined to defend the helpless—he began at last to falter. Some enemies got through. He remembered the naked silence, the quizzical look on Teitelman's face, the hammering questions of the reporters. Each memory caught him unaware, bursting from an unexpected direction. Each slashed him—and vanished into the hills. It was some time before he remembered

Kelly; and then only the flicker of her face against the dune. This was a terrible wound. He had to muster all his resources to defend himself from her, which permitted the others to score at will. He told himself he must make it anyway. He must get through. He fixed his eyes on the exit signs, counting down: Exit 55, three miles, Exit 54, Exit 53. Suddenly she smiled, bored, at Mama's. His breath caught. He took a gulp and gagged. He breathed out: made it.

For a moment there was peace. Then a sign shot toward him— NEW YORK 30 MILES. With a flick of the finger, he thought, just a flick, he could somersault his car into that sign. Friends would bear him down the steps of the church. He remembered pictures taken at the funerals of slain police officers: weeping widows and small children on the front page. Then, suddenly, he remembered his letters to Kelly. His breath caught. He took a gulp and gagged. He breathed out: made it.

Soon he stopped all games. There was room for nothing but his will. He must make it to the city under attack. Along the auxiliary roads that ran parallel to the expressway the lights turned red, so he forced his speed to eighty miles an hour—until he seemed to sail on air. Then he remembered her friendly smile, when they first met at Penelope's. His breath caught. He took a gulp and gagged. He breathed out: made it. But he drove slowly now, like an old gentleman. He did not want to be noticed—please, please. Then he flinched: Jennings, smiling, kissed her gently. Once more he accelerated hard. Swerving in and out of the traffic on his side, he pushed hard against the oncoming cars on the other. He took a gulp and gagged. His breath caught. He cut too sharply, almost cuffing a station wagon. Against, against—the traffic on the other side, at a near standstill, increased his sense of speed. Against, against—he flew against the red lights. In front of him a truck was moving so slowly that he became confused: it must be on the other side. He would roar past it! Hurtling forward he braked at the last moment, then swerved and screeched to a stop on the shoulder. His heart was beating too fast. His eyelids twitched. He breathed out: made it.

He rested a moment. In the distance he saw the city, hazy and gray. He remembered, dimly, the other things—the television show, The Cat's Paw, the axe. They were part of a distant struggle. His heart continued to hammer; but now, inside, he located a dead space, very quiet, where he took possession of an idea. He must sneak into the city. He must succeed through surprise. He must tiptoe to the source.

3

When the telephone rang Kelly looked up, then continued her reading. Soon a buzzer sounded, and the doorman announced Sylvia.

"The article is great," Sylvia said, handing the typescript to Kelly. "*Really* great."

"I'm relieved."

"Really *great*."

"I thought you'd be upset."

Sylvia, walking through Kelly's apartment, glanced out the window. "This is pretty nice here," she said, being kind to the reporter.

"What did you like about the article?"

"Oh, you know, everything."

Kelly peered at her. "In particular. Tell me something you liked in particular."

Sylvia teased the reporter. "Fishing for compliments!"

"No, please tell me."

"I just . . . liked it."

Kelly flipped through the typescript as Sylvia, clicking her teeth, performed several dance steps. "Here where I say, listen to this: 'Sylvia has worked out an elaborate but serviceable fantasy. She pretends she is not a stripper by pretending she is a modern dancer. The money she makes stripping she spends on classes—' "

"I don't mind," said Sylvia, staring past Kelly's shoulder. "That's the writing."

"It's writing about you! I said that about you!"

"Don't worry. It's a really great article. I looked at those magazines you talked about—where it'd be published."

"You know what you do? You're nothing but . . . you strip for a bunch of ugly old men. You kind of like it, pretending you're a modern dancer—"

346

"I am a dancer. You said so at the end. Nobody's going—"

"That's not what I meant! And that studio just wants your money. You know that and I confirmed it. Here in the article . . ." She flipped through the pages again. If she had hurt Sylvia, however, it was only by raising her voice. The substance of what she said, let alone the content of her article, glanced off the girl's mind.

"You can say whatever you want," Sylvia said, taking another two steps. "It's a free country."

"Why the princess act? You're a high school dropout."

"Lot of famous people left school."

Sylvia refused to lose her temper, Kelly realized, because she did not want to jeopardize publication of the article. "Sylvia," she said, becoming calm, "Sylvia, did you read what it said?"

" 'Course I did."

"Didn't it bother you at all?"

"Everybody's got bad stuff written about them. I've never read any article or seen any TV show about somebody didn't have something bad to say somewhere, along with everything else. You have to work your way up."

Kelly sat down slowly. There could be no doubt. Sylvia saw nothing but her typed name, just the celebrity of the page. She did not establish a living connection between herself and what she read; or that part didn't matter. Her interest lay only in the magical connection, the turning of herself into something else— an image, any image—for public consumption. Kelly knew other readers would be more perceptive. But it was Sylvia's reaction that mattered most to her.

"What's wrong?" Sylvia asked. "I told you I thought it was really great. Now we just get the pictures. I heard of this terrific guy. Some of the girls use him to shoot their pictures. He's sort of expensive, but still—"

Kelly tried once more. "You'll probably end up a hooker," she said softly. "You're not going to make it in dance. You should realize that. You don't know enough. You don't really get how it works. Maybe if you understood something about yourself, or if you were truly extraordinary physically, then you could beat out those other girls. But they tell me you're not."

"The teacher says that to everyone—she says it builds toughness."

"Well then," Kelly murmured. "I guess I made you up."

"This guy would give us a special rate. He does that sometimes for young dancers, gives us a break."

"I thought you could learn a little. Not a lot maybe, but a little."

"And this guy, he likes my work. I know he does."

"You're not dumb. You should see yourself, since those men do."

"Come on, perk up!, like my dad says. All this gloomy stuff."

"I guess I made both of us up."

"Sure you feel okay?"

Kelly smiled. "You're the teacher."

There was a pause.

Sylvia smiled back.

"You think I'm kidding."

Kelly began to tear pages in long ragged diagonals. Sylvia grabbed her arm. "You can't do that—are you crazy?—give it to me." Then she shouted, "It's mine!"

"What do you mean 'mine'? I wrote it."

"It's about me."

Kelly tore another page, slowly.

"You're not allowed—"

"Of course I am." She tore another.

Sylvia's painted eyes began melting.

Kelly kept tearing.

"It's really good . . ." Sylvia hopped up and down. "It's—you're not allowed . . ."

"Yes I am."

She kept tearing.

"It's so . . . Come on. It's so . . . so neatly typed. Come on . . ."

Kelly soon stopped. She could not be cruel for long.

"I can help you retype it. I took a course once."

"Please, Sylvia, go."

"But everything's okay, right? You shouldn't be depressed. I told you it's a really great article. You're going to publish it, right?"

4

Kelly stared at the curls of white paper. They reminded her of the strips that children turned into paper dolls—though children used scissors, she thought, to perfect the cut. She laid several of the scraps edge to edge: and the words did or did not match. She had no desire to put the pieces back together, but she would have liked to make something, and she remembered her longing after Oatis' birthday party for a gesture of concentrated and summary power. She stood up and scanned the apartment. Her eyes paused at the history books, which she knew backwards and forwards; at the nearby table, where the wine stains looked like puckered rose petals; at the writing desk, on which a stack of paper stood clean and untorn. Then, without rushing, she left the apartment and slipped into the glinting, blue-tinged world.

Had she forgotten something? She often had that feeling now—an obscure uneasiness that kept intruding on her, the way a half-forgotten dream nags at a morning. Except for this spot of vagueness, however, she examined herself with steely precision. "Obviously," she told herself on Broadway—and the wryness chased the doubt out of her expression—"I am badly made." She was too acute not to see the vanity and rot that passed for ordinary, but too ardent not to love life anyway; her warm hope and cool eye worked poorly together; and they always would unless she changed. She marshaled her attempts that summer to find a way to live with both an open eye and heart. Billy, Oatis—and all that—she had hoped to keep at a determined but friendly distance. She had failed. Jennings she had hoped to make a lover or friend, and with him form a kind of island. She had failed. Sylvia she had hoped to teach and protect, in order to change the world a little. She had failed. She did not want to try anything else. It went against her grain to beg for what she couldn't have.

At the fruit and vegetable stand, where she stopped to browse, something moved and caught her eye. She looked and it stopped: her reflection in a shop window. She put down her bag, then circled a stack of melons to reach the clear and ghostly image. She studied it. She stepped forward to make it expand. She stepped

349

back to make it contract. In the background she saw the mirrored city, no less ghostly and clear—and with one wave of her hand she erased a taxi and with another she restored the melons. She crept closer to the ghost: move her head right and it went left, move her head left and it went right. Were there tears in its eyes? Yes, but not too many. She stared until the tears slowly dried away. Then she admired the reflection: poised and still, near and far, staring back.

She ate dinner in a coffee shop. "You like to read the papers, Miss?" The Greek owner, who remembered her from other meals, handed her a thumbed-through *Post*. She flipped through its pages one by one to please him. Afterwards, very tired, she turned the key in her door and a shadow startled her. From behind a drunk closed in. She whirled around and there was a scuffle—a blur of soiled white, a hot, oversweet breath. Then two seconds of crazy laughter, until he lost his balance. He straightened up slowly. She was as strong as a drunk man, but not strong enough to force him out. "I'm going to stay," Billy said. "Have to stay to make conversation." His eyes were black-rimmed—unlit by recognition, unshaded by memory—fish eyes.

5

Later Jennings found Billy slumped against his door. His hair was tangled and his shirt stained. On his cheek was a bad scratch. "Came to see you," he mumbled. "Decided, come to see you."

"What's happened!"

"Decided to have, come to have a conversation."

Jennings guided him to a chair. Billy sprawled out. "Conversation's what I had, better believe it." Jennings considered him too drunk to be taken home; it would be best if he went to sleep. "Too late for conversation," Jennings said. "I think you should take a nap."

"Trying to get rid of me."

"No, no. I think you should—"

"Conversation with her highness."

"Who?"

"Conversation." He winked. Then his smile tipped into fear. "Didn't do anything."

"What happened! Have you spoken to her?"

He became drunker.

"Conversation's what I had."

He winked again.

"Billy, have you been to see her?"

"Who?"

"Kelly."

"Questions, questions, questions. To hell with questions!"

Jennings dialed her number: no answer. Billy began to whistle.

"Shut up!"

Billy looked hurt.

"Don't believe in fun?"

"What happened?"

"No fun."

"Tell me!"

"Not fair."

Jennings turned away, having almost struck Billy. He wondered if he should go to her apartment. The telephone rang and he seized it.

"Kelly! Thank God! Billy's here."

"I just thought," a voice whispered, "that since we never got it on, you might like—"

"Shut up. What are you saying? What's wrong with you? What's happened?"

"Honey, *relax*, get *nice* and comfortable—"

"Stop it! Can you hear me? Stop—"

"There's just one thing I need, honey—"

"Where are you?"

He heard the sound of traffic.

"What street are you on?"

"Coming to get me?"

"Where?"

"Oooh—" A girlish laugh. "How *romantic*."

"What—"

A recorded voice said, "Please deposit five cents for three minutes."

The connection was restored, but the line went dead.

Jennings shook Billy by the shoulders.

"What happened!"

He rattled Billy's head.

Billy mumbled. The head rolled on the neck.

Jennings shoved him back—passed out. Then he walked to the door, to the window, to the kitchen. Her voice, soft as whore's silk, whispered in his ears. It frightened him that she had refused to give up that voice. And it shocked him that she had not sounded drunk. He tried to think clearly. What could have happened? Had Billy raped her? A man that drunk could not rape anyone, or probably not. He examined the scratch on Billy's cheek—roughed her up maybe. He imagined awful drunken insults, a refusal to leave, a scuffle and flash of anger. Billy was a lot bigger. He shuddered: could Billy have hurt her badly? It was no use imagining, it didn't do any damn good. He sat on the floor with an important and abiding sense of his limited power; with a kind of calm presentiment, too, that was nothing like detachment, for he felt deeply engaged in everything that happened. He stared at the dirt-stained clothing, smudged skin, foul hair. He saw the dim stamp of age in the face of his friend; he could easily imagine him at seventy. Jennings went into the kitchen for a bowl of warm water. He cleaned Billy's face, then put him in his own bed.

The telephone rang.

"Think I might have done something bad," Sylvia said in a rush. "She says I didn't, but I don't know. You said to call."

"What's happened?"

"Can I come see you?"

"Tell me!"

"I want to come see you."

He gave her his address. "Be quick."

Jennings met her taxi at the entrance to his building. "Now," he said, taking her by the arm. "What's happened?" She drew him into the taxi. "It's not my fault. She says it isn't my fault."

The taxi stopped at The Cat's Paw.

"She hasn't . . ."

"I don't think it's my fault. She says so."

His eyes closed.

"You okay?"

He walked through The Cat's Paw. The men moved, as usual, in and out of the booths. There was no sign of damage. Sylvia said

"Here." Jennings stepped into a booth, tried to get out a quarter. Then he looked.

"No . . ." he whispered.

"Oh no . . .

"Yes."

He placed one hand on the glass. He burned and shook with chills. He felt empty, he felt full. Then he was surprised by tears. His thoughts bolted and he turned away. She's strange, peculiar. What's Sylvia done? And Billy, damn Billy anyway. Soon, however, he turned back.

6

Jennings tried to call her. When she did not pick up the phone, he found Sylvia and, pushing past the shop guard, entered the changing room. "I didn't do it, right?" Sylvia said, clinging to his arm. "She said it wasn't me." Jennings could not shake free. He asked, "How could it be you?"

"She didn't like what I said about the article."

"No, that's not enough. Not nearly enough."

"She threw it away."

Jennings took Sylvia by both arms. He looked at her kindly. "This is something else. I promise. You were right to call."

"I thought so. You see, it—"

But he left her, to walk onstage.

She stood naked on the dais. Her body was very still. Only her fingers moved, softly drumming against her thigh. He whispered "Kelly," hardly knowing his voice. She did not answer or look around. Her body was open. Her mind was sealed.

"Kelly."

She did not answer. She seemed to shed wave after wave of light. He stood in her reflection, half blinded.

"Kelly."

She did not answer.

In the unforgiving light, he felt picked out.

"Now . . . let's go now."

She turned toward him. He was startled: a statue had come to life. He took a step toward her. "Let's go now." He considered her temporarily mad. He meant to lead her from the stage, gently. She would receive help; and with rest she would recover. When she looked at him, however, she smiled—a slight smile, very proud, which did not seem mad. "I'm almost done."

CHAPTER

EIGHTEEN

I

On the December morning that Billy and Penelope were to be married, Jennings went to the church half an hour early. He took a seat in a rear corner pew. The minister, the same man who had presided at the reading of Penelope's diary, looked nervous—celebrities and photographers were expected. At the first sign of guests he motioned furiously to the harpsichordist, who began to play baroque music. Among those filing into the church were Teitelman, who nodded to acquaintances already seated; Oatis, who looked as though his work in progress had been interrupted; and Tom, who wore a burnt-rose suit. Because Tom did not have a good figure, Jennings thought, the suit was not altogether successful; it made him look like a polished billiard ball. The model on his arm, however, was perfect.

The attack upon The Cat's Paw had turned Billy into a folk hero. His breakdown at the microphone further increased his stature, since he threw himself on the mercy of the public. He made a full confession of alcoholism and ruled himself out of politics, at least for the near future. The celebrity magazines portrayed him as a wounded hero, a young man of promise who had known early sorrow. The newspapers admired his forthright honesty; too often, they said, well-known personalities pretended to be free of ordinary human failings. During his stay at a private hospital in Massachusetts, Billy had written the story of his life, which he sold to a publisher for an enormous advance. There was talk of a movie in which he might play himself, and his show would soon be syndicated on national television.

Jennings thought Billy looked well, as he stood at the altar. He seemed self-assured, happy, handsome. They had remained friends, but were no longer close. They had only kept up, Jennings knew, to confirm that nothing significant had happened. He also thought Penelope looked well, a picture of radiant angst as she walked down the aisle in an antique purple dress. The purple was one of the untraditional touches about which Penelope had alerted the press. It was better to be natural, she argued, than to pretend to an outdated notion of purity that oppressed women. She herself had become a minor celebrity, the heroine behind the "Love Saves Star from Bottle" headlines. Although she refused on principle to describe the details of Billy's illness, she left the impression of having undergone considerable private tribulation.

The minister spread his arms. "My friends," he said. "Before we begin this . . . joyous occasion I would like to share just two pieces of information with you. The first is that this service has been written by the bride. Her hope, she told me, is to achieve a union of tradition and spontaneity—not, I might add, a bad agenda for marriage itself. She has tried to endow an ancient ceremony with a contemporary spirit, to be respectful of the past but unafraid of the present. I'm sure you will agree with me that she has happily succeeded. Secondly, I hope you have all noticed what a beautiful day it is, with some of fall's fruitfulness still in the air but the crispness of winter just around the corner. A change of season is a wonderful time to make a beginning.

"Will you please rise, then, and join with me . . ."

On another occasion Jennings would have stayed for the service. The person he wanted to see, however, had not come. He was in no mood, as a result, for another performance of Penelope's—not in this poet's church that he remembered too well. He had not seen Kelly since her disrobing, and he still did not know exactly what precipitated her act. Billy, when asked, remembered nothing of his spree: alcohol, he said, had a way of doing that. Jennings slipped outside, into the crush of people hoping for a glimpse of the celebrated couple. Was that Sylvia behind the police barricade, Jennings wondered, three or four deep in the crowd? Yes. He walked slowly toward SoHo; there would soon be a large reception in Penelope's loft, where he could offer his congratulations. He looked around. The minister was right. It was a lovely day, warm but with ice skirting the puddles. He had a sudden idea—to see how she was.

There could be no meeting yet. She had said she was busy on both the dates he suggested, and he refused to press her. Her friends said she was doing well. She had returned to her old magazine, having given up the idea—crazy anyway, the friends said—of teaching adolescents. Her position was responsible and her social life was pretty lively. Jennings walked rapidly uptown, toward the cast-iron building where she worked. Chances were good, he thought, that she would go out for lunch. He could see her then. Perhaps seeing her—even from a position across the street—would tell him what he needed to know. He waited in the bay of a luggage store, where he could watch the entrance of the old building. Its recessed windows looked brooding, he thought, like a person with deeply set eyes. But their stern symmetry was softened by the surprise up or down of the shades. He saw dangling strings and watched people moving around inside.

This stakeout differed from his earlier ones. He was not only willing to meet her, but he also regarded her in a new way. Though he often saw her in his mind's eye standing naked on the stage, he did not admire this image from afar, like a museum picture that remains safely distant. Its beauty for him was of a kind that only the author of an image can know, one in which he himself is implicated, in which the creation cannot escape the life. He could not simply turn her into some sort of art; he had contributed to the real suffering—the thought warmed his eyes with tears—which had animated her act. He could no longer admire, or not easily, any picture of disdain or purposelessness. He did not like art that absolved itself of life or dreams that despised the day.

Was that Kelly?

No.

He was not selfish enough, however, to blame only himself. He granted her freedom and mystery. No doubt each had used the other in a private story. No doubt she was a little unbalanced.

357

(He loved her kind of imbalance.) Certainly he could never know all that had impelled her onstage. Nonetheless, he accepted a measure of guilt. The surprisingly small place where minds touch—that place was important, and he had failed her there.

Was that Kelly?

No.

He hoped to do some worthwhile work, placing in proper relation the many things he knew. But he found it impossible to like himself much. There was something pinched in his heart, something thin and reflected in his character. She was a kind of sun and he was a kind of moon. He loved those who did not have to borrow or steal their light.

Was that Kelly?

Yes.

2

She stifled a shiver like the twinge of a forgotten muscle. "Maybe he didn't see me." She tossed back her hair and took a deep breath. At a traffic light she wondered if he had a job. Would he produce a documentary? Or write a book with the usual ache? Perhaps he would do something good, though even the best rarely did. The light changed. She smiled to herself—remembering, as one remembers something from long ago, how she had picked him out of the crowd at the soup restaurant. She did not go up to him, however, partly because he was probably the same disappointing Jennings, partly because she no longer looked for love. She had not lost her warmth, but it was kept in an inviolable place. She was a person without illusions. She expected nothing. She was done making the effort. Someone else, and only someone extraordinary—but she did not wander for long with such thoughts. Her date wouldn't mind, she thought, that she was late for lunch. He would like the Art Deco restaurant, and he would order the most expensive thing on the menu. Usually she herself began with the pâté. But today, perhaps today she should try something else.

3

The light glanced off the Chrysler Building. He was wrong—he could not tell. She was trim and contained, an attractive woman. What else? He gave up following. It seemed right that, having stood naked and revealed, she should remain a mystery. Yet he could not quite leave it like that. During their summer in the city too much of importance had happened; and too much harm came from not paying attention. He would give her time, but he was determined to stay nearby. He wanted to show her that he understood more than she thought. He wanted to see, once again, the humor in her serious eyes.

At Penelope's, there was a great hubbub. A Japanese chef carved sushi, waiters plied drinks between the laughs, a woman caught her dress on the barbed sculpture. In one corner a D.J. wearing designer sunglasses played oldies on Penelope's new sound system —Chuck Berry, Elvis, Buddy Holly, early Stones. Jennings, smiling, welcomed the sloppy kiss of nostalgia, then joined the crowd. Billy, waving, took him aside for some serious talk. One hand dropped on his shoulder, the other held a glass of fruit juice. Then Billy said loudly, "I want to apologize to you."

"Don't."

"No interruptions. You know now, everybody knows now, that I had a drinking problem. *Have* a drinking problem." He smiled. "And that made me behave badly toward a number of people . . ."

Jennings watched.

Billy was not at home inside his body, he thought, and his way of intimacy—blowzy, ingratiating—remained that of a drinking man. His charm, too, was somewhat impaired. Others would not notice, but Jennings saw the work in what had been effortless. "Now that the drinking's over," Billy said, "we're going to stay good friends."

For a moment Jennings became Billy. He said to the man with the considering eyes and distant smile, "We go back a long way," "We've been through a lot," "Old friends are priceless." A good guy, Jennings, smart and discreet. "Look, if you ever want to come back—"

"Thanks, I'm doing okay."

A commotion kicked up. Penelope wanted to take a picture of herself with the assembled guests—never mind, she said, about the hired photographer. Since there were so many guests, several pictures would be required. She declared, "I want to get this *done!* So nobody gets any cake, no one does any dancing, no toasts, no nothing until . . ." She fiddled with her tripod and timing device, while the crowd hissed playfully. Then she was ready. "We have a minute, a full minute, hurry everybody!" She swooned, like a nineteenth-century actress, into Billy's arms. A number of guests gathered around, and Billy cried out, "Come on, Jennings, get over here!" The old reluctance stole into Jennings; he wanted to make a joke. This soon passed, and he put one arm around Billy and the other around Penelope, to feel the animal under the clothes. He stared out at the party—sharp-eyed (look at Tom, he thought, feeding on caviar), but smiling too. He stared out at the party, but did not forget what was missing in Penelope's picture.

He looked beyond the lens, to the edge of the window. Yes— he quickened to other pictures, other rhythms. For a moment his imagination left him and he saw clearly, as a blind man sees, the intimation behind the surface of the world. Then he turned to tease Penelope.

"Not now!—

"It's about to—

"Hey!"

Beyond the window—beyond Billy who laughed into the lens, beyond Jennings who ribbed Penelope, beyond Kelly who ordered pâté after all—this concealed energy continued its ordinary work. It arranged and rearranged pictures. It formed and re-formed stories. It was restless just to make. It surfaced in delight (laughter in the playground), in boredom (despair in the doorway), in grace (light over water). Its indifference was cruel—and fine, because it permitted so much.

360